DR. THORNHILL'S LAST PATIENT

A NOVEL BY

TOM ULICNY

ISBN-13: 9781795824989

ACKNOWLEDGMENTS

As always, I'm deeply indebted to all those who helped coax this work along and assisted tirelessly with editing, proofreading and their many suggestions. As for the thought-provoking painting used in the cover art for this book, it is an unsigned work that has been in my family for years. I credit it, at least in part, for the idea for this book and would gratefully acknowledge and thank the artist if only I knew who she or he was. Should you, the reader, have any insights on this unknown artist, please contact me via my website. I would appreciate hearing from you.

Dr. Thornhill's Last Patient

CHAPTER 1

July 8, 1920

Abigail stood at her bedroom window listening to Mother's screams filtering up through the floorboards. Trying to ignore them, she peered outside, fixing her attention on the foot-path below that ran out from the porch, between the ragged patches of grass and into the dense woods surrounding the house. Of late she'd spent time walking along it, out among the trees where their nettled branches shielded the forest floor from both sun and rain. A late afternoon breeze caused a rustling in the trees nearest the house. She wished she were out there now.

Turning from the window, she took in a deep breath of regret. The screams had grown more shrill, more desperate, accompanied now by the occasional bang of a cupboard door slamming shut and the thud of what was probably a chair toppling onto the floor.

Hands shaking, Abigail cupped one of them in the other, gripping tightly, forcing herself to be calm. She paced the floor slowly for a time then took to her bed, busying herself with a book, straining in the dim light to make out the words on the page. She'd managed to lose herself in a fanciful story of western adventure then suddenly realized—all had gone quiet downstairs.

She glanced at the clock on the dresser. She'd expected Mother's torment, as she called it, to continue well into the night but this time it seemed to have ended after only two hours. She held her breath, listening. Even the wind outside seemed to have stilled, as if it too expected something more. The minutes passed with excruciating slowness.

Finally, Abigail got up from the bed. Hearing only the pounding of her heart and the quickened pace of her own breathing, she walked to the door, slid back the bolt and pushed it open. At the squeak of the hinges, her heart jumped into her throat. She took a hurried step forward and looked down over the banister to the base of the stairs where she feared Mother might be standing, ready to come up. But no one was there. She placed a hand on her chest and swallowed dryly. No need to be afraid. She'd been through this many times before. With a steadying hand on the railing, she walked to the stairs and started down. The old wood groaned beneath her stockinged feet.

At the last step, she turned into the front room where she saw Mother's knitting, lying where she'd left it, unfinished in her chair. Through the north window the trees outside looked in. She took a calming breath and shook her head. Such a dreary place this was. Walking almost casually now across the bare wooden floor she entered the hallway where she stopped, listening again. Yes, she could hear Mother's slow, raspy breathing coming from the kitchen. She took a few steps more, out to where the hallway ended. She looked in.

Mother stood in the middle of the room with her back to Abigail. Her hair was frazzled. Her yellow house dress was torn at the waist. Beside her, the table and chairs lay tumbled over. Plates, food and broken glass littered the floor. Cupboard doors were swung open. The blue lace curtains Mother had sewn with such care had been torn from the windows and lay in a heap against the wall opposite the icebox. The kitchen had been a mess to begin with but it now looked as if a terrible wind had ripped its way through, sparing nothing in its wake.

All Abigail could think about at that moment was the work it would take for her to put things right. She let out a sigh, a little louder than she'd intended.

At the sound, Mother's body stiffened. She turned slowly to face her daughter, her eyes wide, her yellowed orbs exposed in a frightening way, as if she'd been shocked by something totally unexpected. Her lips began to move, silently forming words that Abigail couldn't follow.

Abigail took a step back into the hallway. "Mother?" she asked tentatively, ready for anything, remembering the time when Mother had come at her clawing and biting like a wild animal. But even that hadn't been as jarring as this bit of strangeness. She fought the urge to turn and run. Rigid with tension, she waited until finally, Mother shuddered and her mouth sprang open expelling a piercing scream that bled into a bitter cry of anguish. Still standing ram-rod straight, tears streamed from her hideously yellowed eyes. With both hands she covered her face.

"Mother?" Abigail repeated.

She'd hardly gotten the word out of her mouth when Mother's knees buckled and, as if finally drained of her last drop of energy, she fell to the floor, her head hitting the rim of a white china plate with a resounding rattle.

Was she dead? Abigail watched carefully. No, at her chest there was still a slight movement. Her eyes were closed and she appeared to be breathing peacefully as if in the middle of an afternoon nap.

Knowing she might have little time, Abigail grit her teeth and moved quickly, setting Mother's chair upright, pulling her spent body up onto it, using the ropes already there to tie her wrists to the armrests. This done, she stepped back, breathless from the exertion but starting to relax.

Was it over? Probably. She pulled the kitchen table upright, set up the other chair, and sat, keeping a safe distance from her sleeping mother who, with hands restrained now, could do her no harm.

Abigail suppressed a shiver. How much better it would be if Mother never woke up. As she'd done many times before, she forced that thought out of her head. She began cleaning up the worst of the mess and worked until there was just enough light to make out her mother's body, still slumped in the chair, still sleeping peacefully. Abigail was about to head back upstairs for the night but decided against it. What if Mother woke up? What if, in the middle of the night, the spell ended and she needed her?

Abigail poured herself some water and drank it down, wiping her lips dry with the back of her hand, knowing what she had to do. She walked back into the front room and spread two blankets down on the floor. For a pillow, she used a winter coat. She spent the night curled up there, sometimes sleeping, sometimes listening wide-eyed in the darkness for the sounds she feared most. But, in that long restless night, those sounds never came. The feeble light of morning was just coming through the windows when, from the kitchen, she heard a soft groan. Abigail roused herself, got up and slowly walked in.

On seeing her, Mother spoke clearly: "I am hungry, dear. Can you get me something to eat?" When Abigail didn't move, Mother smiled grimly. "It's all right, bluebird, I'm not going to hurt you."

Bluebird—it's what she called her to let her know that everything was normal again, that the spell was over and she was no longer a danger. Abigail went to the counter and cut a slice of cornbread. From the icebox, she retrieved a dish of fruit. To be safe, she kept her mother's restraints in place and fed her with a spoon.

Mother ate with gusto, chewing and swallowing ravenously, finishing it all, washing it down with a few gulps of water. She waited while Abigail dabbed her chin with a towel then quietly announced: "I'll be dying today my dear, sometime this afternoon I think."

Abigail wasn't sure she heard her right. "What? You mean *really* dying? Are you sure?" She tried to sound more concerned than hopeful as she prepared then began to eat her own breakfast.

"Yes, dear, quite sure. You know how I get when I set my mind to something."

"Yes, Mother, I know, but..." She caught herself short, looking back at her mother. Was that a smile on her face?

The old woman sat, slouched in her chair, and yes, the corners of her mouth were uplifted as if some secret joke had just crossed her mind. "Don't worry, dear. You'll be free of me soon," she said, her smile fading. After another moment, her expression grew suddenly tense, as if from a cramp, and Abigail feared the start of a new round of bodily tremors. But the tenseness passed and Mother's features grew more relaxed, the softening of the wrinkles in her cheeks causing Abigail to remember her the way she once was.

There had been some good times, back when Father was still with them, when Mother had achieved some degree of fame in professional circles. How proud they'd been for her and how happy they'd been. But too quickly those years passed. Then Father was gone and so was Mother's fleeting fame. Now, as those memories faded, all Abigail felt was emptiness and sadness for her mother, for herself, and for all the years lost.

Mother shifted her weight. Her chair creaked. She hacked out a cough. "Get the book, Abigail. I'll tell you what to write."

Abigail complied and, hours later put down her pen, appalled by what she'd written. Even by Mother's standards this spell had been one of the worst.

With her head tilted against the back of her chair, Mother rested after having talked continuously over most of that time. Then she stirred again. "This house will be yours now, Abigail. Will you live here for a while? You can never sell it, you know. We talked about that. What will you do?"

Abigail knew exactly what she would do, but she hesitated in her reply. When she was a child *Timbervale* had been a familiar and inviting place. The tall trees surrounding it had stood strong, green and stately, dappling the sunlight that always found a way to beam down onto the pitched roof and in through the windows. But, as Abigail grew older, and Mother's condition worsened, the trees seemed to lean further in, their branches bending low over the house as if straining to keep its secrets. Now, they choked off the sun, making each day dank and gray. Mother was right, she couldn't sell the place. But did she really expect her to stay out here alone in the deep woods? Did she really think she could somehow live within these walls, infested as they were with so many dark memories? Knowing the obvious answer but seeing no point in upsetting her mother she simply replied, "I'm not sure."

Mother shook her head. "You're a good daughter, Abigail, but you always were shit for a liar. I know you'll be leaving. I appreciate you not wanting to hurt my feelings, though I don't know why the hell you'd still care about that. Yes, leaving's best for you. You're still young. It's what I would do. Hell, if I were you, I might have left years ago." She tapped her foot and glanced at the clock that sat atop the icebox. "Not long now. Three o'clock should do it," she said with almost a wink.

Abigail stretched out her legs, tired of sitting. "You don't seem too worried."

"Ha. With all the dying I've done over the years, I know what it's like. I have no fear of it. I've looked out into the void many times. I know what's on the other side. The only difference is, this time I won't be coming back." She elbowed herself straighter. "It'll be a relief for me to be done with this strange life I've led. Probably a relief for you too, having me gone at last." Her body shook in a rattling cough.

Abigail stood and held a glass of water to Mother's lips. She swallowed. Abigail sat. And the clock ticked loudly.

At twelve, Mother asked for some bourbon and drank two shots in quick succession, Abigail helping her. Down the old hatch. Mother's face smoothed again, and she fell back asleep.

At one, her breathing lightened, her chest hardly moving. Abigail placed a hand near her mouth to feel the ever so slight breeze in and out—dry, tinged with the smell of the whiskey and only slightly warmer than the air in the room.

At two, without bothering to open her eyes, she asked what time it was. Abigail told her.

"Ha. Still an hour to go."

She'd whispered this so weakly that it took Abigail a few seconds to piece the sounds together to make sense of it. It was so like Mother, running her life and now her death by the clock. Abigail looked around the room: The splintered woodwork, the scarred cupboard doors, the stains on the floor that would never come out. Mother was right, she could never live here. As if to emphasize that thought, the dim light from the window dimmed further and a low rumble of thunder shook the house and rattled the back door.

Abigail got to her feet. From a rusty nail near the door, she grabbed her shawl, wrapping it around her shoulders, pulling it tight against the wind as she walked outside, past the empty clotheslines. Dried out pine needles from years-past made the ground spongy under her feet. Dark clouds raced and the wind whistled as if trying to tell her she didn't belong here. Well, she'd be gone soon enough—her and Mother both.

From the shed a few paces further, she retrieved a tin of kerosene and brought it inside. Opening it, she walked to the kitchen basin where she filled then lit an oil lamp. She brought it to the table and sat back down, her shawl still tightly gathered around her.

The lamplight, or maybe the smell of the kerosene, seemed to revive Mother just a little. She opened both eyes. Maybe one last spasm of lucidity? She spoke gently, almost like the mother Abigail had known from long ago. "You know what to do, don't you Abigail? We talked about it, remember?"

"Yes. I remember, Mother."

"It's important that you do things exactly so, exactly like we talked about. You understand that. You won't fail me?"

Abigail felt a tear forming, her heart melting just a little. She stood and kissed the top of her mother's head, the hair gray and dry, almost brittle like the pine needles on the ground outside; her skin so thin and cold that it sent a shiver down her spine. "I won't fail you."

Mother nodded a few times. "Thank you, dear." She smiled. It was a sweet, almost angelic smile. "I have seen Him," she said. "I spoke with Him. All is good. Everything is finished."

How did she mean this? Abigail wondered but didn't ask. Is she saying that she actually had a little conversation with God? Well, if she believed it to be so, where was the harm in that? She watched Mother's eyes close.

At three, right on time and without a twitch, Abigail's mother, the briefly-famous Doctor Lydia Thornhill, pulled in her last ragged breath. Abigail waited for the next heave of her chest, but it never came. To be sure, she felt for a pulse. She bent closer, lowering an ear just above her mother's gaping mouth, half expecting to be surprised by a curse, or an attempted bite. But there was nothing.

Yes, it was over.

She untied her mother's hands, letting the lifeless limbs fall limp from the armrests into her lap. Abigail knew the restraints had been necessary, Mother herself had always insisted on them after each spell. Still, she winced on seeing the cruel grooves they'd left in her wrists.

She sat back down, the realization hitting her. Mother was at the void now. She was crossing over and she wouldn't be coming back.

A light rain began to patter and quickly build, bringing with it the smell of wet wood and a drip, drip onto the floor. Abigail stared into the yellow flame of the lamp then shifted her gaze to her mother.

There sat the woman who had dominated Abigail's life. Yes, she was finally gone. Abigail knew she should be relieved, just like Mother had said—and part of her was. But, deep inside, Abigail felt dangerous memories swarming. She could almost see them circling, starting to close in. A feeling of utter despair overtook her until at last she stood abruptly and pulled both of her hands into white-knuckled fists. No! She would not allow herself to be condemned by the past. This was *her* life now—hers alone. She reached across the table and grabbed the bottle of bourbon from beside the lamp. She shook it gently, watching the few remaining ounces of amber liquid slosh from side to side. Lifting it to her lips, Abigail tossed her head back and drank hungrily, the heat of the liquor harsh at first, then calming, soothing.

Finished, she dropped the bottle, sending it rolling across the floor until it came to rest beneath the window. Feeling as if she were floating, she walked into the front room and climbed the stairs back up to her bedroom. Not bothering to undress, not bothering to bolt her bedroom door, she got into bed, held the blankets close, and slept.

The storm continued through the night but the next day dawned clear as did the next and the next, enabling Abigail to complete Mother's final instructions. Once done, Abigail Thornhill left the house in the Maine woods and never returned.

CHAPTER 2

March 23, 2017:

"Tell me about your family, Detective Marshall."

"Why? What do they have to do with anything?"

"Maybe something, maybe nothing."

Ben felt like he was caught up in a bad comedy skit on late night TV. When he didn't answer right away, the balding Dr. Byron Howe leaned back, chair creaking, pen poised over a yellow notepad. His brows went up as if reminding Ben the next line was his.

All right then, on with the show. "Only child. Dad bugged out when I was five. Mom died when I was nineteen."

"Grandparents? Aunts? Uncles?"

"Nope."

"You must know something about them."

"Never knew them, never knew of them."

That warranted a note on the pad. "And what do you remember about your father?"

Ben folded his arms. Over his ten years on the force, he'd watched other guys who'd been called up here to the fifth floor for having screwed the pooch in one way or another. In his book, they were fuck-ups, every one. None of them lasted very long after their visit to the shrink. Now it was his turn. Let's see how long he lasted.

One little hitch and his ten years on the force with an otherwise unblemished record didn't count for shit. And it hadn't even been a serious thing—not really. No one had died. No one had even gotten hurt. But that didn't matter. His fate was in the hands of this aging bushmaster coiled up in his swivel chair, staring darts at him, trying to pry an answer out of him. "Worked all the time. Same for Mom," said Ben finally.

"Do you have pleasant memories of them?"

"Nothing I'd call pleasant." But even as he said this he remembered that yes, there had been one time. The three of them went to the ball park—popcorn, hot dogs, the whole bit, just like a normal family, like on TV. It had been a birthday surprise and was one of his earliest memories. A hot sunny day, their seats were in the bleachers so far from home plate he could hardly see the batter. Yeah, that was a pleasant memory. Two weeks after that, Dad left for good. Guess the day at the ballpark wasn't pleasant enough for him to think about staying. Ben shook his head. "They were always having money problems. They blamed me for them." He correctly predicted the next question.

"And what makes you think that?"

He mumbled an answer and did the same to all the questions that followed. The clock on the wall labored toward eleven and, once there, Ben stood.

"One more thing, Detective," said Howe, a finger in the air. "We need your permission to run a DNA test and we'll need to do a little background research."

"Ha. You want to see if I have any loonies in my family tree."

"It's standard procedure. Your family history might be helpful in deciding how best to help you."

"I don't need any help, Doc."

"You're probably right. But it's no big deal. For the DNA part, just get some saliva on this swab and that'll do it. Besides, it's always good to know if there might be a tendency for diabetes or heart disease in your lineage." Howe held out the swab.

Ben snatched it, rolled it around on his tongue. Sure, heart disease, diabetes, *insanity*.

"It's best if you swab the inside of your cheek."

Ben made the adjustment then gave it back.

"Thank you, Detective. I appreciate your time. See you in a couple of days."

"Oh for Christ's sake. Don't you ever get tired of this overly polite, casual chit-chat shit? I'm only here because Captain Nolan ordered me here. We both know that."

Dr. Howe sighed. "You're here, Detective, because you discharged your weapon for no apparent reason. You gave Nolan no choice. He and I and the department are simply trying to understand what happened and why. Your borderline belligerence is only going to slow down the process. Maybe our next session will be more productive."

"Hell, none of this is productive and you know it. You just need to justify your six-figure salary. You'll find out that I can be a lot worse than *borderline* belligerent."

Ben strode out the door and slammed it shut behind him. "The guy's a shit-head," he muttered with a glance at the next victim waiting in the outer office. Ben took the elevator down to the third floor where he grabbed a mug of coffee and weaved his way to his desk, past a few stinging glances from his cohorts in the bullpen. They were probably already calling him crazy-Ben behind his back.

From the desk opposite his, Phil looked up over his glasses.

Ben ignored him for a moment, sat and flipped on his computer, drumming his fingers as it booted up. "He's a shit-head."

"Dr. Howe has a lot of power Benjie. He could have you busted down to beat-cop if he wanted."

"That would be an improvement over this desk-duty shit."

Phil took off his glasses. "You saw a guy who wasn't there and you tried to shoot him. That's serious stuff."

Well, that was true. There wasn't much Ben could say to counter that. He sipped his coffee.

Phil put his glasses back on and resumed his two-finger typing. The guy was closing in on sixty and still had some black in his hair. From a serious work-out regimen he managed to stay fit and trim. He'd been a cop forever and always called Ben 'Benjie' as if he were his little brother. This used to bother Ben but, as partners over the last ten years they'd been through too much for him to really care. With their age difference, they could have been father and son but instead, a brotherly bond developed between them and it had grown tighter each year.

A week had passed since the screwed up stake-out that put Ben in this bind.

It had started out just like all the others: He and Phil on the night-shift, dirty, smelly third-floor room, scope aimed at the second-floor apartment across the street, voice recorder picking up the bug just fine, cold gooey pizza tasting like cardboard, ballgame on the radio in the background. Phil had just turned it up a little as Ben drained his coffee and got up to stretch his legs. He walked past the bed, turned at the door, then headed back to the window. Five steps in one direction, five in the other. He completed the route three times noticing it wasn't even two yet. He was about to sit down when, from behind their target window across the street, a light flicked on. Shadows moved behind the curtains. Phil saw it too. He flicked off the radio and pressed his headphones tighter against each ear.

Shadows on the shade. An old song, wasn't it? Ben could tell there were definitely two people in the room now and they were obviously interacting. He glanced at Phil who gave him a nod that the audio was coming through loud and clear. The shadow-box theater played on. Ben felt his heart beat faster. Maybe this wouldn't be just another wasted night. Maybe they'd finally get the evidence they needed to put one more murderous creep behind bars.

Suddenly, Ben saw movement on the street—a man in a white overcoat carrying an umbrella. A white overcoat? What the hell was that all about? Ben watched him as he walked closer with a meandering gate, almost a limp. The guy lifted the umbrella and Ben saw that he'd been wrong. The umbrella was a rifle and the guy was aiming at something just up the street—something, *or someone* Ben couldn't quite make out.

"Shit, there's a gun," shouted Ben. He pulled his pistol from his side-holster.

The guy held the rifle steady, his back leg angled to absorb the recoil. As if a fog had lifted slightly, Ben could see his target now, a man lying further up the street. He was struggling to get up. Ben had no doubt—the guy in the overcoat was going to kill him.

Instinctively, Ben poked the barrel of his gun through the window, shattering the glass. He fired twice at the gunman.

Gun drawn, Phil rushed to the window, ready to fire then gave Ben a what-the-fuck look.

Ben's vision cleared. He scanned the street—empty now. "He was just down there, Phil. He had a rifle. He was aiming it, about to shoot. I had to..."

"No one's there."

Ben shook his head to clear it. "He could be on his way up." He ran over to the door. He stood beside it, gun pointed up, listening for footsteps. But no one came.

"Shit. Light's out in the apartment," said Phil from the window. "Probably heard the shots. We scared them off."

Ben couldn't blame Phil for including the incident in his report. Shots had been fired and there wasn't any getting around that—it had to be reported. Ben's own report gave a description of the man he thought he saw. The real problem was, this wasn't the first time something like this had happened. A few weeks earlier, Ben thought he'd seen a guy waving a pistol toward a crowd of people. In a flash, he'd gone for his own gun but stopped short of pulling it. The guy with the gun was gone.

Phil had seen the move. "You okay?"

Ben remembered wiping the beads of sweat from his forehead. "Sure, fine, no problem."

Phil had kept that first incident to himself. But Ben knew he was right. He should be taking these hallucinations seriously. But how could they be hallucinations? They were so fucking real.

The captain had pulled Ben's weapon, initiated an investigation, put Ben on full time desk duty and assigned twice-weekly sessions with the shrink the first of which had been this morning. He was lucky to still have his badge. Yeah, he needed to just suck it up, take Phil's advice and be more cooperative with Howe next time.

At noon, Phil left on a case and Ben ate his brown-bag lunch at his desk. The afternoon took forever. Ben left at five.

Outside, the sun was already starting to fade and there was a nip in the late March air. It took fifteen minutes for his five block walk back to his place. He lived in a tiny room on the third-floor of an old Brownstone built back in eighteen something or other. Cracked plaster, bad plumbing and roaches the size of your fist all fell under the heading of historic charm according to his landlord.

He climbed the steps up to the porch, unlocked the front door and opened it a crack. "Ben here," he shouted quickly to Maddie Pembroke, the elderly first floor tenant who was known to pack a loaded 45, ready to shoot at the least provocation. He stepped inside. The smell of her cooking made him hungry as he started up the stairs. Second floor was Robert Roy Rockford, a twenty something hipster who hated being called Bob, preferring the much cooler *Rob-Roy* and preferring it to be spoken as if it were a single word. He had a work-from-home job involving some kind of gaming that he'd once tried to explain to Ben. The guy had a pasty-white complexion which, in contrast, gave Maddie a fetching Florida tan. Ben saw him occasionally in the common kitchen but had never seen him actually leave the building. "Hey Bob," shouted Ben rounding the landing.

Heading up the last flight, he heard the expected commotion coming from his own apartment. He opened the door then dropped to a knee letting Stump, his shaggy, hyperactive terrier, give him a few sniffs and licks. His big black eyes bulged with excitement and his normally flopped-over ears peaked. With paws sliding across the wooden floor, he jumped side to side as Ben came in.

"That's right, Stumper," said Ben. "Time for you and me to go out for a walk." There was a time when Ben hoped Stump might keep the roaches under control but, no, the poor dog, who'd been born with only three legs, lived in fear of them.

Ben grabbed the leash, clipped it to Stump's collar and headed back down. Stump pulled and barked all the way, his lack of a fourth leg not impeding him in the least. Out on the sidewalk, they were off on their usual route. Ben liked this part of the day. It was a good way to unwind and to think things through. Yeah, he'd just make the best of things at work. He'd sit at his desk, do his job and be cooperative with Dr. Howe. He liked his job on the force and he couldn't afford to lose it. Besides, what the hell would he do if not police work?

He saw her from a distance. Brown hair tied back in a ponytail, blue coat with a collar turned up. He'd seen her before. She had a nice face with kind features and brown eyes that held a spark of fun in them. All right, he was probably just imagining the spark of fun thing. He figured her to be in her late twenties.

She was walking fast as if she was late for something and Ben imagined that he might swing slightly into her path, maybe brushing her shoulder with his. "Oh, sorry miss," he'd say, then proceed from there. He wondered if she wore a ring. It was still too far to tell but the gap was closing fast. As he walked, he purposely shifted his gaze as if attracted by something going on across the street but he kept her in his periphery. Just a few more steps now, then a little hitch to the left. It was all perfectly choreographed but, at the critical moment, his shoulder hit hers more solidly than he'd intended. She careened to the side and bumped into a wrought iron fence post. He was about to deliver his 'Sorry miss,' line but she quickly gained her footing and beat him to it.

"Damn it, watch where you're going," she said, spitting out her words without even giving him or Stump a look.

Ben stopped and turned but she was already well down the street.

Stump looked up at Ben.

"Not a word, you dumb dog."

Phil wasn't at his desk when Ben came in the next morning. Probably out working the streets with his new partner, he figured. The guy was a rookie so Phil would have his hands full keeping him out of trouble just as he'd had when Ben first started. The arrangement between Phil and the new guy was supposed to be temporary until Ben got his good-to-go from Dr. Howe.

Ben blew the steam from his coffee and, as he sat, spotted a familiar folder on his desk: *The Ronaldi Brothers*. With a name like that he always thought they should have been a circus act. But no. Bruno and Vito pushed drugs, hookers and hits. They ran their lucrative business in South Boston. He and Phil had had a few run-ins with them over the years. *Have a look,* said the note in Phil's handwriting clipped to the front of the file folder.

Ben opened it. Right on top of the half-inch thick stack of papers and photos was a homicide report. Bruno and Vito had been shot dead, execution style, their bodies found in an alley on the North End. Wow! Must be a new turf war going on, probably by an outside outfit making a move in the South while leaving a clear message to the North-Enders that they might be next. Scum of the earth, all of them, but murder's murder. The Ronaldi boys didn't deserve justice but they were going to get it anyway.

Ben read through the rest of the five page report, making a few notes as he went. He'd just finished with it when Phil came in. "How'd it go with the rook?"

Phil shrugged. "Made a few traffic stops, nothing too challenging. The kid did okay, better than you did when I was breaking you in. He's off doing paperwork." He sat down and took off his glasses pointing them at the Ronaldi folder still in front of Ben. "What do you make of that? Real shocker, huh?"

"Probably just a turf thing. I figure the shooters for outsiders making a move in the south while leaving a clear message that the North End's next."

"Or maybe it was the Easties who wanted to make it look like that."

Ben shook his head. "That's beyond their level of brainpower." He handed the folder to Phil. "I made some notes."

"Thanks. I figured you'd want to see it. I'll be working it with the rook tomorrow. It's going to be a stretch for him. I'll let you know how it goes."

Lunch came and went and Ben spent the rest of the day filling out routine forms and reports. Then it was home again, walk the dog—no sign of miss spark-o-fun, then TV and a dinner of left-over chow mein. Up until a month ago, Ginny would have occupied the couch next to him at this time of day, commenting on the news or out-guessing the contestants on Jeopardy. She was pretty good at it. They'd been together for almost a year. They'd been comfortable together. But maybe that was the problem. Maybe he'd been too comfortable and, one day she'd just left. Ginny had her quirks, but Ben still wasn't over her. He'd called and texted but she'd never replied. He would have gone over to her place but, for all he knew, she'd taken up with another guy. Wouldn't want to walk in on them when...No, wouldn't want that. He stared at the empty couch. Yeah, he was a real idiot with women, first taking Ginny for granted then nearly knocking one over just to get her attention. Pretty pathetic.

He was halfway into his Chinese when he heard a skittering under his recliner. Roaches. He glanced at Stump who'd heard it too. Stump's ears perked up. He took two steps back and barked twice looking back at Ben.

"They're supposed to be your job, you dumb dog, not mine." Ben wiped his chin and got up. He tilted his chair back to see three of them having a great time gathered around a crust of dried bread. He stomped two of them with his slippered foot, the third got away taking the bread with him.

Stump barked from a safe distance.

"Shittin' things. I hate 'em." Ben kicked the squished bodies over to Stump and let the chair down.

Stump eyed the roach debris, his head cocked.

"You're even afraid of *dead* roaches. What good are you?" Ben swept up the mess and retook his seat. He finished his dinner while Stump sulked.

CHAPTER 3

Ben awoke the next morning to the sound of rain hitting the window beside his bed. Half asleep, he parted the curtains and sighed. Not rain—sleet. Shit, winter was back. Beneath the streetlamps he could see a frosty white tinge already trimming the curbs and bushes. He took Stump out for a quick and frigid walk then showered and ate a cereal breakfast. He shrugged into his black overcoat and pulled his Siberia hat on tight. Briefcase and umbrella in hand trotted down the stairs and stepped outside onto the slushy porch. From the dull gray sky that was just brightening, it looked like an all-day thing—one last blast of winter. He popped open his umbrella and turned it into the wind, heading up Elmhurst. He was one block along, starting to think that he should flag a cab, when he heard the sirens.

Up ahead, red and blue flashers cut through the mist. A couple of police cruisers, coming on fast, weaved through the picket line of dumb-ass drivers who didn't have sense enough to get out of the way. The sirens screamed as they passed. Ben eyed the cops—no one he knew. He was surprised when they half-screeched, half slid to a stop only a few hundred feet away. Shit. They were just across the street from his place. What was going on? Ben started walking back toward them. Car doors slammed. Four cops, guns drawn, charged up the steps of a building.

Ben broke into a run, crossing the street.

One of the cops used a ram on the building's wooden door, smashing it open on the second try. All four ran inside. Ben made it to the base of the outside steps. He stopped, staring up at the splintered door. Beside him pedestrians stood gawking.

"Police operation folks," shouted Ben. "I'm a cop. Just keep moving, it may not be safe." Ben felt naked without his gun. What would he do if things went to shit? He spread his arms, guiding the flow of pedestrians out to the far edge of the sidewalk. Out in the street traffic was at a dead stop, blocked by the two police vehicles. Horns honked and in the distance, police sirens wailed. Ben climbed up a couple of steps but couldn't see much. If help was on the way, it would be a while before they'd get here. He glanced over his shoulder. Still no sounds from inside the building. In the floors above, curtains and blinds hid what might be going on behind the windows. He wondered how many people were inside the place.

Ben hooked a thumb into his belt. It had to have been at least five minutes since the four cops entered the place. Usually things went down pretty quick after that. He turned to a man standing next to him. He looked big and burly enough. "Look, I've got to go in there. I need you to keep everyone back. Can you do that?"

"Yeah, I guess so." The man turned around and raised his hands high. His voice boomed. "Okay everybody, let's give the cops room to do their job." He was a natural, must watch a lot of cop shows.

Ben ran up the steps, tossed his briefcase onto the porch and side-stepped the ruined door that hung at an angle from a single hinge. He wondered what happened to his umbrella and figured he must have dropped it somewhere. Too bad, its pointed tip would have given him some kind of weapon. He took a few steps into the darkened hallway where the steam heat overtook the cold. Breakfast smells filled the heavy air. The walls throbbed with low, familiar sounds—radios playing, footsteps, an occasional shout, a kid crying, the low hiss of the steam pipes. Nothing unusual here. Nothing dangerous, so far. To his right, a flight of stairs led up.

Ha, thought Ben, more TV police drama. He found himself humming some dark melody that, in most such shows usually paced the rise in tension that built to a violent climax where somebody died. All things considered, Ben felt amazingly calm. Yeah, can't keep me chained to a desk. He headed up the stairs. Usually he would have had his gun out by now and usually Phil would have been right behind him. Shit. This was so stupid. With each step, he continued his low hum.

From somewhere overhead, five shots banged out in quick succession.

Ben froze halfway up the flight, heart in his throat. He heard a rumbling from the stairs overhead. Someone was coming down at a run. It had to be the perp trying to get away. What happened to the cops? Christ. What now? Phil's favorite stratagem flashed through his head: *When in doubt, attack.*

Ben charged up the stairs, two at a time and made it to the first landing just as a big guy in a Bruins jersey barreled into him. He shoved Ben back with what Ben was shocked to see was the muzzle of a gun. He tried to elbow the gun aside but he was a split second too late.

The gun went off. The loud bang stunned Ben. He fell back against the wall. The guy tried to sidestep him. Ben grabbed the collar of his jersey and pulled hard. The guy staggered back then shoved his gun in Ben's face. But this time, Ben was faster. With his freehand, he latched onto the barrel and twisted it sideways. A deafening shot blazed past his ear. The barrel was blistering hot but Ben held on, pulling it free, sending it rattling down the stairs. Great, now at least this was an even fight. Ben reared back and smashed his fist into the guy's nose. Cartilage crunched and blood spurted. The guy tumbled back, falling two steps down. Out of breath, Ben leaped on top of him.

"Not so fast, you fucker," Ben shouted. "You're not going anywhere."

But the guy was stronger than he looked. He bucked upwards, tossing Ben half off him.

At the base of the stairs, three policemen charged in, guns drawn, shouting: "Police! Police!"

About time, thought Ben with relief. He raised his free hand. "I'm a cop. I've got him. He's right here. The asshole's right here." He rolled off the guy, catching his breath. Funny, he'd thought he was in pretty good shape.

"Good work buddy," one of the cops said to him as they cuffed the perp. "You're a cop?"

"Yeah," Ben reached for his badge.

"Whoa, hold on a minute bud. Looks like you've been shot."

Oh Christ! Ben looked down to see a puddle of red beneath him, some of it trickling down onto the steps. Crap! He knew he should have stayed in bed. He knew it was going to be a shitty day. He tried to sit up.

"Hold on. You just lay still, okay? I've got to go up to check on my partners. You're going to be fine. We have EMT's on the way."

The cop left and Ben slumped back. He had a vague sense of things going on around him. Heavy footsteps thundered up the stairs. There were shouts he couldn't make out. And all the while a pain in his abdomen kept building. He put a hand there feeling blood pumping out. "Oh God, I'm dying." He doubled over and slid down a few steps.

A woman spoke. "Easy there, Detective, we're going to help you."

Ben had no breath. *Better be quick, I'm losing it here.* He tried to say these words but knew they hadn't come out right.

Hands picked him up. He was on a stretcher, he was in an ambulance, swerving, sirens blaring. Then everything went black.

"Thought we'd lost you, Benjie, how you feeling?"

The words echoed in Ben's head. Oh yeah, this is the part where he wakes up in the hospital all better, just a little groggy. Yeah, he was going to be fine. He heard a quiet beeping sound, slow and steady. He opened his eyes but saw no sign of Phil. The dimly lit room was empty. An IV pole stood next to his bed, a couple of green lights flashing in time with the beeps. A display showed his BP: 120 over 60—not bad. The blinds over the window next to his bed were closed, but he could tell it was nighttime. He turned his head feeling restraining connections. Wires? What was that all about? And where had Phil gone?

The door to his room stood open to a brightly lit hallway from which he heard squeaky footsteps. A nurse stood in the doorway for a moment. She took a couple of steps in but all Ben could see was her silhouette. "Hi there," said Ben in the best up-beat voice he could muster. Still, it came out more like a croak.

"Mr. Marshall?"

"Yes, that's me." He tried to clear his throat. "Could I have some water please?"

"Water. Yes, of course. I'll bring it right away."

Then she was gone. Ben closed his eyes. He must have drifted off because when he opened them again in what seemed like the next instant, the room was brighter and his bed was in a more upright position. Beside him a nurse held a straw to his lips. The cool water felt refreshing. He sucked it in almost desperately, some dribbling down his chin.

"Not so fast Mr. Marshall," she said.

Ben sucked in another swallow. He tongued the straw from his mouth. "Thanks," he said, only realizing when she left that there were three other people in the room. One was Howe, another was Captain Nolan in his full blues, hat in hand. Between them and a little behind was a woman. Mid-thirties maybe, curly auburn hair falling almost to her shoulders. Ben found himself thinking she would have made a good *Annie* when she was a kid. But, instead of a red outfit she was dressed professionally, white blouse, black skirt, this was no nurse.

Ben shifted his attention back to Nolan. "Hey, Captain," he said.

Nolan stepped closer. He was a tall African-American with close-clipped military hair and a bit of a weight problem. Ben never considered himself a friend of his but he'd always respected the guy for his decisiveness and for climbing up through the ranks like he had.

"How're you feeling, Ben?" he asked in his raspy tenor voice that Ben always thought didn't quite go with his beefy physique. He put a hand on Ben's just below the IV connection. His fingers felt cold.

Ben noticed a little twitch in the Captain's left eye like he was nervous about something. Probably didn't like being in a hospital. Well, Ben didn't like it either. "Just fine, Captain. Thanks for coming to see me. How're things at the station."

Nolan pulled his hand back. "Doing okay. Hope to have you

back soon."

"Yeah, I know, all that paperwork piling up."

There was that twitch again.

"Bet you're wondering how I ended up in that building."

The Captain looked confused, but only for a moment. He shook his head. "No mystery there. You were on your way to work, you see this thing going down, you step in to help. Did a good job of it too. That guy you brought down had just shot two cops. Your quick action probably saved lives. I've put you up for a commendation."

"How are they? Our guys who were shot? Anyone I know?"

"No, they were from uptown. One shot in the leg. He's all right. The other guy didn't make it."

"Shit."

"Yeah. But you stopped the bastard. You should feel good about that."

"Wish I'd had my gun."

"Look, don't worry about it, man. Just get better." He paused. "Well, just wanted to say hi. I'll catch you later."

Before leaving, he touched Ben's hand again. He'd never known the captain to be sentimental about anything and he was wondering what was up with that when Howe stepped forward.

"Hello, Ben. Glad to hear you're feeling better."

"Hello Byron."

"This is Dr. Silvers, an associate of mine."

Ha, bringing in reinforcements. So she was a shrink too—he should have known.

"Call me Amelia. Pleased to meet you Detective."

"Me too," said Ben. She was a good looking woman. Too bad she was a shrink. He decided to put that fact aside for the moment.

Dr. Howe slid over a couple of chairs and they both sat. Silvers, well all right—Amelia—crossed her legs holding a manila folder on her lap. With her fingers she flicked its forward edge every few seconds. She had her eyes on him. So did Howe. No smiles.

Howe spoke first. "You told the captain you're feeling fine. Is that true?"

"Yes, I *am* feeling fine." Ben did a mental inventory: head, heart, lungs, stomach, extremities; all good. "Just wondering when I can get the hell out of here."

"It should only be a few more days," said Howe.

Amelia stopped the folder flicking and raised her chin, the movement causing her hair to go bouncing. Ben imagined it bouncing under different circumstances—wow, guess he *was* feeling pretty good. That was a fast recovery after being gut-shot. But, that depends, doesn't it?

"How long was I out?" asked Ben. But then he had another thought. "Oh, damn. I've got a dog. He needs to be taken care of. Can you get someone over to my place?" He imagined poor Stump being overrun by roaches.

"I think that's been handled," said Howe. "The person, a woman I think, she's on your emergency call list; she's got your dog." Howe gave Amelia a glance. When she didn't respond he added, "We'll check on that to be sure."

Ginny and Stump had never gotten along. Ben wondered how that was going. "Okay, so how long has it been? How long have I been here?"

"How long does it feel like to you?"

"Jesus, Byron, just tell me, will you?"

"It's been five weeks since you were shot, detective," said Howe.

CHAPTER 4

Ben was stunned. He sat up straight. Five weeks? How could that be? To him it had been maybe five days, tops. He lowered the sheet a little and shifted his hospital gown aside, looking for the first time at his wound. An ugly red gash ran diagonally just below his navel. The stitches or staples or whatever the hell they used were already out.

"Your body is recovering nicely," said Howe.

"I've been out for five weeks?"

"It's unusual in cases like yours but not really that rare," said Amelia.

"So, nothing to worry about?"

"It's more of a concern really," added Howe, as always choosing his words carefully. "You were in post-op for a few days. When your recovery didn't quite go as planned, you were transferred here."

"This is a psych ward isn't it? You've got me in a fucking psych ward." Ben gripped the rails on the bed and tried to pull himself more upright. Too weak to do that, he used the controller to adjust the bed.

"You've been getting the best care possible."

"Look, I was shot in the gut, not the head. What the hell happened?"

"Yes, gunshot to the abdomen. You had no visible head trauma but maybe the guy hit you in the head, or you could have been knocked out when you fell."

Ben played things out: Heading up the stairs, hit the landing, crashed into the shit-head, fell back against the wall, gun fires, struggle, gun fires again and he falls on top of the guy. And, did he fall again? "Yeah, that's probably right," said Ben slowly. He swallowed, his mouth dry again. "I need more water."

Howe hit the call button and, a moment later a nurse came in with it. Ben sucked in a few gulps through the straw then leaned back against the pillow. "I need to get out of here." He coughed a few times.

"Up until a few days ago you've had a tube down your throat," said Howe. "It probably feels a little sore? You'll be on solid food now, I think." He paused. "Look, I want to conduct another session with you. It'll be similar to the one we've already had back at the station. It's all pretty standard for someone who's been comatose for a while. I'd like to start right now if you're up for it."

"Shit, why not? I've already lost five weeks, what's a few more days? Let's get it over with."

Dr. Silvers, that's how Ben thought of her now, pulled her chair closer and opened the folder. "First, we need to fill you in on a few things about the stake-out you were on. The one where you fired your weapon." She paused as if expecting a reaction but Ben gave her none. "We know that, prior to firing your gun, you broke a window. We found a few shards of glass in the room but there should have been more debris on the street below. We found none. It was a fairly large window. It has also been confirmed that two bullets had been fired from your gun but no sign of their impact was found on the street."

Ben shook his head. "The bullets would have ricocheted off the pavement. They could have wound up anywhere. All they would have left was a couple of pits in the cement."

"Yes, you're probably right about that," she agreed. "It was just a minor thing. Probably not important. The glass is another matter."

"Are you saying I didn't break the glass?"

"No," said Howe. "It's just something we can't explain."

"Like the guy in the white overcoat."

"And like you being comatose for five weeks."

Ben felt like he was in a fencing match. "You said that wasn't unusual."

"No, I said it wasn't rare. But, that aside, you had another episode prior to the stake-out, didn't you? Another hallucination I mean."

Ben hesitated, knowing that information could only have come from one place. Shit, Phil. "It...that was a minor thing. I thought I saw something."

"What did you think you saw, detective," she asked.

"I...it was a man in a crowd waving a gun."

"Was it the man in the white overcoat?" asked Howe.

"Shit, you're making it sound like I'm Alice chasing after a white rabbit."

"No Ben," said Silvers, with upsetting calmness. "We're just trying to understand what happened to you."

Ben paused, reigning himself in. He tried to remember that first incident. "No. I don't think...I'm not sure. It could have been the same man, I suppose. Shit. If the two of you are trying to make me think I've lost it, you're doing a good job. Is that what you're doing? Making a case for mental instability so you can pull my badge?"

Both Howe and Silvers kept their expressions blank. "We're trying to help you, Detective," she said finally. "Have you been under a lot of stress lately? Everything okay with your personal life?"

Ben gazed up at the ceiling and adjusted his bed back down a little. "Sure, Doc, everything's just fine with me. How about with you?" When she didn't reply, Ben continued. "Look, I saw something that wasn't there. It was a one-time thing—well, all right, it happened twice. But that was it. I'm fine now. I just need to get out of this fucking place."

"What did you really fire your gun at, Detective?" asked Howe. "Who were you really trying to kill?"

Ben shook his head, convinced this was going nowhere. He stared back at Howe, then at Silvers.

At that moment, a nurse came in holding a plastic tray. "Dinner for Mr. Marshall," she announced setting up the tray then quickly leaving.

Ben uncovered the plate and stared at the food—all soft, mushy stuff.

"You should eat," said Silvers.

Ben felt hungry and sick to his stomach at the same time. He put the metal cover back down. "I was trying to kill a guy who was about to shoot another guy. The other guy was lying on the ground trying to get up."

"You mean he was lying on the pavement," said Howe.

"Yes, he was on the pavement."

"Can you describe him?"

"No. He was all fuzzy, like he was in a fog."

"Why didn't you shout a warning before you fired?"

Ben shook his head. "There was no time," he said quietly. He pressed his hands over his face applying pressure to his tired eyes. "Look, I'm as confused as you are about all of this and learning I've just lost the past five weeks of my life isn't helping."

For a moment, nobody said anything. Ben saw the coffee on his tray and took a sip—weak and cold. As he swallowed, he relived the incident in his head. The shattered glass, pulling the trigger, the recoiling of the gun. "I killed him. I knew it when I pulled the trigger. If I hadn't taken the shot at that moment, he would have killed the guy in the street."

"But they weren't there, were they?" said Amelia quietly. "No one was lying in the street and there wasn't a man in a white overcoat."

"Guess not." He took another sip then pushed the tray out of the way. He felt his fists tightening. "All right, is that it? Is there anything else we need to go over right now?"

Howe sighed and they both got to their feet. "No, I think that's all for now. You should probably rest. Eat something."

Ben was exhausted. After they left, he forced down what food he could, then slept.

Late in the afternoon he was able to get out of bed on his own. Weak and light-headed he held onto the rolling IV pole, glad he could at least make it to the john on his own.

After a dinner of more mush, Ginny came in, bright-eyed and cheery holding a hanger with some of his clothes. "Heard you'll be getting out soon. Thought you might need these." She hung them up then walked closer. "I came to see you a while back but you were pretty out of it."

"So I hear. Thanks for coming." She had a cute face dominated by a broad mouth and a somewhat pointed chin that Ben knew she didn't like. But he did. Her blue eyes were always lively, always darting here and there. It wasn't like she was nervous. It was more like she could just never find anything worth focusing on. The quirk had been a little unsettling to Ben at first but he eventually grew accustom to it and, along with the pointed chin, he considered it one of her charms. But that was back when they were together. Seeing her again reminded him how much he missed her. She wore a sleeveless yellow sundress. "Must have warmed up," he said.

She pulled a chair beside his and sat down. "It's been a warm May so far."

"Oh yeah, for me it's still March." She gave him a token tap on the shoulder. It reminded him that she was the only person who might actually care if he lived or died. Phil would too, but that wasn't the same. A kiss from Ginny would have been nice, but maybe she found someone new. Well, good for her. "I hear you're taking care of Stump. Thanks. I hope he isn't giving you a hard a time."

She smiled. "He had a real attitude problem at first but we eventually came to an understanding: I give him food and water and walk him twice a day and he doesn't pee on my carpet and scare the neighbors like he did at first. He gets a little mournful sometimes. He misses you."

Well, that made three who cared about him: Phil, Ginny and Stump. They were as much of a family as he might ever have and he probably couldn't even count Ginny. What a shit-hole of a life he had.

Her eyes settled on his for nearly a full second. "You *are* getting out soon, right?"

"Couple of days. They want to run more tests. Should be good to go after that. I'll drop by for Stump."

She stayed a little longer then left. Man, he'd really messed up with her. If he'd handled things right, they might be married, maybe even have a baby. But no, he wasn't really ready for kids. And besides, what gave him the idea that she'd marry him even if he did have the balls to ask her? She was the one who'd walked out on him, remember? Yeah, he remembered that.

The IV was disconnected the next morning after which Ben was put through stair-step routines, followed by some work on the elliptical. He had always prided himself on staying in good shape and was appalled at the toll that 5 weeks in bed had taken on his body. Sweating and exhausted, he ate a decent lunch, then rested. Dr. Howe came by in the afternoon and ran vision and memory tests. The day after that was more of the same and Ben was starting to feel like he was getting his strength back. He was as cooperative as he could be with Dr. Howe but the poker-faced shrink never tipped his hand as to how he really thought Ben was doing. Howe would ask questions and occasionally he'd write something down—just like back on the fifth floor.

It was late the day after that when Howe got up to leave. "We should be able to get you released from here tomorrow but we need to do one more thing."

Hear it comes, thought Ben, his eyes rolling back.

"Do you have any objection to being put under hypnosis?"

"Are you serious?"

"It's a way to give us access to areas of your brain that may not even be accessible to you. It might be the only thing that'll shed some light on what exactly happened on the night of the shooting. And it could give us an insight into why you've been out for five weeks."

"I already told you that I'd be willing to take a lie-detector test," Ben reminded him. "You're going with hypnosis instead?"

"We'll do both. The polygraph will be done at the station after you've been released from the hospital." He paused. "So, do we have your approval for the hypnosis?"

"If that's the only thing keeping me from getting back on the job, then yeah, sure, why not."

"Good. You'll be given a consent form to sign before the

procedure and, just so you know, anything we learn from you while you're under hypnosis is inadmissible as courtroom evidence."

"Courtroom?"

Howe gave him a sympathetic look, like a dad might give to a child who'd been caught snitching a cookie. "Look, Detective Marshall, you discharged your weapon into a public street for no apparent reason. That, in itself, is an unlawful act and one for which you could be prosecuted, or at least dismissed from the force."

"No one got hurt."

"Well, you were just lucky about that, wouldn't you say?"

Ben slumped back into his pillow and turned his gaze to the ceiling. "Yeah, Doc. My life's been one piece of chocolate cake after another. That's why they call me Lucky Ben."

CHAPTER 5

In the morning, Ben put on the clothes Ginny brought and had a sausage and egg breakfast. An orderly brought him his keys, cell and wallet. He slid them into his pockets then stood, looking out the window. From a bright blue sky, the sun poured in. He was itching to get outside into the fresh air.

Howe came in at ten. "How're you feeling, detective?"

"I feel good," said Ben from a chair, his fingers laced together. "I'll feel better when I get back to my place and better still when I get back on the job. Any word on my status?"

"It'll be more desk duty for you, I'm afraid, until we can get things cleared up. Just too many unanswered questions."

That was what he'd expected. "But are they bringing me up on charges?"

Howe shook his head and pulled up a chair. "Don't think so, but that's not up to me."

"But it may be up to you if I keep my job or not, right?"

"I haven't written my report yet, but yes, my findings will play a part. I'll be honest with you, Detective. If I were you, I'd be looking into other career options. They're not going to keep you on desk work, not at your current pay-grade. But, you'll still get your citation and the boost in pay that comes along with it, and you'll get a small pension for your service. You're young, it's not the end of the world."

Ben had expected something like this but that didn't make it any easier to hear his fate spoken about so matter-of-factly. His fingers on his lap tightened. He looked down at them, watching his knuckles turning white. So what would he do now? He'd staked everything on being a cop. He wondered how small the small pension would be.

"I'm sorry it's come to this; honestly, I am," offered Howe.

"I still want to take the lie detector test. I'm telling the truth about everything."

"Yes, and we'll go through with that. Based on our conversations, I'm quite sure you think you're telling the truth. Unfortunately, your version of the truth just doesn't fit the facts. And frankly, the mental complications you've had with this second incident do not work in your favor. Right now we don't have a good explanation for your five-week coma."

"Dr. Silvers didn't seem too concerned about it."

"In her world it's more common. She's a specialist in that type of thing."

Right on cue, Dr. Silvers came into the room. Ben hadn't seen her since the first bedside session. She was quiet for a moment as if suspecting she'd been a topic in the conversation she'd just interrupted. "We're ready," she said to Howe.

"Time for the hypno-thing?" asked Ben.

"Yes. We'll be going up to another room, though."

Howe stood. "Barring something unusual, you'll be released from the hospital this afternoon. The captain wants you on the job Monday. We'll run you through the polygraph then. Dr. Silvers will be handling the hypnosis." He took a step toward the door. "It's not really my thing."

"It's not really my thing either," said Ben standing, feeling dizzy for a moment before getting his feet under him.

Howe gave a concerned glance then checked his watch. "Well, I'll see you at the precinct then."

"Wouldn't miss it," said Ben watching him go. "The guy's a shit-head," he said under his breath.

"He's trying to help you."

"I'm beyond help, don't you know? They're kicking me off the force."

She hesitated then guided him out into the busy corridor. "That has more to do with department policy than it does with Dr. Howe. He's just doing his job."

"Like you?"

"Yes, like me." They stepped into an empty elevator and she

hit floor number seven.

"So, you aren't with the force and you're not with this hospital. How did you happen to get involved with my case?"

"What makes you think I'm not with the force or with this hospital?"

"You seemed a little lost back there, looking for the elevator. And, if you were with the force, you would have acted differently around Howe. I *am* a detective, you know. Well I was." He paused. "So, are you going to answer my question?"

She remained silent.

"All righty then."

When the doors opened they took a right down a brightly lit, nearly empty corridor. Her steps seemed tentative.

"You lost again?"

"We're right up here, number 728."

The door was already open. They walked into a small room with a few flowery pictures, a throw-rug, a coffee table and a couple of stools. A couch stretched against one wall and, in the far corner next to where a window should have been but wasn't, sat a well-stuffed leather recliner. Standing to one side of it, as if he were just another piece of furniture, stood a man in a white lab coat, arms folded. He had that fresh out of college look with patches of stubble from a failed beard dotting his chin. "Doctor Silvers? Jim Cook," he said, suddenly animated.

They shook hands.

"You must be Mr. Marshall."

Ben kept his hands at his side. "Hi, Jim."

"Have a seat, would you?" said Jim, directing him into the recliner, handing him a pen and clipboard. "It's our standard consent form."

The leather was cold. Ben checked off a few boxes then signed the single page document.

"We'll be recording everything," said Jim, taking back the clipboard. He pointed to a camera in the ceiling. "And we don't use a swinging watch anymore." He handed Ben a VR headset and a pair of ear protectors designed to completely cup both ears.

The headset fit snuggly shutting out all light. With the ear protectors on, everything went silent. Ben let his head lay back and he started to relax feeling suddenly freed. Freed from the hospital, freed from...everything. Then, he felt something being taped to both sides of his head.

"Just a few electrodes," Silvers told Ben through speakers in the ear protectors. "All right, we're ready to begin. Are you ready, Ben?" she asked in a soft voice.

Ben gave a thumbs up.

"Just lay back. Let your mind wander."

Ben let himself sink further into the chair. All remained black and quiet for a while. Then a faint purple glow appeared before Ben, the headset making it seem like it was floating in the air. The glow remained steady at first, then began a slow throb, pulsing in exact rhythm with the beat of his heart. A low, deep hum joined in as the glow melted from one color to another, to another and shifted slowly from side to side. As he tried to follow its sideways motion, the light began to move steadily closer until both it and the throbbing hum occupied a region that was somehow behind his eyes, somehow inside his head. He felt his head rock slowly left then slowly right in a perfect rhythm over which he had no control. Slowly, his senses faded.

It seemed only seconds later when the ear protectors and headset were removed. Ben blinked. The room was dimly lit and Doctor Silvers was leaning over him.

"Very good, Ben. We're done," she said. "Are you feeling all right?"

Ben breathed in her perfume, a light peach scent that he hadn't picked up on before. Their eyes met and it was all he could do to keep from pulling her closer. Had they been alone, he might have. But no, he wasn't that desperate for female company, was he? Besides, there was Jim, arms folded staring down at him, reminding him that she was a shrink and, for today at least, Ben was just her lab rat.

Gently, she pulled the taped electrode from each side of his head then straightened and took a step back.

Ben swallowed, his throat dry. He spoke slowly. "Yeah, I feel good. That was fast. How long was I out?"

"About forty minutes," said Jim, walking toward the door. The lights slowly came up.

"How'd I do?"

Dr. Silvers turned away from him, gathering her notes, placing them in a folder that he noticed was different than the one from the other day. "You did fine," she said.

Ben got up, feeling a little light headed. "What does 'fine' mean?"

She turned to Jim. "Can you leave us, for a moment?"

"Of course," said Jim. He closed the door behind him.

Amelia—that's how he was thinking of her now—sat down on one of the stools. Ben took the other. "So, am I crazy?"

"I don't like to use the word crazy."

"Not enough syllables?"

"Ben, I believe you. You are quite normal in every outward way and, under hypnosis, you exhibited responses well within the statistical limits of normalcy."

"Glad to hear it."

"But, there was one thing."

He watched the corners of her mouth lift as if she was having trouble containing a secret. He eyed the couch next to him thinking he should be on it right now. "Cut the drama. Just tell me."

"Okay, so here it is. While you were under, I had you relive the shooting. You recounted the events exactly in line with your report, except for one thing. At the very moment you had your gun drawn, aimed through the broken window with your finger on the trigger, you said you heard a voice, a scream actually. Someone, a woman, screamed to you: *Kill him, Ben!* She screamed it twice."

A tingle ran up Ben's spine. Had he heard a scream? He hesitated, then shook his head. "No, that never happened. I just pulled my gun, broke the window and fired. It happened that fast. Almost in the same motion. I'm not one of those guys with voices in their heads." He got up off the stool.

"It did happen, Ben. Under hypnosis, you said it did. Do you want me to play back the session for you? Some part of you remembers the scream. You were very clear."

Ben felt blood rush to his head. "No. There was no voice. I was in control of myself and my weapon. I took the shot." But there he stopped, suddenly not so sure. Crazy things had been happening. He shot a man who wasn't there. He'd spent the last five weeks in a psych ward and now he finds out that there was a voice inside his head. He felt his skin go clammy. "Look, I've got to get out of here." He started walking, hardly feeling his feet hitting the floor or his hand opening the door.

"The elevator's that way," said Dr. Silvers from the doorway after he'd gone a few doors down the corridor in the wrong direction. He changed course and she followed.

"Will you be sending your video to the department?" he asked once they were together in the elevator.

"No. The department will get a report, but the video will stay with me."

"And you'll tell them about the voice in my head."

"Yes. You were in a stressful situation, Ben. For you to hear a voice out of nowhere telling you to kill someone is unusual, yes. But it doesn't mean that you have some kind of actual presence inside you telling you what to do. It might just be a stress-induced thing."

"Shit, I'm a cop. I'm always under stress." He wanted to slam a fist into the steel walls of the elevator and might have if the doors hadn't opened just then.

Silvers got out and took a few steps down the hall but Ben remained inside. He hit the button for the ground floor lobby.

As the doors closed he watched her turn. She ran back, eyes wide. "Ben, stop Ben. You don't understand. I need to tell you..." Her voice was cut off by the closing doors.

Ben let out a breath. It was good to finally be alone. When the doors opened again, Ben followed the signs to the main entrance and walked outside. The sun was warm and the air fresh. He stood on the walkway in front of the hospital just taking a few deep breaths. He pulled out his cell surprised to see it still had some juice. He called Ginny. No answer, must be at work hawking pricey perfume at that trendy store uptown where she worked. Or maybe she'd found a better job by now. He hoped she had. She was a smart woman, too smart to be a perfume pusher. He left her a text letting her know he was out of the hospital and would call back to coordinate a time to pick up Stump. He checked his watch—already two. Funny, it seemed like he'd just had breakfast. He called for a cab.

"Who are you? State your business," shouted Maddie after he'd climbed the stairs to the porch and opened the door to his brownstone. The old woman spoke from behind her door that was open only as far as the chain would allow.

"It's Ben, Maddie. I live here, remember?"

"Ben? Ben? Oh yes, you're the nice boy from upstairs who got shot. I thought you were dead."

Ben stepped inside and closed the door behind him. "Nope, still alive."

"Well, that's nice dear." Maddie closed her door.

Ben hit the stairs with a 'Hey Rob-Roy," at the landing.

"Hey Ben," came the muffled response. The guy probably didn't even realize that he'd been gone.

Ben's apartment was dark, and hot. He pulled up the shades and opened the windows. Sunlight streamed in and a warm breeze carried sounds from the street. Things were medium-grade messy just as he'd left them. He plopped down in his recliner, sat there for a while then realized he was hungry. He checked the fridge—empty except for a jar of strawberry jam. Yeah, everything else would have gone bad by now and Ginny would have thrown them out. He checked the trash. Yeah, she'd taken that out too. He decided to do something nice for her but he had no idea what. He wondered how long it took before strawberry jam turned bad then threw it out.

In the shower he let his mind drift. He wondered if he'd be getting a call from the hospital or from Dr. Silvers after leaving like he did. Then he remembered the expression on her face as she raced back to the elevator. He wondered if she was that concerned about all her patients. He got dressed, hit the street and wolfed down some fast-food. He felt like a double scotch would be a great way to wash down the double burger and fries, but, thinking how the alcohol might screw with the meds already in his system, he resisted the temptation. No, the scotch would have to wait a couple of days—but only a couple.

Back up in his apartment, he spent the rest of the day watching TV. It was dark when he realized neither the hospital nor Dr. Silvers had called. He began to feel good about bugging out like he did. Yeah, it was all about getting his life back under control—his *own* control. Still though, he was curious about Dr. Silvers. How exactly had she gotten involved with his case? And hadn't she seemed a little too concerned about him? But maybe that was just his imagination.

The next day was Sunday. He stopped by Ginny's and, as she opened the door, Stump nearly knocked her over, leaping into his arms. The dog pranced around and woofed and couldn't get enough belly-rubs.

"It was great of you to take him in," Ben said to Ginny. "Hope he wasn't too much trouble."

She shrugged. "He's sure glad to have you back."

"Yeah. I missed him too. Thanks a lot, Ginny." It was pretty lame. He thought maybe he should have said something about missing her too but he knew it wouldn't have come out right: *Sure missed Stump, oh, by the way, missed you too.* He kicked himself for not having gotten her something for her trouble. "We ought to get together sometime," he said.

Her face tightened, her eyes on the floor now. "That wouldn't be a good idea, Ben."

He placed a hand on her shoulder but she pulled back. She handed him a partly empty bag of dog food and a grocery bag with a few doggie toys. Before leaving, Ben had glanced around for any signs that she might have someone living with her but saw none. He wanted her to be happy but he still felt enough of an attachment to her to be jealous if she had someone new. "Well, I owe you. If there's ever anything I can do for you..."

"Sure, Ben. I'll let you know."

On Monday morning Ben tried to behave as if everything was normal. He woke up at the usual time, dressed, took care of Stump and walked to the precinct. The walk felt good. The guys had a welcome-back thing for him in the break room. There were lots of smiles and slaps on the back but Ben knew that everyone was just going through the motions. They all knew he was as good as gone.

At ten came the lie detector test with a nerdy looking guy up on the fifth, two doors down from Howe's office. Ben half expected Howe to show up. But no, it was just him and the nerd and the machine. It took an hour then it was back to his desk where a few folders lay.

"How'd it go?" asked Phil over his glasses.

"All right, I guess." He held up the folders as he sat. "What are these?"

"Stuff from Harriet. She probably thinks you work for her now."

Hard-ass Harriet, Captain Nolan's administrative assistant, was an all business African-American woman who ran her little domain with the stiff demeanor of a sergeant major. She and Nolan were a good fit for each other. Ben knew she came from a military family but didn't know much else. "Shit," he said.

"Shit is right," affirmed Phil.

After lunch, he heard the unmistakable click of her footsteps heading his way. He decided he wouldn't look up from his work right away.

"Captain Nolan wants to see you in his office," she said. She gave Ben no time for a snide remark before marching back to her desk. "*Now*, Detective Marshall," she added without looking back.

"Jesus, she's no fun," said Ben to Phil, getting up.

"Oh, I bet she could be," said Phil watching her go.

Like Harriet, Nolan was all business too. In a month or so," the captain told him, "Internal Affairs will have wrapped up their investigation into the shooting at the stake out. It's official now, there'll be no charges brought against you."

"That's good."

"Yes, that is good. And you'll be receiving a citation for your actions on the Elmhurst incident. It comes with a nice boost in pay that'll be reflected in your pension."

There it was—pension, the word that meant he was officially off the force.

The captain went on. "The best I can give you is three months more of desk duty. I'm sorry Detective Marshall. Really I am. You do have the right to appeal this decision but, frankly, I think that would be a waste of time. You should consider your options. We have a career transitioning program you can take advantage of."

Ben couldn't even remember shaking Nolan's hand when he'd left his office. Even Harriet gave him a sober glance on his way out the door.

The rest of the day was even more of a waste of time than the morning had been. Ben could almost feel everyone staring at him, probably wondering if he was going to go ape-shit about the whole thing. Even Stump that night, seemed to eye him with trepidation.

Ben slept well which he thought was a little odd considering his state of mind. He woke up at the usual time and in the bathroom he stared at himself in the mirror. What the hell was he worried about? The captain was right. He was still young. This wasn't the end of the world. Maybe he'd go back to college and finish that degree of his. What did he need? Another year or two? Sure, he could do that. Why not?

He took Stump out for his morning walk then left for work. Trotting down from the porch, he stared at the tenement across the street where he'd gotten shot. All seemed normal there now, as if the incident had never happened, as if a cop hadn't died on the third floor, as if he himself hadn't nearly bled-out on the stairs fighting for his life. Strangely, he felt the urge to cross the street and go inside. Maybe a part of him wanted to relive the whole thing. And what about the stake out? Did he want to relive that too?

He shook his head. Shit, must be that loony voice inside me playing games. But there was no inner voice, right? He stopped. He stood still, daring the voice to reveal itself. He placed a hand on a lamppost. He closed his eyes and waited, a feeling of dread, almost a nausea, filling his chest. Hearing nothing he took a breath and opened his eyes. He spit into the gutter. Right, no voice. Silvers was just wrong about that.

At the precinct, he punched in on time, grabbed a mug of coffee and said hey to Phil as he sat down. This time Harriet had left four folders on his desk. Opening the top one, he asked Phil what he was up to.

"Oh, the usual crap. Still working the Ronaldi case. Got a line on someone in the Russian mob—a guy named André. No last name, just André. A real pretty-boy though. Should have gone to Hollywood instead of Boston." He handed Ben an 8 x 10.

Dark leather jacket with the collar turned up. It wasn't a good face shot. The photo was fuzzy, obviously an enlargement, taken from a distance. Two other men were with him, their backs turned. "He's got kind of a James Dean look going for him. Who are his buddies?"

"Yeah, we figure him to be still in his twenties. Don't know about the other guys. Our facial recognition software had no luck with them."

"How do you know this is André and why do you figure him for doing Bruno and Vito?"

"We've got a tip. Evidently Andre's been bragging about it. It's like he wants to get the word out on the street that he's the big bad dude now."

"Sounds like a big, bad, *stupid* dude." Despite the unclear photo, Ben could pick out the dominant features: square jaw, perfect nose, mean looking eyes. And, sitting atop it all, was a tangled mass of black curly hair. "You're right, would have been good in the movies. The pic's a little fuzzy too. Maybe his English isn't so good." He handed it back. "Anything I can do to help out? I'll have a little dead time between these things for Harriet."

"Nothing right now. I'll let you know if something comes up."

Just then a shout came from across the room. "Yo, Phil. You ready?"

Phil winced, gave a wave and put on a forced smile. "That's Steve, my partner for the week. Another rookie—third one I've been through since your...thing. Thinks he's Stallone or something." He grabbed an apple from the corner of his desk and took a bite as he stood.

Ben swiveled his chair around and checked Steve out: hat too big, uniform a size too small, hands at both hips, loaded for bear. At least he wasn't chewing on a wad of gum. "Don't be too hard on him."

Phil just sighed as he headed out.

The folders from Harriet were all routine. Filling out forms, checking the right boxes and typing reports. By the end of the morning he was finished and walked them back to her. She wasn't at her desk. Probably out to lunch, he figured. He slipped the folders into her in-box and stuck a sticky note on top with a smiley face on it. Never hurts to be nice. Nolan's door was closed and he imagined her and the captain taking care of a little business inside. No, that wasn't really fair. Nolan's door was almost always closed. Plus, he was a good family man. Maybe he'd taken her to lunch. Wasn't it administrative assistant's day today? She did have a fresh rose poking up from the half-filled drinking glass that sat next to her name plate.

Ben started back to his desk then stopped, a thought triggered by the row of file cabinets walling off Harriet's desk and the captain's office from the rest of the room. He knew that the files often contained information on contract employees and consultants hired by the department on a short term basis. The file drawers were always locked but Ben happened to know where Harriet kept the key. He walked back to her desk and pulled open the center drawer. There it was, a ring with more than a dozen keys. He picked it up. He knew he could get fired for what he was about to do but why worry about that now?

He scanned the labels on each file drawer and found one tagged *Personnel.* Through trial and error, he found the right key and pulled open the drawer. It didn't take long to find a folder labeled *Dr. Amelia Silvers.*

It was a half-inch thick. He pulled it, quickly closed and locked the file drawer then put the keys back where they belonged. On his way back to his desk, he casually glanced around the room. Two guys on the phone, a few more reading newspapers as they munched on sandwiches. No one took notice of him. Well, why would they? As if it was nothing special, he tossed the Silvers folder on his desk. He bought a sandwich from the vending machine and grabbed a fresh coffee. Back at his desk, he stared at the folder for a moment, then opened it.

CHAPTER 6

On top lay a thin stack of pages held together by a paper clip in the corner. The first page listed the particulars of Doctor Silvers' test subject, one Benjamin Marshall. It gave bulleted info on age, marital status, and years on the force. It also included a brief assessment that found him to be in generally good physical health.

The next page gave a brief history of his record at the department followed by a summary of the incident at the stake-out as well as a second summary of the incident on Elmhurst Street and his subsequent hospitalization. Ben skimmed through three pages of things he already knew or expected then flipped to another page headed by the words: HYPNOSIS REPORT.

"What you got there?"

Ben nearly jumped out of his skin. It was Harriet, walking up to his desk. He closed the folder quickly, sliding it under his computer keyboard. "Just something Phil asked me to help out with," he said straightening.

"Oh, okay, that's good. Glad you're keeping busy." She eyed his sandwich. "You going to eat that?"

"Why? You hungry?"

She sighed. "Just don't be leaving any crumbs around. You know how I feel about that. Look, I'll be getting a few more things over to you later today." She paused and put a hand on his desk, her face softening with a grim smile. "I know this isn't easy for you detective and I know it's not exactly fair but..."

"Yeah, shit happens," said Ben through a bite of his sandwich. "That's life, isn't it? Don't worry, I'll make the best of it." Ben hated getting pity from her but at the moment, he just wanted to get back to the Silvers folder.

She nodded in an understanding way, heaved a long sigh that made her substantial chest rise and fall, then walked back to her desk.

Ben wasn't sure he liked or trusted this softer side of Harriet. As her normal hard-assed self she was much more predictable. He finished his lunch as the room got busy again. He opened the Silvers file again, resting it discretely in the crook of his bent knee. He started reading:

HYPNOSIS REPORT

(Digital recording and a full transcript of the session previously provided)

Patient transitioned easily to a deep hypnotic state. Preliminary questioning confirmed that he maintained an awareness of both who he was and where he was. He was easily led back to the incident in question. Subject seemed to relive the events of that night in vivid detail providing information not included in his previously submitted official report. The following is the most pertinent excerpt from the official transcript:

Detective M: *"I'm pacing, window to door then back again looking through the window each time. I see nothing going on in the suspect's room across the street. Suddenly, Phil puts a hand to his earphones and makes a kind of a grunting sound to get my attention. I hurry back to the window. Eventually, two shadows appear on the shade indicating that a second person is in the room. I glance at Phil and he gives me a thumbs up. He's picking up a conversation.*

Dr. S: *Did you actually hear that conversation?*

Detective M: *No. That's Phil's job. I grab the camera and snap a few pics of the window. As I'm doing that, I see something down in the street. It's actually further on up the street and it's just a silhouette in a kind of a fog at first. I can't make it out clearly but, from the way it moves, I can tell that someone is walking, coming closer.*

Dr. S: *This person's walking down the middle of the street? Aren't there any cars coming?*

Detective M: *There were no cars. But there wouldn't have been at that hour.*

Dr. S: *What do you see now? Can you actually see this person?*

Do you hear anything?
Detective M: *I don't hear anything, but the guy seems suddenly to be moving quickly, coming closer very fast. Yes, I see him now—mid-fifties maybe, a little stout. He's in a white overcoat. The coat's unbuttoned and it flares out as he walks.*
Dr. S: *Does he see you?*
Detective M: *No. He seems fixated on something further down the street—something I can't see. Oh, wait, the guy's pulling something up to waist level—an umbrella? No. Shit! It's a rifle. (Agitated) He's pointing it toward that thing he's looking at. I shout to Phil: 'Gun. Gun.' I pull my weapon.*
Dr. S: *You sense danger?*
Detective M: *Yes, but not for myself. I'm afraid he's going to shoot someone in the street.*
Dr. S: *And can you now see what he's aiming at?*
Detective M: *(Shakes his head, still agitated) No, not clearly. But wait, I can just make out someone lying there, off to my right...Yes, it's a man. He's trying to get up. He looks hurt. Shit! The guy's going to kill him. I flick off my safety, break the window with my gun, and point it at the man in the white overcoat. Shit, he sees me.*
Dr. S: *How do you know he sees you?*
Detective M: *He's looking up, directly at me. I can see his face. Pudgy jowls, flat nose, dark eyes close together.*
Observation: *Agitation increases. Subject shifts in his chair. There's a nervous twitch in his right hand.*
Detective M: *The pavement seems to turn greenish. I hear a shout, no, more like a scream. It's a woman's scream. 'Kill him, Ben! Kill him!' she shouts. I fire. Twice.*
Dr. S: *The woman said your name?*
Detective M: *Yes.*
Dr. S: *Did your shots hit the man?*
Detective M: *(hesitating) I...I didn't miss, I know that. But at the moment I fired the second shot, the man was gone. Both men were gone. The street was empty.*

The running dialog went on for another full page that Ben just skimmed through. The report ended with a short paragraph under a separate heading:

OBSERVATIONS AND RECOMENDATIONS

Detective Marshall obviously believes that what he saw on the street that night was real. It is possible that the scream he remembers under hypnosis but apparently doesn't recall when awake, is an indication of mild schizophrenia. That, combined with the influence of certain other factors, such as prolonged high stress, and anxiety over personal issues, can sometimes lead a person to construct entire non-realities. Usually these non-realities are places of refuge but that is definitely not the case here. Though Detective Marshall has, throughout his career, exhibited courage and resourcefulness as a valuable member of the police force, I must recommend that he be confined to desk duty until further study and treatment might render him fit again for active duty among the general public.

So there it was. He'd heard a voice telling him to kill someone. They'd actually used his name and he'd pulled the trigger. But there was something else that bothered him. He re-read the last paragraph and couldn't shake the feeling that Silvers was leaving something out; like her conclusions were a little too brief and not well founded. And what was up with the *personal issues* thing? Still, it was the voice thing that had him most concerned. He closed the folder and put it down. His hand was shaking. He rubbed his eyes. Shit. What the fuck's going on with me? He took a few breaths and refocused on his surroundings just in time to see Harriet walking toward him. He placed an arm over the Silvers folder.

"Feeling all right detective?"

"Sure, just fine."

"Maybe you should take some time off."

"I just got back, remember? No. I'm really all right." Ben pointed to a short stack of folders she held. "What have you got there?"

She placed the stack on his desk. "More work for you. No hurry though. Anytime tomorrow will be fine."

"Great, no problem," said Ben as Phil got back to his desk.

Phil waited for Harriet to leave before sitting down. "You two seem to be getting along just fine," he observed.

"She feels sorry for me."

"I give it three days tops. I don't think she's capable of being nice to anyone longer than that."

Ben found time to go through the rest of the Silvers folder then, staying late, put it back in the files.

At home that night, Ben got on the Internet and learned a few more things about Dr. Amelia Silvers. The next morning, he called in sick.

With only a guard rail separating it from Interstate 90, the campus of Boston University sat just a long homerun shot from Fenway Park. A short cab ride got Ben there and, after negotiating the narrow walkways, he had no trouble finding the Department of Psychological and Brain Sciences where, according to her on-line schedule, Dr. Amelia Silvers would be teaching that morning in lecture hall B01. He joined a line of millennials filing into the theater-style classroom and grabbed a seat in back.

At ten sharp, a computer tone sounded and Doctor Amelia Silvers strode onto the stage in jeans, tennis shoes and a BU sweatshirt looking like she'd just taken a wrong turn off the jogging path, ending up there on the stage by complete accident. She brushed her curly hair back, plopped a thick textbook down onto a wooden table and pinned a wireless mic to her collar. For the next fifty minutes she strode casually between a PowerPoint screen, and a green chalkboard while talking about neurons and synapses and frontal and remedial cortexes. She had an interesting method of speaking Ben thought, at times modulating her voice as if she were reading from a good novel, while at other times using an upraised arm to add emphasis. The students had their tablets out, most taking notes but, from his vantage, Ben could see a good number of them doing online stuff. A few wearing earbuds were even gaming—so much for the upcoming crop of psychoanalysts.

When the computer tone sounded again, Professor Silvers shouted out the next assignment as the room emptied. A few students waylaid her with some questions that she handled quickly as Ben made his way down. He caught her eye at the halfway point.

She straightened abruptly. “Detective Marshall,” she said, watching him walk the rest of the way down and onto the stage. The room was empty except for the two of them.

“I read your report,” he said, stopping a few feet from her.

“Nolan showed it to you?”

“Yes, in a manner of speaking.”

“And what did you think?”

“It’s what *you* think that matters. I’m just the patient. What the hell do I know about what’s going on inside my head? All those neurons and synapses firing all the time.”

“The report wasn’t secret. If you’d given me a chance I would have gone over the hypnosis session with you back at the hospital. You could have seen the tape of the whole thing.”

“You think I’m schizophrenic. They’re going to take my badge because of your report.”

Her cheeks turned a shade pinker. She turned to face Ben more directly. “They might take your badge, yes, but not because of anything I did. You’re the one who heard the screams. You’re the one who fired two shots at someone who wasn’t there. Until we learn more about your condition, you can’t possibly think yourself fit for active police work.”

Well, she had him there. Even Phil didn’t want to partner with him now. But Ben had other questions. “Back at the hospital you said you needed to explain something to me. What was that all about? And right at the end of your report you mentioned something about ‘other factors and personal issues’. What did you mean by that? And, while we’re at it, how did you happen to get involved in my case to begin with?”

In the back of the hall, a few students were starting to filter in for the next class. Conscious of them, Dr. Silvers picked up her things. "Look, I can explain. Yes, there is something I wanted to talk to you about—something you should know. Come on, we can talk better upstairs."

He followed her out of the room, down a wide hallway and into an open lounge area bordered by a couple of fast-food counters. They got two coffees and grabbed a table.

Ben waited for her to begin.

She took a sip of coffee. "All right, first some background on me. After getting my Ph.D. the firm I was with did some contract work for the state. At first, all I did was personnel screenings for high level positions. Boring stuff. Here I was, fresh out of college, looking for a challenge, ready to be the next Freud and all I was doing was screening job applicants. I got sick of it pretty quick. I did some consulting work for the Boston PD. That's how I met Dr. Howe. He and I hit it off, professionally I mean, and because of him, I developed an interest in historical genealogies as they related to certain unusual character traits. I wrote a paper on the subject, got it published and eventually landed the teaching job here at B.U. For nearly a year I lost touch with Dr. Howe, then out of the blue, he gave me a call."

"About me."

"Yes. Well, about your case. At that time you were still in a coma. It seems he discovered something extraordinary."

"That doesn't sound good."

"No, it's nothing bad, really." She lifted a dismissive hand and smiled slightly. "It's about a relative of yours who was once a major influence in the early history of psychology."

Ben shook his head. The last thing he needed right now was a history lesson. "And how exactly is that going to help me? Why would I even care about some long lost relative of mine?"

"Everyone should care about their ancestry. It's what makes us who we are and it just happens to be the whole point of my current research."

"Ah research, that's what's important to all you academics isn't it?—your precious research."

"Don't be so cynical. Research is important."

He held her eyes thinking that, being a shrink, she was probably using a trick right now to make her facial expression unreadable. But maybe that was something all women could do. "And exactly how is your research going to help me?"

"Well the truth of it is, it probably won't help you at all. And it may have nothing at all to do with your present situation. But it's still extraordinary." Her smile returned. "It's about your great, great grandmother."

Ben stared back. Blood rushed to his head. "Look, I don't need to know anything about my great, great grandmother. I just need to find a way to keep my badge and put my life back together. If you can't help me do that, I'm not going to be wasting any more time with you or Howe. The two of you just want to study Ben the lab rat, maybe compare him to his grandmother's lab rat, write a paper and make yourselves famous."

She opened her mouth, then hesitated. For Ben, her wavering eyes said all he needed to hear.

"Yeah, it's true, isn't it?" He stood and for some reason felt compelled to add: "It's really too bad. I kind of liked you in a strange sort of way." He started walking away, fighting off the urge to glance back or go back for his coffee. Great, now he's got her wondering where that thing about me liking her came from.

He took a cab to the stationhouse.

"Feeling better, detective?" Asked Harriet as he fell into his chair and flipped on his computer. She waited for a moment. "You called in sick, remember?"

"Yeah, right. Some sort of sinus thing. Yes, I'm feeling better now." He added a sniff.

He occupied himself with the work Harriet had given him but found himself thinking about what life might be like after the force. He was going to have to update his unimpressive résumé. He imagined the bullet points: Three years of college, never graduated, four years as a beat cop then ten as a detective, got fired. Well, not fired. Officially, he would be retired. He did have the one commendation and he knew that Nolan would give him a good recommendation for any position other than law enforcement. Still, any effective updating of his résumé' would mean stretching the truth.

He imagined himself in a job interview: 'You're a little young to be a retired detective, Mr. Marshall, what made you decide to leave the force?' Yeah, he'd have to work up a good evasive answer for that one. Maybe he *should* go back to school, finish up that Poli-Sci degree. But no, that would take at least two years and more money than he had. Maybe he'd take some time off to get his shit together. He had a few thousand in the bank. It wouldn't last long but, yeah, it would be good to take a few weeks, maybe even a month to just gather himself, get the wind back in his sails.

A few weeks passed.

Phil and his rookie seemed to be working out and Harriet was back to her hard-ass self which was just fine with Ben. He tried to call Ginny a few times, texted her too, but never got a response.

He started drinking. Not much at first, just one or two before bed to help him sleep. After a while he added two more in the mornings to help him get through the day. Nothing serious, he told himself, he could stop anytime.

June went by quickly. He'd gotten into the routine of buying a paper on his way in and reading it at his desk. Occasionally he'd get work from Harriet or help Phil with something but, he was just going through the motions now. He'd taped a calendar to the side of his desk, checking off the days with a red marker, making like he was happy about the whole thing. But Phil knew better, and most of the guys did too. They all knew he was shitting bricks about his future.

It was at the end of the day, with exactly two weeks to go before his retirement became official that Ben pushed open the stationhouse doors and saw her leaning against a lamppost—the curly hair hard to miss. Her eyes locked with his right away. Dr. Silvers had been waiting for him.

"Hi, Detective Marshall. Got time to talk?"

Ben bit his tongue only just able to keep himself from saying something surly. He realized that he was actually pleased to see her again. "Hello, Doc. Sure, I've got some time. Why not?" Pleased though he was, he wondered what she was up to.

"Don't worry, no lab-rat stuff, I promise."

"Look, I'm sorry about that. I didn't mean to..."

"No. You were right about me, Ben. I wasn't being fair to you." She paused. "You hungry? I know a good place."

Ben hesitated only to make her think he wasn't desperate for female companionship. "Sure, why not?"

It was a beautiful late afternoon. At a café, they grabbed some food, each paying for their own then sat at an outdoor table. "You should have gotten a Reuben," Ben told her. "Who orders a salad from a Boston Deli?"

"It's tasty," she said, through a mouthful. "Good for you too. You should have it sometime."

Ben knew she was just trying to get him comfortable before getting to the point. And she was good at it, flashing those brown eyes of hers the way she did as if they were friends. Well, maybe they could be. "So, what did you want to talk about?"

She swallowed and dabbed her lips with her napkin then pulled a thumb drive from her pocket and placed it on the table in front of him.

"Let me guess. That's the video of my hypnosis session."

"It's yours. I know that you've seen the transcript but the transcript wasn't exactly...complete. You should look at the video. Howe was against you seeing it but I think you should—especially in light of a new development."

Ben put down his sandwich.

"Oh, it's nothing bad," she added quickly. "Actually, it's something you might find exciting."

That didn't exactly make Ben feel better. He wondered what could possibly be exciting to a psychologist.

She reached into the messenger bag at her feet and pulled out a thick textbook along with a sheet of paper. She handed him the sheet of paper. "That's a sketch of your family tree based on the information Howe had on you. It wasn't really kosher but he shared it with me a few days ago. It confirms what I told you when we met back at BU—about your great, great grandmother, I mean.

The diagram was a simple pencil sketch showing that Ben's parents were Peter Marshall and Sandra Packard. Yes, that was right. It followed Sandra's line back to her mother, Olivia whose maiden name was Cavanaugh and whose mother was Abigail with the maiden name of Salter. One step further back was Abigail's mother, Lydia, who was married to Daniel Salter. And there the tree stopped.

"Your great, great grandmother kept her maiden name. She was Lydia Thornhill and she died sometime in the early 1920's." Amelia slid the textbook closer to him. "This is the classic: Introduction to Modern Psychology." She opened it to the spot where she had a book mark, tapping a finger on the lower right corner. "Detective Marshall, say hello to your Great, Great Grandmother Lydia."

Ben stared down at the black and white photograph showing an unsmiling woman in profile with her hair tied back. Ben guessed her to be somewhere in her twenties. Her lace collar closely bordered her throat seeming to add length to her neck. Her expression showed calmness but her eyes, fastened as they were on the lens of the camera, had an intensity to them that was hard to describe. Her name was printed in italics beneath her picture. Ben shifted his eyes up the page. The section heading was: *Women in the Reform Movement*. He skimmed the text.

"It says here that she was involved with prison reform."

"She was a pioneer in psychology. Before her, the field didn't even exist as an area of study—at least in America. For a woman to do what she did back then was truly remarkable. She was a person of great courage and compassion."

"Compassion for criminals?"

"There was an institutional reform movement taking place at the time bent on making the penal system in America more effective. Prisons at that time were places of incredible brutality. Among other things, the movement actually promoted the idea of including women in management positions at prisons, the idea being that they would be more naturally empathetic to prisoners and therefore more effective at remolding them into acceptable, productive members of society. Of the women involved, Doctor Lydia Thornhill was one of the most prominent."

"Was she really a doctor?"

"Yes. She obtained a medical degree from the University of Michigan when such a thing was unheard of for a woman. We believe that picture of her was taken while she was still a student. After graduating, she worked for years at a prison up in Maine. It had a profound effect on her. She wrote a book about it." Amelia pulled a much smaller book from her bag and handed it to Ben. "Careful how you handle it, there aren't too many copies left. It took me a few months to obtain this one. "

The book had a green, woven cover. With a fingertip Ben traced the gold-embossed title. Below that, also in gold, was the name *Thornhill.* Not Lydia Thornhill and not L. Thornhill, just Thornhill. He opened the book. The binding creaked. The yellowed pages had a coarse, almost brittle feel that carried with it the smell of old paper. He noted 1890 as the year the book was published. He turned a page and read the first sentence:

I remember the date and the exact hour when normalcy left me.

Ha, thought Ben, just like at the stake-out when normalcy seems to have left him. He closed the book and placed it on the table next to his half eaten Reuben. "You think I should read it."

"Yes, you should read it. But watch your video first."

"What became of her?"

"In her later years she became institutionalized."

"She went crazy?"

"Yes, in a manner of speaking. She developed a condition that came to be known as, *The Thornhill Syndrome* in which it is said, that she dreamed periodically of having experienced death."

"Everybody has nightmares."

"These were more than that. Her dreams were extraordinarily vivid and, on waking, she'd remember them in detail—or so they say. She was a doctor then ultimately a patient at an asylum up in

Maine. After the asylum closed, we believe she and her daughter lived together in a cottage up there somewhere. After Lydia died, her daughter Abigail moved down here to Boston where she led an apparently ordinary life."

Dr. Silvers—all right, Amelia, put a finger on the sheet of paper indicating a phone number at the bottom. "You should call this number. I took the liberty of checking into the Thornhill estate. The Public Records Office told me about the Thornhill house up in Maine saying that its ownership had long since reverted to the state. But, as Lydia Thornhill's direct descendant and I'm guessing, her sole heir, you do have the right to reclaim the house and its contents if you want. You may have some back taxes to settle but, as I understand, the place is located in such a remote area that the state may be just as happy to be rid of it. Maybe you can work a deal."

Ben put down his drink. "Shit. I own a house up in Maine? That's the new development?"

"Yes, if you want it. Having been empty for so long, it probably needs a lot of work. That number is for the State of Maine Office of Records and Deeds. They'll tell you what you need to do."

Ben pictured himself up in the Maine woods, working to fix up the house, waking up each morning to clear country air and hard physical work. It was as if he'd suddenly been given a sense of direction, a challenge of sorts, a place where he belonged. He'd read about guys who'd left big city life to live in the wilderness. Maybe he would become one of them. Yeah, why not?—*Lumberjack Ben.*

"I hope you don't think I stuck my nose where it didn't belong." She took another bite of salad. "So, you think you might call them?"

"Yeah, why not? Maybe I will. I'll be done with the force in two weeks so I might even take the time to go up there."

"Two weeks will also give you time to read your grandmother's book. Let me know what you think of it." She took a sip from her drink. "You can keep the textbook too. Who knows, maybe you'll develop an interest in psychology."

"Don't hold your breath on that. But I do appreciate you looking into all this. And...I'm sorry I had you pegged as a useless academic."

"Apology accepted."

They talked for a time and, as they finished the rest of their food, Ben found himself enjoying her company.

That night, back in his apartment, he opened the textbook and turned to the bookmarked page. He stared at the photograph and, neither smiling nor frowning, a young Lydia Thornhill stared back.

CHAPTER 7

April 8, 1886

The gray-bearded man stood up from behind the camera. "All right young lady, hold very still if you would. He gave her a stern look, then squeezed a black rubber bulb to open the shutter.

Lydia Thornhill held her bland pose stiffly until the man released his grip on the bulb and the shutter closed.

Thank you miss...?"

"Thornhill. First name, Lydia." She spelled both for him then added, "*Doctor*, Lydia Thornhill."

"No middle name? No middle initial?"

"None, thank you." She stood, uncomfortable in the tight dress her mother had picked out for her. She paid and signed a receipt then hurried out the door of the little office that sat at the edge of the university grounds. Were it not for the dress and her tight shoes, she might have enjoyed the walk on that sunny spring morning. Birds chirped noisily in the branches and the campus was bustling. Classes were still in session, but some students were already preparing to leave, most headed home for the summer. She passed a group of boys who gave her a few admiring looks that she properly ignored, but secretly enjoyed, then crossed the commons and made her way up to her second floor dorm room that she shared with three other women—none there at the moment. She pulled off her shoes, struggled out of her dress, hung it up then slipped on a loose blouse and a long green skirt. She opened a window and let the cool air flow in. There, that was better.

She fell backwards onto her bed and lay staring at the white plaster ceiling. The long, hard-fought years of formal education, first at Lindenwood, then Vassar then finally at the medical department here at Michigan, would soon end. Finally she'd be able to count herself as one of the few female medical professionals in America. She was proud of that fact but wondered just what her next step would be. Her grades ranked no better than the upper middle of her graduating class but, unlike most of her male classmates she'd received no offers of employment. Rather than gender, she realized this dilemma could have just as easily come about because of the specialized training she'd chosen to take on: the study of the human brain. She knew she'd been reckless with that choice and always felt it ironic that she'd made it more with her heart than with her own brain. She wanted to be among the first to unlock the secrets hidden deep within the folds of that most remarkable organ that alone set human beings apart from all other species. But she was about to graduate now and there was no going back on her decision. She had to face the grim reality that since surgery on the brain was always fatal, who really needed a brain doctor?

She glanced at the clock on the wall and saw with a fright that she had only five minutes to get to class. She grabbed her things and hurried off, taking a seat in the classroom just as Professor Barnhart stepped up to the podium. His steely Austrian glare seemed to settle on her as it always did, as if asking how she'd ended up here among his real students. As she always did, Lydia glared right back. Being the only female in the class of twenty-eight she knew perfectly well why she was here and not much else mattered. Lydia had to admit that for all the ill-will Barnhart seemed to send her way, his was a towering intellect and she'd learned a lot from the gray-whiskered old man over the last four years.

In June, eight weeks later, her photograph appeared in the university yearbook for the Medical Department class of 1886. The graduation ceremony was held outside in front of a small gaggle of proud parents and admiring relatives. As chair of the medical department, it was Barnhart's job to hand out the certificates.

Lydia felt her heart thumping. To its beat, she marched onto the makeshift stage and made sure to look Barnhart in the eye. Unexpectedly, his expression seemed to soften as she drew closer and she was surprised when he took her hand in his and spoke.

"Congratulations, my dear. Can I trouble you to meet me in my office tomorrow morning at ten?"

Her mouth went dry. "I...yes, of course," she said accepting her graduation certificate from him. "Thank you professor," she said almost as an afterthought. What could he want with her?

Once back at her seat with the rest of the class, Danny Salter retook his seat beside her. He leaned closer. "All right. I saw that. What did the old bastard say to you?"

"It wasn't anything."

"It made you blush."

She smiled and nearly let loose a laugh, feeling almost giddy. She had just graduated. She had just achieved a lifelong dream, but part of what she was feeling was because of Danny. Dashing, debonair, Danny; graduated now as a doctor himself, he'd stood with her through those tough final years of training. She thought of him as her beau and he'd professed the same feelings about her. "He wants to see me in his office tomorrow morning," she finally confided.

"What? Old Barnhart?" Danny asked with a laugh. "And will you go?"

"Yes, of course I will."

"What does he want?"

"Can't imagine."

"I can—the old bastard."

Playfully, she jabbed an elbow into his ribs. "You're terrible."

"I'll stop by tomorrow afternoon and you can tell me all about it."

Lydia's parents were good friends with the Salters and, after the ceremony, they all shared a picnic with the two graduates. It was a beautiful late afternoon, the sun warm, a breeze ruffling the trees, the conversation flowing easily among the six of them along with a few bottles of red wine.

"I'm sure the two of you will go far," said Lydia's father, his back resting against a tree as the others shared the spread-out blankets. "The world's exploding with new ideas and new discoveries in science and medicine. Now that you're graduated, you'll be part of that modern new world. How excited we are for you both."

Lydia smiled lightly at Danny. "We're excited too, although I have yet to receive an offer of employment."

"I have a feeling that something good will come along, my dear," said Danny's father in his usual authoritative but rosy-eyed way. "The population's booming. There'll always be a need for good doctors."

But maybe not brain doctors, Lydia knew her more practical mother must be thinking.

Danny poured more wine for Lydia. "We're still hopeful that we'll both get positions up in Maine at Mount Mercy where we can be together."

"That's up in Portland, isn't it?" asked her mother.

"Yes. Right on the coast. It's very beautiful I'm told."

"We've never been up there," said Danny's mother, making it clear yet again that she disapproved of her son moving so far away. "In fact, we don't know anyone who's ever been there."

The awkward silence was filled by Lydia's mother saying: "Well, shall we eat?"

Following the picnic supper, both sets of parents made a graceful exit leaving Lydia and Danny alone stretched out on a blanket staring up through the branches into the sky. The sun was just dipping behind the crest of a distant hill. The breeze turned refreshingly cool, rustling the leaves.

"We'll remember this day for a long time," she said, a little sleepily. She closed her eyes and felt herself drift. "Oh God, I've had too much wine."

He kissed her gently. "Yes, I believe you have."

"So have you."

"I've had just enough, no more, no less."

She laughed. "You're always so precise about everything." Then she blinked up at him. "Enough for what?"

In reply, he placed a hand on her breast.

Lydia felt her heart quicken. She'd done everything with Danny short of actually losing her virginity. She hadn't expected it, she hadn't planned it, yet somehow she knew beyond a doubt that this was the moment. Yes, it would happen now. She closed her eyes again, pulling him closer so that every inch of her body pressed tightly against every inch of his. She felt her blood rising. Yes, now. Breathless, she pulled him closer still, her lips moving, pressed on his, hungry for him now, excited to feel his body respond.

Lydia awoke alone in her bed the next morning at nine. Her head was pounding. Her mouth was dry, and she was sore, so sore. She sat up remembering the pain, then the sweet ecstasy, then the wonderful oneness she'd felt with Danny well into the night out on that hillside. But the pain as she moved now was excruciating. All part of a woman's burden her mother would have told her. Then, she remembered something else about last night.

Yes, it had been her decision to bind Danny to her in that most intimate, most physical way. And it had been she, not Danny who had controlled the act itself. She'd done so subtly, deftly, and in a natural way, careful not to tarnish his delicate male ego, careful not to reveal that it was she, not he, who was going to control their relationship from this point forward. This thought gave her a spark of pleasure and she managed a slight smile.

Gingerly, she rose from the edge of her bed. Agatha, who everyone called Aggie was still curled in her bed quietly snoring. The other two beds looked as if they hadn't been slept in and, as she dressed, Lydia wondered about where her other dorm-mates might have spent the night. Maybe they were waking up sore too.

She decided against her good dress. She put on her most comfortable white blouse and blue skirt and blue leather flats. If Professor Barnhart disapproved of her lack of formality, well that was just too bad for him.

His office was a twenty minute walk across campus and, on the way she ate an apple, tossing its core into the bushes that ringed Camden Hall. She winced a little climbing the steps and, once inside, found room 108. She pulled her blouse straight then knocked softly on the door, thinking only then that she might still have some apple debris on her chin. She ran a wrist across it as the door opened.

"Lydia Thornhill to see Professor Barnhart," she said to the plump, matronly woman who stood unsmiling in the doorway.

"Do you have an appointment?" she asked in a thick Austrian accent.

"Yes, at ten."

"The professor said nothing to me about that. You are not on his schedule."

"He asked me to see him just yesterday."

Her eyebrows dipped as she sighed. "Very well. Please come in."

Through an inner doorway, Lydia spied Barnhart standing behind his desk, waiving good-naturedly. "Ah, Miss Thornhill. Thank you for coming. Please, please show her in, Frau Becker."

Lydia shook hands with him and they both sat.

"Would you like some tea? Coffee perhaps?"

"No, thank you. I'm fine." She folded her hands in her lap.

Barnhart gave a nod to Frau Becker who left, closing the door behind her. He then sat back in his chair. "Please, relax my dear. You no longer have anything to fear from your old professor. You have graduated now and, in a couple of years perhaps, you and I might well be considered colleagues. That is, of course, if you continue to work hard."

"I always work hard, professor."

"Yes, I have seen that. And that is the reason I wanted to talk with you." He reached into a drawer and pulled out a pipe. He tapped out its bowl, filled it with fresh tobacco then lit it, bringing it into billowing life with a couple of puffs.

The aroma reminded Lydia of her father. She felt some of the tension in her shoulders bleeding away.

Barnhart took the pipe from his mouth. "I know that you have always had a great interest in the human brain. Why that is?"

Funny, she thought, it was the same question her own father had asked when she'd first applied to the university and it was an easy one to answer. "It's the most important organ we have. It's what makes us who we are. I want to understand the brain because I want to understand people, and I want to understand myself."

Barnhart nodded. "Yes, very good. Your reasoning has always been brief and to the point. Most of your classmates would still be prattling on about the mysteries of the human body and their desire to make sense of it all. I'm sure you share those same feelings but you seem to have a way of boiling things down to their essence. Over the years I've had you as a student I have always admired that about you."

"Forgive me professor, but I can't think of a single time that I've felt admiration of any kind from you."

"Well, perhaps admiration is too strong a word. As you know, a professor must always keep a stiff demeanor as well as a certain distance when dealing with his students. I know that I can be a hard taskmaster. Still, the competent grades you've received from me should count for some measure of what one might call, admiration. Am I right?"

Lydia winced slightly at the word *competent*. "Why yes, I suppose that's true, if that was your intent. Your assessments of me have, at the least, always been fair." She felt tension building again and she struggled to keep her hands relaxed in her lap.

He took a couple more thoughtful puffs, his eyes on hers. "I have an opportunity for you, Miss...no, sorry, *Doctor* Thornhill. Have you ever heard of The National Congress of Penitentiary and Reformatory Discipline?"

Lydia swallowed—Penitentiary? Reformatory? Her expectations, which hadn't been high to begin with, fell further. "No, I haven't."

"It's been some time ago now, but I took part in their meetings. What they proposed then was a complete revolution of our penal system; to have as its primary goal, not just incarceration, but reform. You may have heard about the great new reformatory in Elvira, New York. That institution came about as a direct result of the National Congress. Another result of the congress was what they called a Declaration of Principles. One of those principles, you may be interested to learn, expounded the need to involve more females in the administration of penal institutions." He chewed on his pipe for a moment. "Is this something that you think might interest you?"

"I...I would be working in a prison? That's the opportunity?"

"You would be working as a *doctor* in a prison. And, one other thing, the prison is located in the state of Maine, not far from Portland." The old man held up a hand, delaying her response. "I don't often meddle in the personal affairs of my students but, I'm afraid I'm guilty of it in this case. Yes, I am aware of Mr. Salter's closeness to you and about his offer from Mount Mercy. The prison, you'll be happy to learn, is only a short distance from that hospital." Professor Barnhart smiled. "You are happy about that, yes?"

Lydia's mind was spinning. Without intending to, she spoke her unfiltered thoughts. "A prison? How could I be happy about working in a prison?"

Barnhart smiled. "What better place to study the workings of the human brain? The criminal brain?"

"I would be treating murderers and rapists..." Lydia cupped her hands more tightly to keep them from shaking. Was it dread she was feeling at the prospect of working among such criminals? Or was it outright fear? She swallowed dryly. Treating prisoners? Is that all that would come from all her years of formal education? No! She would not do it.

The professor's smile thinned. "You can think about it if you like but I'll need your answer by the end of the week." He slid over a sheet of paper. This will give you all the particulars: Travel, accommodations, pay, and the duties that will be expected of you." He stood up and so did she. "This is a big opportunity for you, Miss Thornhill. I hope you will choose to accept it."

"Yes, of course," she mumbled in a daze. "I appreciate the

offer very much. Thank you Professor Barnhart."

They shook hands and Lydia left. Outside, she paused for a moment at the base of the steps. She turned to see Professor Barnhart watching her from his window. He touched a hand to his forehead and she nodded back. What should she do about this offer? Her mother would be appalled, her working in a prison, so might Danny. Still, it was in Portland, and it was the only offer she had. She took a deep breath and started back across campus, the earlier pain forgotten, her strides lengthening as she walked.

CHAPTER 8

Ben drained his scotch. It was nearly eleven, his room dark except for the glare of his computer screen. He picked up the thumb drive and plugged it in. It contained a single video file named *Marshall.* He clicked on it.

The scene came up. He saw himself seated in a chair with the VR headset and earphones in place. Amelia sat on a stool in front of him. The other guy in the room must be off-camera, Ben figured. He clicked PLAY and a digital display in the lower left corner of the screen giving the date and time, began counting off the seconds.

Amelia's voice came up. "Can you hear me Detective Marshall? Do you know who I am?"

"Yes. You are Doctor Silvers."

"Do you know where you are?"

"In a hospital."

After a few more formality questions, Amelia began asking about the stake out. "Where exactly were you that night? Can you imagine yourself back there? You're in the room with your partner. It was dark..."

"Yes, a seedy place, smells like garbage. We have eyes and ears on a room across the street." Ben heard himself give the specifics about the room they were in, the street below, the room across the street and the guy they were surveilling. Ben's hypnotic-self described things vividly.

"Did anything unusual happen?"

Ben watched himself pause for a long moment and take a few

deep breaths as if he was afraid of what he was about to say. He went into the description of what happened exactly as was detailed in the report. Ben watched himself start calmly enough then get more and more worked up, his body moving in a jerky way as he fired off his words. Shit, it sounded like he was going hyper.

As he watched, Ben took another hit of scotch. His description played out: seeing the man in the white overcoat, seeing the man lying in the street. Then Ben saw himself nearly jump from the chair shouting, "A woman screams to me— *Kill him, Ben! Kill him!"* Ben saw his body tense. His breathing labored.

At that moment Amelia had leaned closer. "It's all right Detective Marshall. Nothing can hurt you now. You're just remembering things that have already happened."

The hypnotized Ben took a breath.

"You hear a woman's scream. What do you do then?"

"I pull my weapon, and flick off the safety. I shout to Phil then break the window with the barrel. I fire, twice. Shit, I know I hit him."

"All right Ben. Let's back up and slow things down now. You saw the man in the street. You saw him raise his weapon. Did he fire at you?"

"No. He was aiming at the guy lying in the street."

"Did you see the gunman's face?"

"Yes. He was looking up, directly at me. I could see his face. Pudgy jowls, flat nose, dark eyes close together."

"And did you recognize him?"

"No. But *she* did."

"She? The woman whose voice you heard? How do you know she recognized him Ben?"

He shook his head. "I can feel it. I can feel her panic. She's afraid. I have to protect her."

"But you said the gunman was aiming at a man lying in the street."

"Yes. I...I don't know. I guess I had to protect him too."

Amelia straightened in her chair. "So there are three people in the street: The woman, the gunman and the guy lying there. Do you recognize any of them?"

"No, that's wrong. Only two people are in the street—the gunman and the man lying there. I can't see the woman."

"But did you recognize her voice?"

"No."

Hypnotized-Ben wrung his hands, breathing faster now, slumped back in his chair, his body shaking.

"The man's gone now, Ben. You're safe from him now."

"Yes, that's right," said Ben catching his breath. "I'm safe and so is she."

"Who is she, Ben?"

He shook his head. "I don't know."

Amelia turned to the camera and raised her hand. "Okay. That's enough. I'll bring him back."

The lights came up. The screen froze on her image.

In the darkness of his room, Ben backed away from the computer, his hands cupped to his knees. He sat there for a moment, then concluded: "Shit. I *am* nuts." He pulled the thumb-drive and tossed it into the trash.

The next day at the station, he called the number Amelia had given him for the office of records in Maine. After being transferred twice, he was told that he would need to go, in person, to their office with the proper documentation to register his claim on the house. "You understand," the woman had added, "that your claim would only be honored for the house, its contents and for the land immediately surrounding the house by no more than 100 feet in all directions." Ben told her that would be just fine and that he'd try to stop by in a week or two.

"You're going up to Maine?" asked Phil after he'd ended the call.

"Yeah. Turns out I had a relative there I didn't know about. I may have even inherited some property up there in the woods. I thought I'd check it out."

Phil shrugged. "Not a bad idea. Hunting and fishing's great up there if you're into that kind of thing. And, even if you're not, it'll give you time to get your head straight with everything. I'll bet you come back a changed man. Hell, maybe you'll like it up there so much you won't come back at all. You never know, right?"

"That's right, I guess you never know."

On his last day at the department, Captain Nolan gave a little speech and offered a coffee toast after which, Ben said a few words—very few. He thanked the captain, he thanked Phil and he thanked everyone who'd taken the time to gather around his desk. Harriet brought him flowers in a vase. He gave her an awkward hug, got a few slaps on the back, signed a few forms and sat through an exit interview from a young guy in HR whose total lack of life-experience didn't stop him from dispensing what he thought was helpful transitional advice.

Phil and a few others, took him out to lunch. Ben had a couple of drinks that brought him up to a good buzz and it was late in the afternoon by the time he walked home alone, officially done with the force. Once there, he hit the scotch again, went to bed early and slept through the night until seven when Stump's bark and his scratching at the door got him up. Ben rubbed his eyes awake to a blazing headache. He showered, standing with eyes closed for a long while, letting the hot water run off his face. As he dressed, Stump's barks grew more insistent.

"All right, all right buddy, I'm with you now, ready to go." Feeling better, and hungry, he grabbed the leash then saw the Thornhill book sitting on his kitchen table. "Might as well see what old Lydia has to say." He picked it up and left. The fresh air brightened his mood and he took Stump out on a route different from their usual. It was a big adventure for him—new scenery, new dogs to bark and sniff at. Ben stopped at a café and got a breakfast sandwich that he ate at an outside bench. He checked his watch. He'd normally be out on an assignment with Phil by this time. Not today. He looked around at the other bench-sitters, pigeon-feeders and dog walkers—all old. All probably wondering who this young new guy was.

Ben knew he shouldn't be here. He didn't belong here. He

should be up in Maine, fixing up that house. Right, *Lumberjack Ben,* living off the land. He shook his head. No, that didn't feel right either. What did he know about living off the land?

With the hangover still fogging his head, he picked up Grandma Lydia's book and opened it to page one:

I remember the date, almost the exact hour that the feeling of normalcy left me. It was September 29th 1886, nearing midnight. As a medical doctor in the Portland Reformatory for Young Men, I am about to participate in the execution of a prisoner named Timothy Beckham. I am in his cell along with two guards and a priest. The prisoner's eyes study mine, their whites tinged yellowish-red, the black pupils distorted and dilated. Like twin whirlpools in a stream dancing over a sinkhole, his eyes draw me in. I hesitate then, as I am obliged to do, move closer. Then, within an arms' reach of him I take one fatal step more.

At that moment I feel a shock, stabbing and brief. I am blinded by a brilliant light and, for the briefest instant, I see a shadow move against that light. A sound, shrill and piercing, hits me with a jarring force and I feel lifted up as if by a powerful wind. Then, suddenly, all is quiet, the wind is gone. The light is gone. The eyes of Mr. Beckham still stare but without the magnetic pull they'd exhibited only an instant earlier. I see in them only a single emotion and I am surprised to diagnose it as—Gratitude.

He nods as if knowing, as if understanding what had just happened.

I sense the air around me going stagnant. I feel my body sway.

"Doctor Thornhill?" asks one of the guards standing next to me.

I correct my balance and refuse the arm he offers. I return to the necessities of the moment.

In this new world of mine at the State Reformatory, I'd realized on my first day that the Hippocratic Oath does not apply here. Or rather, there exists a slightly different and much simpler version of it: Do no harm—others will do that for you.

I reach out a hand. I unfasten the top buttons of Mr. Beckham's prison shirt, brushing his bare chest with my fingertips. The physical contact is brief but almost electric. My mouth goes dry. The stethoscope I place over his heart is quite unnecessary for I already feel his cardiac rhythm: thump, thump, thump, feeling it to be in cadence, beat for beat, with my own. I place a thumb on his wrist. I take a quick look down his throat. No congestion, breathing fine. I back away.

"How are you feeling, Mr. Beckham?" I ask as protocol requires.

He gives no reply.

His face seems kindly to me, too kind to be the murderer the jury says he is. I want to ask him if he really did kill all three members of his own family on a summer's day last year. But I don't. I wonder how his last meal was. I see a little of it stuck to the whiskers on his chin. But I don't ask that either.

Instead, I take a step back. "He appears to be in good medical condition," I say to those listening: a priest and the two guards.

Timothy Beckham doesn't talk and for a long while he keeps his eyes on mine, his face now not so kind. I think maybe he'd like to kill me. I find myself conversing with him in my head. Would you like to kill me, Mr. Beckham? Now, now, there'll be none of that, I reply with my eyes, just beginning to learn the language of this strange world where my power over him and the other miserable creatures here is complete and absolute.

With Mr. Beckham's chains clanking at every step, we walk down to the basement and into the execution room where a small group is gathered sitting comfortably in utter quiet as if in a theater waiting for a show to begin. There is a foul smell in the unmoving air. We ascend the gallows stairs. Mr. Beckham falters but eventually takes his position. A black hood is placed over his head. My breathing becomes labored, my vision seems to blur.

The noose is looped over his head. My eyes, struggling to focus, go to the clock. We wait for the last minute before midnight to tick away. When it does, my eyes close, I lean heavily against the wooden railing. After some consoling words from the priest, I hear the floor drop out from beneath Mr. Beckham. I hear him fall. I hear the rope spring taut, almost vibrating with a low hum. Somehow, I feel Mr. Beckham twist and struggle for one last breath almost as if it were my own last breath. I struggle to keep my footing then open my eyes.

I tell my lungs to work again. As if confused, they pull in a desperate breath and then another. It's as if my own life had been stopped for an instant but, as if reborn, can now begin again. I collect myself and, as before, go back to the necessities of the moment.

I take the gallows stairs down and approach the hooded body, still swaying on the rope. I perform my examination and announce with an air of professionalism: "The prisoner is deceased." I stow my stethoscope and leave the room. I return to my office and, almost in a trancelike state, I write up the certificate. Cause of death: Strangulation resulting from hanging. Or, I wonder, was his uncaring mother the real cause? Or maybe the cruel and abusive father? Or maybe a hundred other things that led Mr. Beckham from his cradle of perfect innocence to this unfortunate end?

My life went on after that experience but I knew in my heart that something within me had changed. I was no longer the young and naive wife and doctor I'd once been. I was different.

I was no longer normal.

Stump tugged at his leash, yapping at a passing dog. Ben closed the book and pulled him back. "Sorry," he said to the other dog owner who was already a few steps away, out of earshot. With a snort, Stump accepted the treat Ben gave him and sat back down at his feet. Ben looked down at the book.

Those were strange words from his great, great Grandma Lydia. He wondered why Amelia thought it was important that he knew about her. Maybe she figured that Ben, like anybody else, would get a kick out of knowing that one of his ancestors was somebody famous. And then there was the Thornhill house. Why did Amelia go to all the trouble to find out first, that the house even existed and second, to find out that Ben, as Lydia Thornhill's only living heir, was its rightful owner?

Might she actually care about me? Ben asked himself. No, probably just feels sorry for me. Still, maybe something good could come from that.

Stump barked.

"I know, stupid huh?" Ben drummed his fingers, eying his half-eaten breakfast sandwich. He was no longer hungry. He tossed it, grabbed the book and walked home slowly. He brewed a pot of coffee and, with a cup in one hand and Grandma Lydia's book in the other, lowered himself into his recliner.

It was dark, the pot long since empty by the time he closed the book, finished with all 153 pages of it. His mind was a whirl of Lydia Thornhill's prison experiences which collectively came across as a bare-faced indictment of the 1890 penal system and even of the part she played in that system. How could she write those brutally honest words about herself? About her innermost feelings? About what eventually became her obsession for complete power over others? Then he thought maybe she wasn't being honest at all. Maybe she was just teasing with her words, playing them into the readers' own dark fantasies. It would have helped her sell more books after all. But, then again, her words rang much too true for that, didn't they? After all, the psych community seems to still take her seriously enough to warrant a mention in today's textbooks. Or was she mentioned there for a completely different reason?

It was too early for bed. Ben's stomach felt a little unsettled, but he wasn't hungry. He found himself staring at the few shots left in the bottle of scotch on the counter. Sure, go ahead, drown your sorrows, Ben. Get drunk. See if anyone cares. No one will, you know; not Ginny, not Amelia. Stump might if you got drunk enough to forget to feed him. He thought about tomorrow. No work tomorrow, or the next day, or the day after that. No reason to get up in the morning. No good reason not to get wasted tonight. Shit. It seemed he had a choice here: Either lose himself in drunken self-pity, or... Or what? He gave a shrug—or head up to Maine.

He smiled at the thought, gave a shrug, then grabbed the bottle by the neck and poured it into the sink. Getting drunk was the one thing he *wasn't* going to do. He dropped the empty bottle in the trash.

He looked down at Stump. "What do you think, buddy? How 'bout a road-trip?"

Stump peaked one ear—noncommittal. Probably hungry. Ben freshened his water bowl and poured him some food. Maybe food would do himself some good too, thought Ben. He popped a frozen pizza in the oven, watched the news on TV and went to bed early that night.

CHAPTER 9

October 20, 1886

Lydia sat at the desk, her pen moving fast over the page, the blue ink flowing. Lost in her thoughts, she wasn't prepared for the arms that encircled her from behind. She jerked upright.

"Oh, sorry to startle you my dear," said Danny. He gave her a kiss on the cheek. "I thought you heard me come in."

Quickly she covered her writing with a blank sheet of paper then swiveled her chair around. Danny straightened and she smiled, feeling the slightest of twitches in her lower lip—too slight for him to notice, she hoped. "No. I didn't hear a thing. You know how I get sometimes." She cupped her hands in her lap.

"Yes, I do know. It's like you're in a world of your own when you're writing. You *are* all right though, aren't you?" His eyes were on the desktop behind her.

"Why, yes, of course I am." She drew his gaze to hers, rose from her chair and gave him a kiss. "Now tell me about your day."

She sat again as he shrugged and leaned against the side of the desk. He loosened his collar and sighed. "It's a hospital. The sick people are getting sicker and only a few are getting better. It's frustrating. Sometimes I wonder why I ever wanted to be a doctor."

"It's what you're good at, that's why. Besides, you're just starting your career, things will get better. I know they will. They're making new discoveries in medicine almost every day now. Who knows, maybe one day you'll make one of them yourself."

He smiled and kissed her forehead and Lydia felt a release of tension inside her. Danny still had the power to do that and she knew that she had the power to do the same for him. They'd been married for two wonderful months now and were still settling into their two-bedroom living quarters at a boarding house in town. He pulled a chair up to hers. "And what about you? How are things at the prison? Are you keeping all the criminals happy?"

Her mouth went dry, knowing that some of the things going on at the prison had to remain her little secret. Its sprawling grounds lay fifteen miles out of town and her arrangement required her to room there in four-day stretches, actively on duty or on call over that entire time. She was allowed two days off before each four-day stretch began. Only six hours earlier, she'd come back from her third stint. "It's a reformatory, not a prison," she corrected him. "And, yes, the inmates are all doing reasonably well." All except for Timothy Beckham, she thought. But Danny didn't need to know that.

"So, what maladies do you cure them of? Were you able to conduct any brain surgeries yet?"

She smiled at his joke. "Not yet but, if the opportunity presents itself, I'll be sure to take advantage. No, my days are filled with rashes, lice, cuts, bruises and broken bones. It's probably not much different than what you see at Mount Mercy. It's medicine. It's what we're both good at, you and I."

"You must be exhausted from four days straight of it. I thought I'd come home to find you napping." He checked the time. "They're still serving supper downstairs. We'll have to hurry though. Are you hungry? I'm famished."

"Why yes, I *am* hungry." Funny, but she hadn't even noticed. "Just one moment." She turned back to the desk and capped her pen. She blew lightly across the page she'd been writing, blotted it dry, then folded it over, tucking it into the pocket of her skirt. "A letter to mother," she explained, the lie sticking in her throat only for an instant.

Two mornings later the expected shout came up the stairs: "Carriage for Mrs. Salter." Even though Lydia had kept the Thornhill name, the matron of the boarding house insisted on calling her Misses Salter. This was a nagging irritant for Lydia but it was fruitless to argue the point, especially at five in the morning.

Already dressed, she gave still-dozing Danny a kiss goodbye and trotted down the stairs, pushing her way through the front door into the darkness where the late October chill cut her like a knife. She was pleased to see the extra blanket inside the carriage as she climbed in. A gentleman inside put down his newspaper and offered his gloved hand as she turned to take her seat. "Good morning to you, sir," she said, her breath frosty as she bundled up. She'd met him on her first ride out to the reformatory but couldn't remember his name. Apparently the elderly man was to be a semi-regular morning passenger, but not to the reformatory.

"And good morning to you, Miss...Thornhill is it?"

"Misses Thornhill actually." She sometimes wished she'd just gone with Salter. The carriage pulled out, bouncing and rattling over the cobblestones.

"Yes, I remember from our last ride together that you work at the prison," he said.

"Reformatory, yes I do. And you teach at the college." At least she remembered that much about him.

"It's a nasty business," he said.

"Oh? You don't like teaching?"

"Ha. On the contrary, I love teaching. But I suppose you knew I was referring to whatever it is you do at the reformatory."

"I'm new there. I'm a doctor. And I wouldn't call our work nasty. We try to correct the behavior of prisoners, not just incarcerate them. We try to make them fit for society."

"They seem to hang more than is necessary. Hung one just the other day. It's right here in the paper. The man had killed some people with an axe. Had to be done away with, I suppose. Still, to my mind, it's a nasty business."

"Yes, well some of them are incapable of reform." Lydia wished he hadn't brought up the Beckham execution. In vivid detail, her mind flashed back, her stomach fluttering at the thought of it. She stiffened, turned and watched the buildings go by, making it clear that she was in no mood for conversation.

Once beyond the city-limits, the road turned bumpy and, after a few more miles, they reached a three-story brick building. With a shout, the driver halted his team.

"My stop," said the man, folding his paper and grabbing his satchel. "Good day to you Doctor Thornhill."

"And to you, Mr....sorry, I'm not good with names."

"That's quite all right. We've only met the one time. I am Professor Horace Wickersham. If you forget again, I *will* be offended."

"I won't forget," said Lydia through a rigid smile as he got out and headed up a stone walkway toward a large three-story box of a building in which every lamp at every window seemed to be lit. Not much of a college, she thought. Not at all like the stately halls of Michigan. She wondered briefly if she might be turning into a snob, dismissed that thought then gathered the blanket more tightly around her. At another shout from the driver, the team pulled out.

Ten bumpy miles later the carriage veered to the right and bounded up and onto the smoother gravel of the long circular drive that wound up a gentle hillside and onto the grounds of the reformatory behind which the eastern sky was just starting to pinken.

As if pretending to be a footman at some fancy country estate, a man in a gray prison coat opened the door for her but kept his eyes down, "Good morning Ma'am," he said in a deep voice as he helped her out. She'd worn no gloves and, at the touch of his cold callused fingers, she reflexively drew her hand back. She hesitated, then grasped it again as she stepped down. "Thank you, sir," she said before remembering that, as she'd learned on her first day, you never thanked a prisoner for anything and you certainly didn't call them sir.

A light snow was starting to fall, slickening the walkway and she was careful to keep her footing. Two guards loitered at the base of the outside steps, each with a rifle, each casually chewing on wads of tobacco thick enough to bulge out their cheeks. She walked past them up to the door where another inmate opened the door for her. In more proper form, she took no notice of him.

Inside, the large lobby was well lit from gaslights fixtured overhead. It would have resembled a busy hotel lobby were it not for the armed men in black uniforms stationed here and there at the hallways that ran out from it like the spokes of a wheel. Lydia walked to the center of the room where Mrs. Morgan, the only other woman in sight, sat behind a heavy wooden desk. Lydia traded good mornings with her and obtained a yellow medical-staff card on a string that she looped around her neck, then headed down the main corridor.

A few turns took her to the door of the infirmary where a long line of inmates stood waiting. "About time, missy," one of them grumbled.

She sighed to herself. It was going to be a long day. It was going to be a long *four* days. She marched inside and hurriedly put on her white coat.

"Why so many today, Sam?" she asked her beefy orderly.

Sam shrugged and looked up. "Fight broke out last night over something or other. One guy's dead. We've got some with broken bones, some with cuts—nothing too serious."

"Somebody died? Do you know who? Didn't the guards try to stop it?"

"Don't know who died but, no ma'am, standard policy is to just let 'em fight it out until they get tired, then move in. At least that way the guards don't get hurt."

Lydia sighed again. "All right then, start them rolling."

First up was a broken forearm that needed setting. Despite her small frame, Lydia had learned to leverage her weight against her grip to move bones apart and reposition them. When it went well, it was a simple procedure. This one did not go well.

"All right now, this is going to hurt," Lydia warned the prisoner, just a boy who couldn't have been more than eighteen. He nodded as she carefully positioned her grip on his arm, his skin slick with sweat.

Lydia pulled hard. The boy grunted. She could feel the bones at the break move apart slightly, but not enough. She relaxed, re-gripped, and tried a second time. Finally, she called Sam over to assist.

By this time the boys' arm and wrist were dripping wet. He had not yet let out a scream but he was panting heavily, eyes squeezed shut. Lydia glanced at the name on the medical form.

"Sorry Jerimiah, we're going to have to try this again. With some help this time. Are you ready?"

Jerimiah nodded, his face tensed in an ugly expression that made Lydia wonder what his crime had been. Could this be the look taken on by a murderer as he killed his victim? Could pain and hate be so tightly interwoven that they left the same angry facial scrawl?

"You ready?" she asked Sam.

"Sure thing, Doc."

Lydia took a breath. She dried her hands then took her grip and put all of her weight into the pull. She felt the bones move again, but more now with Sam helping. Straining, keeping up the tension, she turned the boys' forearm slightly, lining things up.

"Fucking God damn Christ!" screamed Jerimiah.

"Almost there," shouted Lydia. "Hold on, Jerimiah." She eased up just a little and felt the bones move into position. "There, we go," she said with mild satisfaction. She glanced at Sam and slowly released the tension, then let go completely.

The boy was shaking, bent over, whimpering, tears flowing. Lydia felt herself shaking a little too. She calmed herself then examined the break with her fingers. "Feels good, thanks Sam," she said. "He'll need it bound with a splint. Can you see to that?"

"It still hurts," cried the boy.

"That's normal," said Lydia with as much compassion as she could muster. "The bones are where they need to be now. Your body will do the healing." Sam led the boy off. "And try to stay out of trouble," she yelled after him as the next patient was ushered in.

One dozen patients, a quick bite to eat, then two dozen more shuttled in and out until, finally, Lydia was startled by a loud clang. She glanced at the clock—8PM already. She sank into her chair, exhausted. She felt like sobbing. And, more than that, she felt like running away from this place as fast and as far as she could.

"Goodnight, Doctor Thornhill," said Sam, the door closing behind him.

"Goodnight," she mumbled knowing she'd still be on-call through the night. Eventually, she got to her feet. The air was thick with the smell of sweat and urine. Despite this, and despite her fatigue, she loitered there, suddenly curious. She walked to Sam's desk where the day's paperwork lay in a wooden tray. She thumbed down to her first patient, Jerimiah Foley. And there, written next to the words *Guilty of:* was the single letter *A* which she knew stood for arson. Well, at least they wouldn't be hanging him for that. And, even if they did, they'd wait until his arm healed.

She wondered why she cared. She closed her eyes, resting them, her mind still on Jerimiah Foley. In a dim light she seemed to see him now, his face a little older, lacking its boyish features. Then, somehow, blood appeared on his cheek and his face took on a look of terror, his eyes wide with fear. Suddenly, more blood came, this time from his mouth, streaming out unabated. Sickened, Lydia squeezed her eyes tightly shut, but still the scene played out. Jerimiah Foley was dying and she was watching it happen.

As if in denial, Lydia forced her eyes open. She steadied herself against Sam's desk.

She refocused on the medical form she held. *I'm just tired. And yes, hungry. I need to get something to eat and I need to go to bed.*

She had her meal with some of the night staff then turned in for the night. Being the only female doctor, she had the luxury of a room to herself where it was quiet and dark. She lay there exhausted but her thoughts kept her awake. Giving up on sleep she got up and lit the lamp. From her purse, she pulled the pages she'd written while at home.

Her words about Timothy Beckham frightened her and, rereading them she wondered and she worried. What had he done to her? And how was it that she could so intimately feel his pain and despair at the moment of death? What was this place doing to her? She was repelled by the words she'd written. She'd gone too far. Maybe some things shouldn't be written about. She eyed the flame of the lamp. Yes, she should burn these terrible pages into ash. But she found that she could not.

She was convinced of the truth in the words she'd written. And this made her wonder: What about Jerimiah Foley? What of the death vision her mind had conjured up for him? Was there truth in that too?

CHAPTER 10

Ben felt free. Driving along in his rental car, wind in his hair, Stump in the back looking over his shoulder, he had no obligations, no commitments, and there was no place he had to be. He remembered feeling that way the summer after graduating from high school. What was it he had in mind to do back then? Oh yeah, he was going to be a singer-songwriter—just he and his Washburn electric, going out on tour, wowing crowds and making a name for himself along the way. He'd come across his old guitar a few months ago, its neck sticking out of a pile of old clothes in the back of the closet. He hadn't thought much of it then, but now he was sorry he hadn't brought it along. He wondered if he could still play a C-chord.

Of course, the singer-songwriter thing hadn't worked out, but things were different now. He was older and smarter, he had some money to his name, and he had a house up in Maine. Re-starting his life up there was no stupid high schooler's dream. With a half-decent job to supplement his pension he really could make a go of it. Besides, this was just a trip to check things out. If things didn't look good, like if the house was a run-down ruin, he would just go back to Boston and make a go of it.

He reached over and gave Stump a head-scratch as if soliciting his support. "That's right, isn't it boy? We've got options."

After reading her book, Ben decided that he'd not only inspect the house but he'd also learn more about Grandma Lydia herself. In her book she'd mentioned that she and her husband Danny had lived in a third floor apartment on Norwood Avenue in Portland.

The Internet showed that Norwood Avenue still existed and was only three blocks long. A street-view showed that, if her building still stood, it could be only one of two along that three-block stretch. The likeliest of these was now a bank, the other, a furniture store. He really had no idea what he might find there but Portland was on the way to Augusta where the historical records and property deeds were kept so why not stop by for a look?

It was a little after 9pm when he drove past the bank and saw it was in the process of being torn down. Well, he'd have to pin his hopes on the furniture store then. He pulled up to the place at 298 Norwood and got out, not surprised to see that it was closed and wouldn't reopen until ten the next day. He eyed the building while stretching his legs. The three-story brick structure took up a third of the block. It had the appearance of once being stylish, with tall grooved columns of gray cement which, on the lower level, separated large windows displaying furniture. Bright red and white banners in each announced the latest blowout deals. Above this first level, two rows of dark and dirty smaller windows defined the upper stories. The building looked just like the picture he'd seen on the Internet.

Ben leashed Stump and, under a blinking yellow stop-light crossed the street for a better look at the whole place. With its faded bricks and chipped cement, the building looked old enough to have been around in the 1880's. He guessed it had undergone several renovations to take it from its original boarding house layout to its present design. Ben looked up the street. There wasn't a soul around. This was an older part of town, plenty of crumbling storefronts with their neon signs buzzing and blinking nervously and three out of five streetlamps burned out. Lydia Thornhill would probably have been appalled to see her old neighborhood in its present state.

A police car did a slow roll-by, paying him no attention and a cool breeze kicked up. Ben thought about where he was going to stay tonight. He supposed he should have called ahead for a motel but he hadn't. He also hadn't had dinner yet. He'd just finished off a bag of Cheetos and his stomach was growling. Stump was growling too.

A three mile drive got them to a cheap motel that looked like it might be pet-friendly. To this question, Ben applied his don't ask, don't tell policy. The place wasn't too much of a dump—bed, bath, table, and a small flat-screen TV. What more did he need? Ben bowled-up some food and water for Stump then found a diner within walking distance. He slept-in the next morning, had breakfast, and walked into the furniture store at 10:05.

"Can I help you, sir?" From behind a counter midway back, a boy beamed with a fresh out of high school smile.

Ben beamed right back. "Thanks, no. Is your manager in?"

"I'm sure I can help you with whatever you want, sir."

"All right. I'm interested in leasing the top floor of this building. Can you show it to me please?"

The kid swallowed the smile. "Sorry, I'll get my manager."

As he waited, Ben eyed Stump through the front window. Leashed to a parking meter his head was cocked as if trying to figure out his new surroundings. He didn't pay much attention to the few passers-by.

The manager, an older, stocky woman who looked like she should have retired years ago, came out and introduced herself as Helen Bolden. "I understand you're interested in leasing some space?"

"First, can you tell me how old this building is?"

"When it was built, you mean? Well, I don't know for sure. I do know it's been around for more than a hundred years. Is that important for some reason?"

"No, I just like old buildings. Do you own the place?"

"Oh no, I just manage the store. We do use the second level for storage though."

"But not the top floor?"

Helen shook her head. "No. I've never been up there. I don't remember anyone ever going up there." She scratched her head. "Well, now that I think on it, maybe there was some electrical work done up there a few years back. What did you want it for?"

"I represent some investors who may be interested in it. Maybe to convert it into some loft apartments but I don't know for sure. Do you mind me checking it out, taking a few pictures?"

"Well no, I don't mind." Her face turned a little sour. "I won't be going up there with you though. It's a bit of a climb and I have kind of a hip thing going." She gave that part of her body a pat. "You got some ID?"

He gave her one of his cards from the Boston PD. "That's my day job," he explained. "I'm just doing some friends a favor."

She nodded and gave a shrug. "All right then, let's go."

He followed her into the back of the store, then up a dusty staircase to the second floor where boxes were stacked atop one another nearly to the ceiling. She pointed up a second flight of stairs. "Third floor's up that way. The door's unlocked, I think. The lights should be working but you shouldn't need them—plenty of sunlight coming through the windows. You okay then?"

"Yeah, thanks. I'll be fine."

"I'll just go back down then—customers you know." She seemed glad to be leaving.

Ben headed up the stairs, a crooked arm in front of him fending off cobwebs that dropped from the ceiling. The stairs creaked. The closed door at the top was dark except for the line of sunlight at the bottom. It was like the many other doors he'd confronted as a cop except, in this case, he was fairly certain there wasn't a guy with a gun on the other side. Like Helen thought, the door was unlocked. He shoved it open and stepped into what may have once been the boarding house home of Lydia Thornhill and her husband Danny Salter.

There were more cobwebs but he ignored them now as he walked to the windows. Plenty of light was coming through but the glass was frosted over with dirt.

He turned and checked the floorboards. Although this floor was one large open room now, he could see the markings where a hallway and some interior walls of individual apartments must have been. He had no idea which of them might have once belonged to his grandmother. He sensed from the floor markings that he was standing in a parlor with maybe a small kitchen off to one side and a couple of bedrooms off to the other. "Hello Grandma Lydia," Ben muttered under his breath, feeling like he was playing the part of a modern-day Sherlock Holmes searching for clues from which he and only he could draw startling conclusions about some crime once committed here.

But there hadn't been a crime here. No, he was just trying to get the feel of the place that his great, great grandparents had once called home.

Something on the floor, near the center of the room caught his eye. He knelt over the spot and, with his hand, swept away the dust. It was nothing. Just the dark ragged edge of a stain that hadn't been cleaned up. Still on his knees, Ben looked up to the tin-tile ceiling and saw a round mounting fixture from which a chandelier might have been hung over a dining table. He shook his head examining the stain again. Probably just some spilled gravy. He stood up and did a slow walk around the room, covering every inch looking for marks, gouges in the walls or floor but saw nothing of any real interest. He took a few pictures with his phone, then left.

"Dirty up there, huh?" said Helen on seeing him back in the store area.

"Yeah, just a little."

"So, are you interested in the space?"

"Maybe. I'll get back to you." He took her card and was glad to get out into the fresh air where Stump sulked, his jaw flat on the sidewalk.

"Yeah, buddy, my bad. This was just a waste of time."

He took the main route out of town past the hillside site of the old penitentiary, long-since replaced by a sprawling housing development. A little more than an hours' drive up 295 got them to Augusta.

In the State of Maine, birth and death certificates and some tax and property records had been digitized back to 1892. Older records and those defined as less-vital were kept in the State Archives located a few blocks from the capital building and that was where he needed to go. Ben had no trouble finding the large, Romanesque building. He parked, gave Stump a pat and walked inside. After passing through a security check-point, he found his way to what he hoped was the right office.

"Name please?" a young woman asked from behind a counter.

"Ben Marshall. I emailed your office last week about looking up some ancestral information. I filled out one of your forms. He handed her a paper copy of the email he'd sent.

"You're interested in...Lydia Thornhill?"

"Yes. I'm her great, great grandson."

"So, the information you need is for personal use?"

"Yes. That and, as I said in my email, I'm working with a professor at Boston University who also has an interest." He added that last part with an air of professionalism.

With a funny expression, like she'd had one too many prunes for breakfast, the woman looked back at her screen. "That would be Dr. Amelia Silvers, Professor of Psychology?"

"Yes. That's right."

"And what's your relationship with her?"

Ben kept up his smile even though he felt a bureaucratic run-around coming on. He sure wasn't about to admit to being her patient. "I'm helping her with a project of historical interest." He glanced at her name tag. "Is there a problem, Cindy?"

She sighed as if the weight of the world were on her shoulders. "We get a lot of people coming around here wanting to check out their ancestors. You know, just for fun. It's a waste of our valuable time. We can't have that. I'm sure you understand."

"Perfectly. I can assure you this isn't for fun."

At that moment, another 'customer' came in. "Just have a seat ma'am. I'll be with you soon," said Cindy, looking a little bothered. She turned back to Ben with a questioning expression.

Ben cleared his throat. "Like I said, Dr. Silvers and I are collaborating on a historical project. My great, great grandmother, Lydia Thornhill, lived in Maine from 1886 until her death. She worked at a state prison and then a state-run insane asylum, both not far from Portland. I think she died in the twenties. She also had a rare medical condition. Here, I have Dr. Silvers card somewhere." He began checking his pockets for a card he knew he didn't have.

Cindy heaved another sigh and held up her hand. "No, that's all right." She pressed a button and a door to Ben's right clicked. "Come on back."

She met him at the door and guided him past a few desks, through another door and down a flight of stairs. "Nothing personal but, do you know you have cobwebs in your hair?"

"Oh, sorry. Thanks for telling me." He brushed them out with his hand as they entered a room filled with tall shelves, each loaded with string-tied black and white banker boxes.

Cindy turned down an aisle, walking slower now, gazing up at the boxes. "Thornhill should be through here. Yes, Thornhill, Lydia. Whoa, she's got a box all to herself. Who'd you say she was?"

"My great, great Grandmother."

"No. I mean what did she do? Was she famous or something?"

"She was a doctor in the 1880's. She worked at a prison and at an asylum."

"Ha, a woman doc that long ago? Cool, I like her already." She pulled down the box and, with Ben following, had no trouble carrying it to a table at the end of the aisle. She deposited it there with a thud. "You'll likely find more stuff on her by looking up the files for the prison, the asylum too. That'll be in the State Business Records area in another room down the hall. If you need anything from there, you'll have to fill out another form." She pointed. "See that black buzzer? When you're done with this box, hit the buzzer. I'll come down and put it back on the shelves. That way we make sure nothing gets lost and nothing gets misfiled. You can take all the notes and pics you want but don't even think about trying to take anything out with you. We've got cameras everywhere down here and I'll be watching you. I mean when I'm not busy with other stuff. When you're done, just put everything back in the box, *neatly* and in the right order and hit the buzzer when you're done. Got it?"

"Got it, thanks."

She headed off, footsteps fading, door closing.

Ben unwound the ties at both ends of the box, lifted the top and breathed in that old-paper smell. He ran his fingers over the top, uneven edges of papers and files that stood on edge not quite filling the box. He pulled the first page from the first folder. It was her birth certificate, well *Notification of Birth* as it was called back then. The yellowed page was rough and worn, its fold marks nearly severing the paper. It was dated 18 June 1858, only three days past his own birthdate. Ha, now there was a coincidence. He stared at the page. Nothing else unusual; no mention of any complications. The birthplace given was Blue Hill Michigan. No specific address, just Blue Hill Michigan. The parents were listed as Thomas and Maria Thornhill. He pulled out his cell and took a photo of the document then went onto the next folder. He checked the time. He'd better get a move on if he wanted to finish up today.

Education documents followed and Ben just checked them briefly, not even pulling them out. He noted that all Lydia's pre-college work was done in Blue Hill. After that, she went to two colleges, the second being Vassar. She followed up on those studies in the medical department at the University of Michigan and that warranted a folder all to itself. Ben pulled the file and flipped through the pages one by one.

Enrollment records, fields of study, assessment letters, then came a thick document bound in its own folder with a title on the front: Conjectures on Human Consciousness, by Lydia Thornhill. A note scrawled in the upper right corner read:

An impressive discourse.
Barnhart

The document looked like it had been typeset and printed. Didn't they have typewriters back then? Maybe not. Ben wondered if he should photograph each one of its twenty-something pages but decided on only the first couple.

Following this, were a few more bound documents and again Ben took photos of only the first few pages. The last document was a handwritten letter of recommendation from Professor Barnhart to the warden of the state prison in Portland, Maine. It sang the praises of Doctor Lydia Thornhill and made mention of her interest in the inner workings of the criminal mind. Ben closed the college folder and put it back in the box.

Prison records were next. They included dozens and dozens of forms with the names and dates of all those treated by Doctor Thornhill. Also documented were the deaths occurring from both executions as well as from more natural causes that had occurred during her time as presiding physician. The last of these was a certificate for the death of a Jerimiah Foley on April 11, 1893.

There followed a single-page Letter of Dismissal, addressed to Doctor Lydia Thornhill and dated July 12, 1893. It was short and not very sweet:

Doctor Thornhill,

Due to circumstances involving the dereliction of your responsibilities, your lack of discipline, your radical mistreatment of inmates, and your continual confrontations with authority, you are hereby relieved of your duties as physician here at the Portland Reformatory. This dismissal is issued with malice and with the hope that it will serve as a warning to any organization that may consider employing you in any capacity in the future.

Yours Very Truly,
Allen J. Brown, Warden and Chief Administrator.

Wow, poor Grandma Lydia, thought Ben, wondering what she might have done to deserve those fiery words. He checked the dates. She had been at the prison for seven years and would only have been in her mid-thirties—about the same age as he was right now. Not a good age to have your career turn to shit.

Ben took a photo of the damning letter then reread it. He was startled by the sound of a door closing and footsteps coming his way. He glanced at his watch, surprised to see it was already nearing five. "Just finishing up," he told Cindy as she rounded the corner.

"Find what you were looking for?"

"I don't know. Maybe." Ben started picking up the papers and folders that were scattered around the table.

"They have to be in order so be careful with those. And you can't take anything with you, I told you that, right?"

"Right." As she watched, he filed the loose documents more carefully then placed the lid on the box.

"Great," said Cindy. She tied the lid down and re-shelved the box.

"I'll be back tomorrow. You know, for the business records. Is that all right?" asked Ben on the way out.

"Some of those records would have been in her personal file. You didn't see them there?"

"I saw them for the prison but not for the asylum."

"That's a little odd. But no, it shouldn't be a problem, you coming back. Just don't come before ten. Do you know the exact places where she worked?"

"The Portland State Reformatory, then The Windward Asylum for the Insane."

"We should have them but, you never know. All right then, see you tomorrow."

CHAPTER 11

May 18, 1894

"Push, Lydia. Harder, you must push harder!"

"Any harder and my guts will be flushed out," Lydia gasped. The pressure that had been rising and falling through the night now tore through her. She couldn't breathe. She braced her feet more tightly against the footboard and arched her back almost retching with the effort. Over the crest of her stomach Lydia could see Danny, his eyes frantic. He'd delivered babies before, of course, but never his own.

"I see it! I see the baby," shouted Danny. His hands pressed her stomach, feeling for the profile within. "Wait, I think there are two."

"Twins?" She hoped she sounded surprised at what she'd long suspected but never told anyone.

"Yes darling, I think so." Danny gave a nervous laugh and repositioned himself.

Lydia felt another huge contraction building like a wave inside her. She gulped air in and spewed it out. "This is it Danny, I can feel it. She's coming now. Right now..." Her words ended in a scream. Her body stiffened and shook as if she was coming apart. She squeezed her eyes shut and let loose a loud guttural sound through contorted lips. Suddenly, the pressure lessened and the pain eased. She felt blessed relief until realizing that the room was silent.

Lydia forced her eyes open, blinking away the dried residue from her tears. Danny held a warm compress to her forehead. He had a shaky smile on his face.

"We have a beautiful baby girl, my love," he whispered, gently kissing her lips.

All Lydia could do was nod and force a smile of her own. Danny propped her head up and gave her some water. Now she could speak. “The boy, he didn’t survive did he?”

Danny brought the baby over. “Here is our daughter, bright pink and healthy.” He paused. “No, our son didn’t survive. How did you know?”

“Mothers know these things,” said Lydia, taking the child she knew they would call Abigail in her arms, her bare skin on hers. That’s right. She’d known about the boy and had not been surprised. And she wasn’t disappointed. She’d first sensed the struggle within some months ago. One of them had to die so the other might live. She’d wondered why this was so, but had no answer.

Life had been hard for her since leaving the reformatory. But the cause for her difficulties wasn’t the harshness of her dismissal. “I felt I was doing some good there,” she told Danny one night when he’d asked. But that had been a lie, the same lie she’d been telling herself for her first few years there. After assisting in six executions she’d written and published her book which she’d intended to be a treatise on how the dead and dying could affect the living. Instead, it had been received as an indictment of the prison reform movement and of the Portland Reformatory in particular. After a flurry of endorsements from leading political figures, she’d been invited to several speaking engagements all of which were well received and all of which put the Portland institution in a bad light.

Late in the year 1887, the Maine legislature officially banned criminal executions in the state. No longer would Lydia take part in publicly sanctioned killings. No longer would she examine a prisoner and pronounce him fit to die. No longer would she look into a prisoner’s eyes knowing that in some way she was about to share the pain and agony of his death experience. She supposed she should have been relieved. She should have at least taken some pride in knowing that her book and her activism may have helped bring about the ban on executions. But, to her horror, she found herself to be strangely and secretly...disappointed.

Lydia's outspokenness and the resulting publicity were the reasons for her firing—at least that's what she told Danny. She never showed him the dismissal letter she'd received from Warden Brown and she never let on that there might be a deeper, darker story behind her departure.

As head of the infirmary at the reformatory, Lydia had been in a perfect position to show sympathy and kindness to prisoners she knew were about to die. There was nothing wrong with that of course, but with Jerimiah Foley she had crossed a line running well beyond sympathy and kindness.

She hadn't forgotten her years-ago vision of him at the gallows and had never doubted his fate. As if bound to him by that secret knowledge, she began to feel for him an almost maternal love that one day blossomed into something quite different.

That day had been a busy one and Lydia was near exhaustion when Jerimiah, her last patient, limped into the clinic. He had a habit of getting into trouble with the other prisoners, often needing her attention for one thing or another.

"What is it now, Jerimiah?" she'd asked, watching him from her desk, a hand propping her head up.

"My foot hurts something fierce, ma'am."

She glanced at the clock then gave a sigh. "It's all right, Sam, I can handle this one by myself." Lydia knew that prison protocol prohibited her from being left alone with a prisoner but she and Sam had bent that rule with the harmless Jerimiah before and he made only a mild objection before grabbing his coat and heading for the door.

"Stubbed your toe on something?" She asked, the two of them alone now.

"Yeah, something like that." He removed his shoe and stocking, exposing a dirty, smelly foot that, on one side, looked deformed.

She held it with both hands, shifting her fingers, he wincing as she felt the distorted bones. "You don't wash very often do you?"

"I get hosed down a couple of times a month just like everyone else ma'am. This is pretty much as clean as I get."

She did her best to repair the damage and wrapped the foot tightly in a bandage. "You'll need to stay off of it for at least six weeks. Here, I'll write the order." She scribbled a note and handed it to him. "Just show this to the guards."

"Thanks ma'am, but it'll take more than this to keep me off the work detail."

"Sorry, best I can do." She started her usual kindness and sympathy routine but felt a strange rush of blood that sharpened her senses. A voice from the back of her head cautioned: 'No, Lydia. Stop. You can't. You shouldn't.' But it was drowned out by another: 'Yes, you can. He needs you Lydia. The boy needs you.' 'Yes,' she reasoned, 'the boy needs me. I can help him.' She felt her heart pounding as she watched her hand. As if controlled by an external force, it gave his hand a reassuring squeeze then rose gently to his shoulder where she felt his muscles tense under his shirt. With the tips of her fingers, she applied some pressure and moved her fingers in a slow, circular motion. She watched his face. His eyes were closed now and she realized he was holding his breath, perhaps lost in the gentleness of her touch, perhaps wondering where her hand might go next.

Her fingers moved from his shoulder, rising to give a lingering brush of his stubbled cheek that just touched the corner of his lips. That first voice, faint now, cautioned her to stop but she could not. She cradled his face in her hands then bent closer, her face so near to his that she could feel his breath on her lips. She let her breast brush lightly against the side of his arm. Slowly, she shifted her gaze from his face to his torso, then down further. She smiled slightly then watched his mouth open as if he were about to let out a moan.

And, at that moment, she pulled away.

"I'll write you another script," she said as if nothing had happened. "Come back next week and I'll examine your foot again to make sure everything's healing properly. Make it late in the day."

For a moment, Jerimiah didn't move. He opened his eyes.

Ignoring his stare, Lydia handed him a crutch. "This will help you get around."

Still, he didn't move.

"That's all," she prompted. "You can go now."

He cleared his throat and stood, then hobbled to the door where he turned. "Th-thank you, ma'am."

"When you come back, make sure you are hosed first." Lydia said this without a glance as he closed the door behind him.

So yes, she'd crossed the line that day as she had many times since.

Her affair with Jerimiah went on for two years and over that time she was able to keep it secret from the warden and from Danny. She was careful. At first, she rationalized her actions, calling them acts of kindness stemming from her sympathy for the boy and for his unfortunate circumstances. On rare occasions she sensed there to be something wrong and vile in her actions. In those brief moments of weakness she was genuinely shocked by the subtle streak of depravity that seemed to be growing deep within her, giving her pleasure in, and eventually a terrible need for what many would consider deeds of evil. And no, it wasn't sympathy she felt for Jerimiah, but it wasn't love either. It was nothing like the feelings she still had for Danny. It was something she couldn't define. It was something stronger, something irresistibly pleasurable. And how could that be evil?

Then came the night Lydia would forever remember.

With the help of several cups of meadowsweet tea, she was able to make it through the day but decided to forego supper, retiring straight to her room where she fell onto her bed and tried to sleep but could not. An hour went by, then two. A female orderly came by with some soup that she forced down.

"You look terrible Doctor Thornhill," said the young girl whose name Lydia should have known but at that moment couldn't recall. "Can I get you anything else?" the girl added.

"No!" Lydia snapped causing the girl to jump. "Please, just leave me be. I am all right."

Alone again, Lydia fell back onto her bed. As if drunk, her head was spinning. She ran a hand across her forehead surprised that it was covered by beads of sweat. Did she have a fever? No, she was quite sure of that. But something was dreadfully wrong. She was about to get up to call the girl back but at that moment heard a disturbance in the hallway—footsteps, hurried footsteps, coming closer. Suddenly, dread filled her heart. She braced herself and, after a single knock, the door burst open. An out of breath guard stuck his head into the room.

"Doctor Thornhill, you're needed right away. There's a man in the infirmary. We need you. We think..."

For a moment, Lydia didn't move. Then, forgetting about her sickness, forgetting about everything, she sprang out of bed, grabbed her coat and, at a run, followed the guard down the hall back to the infirmary.

"Make way. Make way," shouted the guard as he pushed open the door, Lydia just behind.

The three other guards inside parted quickly revealing a man lying on one of the beds. She stopped, stunned. It was Jerimiah.

His head was bloodied but Lydia saw right away it was his chest that needed her attention. His breathing was more of a gurgle, blood pooling and dripping down.

"He took a terrible fall," said one of the guards unconvincingly as Lydia came up to the bed.

Her mind was spinning again, in a split second flashing past each of the carnal interludes she and Jerimiah had had together. They'd been more than that, hadn't they? God help her, she really did care about him. What would she do without him?

"Doctor?"

"Help me with his shirt," shouted Lydia, abruptly moving into action. Breathless, she started tearing at the buttons until, from the other side of the bed, a guard grabbed the blood-soaked shirt by its collar, ripping it apart, exposing a bloody lake beneath.

Lydia almost staggered at the sight. His rib-cage had been crushed, blood spilling onto the floor at each gurgling breath. But she was all business now. With her fingers, she probed past the torn flesh, feeling her way through the fractured ribcage to the lungs and the other internal organs. As she did this, she looked at Jerimiah's face. Blood streamed from his mouth and she realized that she was now living the years-ago vision she'd had of this very moment. And she also realized there was nothing she could do to save him.

Slowly, she pulled her hands back, letting them fall to her side as she took a step back and straightened. The guard across from her pleaded with her to do something but she barely heard him.

She was still looking at Jerimiah's face. His eyes were wide with fear. She moved closer to him, her eyes now gazing into his. She could feel his failing breath on her chin and she could smell the bloody vapors he exhaled. She held his eyes with hers then reached down for his hand and held it too. And, in that moment, she felt the fear and the pain drain from his body—*into hers*. His eyes grew calm. With an effort, she spoke softly to him. "I am here, Jerimiah. It is over. You will suffer no longer."

Lydia felt his hand grip hers as a burning, suffocating pain hit her chest, squeezing the breath from her lungs. She felt her body shake, fighting for another breath, but still, she held his eyes with hers. She stood transfixed, as if frozen in time. My God, I'm dying too, she thought for an instant. But Jerimiah's grip on her hand suddenly loosened and at the same moment, her lungs were freed. Her knees gave way and, gasping for air, she fell to the floor.

If she'd lost consciousness, it hadn't been for long. "There's nothing I can do for him now," she mumbled, a guard helping her up.

"You all right Doc?" he asked.

She took a deep breath. "Yes. I'm fine. Guess I just slipped on the blood on the floor."

"He's dead. There'll be an inquiry," said another guard.

Lydia nodded. With a hand on the bed, she stared down at the body that had once held the life of Jerimiah Foley. She could see a certain calmness in his face as if pleased with his escape from this terrible place. Well, maybe it was for the best. Maybe it was time she made her escape too.

"You told me he fell," she said, turning to the guards. In each face she could see their fear and, in at least one, she saw the hint of a threat. "I will make sure my report of his death reflects that."

After they left, Lydia stayed, cleaning the body, then the floor. Pulling a clean sheet from a cabinet she covered Jerimiah and the bloody bed. In the slow walk back to her room, she was not surprised that she felt no hint of the sickness that had hounded her all that day. She knew the cause of it now.

It was nearing one in the morning when she completed the certificate of death, signing her name as the presiding physician. That done, she put on her heavy coat and found her way outside, into the silent, frigid night where the stars shown down and her tears for Jerimiah and for herself could fall unseen.

She walked slowly and in no particular direction, eventually coming to the crest of a low hill where the grass grew taller. She slowed then stopped, breathing-in the cold night air, turning to look back at the lights of the reformatory. There was an evil in those buildings. She knew it as surely as she knew there was an evil within herself. Perhaps, like dirty water in a laundry, a residue had been left by the steady stream of flawed men who'd lived there then left after supposedly being washed clean of their sins. Somehow, their evil remained within those wall. And somehow, that evil had infected her.

Lydia raised her eyes to the stars. With a chill in her bones not caused by the cold, she realized that, in the same way she'd been changed by the execution of Timothy Beckham years earlier, she'd just been transformed yet again by the death of Jerimiah Foley. Yes. She was certain of it. She had just taken one more step away from normalcy. She wondered where that divergent path might lead and she had no answer. She only knew that now, there was no turning back.

The next day, she confessed her relationship to Jerimiah Foley to a shocked Warden Brown who issued her dismissal letter two days later. Little Abigail arrived eight months after that.

With Danny's good position at the hospital, they could easily afford the loss of her income and so, for the next three years, Lydia played the role of housewife and mother. For her it was cooking, cleaning and diaper-changing. No longer was she exposed to the evils of the reformatory. But she often thought about them and about the part she'd played years earlier in the executions. And, heaven help her, it was the absence of those things that made this mundane life of hers so impossibly difficult.

It had been Danny's father's idea to build the cottage in the woods. "A place nearby for us to share our summers with you," he had said to his son.

"Good idea," Danny had agreed with a glance at Lydia who forced a smile and said that she loved the idea.

Lydia had always gotten on well with the Salters but she wondered how, having them so close for three months at a time would affect that relationship. For one thing, she knew that his mother resented her not taking the Salter name. Other issues were bound to come up, especially when it came to child-rearing matters. Still, it might be nice to have another woman to talk with during the day.

The foundation for the house was laid in the spring of 1899. The lumber, cut from the surrounding woodland and seasoned the year before, went up quickly with the walls, roof and interior finished by mid-July after which a formal christening of the place was held.

The sun was bright that day. Danny's father had just twisted the cork off a bottle of French wine which he poured for all present, making sure to include a small taste for little Abigail. He raised his glass as they gathered beside him on the front porch facing a photographer he'd hired for the occasion. He spoke in a loud voice: "I name this cottage *Timbervale*. May its sturdy walls give us shelter and may it be a place for our family to grow and prosper for generations to come."

"Hear, hear," shouted both Danny and Lydia as the photographer raised his hand, igniting his flash-powder in a puff of white smoke. They held their pose until the photographer lowered his hand.

"I need one more," said the man, hurrying to pull out one plate, sliding in a new one and preparing a new line of magnesium granules.

Everyone raised their glasses again as the powder flashed.

Lydia surprised herself by being delighted with the place at first sight. Its exterior walls of bright red, rose two stories high, with a covered porch and numerous windows. Inside, ample sleeping spaces, a large front room and a spacious kitchen made the house practical while retaining a rustic charm that made her feel a part of the place from the moment she walked in. What a wonderful home it would be for her and Abigail, she thought but did not say. True, it was a summer residence for the Salter's but she was quite certain that one day it would be hers and Danny's. She was also quite certain that one day, it would be hers alone. It never occurred to her to wonder how she knew these things, it was something she had just grown to accept.

The house sat in a clearing on a ten-acre plot of otherwise dense woods. A dirt two-track led off the property and around the marsh out to the road that wound its way east down the hillside out to the town of Randell then out to Portland with the reformatory halfway between.

On the afternoon of the christening, Lydia worked well with Mrs. Salter in preparing and serving a dinner of roast lamb and porridge-potatoes after which she joined everyone on the porch as the last gleam of the sun faded.

"It'll be hard getting out here in the winter," said Lydia.

Mr. Salter sat in a rocking chair that creaked softly as he puffed on his pipe. "Oh, I don't expect we'll be up here at all in the winter. The snow drifts'll be up over the windows by December and won't melt till late April. The place'll have to be boarded up solid each year. I've got a man a few miles away in Randell to help with that. He'll come up in early November and then again in early May."

"A shame not to live here year-round."

Mr. Salter stopped his rocking. "You think you'll like it here, do you?"

Lydia sat on the first step off the porch. In the dimming light she turned to face him, barely able to make out his features. "Oh yes, I love it already."

She turned again, staring off to the eastern horizon where stars were blinking on and the light from an amber moon was just starting to break through a woods alive with the gleam of fireflies and a full chorus of crickets and frogs. She had spoken truthfully. She did love this place.

Lydia, Danny, and Abigail spent the rest of that summer at *Timbervale* parting with the Salters in mid-September to return to their boarding house in Portland. One week later, the Salters left *Timbervale* and never set foot there again. Both were killed when the train they were riding back to Michigan derailed.

CHAPTER 12

Ben rubbed his tired eyes, glancing at Stump who snored a few paces away beside the motel room door. It was nearing eleven on their first night in Augusta and Ben had just sketched out a time line for Lydia Thornhill based on what he knew of her life so far. He looked back down at the single sheet of paper:

Born June 18, 1858
College years: 1878-1886
Employed at Portland Reformatory in 1886
Assisted in 6 executions
Published her book.
Fired from Portland Reformatory in 1893.
Gave birth to Abigail in 1894
Hired at Windward Asylum in 1900
Interred as a patient there in 1908
Died in 1920

There were way too many gaps. If he was lucky he might be able to fill in a few of them with any new information he might find the next day. Or, maybe not. He sat back in his chair wondering why he'd become so curious about his great, great grandmother. It wasn't like him to be the least bit interested in family history. Hell, he never even knew much about his own mom and dad and here he was researching someone who died almost a hundred years ago. Well, there was the house. Yes, he was curious about that.

He was putting away his notes when he came across a print-out he'd made before leaving Boston. It was billed in Wikipedia as the layman's definition for *The Thornhill Disorder*. He read through it again:

An extremely rare condition in which the subject is convinced they are dying and actually undergoes what they believe to be the dying experience even as their body continues to function and remain perfectly healthy. In its most common manifestation, the subject believes they are being violently assaulted by something or someone or that they are in some other life-threatening danger. They scream in panic and become extremely violent as if in excruciating pain and agony until the dying process runs its course, ending in a so-called death-sleep that might last as long as several days. A subject awakened from this sleep may recall all or nearly nothing of the experience yet, in either case, they live in terror of another episode coming on. Some subjects endure them almost weekly while, for others, they might never reoccur.

The disorder is named for Doctor Lydia Thornhill who, in the early 1900's, contracted the condition herself. There is no known cure.

Ben undressed and turned out the lights. Climbing into bed, he imagined how hellish life must have been for Grandma Lydia. He expected to be done researching the archives by late morning the next day so that, sometime tomorrow he could be standing in the house where she died. The thought sent a chill down his spine.

At 10:15, Cindy guided Ben down the stairs and through a corridor into a room different from but identical to the one he'd been in the day before. As he looked on, Cindy surveyed the business archive shelves. "Let's see, Windward, Windward. Yup, here it is." She grabbed it handily and put it down on a table, wiping the dust off her hands. "Well, you know the drill," she said, walking off. "I'll be back down to check on you in a couple of hours. If you finish before that, just hit the buzzer on the wall." She was nearly back to the door by the time she added that last part.

Ben opened the box. He started flipping quickly through the musty contents until he reached the institutional records dated close to Lydia's arrival there. At that point he slowed, examining each page until finally coming across her record of employment dated December 13, 1900. Ben recalled that she'd left the Reformatory back in 1893. He wondered how she'd occupied her time in that seven year gap.

He took a photo of her employment papers only then noticing her marital status: Widowed. What happened to Danny? She listed Abigail as her daughter, age six at the time and it also listed the town of Randell as a secondary residence. He ran a finger under his collar. It was hot down here in the basement and he was starting to sweat.

Along with the employment papers, there was a photograph of Lydia. It showed her face drawn and stern, even more so than the photo he'd seen of her from the text book. Her eyes shot through the camera lens, sending a shiver through Ben as if warning him of the risks in looking further into her secrets. She wore her hair up in a way that accentuated her high forehead. Her nose and mouth were fixed and angular as if they'd been carved in place. It struck him that here was a woman with some serious things on her mind.

Ben shuffled quickly through the rest of the box coming up with only two other interesting documents. One was a form documenting Lydia Thornhill's dismissal as a doctor at Windward, the reasons being physical and emotional instability. The second was a form dated only a few days after the first, admitting her to Windward as a patient, her condition predictably being physical and emotional instability. A Doctor A.C. Carp had signed both forms on the same day. Abigail Thornhill, representing the next of kin, had signed the second. Wasn't Abigail still underage then? Ben wondered about that as he took photos of both documents then looked up when he heard Cindy's squeaky footsteps coming his way.

"Look, sorry to rush you but something's come up and I need to leave for the day. I can't leave you down here while I'm gone. You done yet?"

"Yeah. Just finishing up." Suddenly Ben was anxious to be through with this place. He had a few papers and folders on the table and, conscious of Cindy's watchful eye, put them carefully and neatly back in the box. It was only by chance that he caught sight of a thin sheet of paper that had gotten itself curled up at the bottom of the file. He pulled it out and saw the orderly handwriting that covered the page. It was a letter addressed to Abigail Thornhill.

Cindy held the cover to the box. "Sorry, Mr. Marshall. I hate to rush you, but you've already had all this time, I..."

"No problem, just one more second." Ben quickly snapped a picture of the letter then placed it back in the box. Quickly, Cindy put the lid back on, hefted it down the aisle and slid it back on the shelf. "What came up that you're suddenly in a hurry?" he asked on the way up the stairs.

"Oh, just a dumb personal thing. My stupid boyfriend got himself into...well, I can't really talk about it, but I've really got to go. Sorry."

He followed her up to her desk. "Before I leave, do you know of a town called Randell? It should be around here somewhere."

"Nope. Never heard of a Randell. That doesn't mean anything though. I don't get out much. Spend my days in the office, hit the Y in the late afternoon and watch TV at night." She grabbed her purse then ushered him out into the hallway. "That where you're off to now? Randell? Just Google it and it should come up. Hey, I thought you were a detective."

"Yeah, I'll check that. I'm off to the Office of Property Deeds right now."

Cindy threw a thumb over her shoulder without breaking stride. "Two doors down the hall, back that away. Ask for Jeff."

"Thanks, you've been a big help."

"Just doing my job for the wonderful State of Maine."

At the Deeds Office counter, Ben asked for Jeff who appeared a moment later. An older guy with stringy gray hair and a gray mustache, he wore suspenders over a red flannel shirt. Ben asked him about Randell.

Jeff ran his fingers through his hair. "Well, there's a Randell up near the border."

"The Canada border?"

"Yeah, up there."

"No, that's not it," said Ben. "There would have been a plot of land not far from here, close to a town named Randell. The land was owned 100 years ago or so by a Lydia Thornhill or maybe her husband Danial Salter. Do you have any records on that?"

"Hundred years, huh? Well, we should have it somewhere in the historicals." Jeff walked to a desk and started punching keys on a computer.

Ben waited, turning to glance through a window that overlooked the parking area. He wondered how Stump was getting along cooped up in the car with the windows only open a crack.

"Well, hello," exclaimed Jeff finally, staring at the computer screen. "Randell, just like you said, close by too. Well, it's not there anymore though. Town must have folded during the depression. It's all state park land now." He hit a few more keys. "Yes, and here's a deed. It's made out to an Abigail Thornhill, not Lydia. Ten acres is all. Too small for a farm. You said your name's Marshall. You related to the Thornhills?"

"My great, great grandmother was Lydia Thornhill, her daughter was Abigail. They had a mailing address in Randell."

"Must have had a shack there on that little plot, I suppose. Back then all the mail for the surrounding area would have been delivered to the town. Mail slots at the general store, that's how they did things back then, just like on *The Walton's*. Oh, you probably wouldn't know about them. Want the coordinates so you can GPS it? Says here you can get fairly close in less than an hour from here. It'll be a bit of a hike off the road though."

"Coordinates would be great."

Jeff collected two sheets of paper from his printer; one, a copy of the deed, the other the GPS info. He handed them to Ben. "This is nothing official or anything, me giving you a copy of the deed. If you want it signed over to you officially, you'll need to have documentation, you know, that you're really related to the Thornhills. Might be a little sticky though, getting it through the state park folks."

"Right now I just want to have a look. Thanks for your help."

"I think they had a good rain out that way a few days ago. You might want to buy yourself a good pair of hiking boots."

"Thanks, I'll do that," said Ben, knowing he wouldn't.

Stump was pissed and let Ben know it. After being let out for a short while he resisted Ben's shoving him back in the car. Ben set the GPS coordinates and pulled out of the lot, while Stump lay slumped and sulking, head resting on the passenger side seat cushion, his big sorrowful eyes looking up at Ben as he drove.

"You're such a baby sometimes. I had important business to take care of." Ben dug a treat out of a bag and tossed it to him then put the windows down, letting the air roar in. Stump chewed the treat and slowly his ears perked up. He sat up, the wind ruffling his fur. "Yeah, that's better, right boy?"

Stump woofed.

It was three in the afternoon when Ben pulled off the highway onto a gravel road. Open fields bordered both sides for a few miles before the road grew twisty, climbing slowly up where the trees grew taller, crowding the narrow road. According to GPS he had about three more miles of this before he'd have to get out and walk the rest of the way. Well, at least Stump was going to like that part.

He passed a sign announcing his entry into Forestside State Park:

No hunting, No littering, No open fires. Camping permitted only in designated areas. Have a good time.

Ten minutes later, the GPS announced that his destination was 3.2 miles off to the right of the road. Ben angled his car as close as he dared to the road's edge, beside a drainage ditch.

He killed the engine, got out, and peered off into the woods while Stump drank some water from the ditch. Taking the hint, Ben grabbed a full bottle of water from the back then locked up the car. Looking into the woods again, he realized that Jeff had been right about the boots. He leaped over the ditch as Stump splashed through, shaking off the water on the other side. Ben pulled out his phone. The power in his cell was good but the signal strength was low. If he lost the GPS signal, he'd be in trouble. He switched to compass mode, checked their heading, and started out.

With a slow and steady uphill grade, the ground grew mushy with crumpled leaves and green moss. The sounds and smells brought back a forgotten memory when he couldn't have been more than five or six. Ben was running to keep up with the long strides of his father. They were tromping through a woods much like this one. But that was all he remembered. Where had that been? Where were they going? Strange, he thought, that he had only the barest recollection of it.

Eventually, the ground firmed up. Ben stopped and looked behind him. There was no sign of the road, just tall pines in all directions. Pinecones, and rust colored needles covered the ground. The Christmas-tree scent was everywhere. Insects buzzed and squirrels and gophers scurried. Every now and then a deer appeared with ears perked, staring back with curiosity while Stump barked and growled as threateningly as he could. The trunks of the trees ran bare as electrical poles for the first twenty feet or so, spreading their branches further up to complete a dense canopy over the forest. Ben knew the sun was shining in a blue sky. But here on the damp forest floor only a dim ambient light was able to make its way down. He imagined the nights here to be black as coal. He checked the time—nearly four. Still plenty of time.

The signal strength on his phone was fading. GPS told him he'd walked only 0.8 miles. At this rate, he might get to the house by 5:30. Okay, that's good. Stump looked back at him, barking, anxious to get going again. "Right, boy. On we go."

At five, Ben lost the GPS signal. Except for the compass on his phone, he was on his own now. He kept his direction constant until, up ahead, he spotted a patch of bright sun. It had to be a clearing. He quickened his pace as the ground leveled and he broke out from the trees into a grassy glade. He was glad to see the sun again but worried when he saw how far down it sat in the west. If he was smart, he'd start back now. Yeah, that's what he should do. He'd scout this clearing then head back.

But he should be close to the house by now, shouldn't he? Yes, it should be just ahead. Scanning the bright greenery on the far side of the clearing, Ben saw no sign of a building that might be the Thornhill place. He did see that the glade doglegged off to the north but his view of where that led was hidden by the encroaching trees. Yeah, he should at least check that out.

Worried that he could easily lose his way out here, Ben looked for a way to define his present location, knowing it to be the point closest to the road. To get back, he'd have to find this spot where he'd exit the clearing and make his way back through the woods to his car. He looked for an identifying landmark. He would need two of them.

He spotted a hilltop to the east and another to the south east. That's it, he'd take a compass reading of both to mark his position. Yeah, that's not so tough. He took the readings, wrote them down then set out, following the line of trees off to where he had a clear view of the dogleg. He hadn't gone far when, off in the distance at the opposite edge of the clearing, he saw a break in the trees. Was that a trail or road? If so, the house might be just beyond it.

To get there, he'd have to work his way around the clearing, or he could take the shorter route, that cut directly across it. He glanced back to where he'd broken out of the trees already a few hundred yards behind him. Yeah, there was always that third choice, head back now and come back tomorrow morning.

Shit, that would be a wimpy thing to do. Stump looked up at him, head cocked.

"You up for it boy?" asked Ben, noticing a few cattails poking up over the tall grass near the center of the clearing. Yeah, it was probably marshy out there. But they couldn't go back now, could they? The house, his house was so close. So his feet got wet, what's the big deal.

Decision made, Ben strode off down a shallow embankment heading directly for the spot he'd seen across the clearing. About ten steps out, ankle deep water filled his tennis shoes. Shit. He picked up Stump, carrying him through the chest-high grass where dragonflies the size of small birds hovered attentively. There could even be snakes out here, Ben realized. He hated the slithering things and took the longest possible strides to minimize the chances of stepping on one. Ugh, it gave him shivers. In his arms he felt Stump trembling too. With him being afraid of a little cockroach, what would he do if confronted by a snake?

After a while the water rose to calf depth and Ben had to be careful to keep the mud from sucking off his shoes as he slogged onward. He kept his eyes on the spot in the woods on the other side where he'd thought a path or road might be and slowly it got closer. At the halfway point he stopped to catch his breath. "Well, it's not the dumbest thing we've done, right Stump? Don't worry, we'll be okay." He glanced at the sun that seemed lower than it should have been. Shit! He started out again.

Stump was getting heavy and Ben had difficulty keeping his balance but he kept sight of the break in the woods and slowly made it to an upslope where the water grew shallower and the footing easier. Huffing and puffing, Ben took a few more steps up to dry land where he tumbled to the ground, exhausted. He stared up at the blue sky as Stump licked the side of his face. "I'm okay, boy. Don't worry. I'm okay." He sat up and looked down at his feet—two big mud-balls of black, earthy mush. He pulled off his shoes, shook off the mud and wiped them as clean as he could on the grass. He did the same with his soaked-through socks.

He put his socks and shoes back on and stood, hands on hips. With his back to the clearing he peered into the woods and saw the footpath that led off into the dark woods. There was no sign of a house. He checked the time. Almost 7. Crap. Even if he left now, there was no way they'd make it back to the car before dark. That's it then, he and Stump would have to spend the night out here with no food and only his half-filled bottle of water. It would be cold soon and he had no matches to light a fire.

"Okay, boy, I got us into this pickle but it'll only be for one night. You and I can do that, right? Let's see if we can find that house of ours." He started out. Stump gave a little whimper then caught up, staying a few steps behind.

Ben walked into the woods following what appeared to be a crude path long overgrown by a blanket of moss and weeds.

Branches rustled overhead as a breeze kicked up giving him an eerie feeling like he was getting close to… something.

Stump growled, sensing it too. He hung back, keeping Ben between him and whatever might be up ahead.

Ben slowed his walk, peering ahead through the trees. His heart was thumping. Twenty paces ahead, against the faded green pines, he caught sight of a large, dark shadow. He drew closer, then stopped. Just ahead stood a two-story wooden structure. The roof leaned in on itself as if it were about to collapse. The railing that must have once lined the wooden porch lay on the ground. The front door hung askew on a single hinge and all the windows that Ben could see were broken. Gaping holes pock-marked the walls where the wood had rotted through. Vestiges of faded red paint still remained here and there on the siding. The structure resembled a house of cards that might come tumbling down with the least disturbance. Ben took in a breath. This was it. Here was the house that had once belonged to his great, great grandmother, Lydia.

CHAPTER 13

With his foot, Ben tested the first of the three steps that led up onto the porch. The wooden planks groaned but held as he climbed up and walked to the door which, angled as it was, allowed him a look inside the house. All he could see was darkness. He gripped the door intending to swing it aside when the one good hinge gave way and the door fell flat onto the porch with a crash.

At the sound, birds fluttered and called out. Ben jumped back. Stump barked. And, from inside the house, there came a rustling.

Ben froze, listening, but heard nothing more. "All right, just a few animals inside. Small ones, right Stump? We're okay." He swallowed, then wondered what he was so worried about. "Shit, it's just a house." Straightening, he walked inside.

His eyes adjusted slowly. He stood in a large room dominated by a massive stone fireplace that took up the whole of one wall. Two overturned chairs, lay before it with a table between. Against the opposite wall a staircase led upstairs. A dark leather sofa stood beside a hallway that led back into the rest of the house. His footsteps crunched over shards of glass and other debris he couldn't see in the dim light. He followed the hallway into the kitchen. Ha, was that a hand pump next to the sink? He walked to it, grabbed the handle and gave it a yank but it wouldn't budge. Through the broken window above the sink stood the trunk of a tree, so close he could have reached out and touched it.

Ben opened a few cupboards, finding a sack of moss-eaten flour and some unmarked tins of food. The oak icebox was empty. He looked at his watch then glanced at Stump. "After eight already. Sorry, boy, we missed *Jeopardy* again." Off the kitchen was a mud room and a walk-in pantry, its shelves bare except for a thick layer of dust. The floor was littered with debris but, like the front room, it was too dark to make out much of what was lying there. He could have used his phone in flashlight mode but didn't want to waste the power. Besides, everything would still be there in the morning as would the staircase that led upstairs. He'd check everything out then.

He leaned his back against the sink. So far, the Thornhill residence didn't look too promising. Well, what had he expected? The place had been empty for almost a hundred years. He found a corner in the kitchen, cleared a spot on the floor and sat down. He took off his wet shoes and socks, thankful that they had at least some shelter from the elements. He laid back, his laced fingers serving as a pillow. Thinking better of it, he took off his shirt, rolled it up and rested his head on that. Stump came over and put his head on Ben's knee. Before long, the tired dog was snoring lightly.

Ben kept his eyes open, listening to the gusting breeze outside and the creaking of the house around him. He looked at the walls beside him and at the ceiling above wondering if they might come crashing down at any moment. Well, there was no point in worrying about that. He gave Stump a pat on the head, then closed his eyes.

Ben awoke to a wet tongue licking his face. "Okay boy, okay, I'm up, I'm up." He shooed Stump away and rubbed his eyes awake, amazed he'd slept so well. He sat up, then stood and stretched, working the stiffness out of his body. His back was sore. He looked out the window and, through the dark shroud of the trees overhead, he saw a few spots of bright sky. His watch told him it was 6:30.

His stomach rumbled. He drank down the last of the water then looked around the room, seeing it better in the morning light, albeit dim.

Plates and dishes, most broken, were scattered around the floor. Shards of china and glass lay everywhere. An empty whiskey bottle lay against the baseboard. Ben stepped carefully over to where he'd left his socks and shoes—still damp and stinky. He put them on then walked into the front room where the fireplace took up nearly the whole of one wall. It had probably been 100 years since the last fire contributed to the charring on the stones that framed the hearth. A pile of black cinders from that fire lay between the andirons. From the low whistling sound coming from the chimney above, he could tell the flu had been left open.

Then Ben turned.

He nearly jumped back from what he saw on the dirt-stained wall beside the staircase that led upstairs:

SAVE THEM
SAVE ME
SAVE YOURSELF

The words were boldly scrawled in faded black paint.

Shit. What the hell is that supposed to mean? Had Grandma Lydia written those words? Who did she think would be reading them? Ben realized that his hands were shaking. He reminded himself again that this was just a house and, as long as there were no bears inside, there was nothing to worry about. He stared at the words on the wall then realized that, from their position, the three-line message seemed to be directing him up the stairs.

He crossed the room, debris crunching under his feet. He put a hand on the staircase railing. The steps were splintered but otherwise, looked solid enough. Ben tested the first step, then the next. Slowly he climbed up, taking care to place his feet close to the wall where the structure should be strongest, all the while keeping a hand on the railing. The wood creaked under his weight but Ben made it to the top where he turned.

He saw three closed doors equally spaced along the wall to his right with a fourth, this one open, facing him beyond the railing of the stairs. Just like the old game show, thought Ben, pick the right door, win a prize. Except, in this case, the right door was already open. He walked forward in short, slow steps. He had his eyes on the open door, past which he saw the side of a wooden dresser and the footboard of a bed. If the floor was strong enough to hold those, it should be able to hold his weight with no problem, right?

Ben moved closer. Up until then Stump had been as tentative as Ben, climbing slowly up the stairs, staying just at his heels as he walked. Now, just as Ben got to the open doorway he charged ahead, leaped as high as his three legs would allow, and landed flat on the bed in a cloud of dust. He looked back at Ben as if asking why they hadn't slept here last night.

The bed was neatly made. Above the headboard, green-needled branches poked their way through a broken window, waving in the light breeze that wafted in. On the wall, beside it, whitened rectangular spots showed where two pictures had once been hung. Yes, there they were, on the floor, long since fallen, both, face down. Ben was about to reach down for the closest of them but, at that moment, spotted something more interesting lying on the dresser.

It was a small black box of pebbled metal with a leather strap on top and a metal lever near one end. On its side were the words: *Kodak Brownie*. He picked up the old camera and brushed the dust from its textured surface. He checked the lens and the viewing windows, wiping off the grime with his thumb then noticing on the end opposite the lens, a window through which he could just make out the number seven. He had seen cameras like this before in antique stores. Had there been seven pictures taken or were there seven pictures remaining on the role of exposed film inside? He was unsure of that, but was sure that he'd be taking the camera back with him.

He went through the rest of the room. He opened each of the dresser drawers—empty except for a few moth-eaten garments. He checked the pictures laying on the floor. One was the print of a praying Jesus, the other was a faded but decent-quality photograph of the house with a gathering of people standing clustered on the porch and down the front steps. The place had been impressive back then, standing tall and stately in front of the trees. He looked closer. Among the people gathered on the porch, he immediately recognized Lydia. She had a genuine smile on her face this time and, in a white blouse and long dark skirt, struck a confident, almost provocative pose. Beside her, tall and stern, stood a man who must have been Danny, her husband. In front of them stood a little girl who must have been Abigail. An older couple stood off to their right. Ben smiled grimly at their images. Of the house they'd once been so proud of, there wasn't much left.

He walked out of the room, camera and photograph in hand, then went through the other upstairs bedrooms and through the rest of the house. He found nothing else worth the trouble of bringing back and, as he left through the front door, he glanced again at the message on the wall beside the stairs. Those were Grandma Lydia's words, he was sure of it. But what did they mean? And who had they been written for?

He hesitated, then stepped outside and down off the porch. He walked a dozen paces further then turned to face the old house at what must have been the location where the photographer had set up his camera and taken the photograph Ben held. He tried to imagine those same people standing now on this crumbling edifice. They were his ancestors and, though he never knew them, Ben was sure that each of them held fond memories of that day when the picture was taken so long ago.

On the way back, Ben and Stump took the long way around, skirting marsh. His shoes were still wet and he didn't want to get them any wetter. It was a clear day and, after making it to the other side of the clearing, he could easily see the distant hilltops. He took his compass readings and, through trial and error, found the spot where they needed to strike off into the woods. It was late morning by the time he and Stump emerged from the trees and stepped over the drainage ditch onto the road, exhausted, thirsty, and hungry.

The car was nowhere in sight but, since his compass readings were just approximate, this didn't come as a surprise to Ben. With his cell battery fading, he was just glad to have found the road. He wiped a sleeve across his forehead. "Here boy, you decide. Which way do we go? Left or right?"

Immediately, Stump started off to the left apparently happy to be in the lead this time. Ben followed, hoping he'd guessed correctly. Ten minutes later, having just rounded a second curve in the road, Ben saw the glint of a windshield in the distance. Stump started barking and broke into a run. With relief, Ben saw that it was indeed his Ford Focus, still angled off on the edge of the road. "Good boy. Good boy," said Ben when he finally caught up.

After giving Stump some food and water and drinking a full bottle himself, Ben drove back to the highway where, at the first opportunity he got some coffee and fast food. Then, it was back to Portland to the same fleabag of a motel they'd stayed in a few days earlier. Ben showered, hit a diner, then conked out on the bed. It was only as an afterthought that he plugged in his dead phone.

Its ring woke him at 7 the next morning.

"Ben?"

"Yeah, who's this?"

"It's Ginny. I've been trying to reach you. Are you all right?"

Ben was still bone tired and his legs ached. His head fell back onto the pillow. He closed his eyes.

"Ben, you there? You're alive then? Oh man, that's great. I..."

"What? Slow down Ginny. You're not making any sense. Of course I'm alive. Why wouldn't I be?"

"There's been a fire at your place, Ben. Don't you know about it?"

"You said fire." Ben's eyes popped open. "What? A fire? Where? At my apartment you mean?" He swung his feet around and sat up on the edge of the bed.

"Yes, your apartment. It was terrible, Ben. Three people died, two in your building, one in the neighboring building."

"Holy shit!"

"They're still checking the place. I was afraid they might find...might find you inside too. Where are you?"

"Oh God. It had to be Maddie and Rob that died. Shit. Yeah, I'm up here in Maine—Portland. I...I decided to take a little vacation. But...Jesus Christ!"

"Well that was lucky for you." She hesitated. "I'm so glad to hear your voice, Ben. I still care about you, you know."

"Yeah, I care too." Ben took a breath then got to his feet. "Shit. I can't believe it. "You're right. I was lucky not to be there. Poor Maddie and Rob. Oh man, that's terrible." He slumped into a chair. "I can't believe it. Ginny."

"I'm just glad you're all right. We've been through a lot together you and I, and we've had a lot of good times. Maybe we should get together again. You know, just for a bite somewhere when you get back? I'd really like to see you. I was so scared when I thought you were...gone."

"Yeah, that'd be good. I'll get with you when I'm back." He swallowed hard. "Thanks, Ginny. Thanks for caring about me. I...I care about you too."

She ended the call and Ben put the phone down. He walked into the bathroom and splashed some water on his face. His mind flashed back to the words on the wall of the Thornhill house—two of them in particular:

SAVE YOURSELF

Is that what had just happened?

Ben showered and shaved slowly, his mind elsewhere. He was torn about what to do next. He should probably call the insurance company and file a claim. But no, the landlord would take care of that. But yeah, that's it, he should call the landlord. He did that, leaving a rambling voicemail saying that he was still alive, out of town, expecting to return soon and would be in touch then.

Still holding the phone, he thought that maybe he should just head back right away. He wasn't close to either Maddie or Rob but he still should go to their funeral, right? Yeah, he should at least do that. He thought about what it might have been like for them, being burned to death, and he cringed. God almighty, that's right, it was just luck that he wasn't dead too. He put down the phone then saw the Thornhill camera sitting on the table.

"Wow, I haven't seen one of these things in a while," said elderly Sam from behind the counter at Sam's photo-shop a few miles from the motel. He stared at the camera he held. "Still loaded. Bet you want it developed."

"Do you think the film's still good?"

"Could be. Depends on how old it is."

"It might be as old as a hundred years."

"Is that right? Well, I wouldn't give it much hope then. Still, you never know. Back then, film wasn't as light-sensitive as it is today." He put his glasses on and inspected the camera more closely. "I don't see any damage to the case." He tested a knob on the side but it wouldn't budge. "Back then you had to pull the shutter leaver then turn this knob to advance the film before taking another picture. Looks like someone took six exposures, advanced the film, but never took the seventh. That's what this number here is." He pointed to the number 7 behind the small circular glass. "Should be maybe six shots left. Here, I'll take your picture just to make sure it's working. That all right?"

"Sure, why not," said Ben.

Sam cleaned the lens then aimed it at Ben. "Now stay still. Exposure time on these things was pretty long back then. If you move, it'll come out blurred. 'Course it might be blurred anyways." He took the shot. "Shutter's got a gritty feel to it but it seemed to work fine."

"Can you do this right away?"

"Oh, you want to wait for it?"

"Yeah. I'll pay extra."

Sam shrugged looking around at his empty store. "Nah, that's all right. I'll do it right now. If anyone comes in tell them I'll be right back."

"Will do," said Ben.

A few seconds after ducking into a back room, Sam called out to Ben. "They'll all be black and whites, you know that, right?"

"Yes, that's fine."

Sam reappeared 30 minutes later, the camera in one hand, a yellow envelope in the other. He handed them both to Ben. "You got lucky. The images aren't what you'd call sharp but you can still make them out. Twenty bucks okay with you?"

"Yeah, twenty's fine." Ben paid with a credit card then opened the envelope and took out the photographs, laying them out on the counter one by one. The first five were photos taken around the Thornhill house. In one of them an elderly woman sat on the porch wearing a dressing gown. Her sunken eyes stared at the camera and, though the rest of her features were indistinct, she held a stoic expression. Her features were unmistakable. It could only be Grandma Lydia, the photo taken maybe only days before her death.

Ben flipped to the next photograph. Here was Grandma Lydia again, this time with her eyes closed and her mouth gaping wide. Arms folded, she lay flat on her back in a freshly dug hole in the ground. Ben looked closer. Her arms were folded over something. It looked like a package, or maybe a large envelope.

"Negatives are there too," said Sam who then inquired, almost in a whisper, "Do you know who she was?"

"She was my great, great grandmother."

"Guess you're doing this as kind of a family history project? Lots of people into that these days, most of them old like me. You look a little young for it."

"I'm not feeling so young these days." Ben glanced at the fuzzy photo of himself taken by Sam only a moment ago, then looked again at Grandma Lydia in her grave. He laid it flat on the counter then took out his phone and snapped a photo of it. He texted it to Amelia with a message:

I'm up in Maine researching my Grandma Lydia. Driving back now. Thought you'd like to know. Here's a pic that might interest you.

Ben put everything back in the envelope, thanked Sam then got back in his car. He'd only gone a few miles south when his phone went off. He smiled, recognizing the number. "Yeah, this is Ben."

"Mr. Marshall, this is Dr. Silvers. I just got the photo."

"Yeah, I just sent it." He'd expected her to call back, just not this quickly. He wished she'd stop with the Mr. Marshall crap and wondered how long she'd keep it up.

"Where did you get it?"

"It's from an old camera. I just had the film developed."

"So that's really Lydia Thornhill?" Ben could hear the excitement in her voice.

"Must be. I found the camera in the old house she had up here." Ben flashed a grin at Stump. That's right. There was nothing better than knowing something that a pretty woman was dying to know too.

"She's holding something. Did you notice that? It looks like her arms are wrapped around a package."

"Yup. Saw that."

"Do you know where the grave is? Is it in a regular cemetery?"

"No. I think it's just in front of the house. You can see the edge of the porch in the photo."

For a moment, there was silence on the other end. "Where are you Ben? Where are you right now?"

Ha, there it was, she'd finally called him Ben. "Still in Maine. On my way back to Boston."

"Ben, listen carefully. I think I know what's in that package."

"How could you possibly know that?"

"Her journals Ben. There've been rumors about them for decades. She started them at the asylum. That's what's in that package. It's the only thing it could be. Do you know how important this is?"

Ben slowed the car. "Why would she have them buried with her?"

"I don't know." She paused.

Ben waited for a moment then nearly swerved onto the shoulder as the thought hit him. "Shit! You want those journals. You want me to dig her up, don't you?"

"What? No, Ben. Of course I...Well, not her, just the journals." She hesitated again. "You don't realize how important they could be. But Ben, it's got to be up to you. You're her direct descendant."

"I'm not digging up my own grandmother."

"It would be just her journals. We would be respectful to your grandmother's remains. Ben, those journals could be one of the most important discoveries in the history of psychology. They could end up helping a lot of people."

Including Dr. Amelia Silvers in her struggles to make a name for herself, thought Ben. Then he realized something else. "You said we."

"What?"

"You said *we* would be respectful of her remains. Are you saying that you'll come up here and help with the digging?"

There was silence on the other end.

"Hello?" prompted Ben.

"Yes, all right, yes, I'll help with the digging. I don't like it any more than you do, but it's the right thing to do. I can be in Portland tonight. I'll bring a colleague who'll take photographs and act as a witness."

"A witness?"

"Yes. Probably a grad student. They'll authenticate everything we do to prove that none of it's fake." She paused again. "Ben, don't worry, we'll be respectful."

"So you'll be up here tonight?"

"If I can arrange it, yes. Look Ben, I'll understand if you're not good with this. You can refuse if you want to but..."

"Jesus Christ, Amelia, of course I'm not good with digging up my grandmother. Who would be? But, something tells me it's the right thing to do. Besides, I just found out that there was a fire in my building that killed some good people I know, so I'm really not that wild about going back there right now."

"A fire? Oh my God."

Ben went over the few details he had and she gave her sympathy, after which the line went quiet.

"So when can you get here?" he asked.

"You're comfortable with...?"

"Yes, yes. Stop asking me that. Anyway, now that I think about it, Grandma Lydia must have wanted someone to see her journals. Why else would she have had Abigail take a picture of her in her grave? And why would she have left the camera where someone would find it?"

"All right then, good. Look Ben, this is all kind of sudden but it comes at a good time. I've got a few days without classes. I've got to make some calls. I'll check back with you when I'm on my way." She ended the call.

Ben thumbed the steering wheel and gave Stump a glance. "Well, I suppose even that fleabag motel of ours beats going back to a burned out apartment. Right boy?" He sighed, thinking how easily he could have died in that fire like Maddie and Rob. No, he really didn't feel like going back to Boston right now.

He took the next exit and headed back to Portland.

CHAPTER 14

December 8, 1900

The elderly Dr. Cyrus Woodhouse looked up from the sheet of paper he held. "I see, Dr. Thornhill, that your last place of employment was the Portland State Reformatory not far from here."

"That's right. But I believe you already knew that." Lydia sat stiff and straight while keeping her facial features relaxed and confident. Financially, she didn't really need this position at the Windward Asylum yet she wanted it desperately. She kept her hands cradled in her lap, her fingers tightly laced.

He put the paper down. "Yes, I was aware of your background and am frankly impressed that someone with your...notoriety would consider a position here at the Windward Asylum. But it says here that you were dismissed from the Reformatory because of what Warden Brown called, questionable behavior? Can you explain that please?" His eyes held hers for a moment then dropped to her hands as if reading in them her true emotion. But no, Dr. Woodhouse wasn't quite that sophisticated, was he?

Just the same, Lydia smiled gently and shifted her hands, cupping them loosely, one in the other. "That was Mr. Brown's view. Owing to my years of formal training and Mr. Brown's entire lack of it, we had many differences of opinion. When I published my book about criminal behavior and my experiences with a rehabilitation process that too often ended with an execution, he took it as an indictment of his institution and of himself personally. While that hadn't been my intention, most others took it that way too, and this led to many reforms not only in Portland but across the country. Yes, I did achieve some notoriety for my views and Mr. Brown resented me for it. That is what led to my dismissal."

Left unsaid by Lydia was the fact that her formal training had taken place at the University of Michigan, the same college attended by Woodhouse. But he was already familiar with her academic credentials and she thought it best to let them speak for themselves, perhaps balancing out Brown's damning letter.

"There were no other factors in your dismissal?"

Without hesitation, Lydia lied. "None that I am aware of but, to be sure, you would have to ask him that." She added this last part knowing that Brown was currently out of the country and would be for the next two months. She also knew that there was no written record of her indiscretions at the reformatory. Only Brown knew of them.

Woodhouse leaned back in his chair. "I have read your book and was very impressed by it. But I do know that others were not impressed and, at your dismissal, were not so kind in their views." He peaked his fingers letting that sink in, then straightened and pulled open a drawer. From it he pulled out a newspaper clipping. He held it up. "Perhaps you have seen this?"

Lydia tried to keep her cool demeanor, but inside she was seething. Yes, she had seen the article. It was short but scathing and she remembered it word for word:

A BLEMISH REMOVED

With all the progress made across the country in the construction and the enlightened administration of our penal facilities, an undeserved blemish had been placed several years ago upon our own stellar facility here in Portland. That blemish, took the form of a book written by Mrs. Lydia Thornhill. Though it received premature acclaim, that

> publication has since been exposed as the false and vindictive ramblings of a demented woman who professes herself to be a trained medical doctor. All knowledgeable professionals view her opinions and her writings with distaste, and her recent dismissal from the Portland facility as her just desserts. Yes, the blemish has been washed away and we can all take solace in knowing that the small matter of Lydia Thornhill has been put to rest.

"That article was written by a third rate journalist who happens to be Mr. Brown's own brother-in-law," said Lydia. "I will not dignify it by saying more."

Dr. Woodhouse put the clipping down and fiddled with his gray beard. Lydia wondered if he believed her about the brother-in-law thing but decided that to be of little consequence either way. This was not a polished man in front of her. He wore his tie a little too tight, the same with the belt around his waist and the same with his stylish shoes that almost pained her to see how they crimped his feet at every step. Lydia had taken note of these things at her first sight of the pudgy, late-sixtyish, overblown authority-figure as he'd stood in front of his wall of framed awards and diplomas welcoming her into his office with a limp handshake.

Lydia also knew that Doctor Woodhouse had other things on his mind. Eyeing the shiny layer of sweat on his forehead, she wondered if maybe he'd had a fight with his wife that morning. Or maybe he was worried that he wasn't getting the proper respect from the people he employed here at this venerable institution. Analyzing these thoughts on a flash, she gave him a confident smile and waited for his next question.

"I see from your papers that you are a widow and you have a daughter."

"Yes, Abagail. She's six."

"Working here will substantially reduce the time you'll be able to spend with her. I would think you might be worried about that?"

"I've raised Abigail to be a very capable young girl, able to devote long hours to her studies. She will hardly notice my time away from her."

"Only six and she's already absorbed in studies?"

"She's very smart for her age."

"So, she will be alone for hours at a time?"

"I am a good mother. My daughter has her books and next year she will be enrolled in a private school." Lydia fastened her eyes on his now and spoke deliberately. "It is not something you should be concerned about. Dr. Woodhouse."

He spread his hands and stood. "Very well then, Mrs. Thornhill, we'll notify you of our decision in a few days."

"Thank you for your time, Dr. Woodhouse. I'll be delighted to work here under you." She accepted another limp handshake, then left his third-floor office.

She took the stairs down one level intending to leave, then saw that a normally locked door had been propped open by a chair. Probably the custodian looking to make his floor-mopping job a little easier. She did not hesitate. She walked through the doorway into a long hallway where male patients in wrinkled gray gowns shuffled and medication carts manned by white uniformed orderlies rattled over the tiled floor. The stink of sweat and urine was in the air but Lydia was unbothered by it as she walked, glancing through windowed doors that gave a full view of all six beds to a room that was apparently the norm here at Windward.

She knew that, at the last count, the sprawling facility was home to 857 men and women, each interred here because of a mental deficiency of one kind or another. 'Mental deficiencies', that's what they liked to call them. But she knew better.

She came up to a middle-aged patient who was leaning against the wall, head downcast. She stopped. She tried to catch his eyes which, she noticed, blinked twice as if bothered by her attention. He stood as still as a statue, yet Lydia could feel something else going on behind his mask of dormancy. She glanced at his nametag.

"Pleased to meet you, Jim," she said, knowing he'd heard, despite his stony expression.

Along the hallway, she approached a number of other random patients in the same way, greeting them by their first name, each time getting the subtle response she expected. On reaching the end of the hallway, she retraced her steps back the other way and left the building. Yes, *Windward* would do just fine.

Lydia received the acceptance letter the following week.

Across from her, Abigail looked up from her bowl of soup. She was such a beautiful child, sitting in her blue sailor outfit, her black braids hanging down in front of her shoulders, a drop of soup clinging to her chin, her big blue eyes questioning her mother.

Lydia tucked the letter back into its envelope and placed it on the table. "Remember we talked about me needing to be gone for part of the day?"

"Yes, I remember. You need to go and help people."

"Yes, that's right. In a few days, that's what I'll be doing." Lydia leaned closer and, with her thumb, dried Abigail's chin. "Is that all right? Mrs. Murphy from downstairs will be up to look in on you every now and then."

Abigail shook her head. "I don't like her."

"Well, she won't be up here much and she won't make you do anything you don't want to do. She'll just make sure you're safe."

"Safe from bad people? Like the ones who killed Daddy?"

Lydia sighed at the thought. "Yes, that's right dear. Safe from them. Is that okay?"

Abigail went back to her soup. "It's okay."

Lydia stood. With all the skills she'd developed in understanding people she thought it odd that she'd not yet been able to understand her own daughter. She attributed this to Abigail slowly becoming her own self as she grew. Yet she felt estranged from her; familiar with who she was at the moment while wary of the young woman she would one day become, and even more wary of the questions she might ask.

Though Lydia loved her daughter as deeply as she could love anyone, it would be a relief to be away from her. And, it wouldn't come as a surprise when she one day learned that, even back then at the tender age of six, Abigail had felt the same.

Lydia's first day at Windward was predictable. Dr. Woodhouse took her down to her first floor office, empty except for a desk and chair and two side chairs. Through a single window behind the desk, an apple tree, planted in a wide expanse of green grass, looked in. "You can decorate the walls however you like but at your own expense—pictures, diplomas, curtains, that kind of thing. Nothing unprofessional," he'd told her. "We'll have your name and position posted on the door in few days."

She spent the morning filling out forms and reading and signing policy statements. She had lunch with Dr. Woodhouse in the staff cafeteria where she attracted and returned a few stares.

In the afternoon, Dr. Woodhouse took her along on his rounds, introducing her to the staff at each orderly station on each floor. Though not a priority for her, she memorized the names and faces, their manner of handshake, their mannerisms and style of dress. Their every twitch and shrug told its own story that she casually filed away in the back of her mind. Of course they all viewed her with some degree of suspicion and some, even as a threat—no surprise there.

Near the end of the day, back at her office, Dr. Woodhouse introduced her to her nurse-assistant.

Ellen Maxwell was mid-aged and stout and, as Lydia learned later, she walked with a slight limp that gave her a signature thumpity-thump sound as she rambled the hallways. She wore her graying, wiry hair in a bun and she smiled too much for Lydia's liking.

"Pleased to meet you, doctor," she said in a bubbly voice, her gray-blue eyes shifting from Dr. Woodhouse, catching Lydia's and holding them in a quiet, comfortable way that, oddly, put Lydia immediately on her guard. Of all those she'd met, she sensed that Ellen was one of the few who actually wanted to be here. Now why was that? Was it for the same reasons as Lydia? Ellen's large hands were callused and, in their handshake, gripped Lydia's like a vise causing her to wince.

"Oh, sorry. I do that all the time," said Ellen, smiling. "I've developed a strong grip from pulling weeds. I do a lot of gardening here in my spare time."

"Here?"

"We have a large garden in the back," explained Dr. Woodhouse, smiling as well. "Some people call us Windward Farms."

Lydia nodded. "Sounds better than Asylum." She turned back to Ellen. "I'll look forward to working with you. I mean with patients. I don't really do gardening."

"Some of the patients find it therapeutic. I just like to grow things—like to eat too." She patted her midsection. "I'll take you out there sometime. You might change your mind."

Dr. Woodhouse gave her an uncomfortable grin. "Ellen is a woman of many talents and is one of the few non-doctors to have access to our entire facility. Everyone calls her Ellen-Magellan since her duties through the course of a single day sometimes take her on a complete circumnavigation of the entire building."

"I'll be here in your office at eight tomorrow and you can join the voyage," said Ellen with a toothy smile.

"I'd like to interview each of the patients first."

Ellen lost her smile. "What was that? You mean all of them?"

Dr. Woodhouse wasn't smiling either. "We have more than 800 patients, Dr. Thornhill. How can you possibly expect to..."

"I want to meet all of them. I want to know their names and I want them to know mine," said Lydia calmly, her eyes on Woodhouse. "You told me that I'd have free reign in the performance of my duties. If that's not in fact true, then there is no need for me to be here."

"No, no. I meant what I said. But interviewing each patient is hardly practical."

"I disagree, doctor. Ellen, we start tomorrow. Six patients to a room, we'll spend an hour in each room. I'll need a few notebooks and a good pen."

"Yes, doctor," said Ellen.

Lydia smiled inwardly at the ease with which she'd won this first battle.

She was well into her third week at Windward and well into her third book of notes when she first met Silent Margaret.

Not much older than Lydia, the woman sat next to her bed in a chair by the window and, while her roommates all stared at Lydia when she and Ellen walked in, Margaret seemed to be oblivious to their presence. By now Lydia was familiar with the hierarchy among the patients. A bed by the window was a prestigious spot, a sign of Margaret's authority at least among her roommates. She also noted that, a few of the women gave Margaret a glance as if asking how they should react to these intruders.

Lydia was drawn to her immediately.

"Name's Margaret Wheeler. Never known her to say a word," Ellen was explaining. "She just stares. Eats too, so I know she at least wants to stay alive. God knows why. She's been here three years. Just like that. Just staring."

She might have once been pretty, with her noble yet feminine chin, her well-formed nose and her slight build which, at the moment, was covered by a bed-shirt from the waist up and down from there by a brown blanket. Three years was a short time to qualify for window bed, thought Lydia. Maybe that had just been a random thing. "Hello, Mrs. Wheeler. My name is Lydia Thornhill. Would it be all right if I sit? I'd like to ask you a few questions."

Margaret Wheeler turned her head slowly, her charcoal eyes remaining fixed in their sockets as if only capable of focusing on that which was directly in front of her nose.

Lydia pulled over a chair then drew Margaret's eyes to hers. Slowly, she extended her hand and placed it atop Margaret's on the armrest. At the touch, Margaret didn't flinch but something subtle, nearly undetectable, had changed and it was reflected in the woman's eyes. Had the dark gray of her irises suddenly merged with the deep dark of her pupil to become a shining, almost iridescent black? Unsure of what had happened, or indeed, if anything had happened, Lydia felt her own heart pounding. Her mouth felt parched. She kept her eyes fixed on those of the silent woman, her hand on hers.

"Where are you Margaret?" Lydia asked, her voice low, her tone wavering. She forced herself to remain analytical. "You aren't here with me are you? Where are you? What is it you see?"

Margaret's lips remained thin and tight but trembled as if fighting back a torrent of words trying to pass through. Then, as clear and as startling as a gunshot, Lydia read Margaret's eyes: *Stay away from me!* they shouted.

"Why is that, Margaret? Why do you want me to stay away?" Lydia asked in a whisper.

Again, the woman's lips trembled. They opened as if she was about to speak. But no, she again let her eyes speak for her. They went wide and again Lydia heard her words clearly:

I AM DANGEROUS!

In that instant, Margaret turned away and, for Lydia, it was as if a door between them had just slammed shut. Margaret's hand went suddenly cold. Lydia pulled her own hand away and remained perfectly still for a moment, then got up. Without a word, she left the room.

Ellen followed her out and met her in the hallway. "She's a strange one, Margaret is." Then, looking at Lydia more carefully. "Are you all right?"

"Yes. Yes, of course, I'm all right."

"You don't want to talk to the others?" Ellen cocked her head back toward Margaret's room.

"Maybe tomorrow," said Lydia rubbing her temple. "I'm sorry, I guess I am feeling a little under the weather. We'll carry on with it tomorrow. I won't be needing you any further today, Ellen, thank you."

Ellen shrugged but held her look of concern. "That's fine with me, doctor, but maybe you should get some rest."

"Yes, maybe I should." Lydia walked quickly back to her office alone and closed the door. Had she really communicated with that woman? Or was her own mind playing tricks with her? She thought about those iridescent black eyes and the flash within them that seemed capable of illuminating Lydia's very soul. She shivered, knowing she'd experienced that same flash so many times before at the reformatory. Margaret was right, she was dangerous. The trouble was that Margaret Wheeler was exactly the type of patient that Lydia had hoped to meet.

The next morning, Lydia resumed her interviews, purposely avoiding Margaret's room and purposely avoiding Ellen's stare that questioned why that was.

A week passed before Lydia again approached Margaret's room. With Ellen beside her, she stood by the door, hesitating.

"Doctor?" asked Ellen.

But Lydia hardly heard. What was she afraid of? Wasn't Margaret the reason she was here at Windward? Didn't she possess the same look, the same electric aura as those of a prisoner at the gallows, knowing he was only moments away from death? She should be excited right now, not fearful. But, undeniably, Lydia was both. Sensing there'd be no turning back, Lydia opened the door to Margaret's room and walked in.

There she was, staring as before, sitting by the window that was lightly spattered by the rain outside. Lydia caught Margaret's jet-black eyes and in them could not sense the hostility she'd expected. Could it be that she was actually pleased to see her again? No, maybe not pleased, but...relieved.

Lydia knelt on a knee in front of her. "Hello Margaret. Do you remember me?"

Her eyes said she did.

Lydia reached out a hand and laid it on hers as before. But, unlike before, the skin to skin contact generated an immediate warmth that seemed to build. Lydia knew that something was happening but did not know what. She stared at her hand that seemed to radiate heat. She tried to pull it away but could not. The fear within her rose, a terrible nausea building. She felt her senses slipping away and everything around her seemed to turn a brilliant white. Gone were the features and sounds and smells of Margaret's room.

Painfully, Lydia's eyes adjusted to the new brightness. As if enveloped in a dense white fog she perceived a blurry, irregular band of grayness stretching around her and into the distance. As she tried to bring things into focus she began seeing streaks of lights and darks reminiscent of an impressionistic landscape painting. She tried to discern those features, to judge their distance, but she could not. A few seconds slowly passed before a low whistling sound began to build and a strong wind began to blow. It streamed through her hair cooling her body.

Then, the wind and the whistling were suddenly gone and she was back in Margaret's room, still staring at the woman's eyes.

Lydia pulled back her hand and stood. Without a word, she slowly backed away from Margaret, broke eye-contact, then walked out of the room.

"What happened in there?" asked Ellen when they were both out in the hall. "I've never seen her act like that."

Lydia felt her lips spread into an involuntary smile as the revelation hit her. "She tried to take me into her world."

"Her world? What do you mean? Her world's right here. She just doesn't know it."

Lydia shook her head. "No, her world's not here."

"So Silent Margaret has a world all to herself? And here you are talking like that's a place you'd like to go."

"Did you notice her eyes?"

Ellen scratched her head. "Well, I'm not sure what you're talking about but I did notice that from the time you got down on a knee in front of her until the time you got back up, she didn't blink. And I noticed something else too. You didn't blink either." She paused. "Doctor Thornhill, I've been a month following you around from room to room to room. You're not like the other doctors. You study these patients almost as if you're looking for something, or maybe even some*one*, in particular. Is Silent Margaret that person? And, if she is, what happens now?"

Lydia re-formed her half-smile. "I don't know," she said honestly.

Ellen lowered her voice. "I'll tell you the truth, doctor. I've seen patients act like you sometimes. Sometimes it's as if you are more like *them*, than us."

Lydia's heart blazed at the insight. She realized that she had underestimated this woman. "We're done for the morning, Ellen. Here, give me my notebook." Lydia snatched it from her then hurried back to her office and closed the door. She sat, holding the notebook to her chest. She thought about her days at the reformatory infested as they were with evil and death. She thought about the palpable fear of a prisoner as he climbed the gallows steps. She thought about the feel and the scent of his freshly hung body. She thought about Jerimiah, and she thought about Abigail's twin brother born dead.

'Why would those thoughts intrude now?' she wondered, almost shaking. She put down the notebook then reached out and touched it as she'd touched the hand of Silent Margaret. Where had she been for those brief moments in Margaret's room? Through that fog, had she really glimpsed a different world, fleeting and vaporous? A world that somehow floated unreal, yet real? A world presently inaccessible to Doctor Lydia Thornhill, but there just the same? Or had she simply gone a little dizzy from the strains and stresses of working at the asylum?

Lydia brought both of her hands to her face, comforted momentarily by the darkness and by the light pressure of her fingertips on her closed eyelids. She breathed deeply and, on opening her eyes, sat up straight, back to being Doctor Thornhill, back to take on the impersonal analytical duties of a medical doctor.

She pulled her notebook closer and took up her pen. Then, thinking better of it, she slid the half-filled notebook aside and pulled from her desk a fresh one. She opened it to the first page, blank and sterile, and began to write.

CHAPTER 15

From behind the wheel of his Ford Focus, Ben watched Dr. Byron Howe. He stood outside, hands on hips in front of his motel room door. He wore a pair of oversized jeans and a Princeton Tigers sweatshirt looking like a well-trained Shakespearian actor who'd suddenly found himself demeaned to the level of an off-Broadway revival of *Hair*. It was 6AM and he was frowning at Ben's car. "I don't understand why we have to start out so early."

Stretched out in the backseat behind Ben, Amelia sighed and shouted back. "We went over this yesterday, Dr. Howe. Ben says it's a long hike off the road and he doesn't want to spend another night there. He says it's a spooky place. Frankly, I don't want to spend the night there either."

"You sure he's up to this?" Ben asked her, watching Howe shrug then do a few deep knee-bends.

"He's in better shape than he looks—ran the Boston Marathon once. At least that's what he told me."

Finally, Howe got in, riding shotgun. "How about stopping for a breakfast sandwich and coffee?"

"All part of the plan, Byron," said Ben. "You all right there Stump?"

Stump woofed from the way-back and they started out.

Ben hadn't been pleased to see that Amelia's impartial, professional observer turned out to be Dr. Howe. She'd explained to him that a BU grad student wouldn't have been impartial and that Howe had been the only one available on such short notice. He guessed that made sense and, looking at the bright side, Howe would hardly be much competition for Amelia's affections should things tilt in that direction. Not that he expected this. In fact, he found himself thinking more and more about Ginny and their last conversation over the phone. Still, that bouncy red hair was distracting. It was probably just as well that she wore it tucked under a BU baseball cap this morning.

Two hours later, they pulled over to the side of the dirt road that was all too familiar to Ben and Stump. They all got out and, as they gathered their things from inside the car, Stump sat on the gravel by the rear wheel looking off into the woods, ears cocked.

"He seems a little reluctant," said Amelia.

"He gets squeamish sometimes. He'll be all right once we get going," said Ben, hoping the same for himself. At least this time he was prepared with decent hiking boots and a backpack full of goodies. And he had company.

Amelia had a pack of her own and Howe carried a small duffle bag with a meter-stick slid between the handles.

"Be sure to take plenty of water," said Ben as he set up the GPS in his phone. He checked the time. "This thing says it'll take two and a half hours to get there. Figuring everything, we should be back here about four, maybe five o'clock." He picked up the collapsible shovel he'd bought the day before and closed the trunk.

"Two psychologists and a police detective go off into the woods, sounds like the start of a good joke," said Amelia as they started out.

"Can't wait to hear the punch-line," said Howe.

Without much small-talk, they tromped through the woods at a steady up-hill grade taking a water break every half-hour or so. On reaching the clearing two hours later, Ben looked skyward. "It's not supposed to rain but I don't like the look of those clouds."

"Smells like rain too," said Howe.

Ben waved a hand across the clearing. "The house is straight out across this marsh. We'll stick to the edge of the woods and work our way around."

"Sounds good," said Amelia. She took off her hat and ran a wrist over her forehead. "I don't mind a little rain either, it'll cool things off. Let's get going."

"Just give me another minute or two," said Howe legs crossed, sitting on his duffle-bag. He took another drink from his water bottle then stood. "Guess I've been spending too much time at the desk these days."

"The terrain's pretty flat from here on in so the worst is behind us," said Ben with another glance at the clouds.

A slow drizzle was just starting when they reached the point on the other side of the clearing where the foot path led off into the woods. "Looks a bit like *Fangorn Forest* in there," said Howe, hands on hips, staring into the dark woods.

"What's *Fangorn Forest*?" asked Ben.

Howe smiled then put on a ghoulish look. "It's a place in Middle Earth. Lots of spooky things in *Fangorn Forest* at the foot of the Misty Mountains."

Ben gave Amelia a glance and got an apologetic look in return. "The house isn't far," he said, leading the way in.

A musty smell floated in the still air. The light rain had not yet reached the forest floor. The quiet of the woods and the weight of his gear gave Ben a feeling of dread both for where he was and for what he would soon be doing. He moved slowly and stopped when he saw the house.

Howe broke the silence. "When you said the place looked a little spooky, you weren't kidding, were you? It looks straight out of a Stephen King novel."

"We don't have to go inside," said Ben, still not moving.

"Yes, we do," said Amelia walking up to the porch. "Everything here has to be documented."

"Right," said Howe, joining her. He put down his duffle bag, pulled out his SLR and took a few shots.

Ben walked forward and pulled out the collapsible shovel, tossing his pack onto the porch next to Amelia's. He just wanted to get this over with. The light patter of rain began to dot the dry ground. He unfolded the shovel and tightened its joints. From his pocket he pulled out the picture of Lydia in her grave. He stared into her eyes. "Sorry Grandma," he said with a sigh.

Holding the photograph up in front of him, he matched the image of the porch in its upper left corner with the actual edge of the porch. He then walked a few steps forward where he cleared away some of the pine-needles then planted the tip of the shovel on the spot. "Her grave should be right here."

Amelia didn't say a word. Howe snapped off a few more pictures.

Ben tucked the photo into his pocket. He took a breath then put a foot on the shovel feeling it sink almost too easily into the dirt. He tossed aside the small amount of earth then mechanically repeated the process, not putting his full weight into it, allowing the shovel to sink only a few inches deep at a time, each time expecting to hit some part of what was once Lydia Thornhill.

The rain picked up.

"Ben, you need to hurry," said Amelia from the porch. "We don't want everything going muddy on us."

He gave her a nod and but kept digging at his own pace. Finally, he hit something solid. He swallowed hard, then got to his knees. He tried to ignore the snap of Howe's camera as he dug with his hands, clawing at the dirt, loosening it then sweeping it aside until he suddenly drew back. He rested on his haunches, his stomach in a knot. "Oh God. Here she is," he said in a whisper, suddenly feeling that he shouldn't be doing this.

Amelia came down and knelt beside him. "Do you want me to help you?"

He shook his head, then again bent into his work, shivers running down his spine as he exposed...oh God, was it her skull? Yes, first a cheekbone then, oh shit, there was an eye-socket.

"Dig down here," said Amelia, pointing at an area a foot or so down from the skull. "Do you want me to do it?"

Ben took a breath. "No. I'm all right. I'll do it. Never dug up a grave before."

"It's a first for me too," said Amelia.

Ben stood. He picked up the shovel and dug more aggressively over where Grandma Lydia's chest should be. Before long he dropped to his knees again. Again, he clawed at the dirt, slowly exposing the bones of Grandma Lydia's hands. He tried to work around them down to what he knew those hands were grasping.

"That's it, Ben. You're doing fine," said Amelia, the rain still harder now.

He swept aside more dirt, mud now, and came to a brown and

wrinkled surface. He shivered, thinking it to be a layer of skin but saw that it was a woven fabric. "It's canvas, I think."

Just then, Ben felt a hand on his shoulder. He nearly fell back, then realized it was Howe.

"Here, stop," he said. "I need to get a shot of this."

"Shit, I...okay, all right." Ben shook his head and skootched out of the way as Howe placed a meter-stick onto the exposed canvas. He took three shots from different distances and angles then picked up the stick.

"All right. Let's get this over with," said Howe.

Ben dug. Knowing the shape and general size of what Grandma Lydia was holding, he quickly exposed it. Howe took more pictures as the work progressed.

"Can you get it free?" asked Amelia.

Ben swallowed. He used both hands and pulled up on the canvas package, gently at first, then harder. It shifted. His stomach twisted. Grandma Lydia's brittle finger-bones snapped, their fragments falling aside as he slid the package out. Still kneeling, he held the package for a moment then clutched it to his chest, reverently, holding it in the same way that Grandma Lydia had been holding it for so long. He glanced into her eye-sockets, imagining her staring back, then stood and handed the package to Amelia.

"I'll lay her back to rest," Ben said quietly. The rain was falling hard now, streaming from the bill of his cap. Howe and Amelia retreated to the shelter of the porch as he finished covering up the grave. Done, he tossed the shovel aside and bent low to lay a palm on the fresh mud. "Don't worry, Grandma," he said. "We'll do right by you." Drenched, he walked up onto the porch beside Amelia.

She put a hand on his shoulder. "You all right?"

"I didn't expect to get this emotional."

"She was your great, great grandmother, Ben, it had to be emotional for you. Just knowing the little I do about her, it was emotional for me too. Howe has the package inside."

The wind began to blow, the porch offering little protection. They walked inside, dripping. Howe sat in the front room on a wooden chair, the canvas package on the table in front of him. "I took a few pictures around here." He pointed to the words painted on the wall. "What do you make of that, Detective? You saw those words when you were here before, I assume?"

Amelia turned then froze, just staring.

"Yes, I saw them," Ben said quietly. "I don't know what they mean. But I do know, if I hadn't been up here, I'd be dead right now."

"Killed in the fire, you mean," said Amelia, taking a few steps closer to the wall, running a hand lightly over the words.

"And you think that's where the *Save Yourself* thing comes in?" asked Howe.

Ben shook his head. "I don't know."

"The fire had to be a coincidence, Detective," Howe went on. "You were lucky, that's all. Besides, even if she had intended those words for you, she's saying you have to save others and then save her before you can save yourself."

Ben hadn't thought about any possible significance to the order of Grandma Lydia's words. His mind flashed back to when he'd unearthed her skull and stared into those empty sockets out of which her eyes now seemed to stare back. He felt a little unsteady, then caught himself and took a breath. He found himself coming to a harsh conclusion. "My grandmother was a dying old lady when she wrote those words, senile, maybe worse. There's no future in trying to make sense of them."

Howe, nodded in agreement while Amelia walked from the wall back to the table where the canvas package lay. She placed a hand on it. "If there are answers anywhere, they will be in here. The fabric is wet from the rain but there's a brittle feel to it so it must have been kept fairly dry all these years. We've got a good anthropology group at BU, it's probably best that we have them unwrap it."

"I will be the one to unwrap it," said Ben with sudden conviction.

"I wouldn't advise it," said Howe. "You could easily damage what's inside."

"I will open it," said Ben.

Ben saw Howe give Amelia a glance.

"All right. You'll be the one to open it," agreed Amelia. "But not here. We need to get back."

"We're not going anywhere until the rain dies down," said Howe.

Ben started to breathe easier then tensed, looking around. "Where's Stump?" He turned, looking outside. "I hope he's not out there."

"Relax Detective, he's right here. He came inside with me." Howe pointed under the table where Stump lay head on paws, resting gloomily. "He has a lot of sense, that dog of yours."

They sat and waited. The rain continued hitting the old house hard, sounding to Ben like the static from an old television. Water that had been falling in drops through gaping cracks in the ceiling, now fell in steady streams.

"I'm going to take a look around," said Amelia.

Ben went back out onto the porch. The wind howled and the tall trees swayed but out toward the clearing, he could see spots of sunlight on the green grass. Slowly, the sky began to brighten and the wind calmed. Then, not much later, as if turned off by a faucet, the rain stopped.

No one talked much on the way back to the car—Ben and Stump leading the way, Amelia following, carrying the canvass-covered package, Howe bringing up the rear, using his meter-stick as a walking stick that gave a distinctive tick sound every time it hit the ground. They were all still drenched from the rain, and now the sweat from exertion and from the hot, moisture-laden air only added to their discomfort. It was nearly six when they found the car, each guzzling water from fresh bottles while wolfing down a couple of energy bars.

"I see why you wanted the early start," said Howe to Ben, wiping his chin as they climbed in. "This was more of a trek than I thought."

"Thought you were a marathoner," said Ben starting the car, turning the AC up to max and pulling out. The drier air from the vent felt great, warm at first but cooling fast.

"To be honest, that was many years back," said Howe, buckling in.

Through the mirror, Ben gave a glance back to Amelia who seemed unnaturally quiet. He caught her eye and she gave him a thin, *I'm good*, smile, but said nothing. Probably has the same thought rattling around in her head as I do in mine—*What have we done?* Well, like a bunch of drunken teenagers screwing around on a Halloween night, we just vandalized a grave site. That's a criminal offence in every state in the union. That's what we did.

Ben took the dusty road back to the freeway then gunned it down the entrance ramp, glad to be leaving the Thornhill house, hoping he'd never have to go back.

It was already getting dark by the time they got back to the motel. They gathered in Ben's room, standing around the canvass package that Ben had placed on the table.

Howe turned on all the lights then closed the drapes. "I really wanted to shower first," he complained, wiping his hands on his pants. Getting no support for that idea, he sighed and began checking his camera.

"It looks like there's a wax seal around the edges," said Amelia, feeling the canvass surface. "If we're lucky there'll be no water damage inside."

Howe snapped a photo and checked the result. "Okay, we've got enough light. We'll do a high-res video and will be recording audio too so keep your comments professional please. I will begin the commentary. Are we ready?"

"Yes," said Ben, his throat dry.

"All right, recording, NOW." In a slow, solemn voice Howe gave the date, time, location, the names of the people present and the purpose of the video ending with: "You may proceed, Detective Marshall."

Ben bent closer to the package and carefully tucked a finger under the edge of the canvas. He pulled gently, the wax seal brittle, peeling away easily as he ran his finger along the seam. That done, he folded the fabric back as if he were turning a page in a book. The wax broke at the top and bottom edges exposing a second layer of canvass.

“She protected it well,” said Amelia.

Ben turned the package over and found the seam in the second layer. Breaking the wax seal in the same manner as he had the first, he pulled the canvas back exposing what appeared to be a stack of notebooks, each about half an inch thick, each bound in thin black cardboard.

“Her journals, just as we thought,” whispered Amelia, “four of them.”

“Turn them over,” said Howe, “you have them front side down.”

Carefully, Ben lifted the notebooks as Amelia cleared the canvas from beneath leaving flakes of reddish wax on the table, some dropping onto the floor. Ignoring the mess, Ben put the stack down and saw a faded label centered on the first notebook. In neatly printed block characters it read:

THORNHILL JOURNAL I

He fanned out the other notebooks exposing the labels on each.

“Yes, there are four Thornhill notebooks,” commented Howe in a dramatic whisper, keeping his camera running. “Each is numbered, one through four. All appear to be in excellent condition.”

Ben picked up the first journal and sat down on the edge of the bed.

Hurriedly, Howe repositioned himself so that his camera now looked over Ben’s shoulder.

Ben turned the cover exposing a page filled with bold, stylish writing.

Howe continued with his commentary, excitement tinging his voice: “The writing is clear, the page pristine. The date of the first entry in January 5th 1900.”

Conscious of Howe’s heavy breathing near his right ear, Ben

closed the book and looked back at the camera.

Howe took the hint. "This concludes the video documentation of what right now truly seems to be the discovery of the Journals of Dr. Lydia Thornhill. Further documentation will take place as part of a thorough, professional, examination process which will begin as soon as possible." He clicked the camera off and put it down. "Didn't really expect you to glance back like that, Detective. But, no matter, we can edit that out."

"This is a tremendous find," said Amelia, her fingertips brushing lightly over the second journal. "It'll take years of study to go through it all."

Ben barely heard her. His heart was beating fast. He felt the heft of the journal that lay closed on his lap. The air in the room felt suddenly stale. He put the journal aside and stood. "Just give me a minute," he said, heading for the bathroom where he splashed some water onto his face. He looked at himself in the mirror. His face, gaunt and stubbled, stared back. Beads of water glistened over smears of dirt and sweat. His eyes were reddish. Shit, he was a mess. Just tired though, right?

But no, he knew it was more than that. He took in a deep breath. Lydia's image, young and vital as he'd first seen her in the textbook, flashed through his mind and he felt a certain calmness at the thought of her as she must have been back then, only a little younger than he was now. Yes, that was how he should remember her. He wet his face again then toweled dry. He filled a paper cup, drained it in two gulps, then retook his spot on the bed and picked up Journal Number I. "Okay, I'm just going to read the first few pages aloud. No camera this time though, all right?"

"You don't have to do this, Ben," said Amelia.

"Yes, I do."

CHAPTER 16

Ben opened the cover to Journal Number I. "Okay, this is dated January 5, 1900," he announced, then began reading:

I am Doctor Lydia Thornhill. For four weeks I have been a physician at the Windward Asylum near Portland Maine. Prior to that I spent years at the state reformatory and more years on my own, studying and speculating on mental disorders in all of its many forms, searching for a common trait, hoping to find a common cause and hoping against hope, to ultimately find a cure. The professional papers I've written related to those efforts remain unpublished, all having foundered in a peer review process favoring only work supportive of conventional thinking. Sadly, both in medical circles as well as in society in general, there is an aversion to the study of abnormalities of the human mind. It is an aversion stemming from the fear that each and every one of us has when confronted with our latest lapse in judgement, or our latest lapse in memory and we ask ourselves: Am I really normal? The truth is that every one of us is susceptible to mental disorders and that these disorders come about as the brain, like any other physical organ, degrades with both stress, with age and with perhaps a dozen other factors.

Based on my past studies and on an incident that occurred just this morning, I have begun to speculate that there may be a peculiar condition in which the brain can leap, for brief periods of time, into a heightened emotional state where for some, the physical world might melt away replaced in an instant by another world, just as real as the first, but in many ways different. While in this state, a patient would feel themselves to be completely logical and rational in their actions but, to an observer, such as a doctor still locked into his or her own reality, those actions are anything but logical and rational. To the doctor, those actions are those of a person with a mental disorder.

I am early in my investigation. The purpose of this journal is not to present opinion or to argue truths over falsehoods. My purpose is to provide a detailed record of my experiences here at Windward. I live both in awe and in fear over what additional experiences I might have and to what conclusions they might lead but, dear reader, I am compelled to compile the facts as I alone see them.

The incident from this morning, is the first case in point:

At approximately 10:05 this morning I enter room 106 with Nurse Ellen Maxwell. It is my second visit here, the first being just last week. As with all the other rooms at Windward, this one is occupied by six patients, in this case all female. On entering, I am immediately aware of a woman who sits alone in a chair by the window. She stares not through the window but at the blank plaster wall on the far side of the room. She seems not to notice my presence but I somehow feel certain that she knows I'm there. As on my first visit here, I walk directly to her.

She's known to the staff as Silent Margaret. She is 48 years of age and has written several books on historical topics. Her full name is Margaret Wheeler. She has been a patient here for 12 years, originally admitted after a bout of violence with her husband as witnessed by her three children. She hasn't spoken or written a word since being admitted yet, as I would learn, she is capable of communicating in other ways.

In a chair I sit nearly knee to knee between her and the wall at which she continues to stare, still undisturbed by my presence. I re-introduce myself then ask: "How are you today, Margaret?" There is no reply. I study her eyes. The whites are pure, the irises, a dull charcoal. The corners of her eyes are relaxed and her demeanor seems entirely passive as if she doesn't see me at all.

Then she moves.

Her hands which had been laying relaxed in her lap now take hold of the front edge of her chair. I reach out my hand and touch hers then look back at her eyes and see that they've widened. The irises have changed from charcoal to a shiny black. As I watch, her pupils dilate and her irises change again, becoming thin floating rings of turquoise. I am unable to tear my gaze from them. From behind me, I feel a chill. I feel her eyes enlarge, as if they are trying to pull me in. I feel my heart jump. Cold envelopes me. I resisted at first, but then, weak as from too much wine, I relax. Suddenly, of their own volition, my eyes snap shut.

Where I am at that moment I do not know. There is a fog of bright white all around me, and in the far off distance I see the vague hint of something dark and foreboding. I struggle to bring it into focus but the fog thickens and, within a few seconds, the dark thing vanishes and I am left floating as if I'd somehow left my body behind. I remain suspended like this for a few moments then, suddenly, all is dark and the chill is gone. I feel my senses return and I open my eyes to find myself sitting as before in front of Margaret, her eyes normal again, staring as before.

I am shaken by this experience. With an effort, I turn away from Margaret. I rise and walk to my office where I now write with a heavy hand, uncertain as to what had just happened but certain that, when I revisit Margaret, something similar will happen.

And maybe there will be something more.

Ben looked up from the page. Amelia and Howe both stared back at Ben, silent as if still absorbing the words he'd read. Ben was still absorbing them himself. He thought back to his grandmother's book, specifically the incident where she'd lost her sense of normalcy. She'd been in her early days at the prison back then, years before she'd written these first pages in her journals, yet it seemed as if that experience with the prisoner about to be hung held an eerie similarity to her experience with Silent

Margaret.

Stump barked. Tail wagging, he stood by the door.

"I better take him out," said Ben, laying the journal aside and getting up from the edge of the bed. He was glad for the diversion.

"Do you mind us reading ahead?" Amelia asked, picking up the journal.

Ben shrugged. "Knock yourselves out. I just felt I had to be the one to read that first part. Don't know why, it just felt right." He leashed Stump and left.

Outside in the cool air Ben was glad to be alone with his thoughts. He guided Stump out to the grass beyond the lights of the parking lot. After the stuffiness of the motel room, the air was refreshing and a few stars were visible between the hovering clouds. He wondered why his grandmother decided to take her journals with her to her grave. She couldn't possibly know they would one day be discovered by one of her descendants a century later. So why did she do it? He thought about that first passage he'd just read from her journal, mentally joining it to what he already knew about Grandma Lydia through her book. She'd been impacted at the reformatory, first by Timothy Beckham, then by Jeremiah Foley—both men dying before her eyes. And now there was this Silent Margaret at the asylum. Those three people each had a pivotal effect on the normally stern and analytical Doctor Lydia Thornhill. He wondered how many more such people there might have been in her life.

He swatted a mosquito. A truck roared by on the road. Stump barked then glanced expectantly up at Ben.

"You done already boy? Yeah, suppose we'd better go back," agreed Ben. He checked his watch and saw that they'd been out longer than he'd thought. He took his time walking back across the lot and, approaching the motel room door, he heard Howe's muffled voice coming from inside. Ben listened for a moment then, unable to decipher any of what was being said, opened the door to find Howe seated with one of the journals opened on his lap. Amelia stood beside him and both looked up almost guiltily when he walked in.

"Hope I'm not interrupting," said Ben closing the door. He unleashed Stump then glanced first at Amelia then Howe who still hadn't said a word. "What? Did you find something?"

Howe cleared his throat. "I skimmed ahead in the first journal, the one you were reading, then turned to the end of it."

Ben reclaimed his spot on the bed. "And?"

"Either your Grandma Lydia had a very active and vivid imagination, or..." Howe shook his head. "It seems she went back to this Silent Margaret person many times to probe the woman more closely. Each time though, the woman simply stared back, not talking and in no way having the unusual effect on your grandmother that she'd had at their first meeting. Like I said, I just skimmed ahead so I probably missed a few things."

Amelia picked up the journal. "After those early meetings with Margaret, your grandmother started having dreams, nightmares really. Terrible ones, each about someone dying. She thought the dreams might somehow be connected to Margaret so eventually, after a lengthy absence, she visited her again."

"And...?"

"Well, I'll just read," said Amelia. "These are the last few pages of the first journal. This entry is dated January 8, 1902:

I sit in front of Margaret as I have so many times before. I hold her eyes in mine and after the briefest of moments, my eyes close and I am gone. I somehow know that Margaret is no longer with me. I am shaken at first, then slowly, my senses seem to calm me.

I feel on my skin a sweet summer's breeze, warm and refreshing. No longer can I sense the oppressive airs of the asylum as they'd been replaced by the smells of freshly mowed grass. I feel the sun on me. Insects buzz. As if controlled by an outside force, my eyes open.

Under a sky of clear blue, I am standing in an open field that stretches completely flat out to the far horizon. But no, I am not really standing since, when I look down to where my feet should have met the ground, I see only the ground. I cannot see my own body. All my senses tell me that I am in this place and yet my body, it seems, is not there with me. It is all too vivid to be a dream and I wonder, 'Might I be dead?' Then, I hear the crunch of dried grass behind me and I turn.

No more than three paces from me is a boy. He is running hard, breathing heavily, his eyes wide with fear. As he passes, his head turns toward me and I can see more clearly his frightful expression—his mouth is distorted, stretched wide, his fat cheeks are streaked with mud and tracked with tears. His blond hair is matted with dirt. Then I see that he is hurt. From the side of his head, blood runs fresh and glistening. I am certain that he senses my presence and I call out to him but find that I cannot make a sound. He hesitates as if distracted, then falls.

Trying to get up, he begins sobbing. I try to help but cannot.

The crack of a gunshot startles me and I turn again to see a tall man, finely dressed as if just back from Sunday church. He stands perfectly still, the stock of a rifle pressed to his shoulder. White smoke rises from the barrel that appears aimed at the boy.

I turn to the boy who is still lying on the ground. Except for the head wound, he appears unhurt and I conclude that the man's shot has missed.

The man shouts. "I'm going to kill you boy. Start saying your prayers." He lowers the rifle and begins taking long strides closer, about thirty paces from us now.

Beside me, the boy sobs but makes no more effort to get up. I see now that he has banged his knee against a rock. He lays there, his body shaking. I try to bend over him, and again try to help but cannot. The man is nearly on us now. I want to scream. I want to tear the weapon from his hands but I cannot.

Five paces from us, the man stops. He points the rifle down at this poor boy. God no! I shout soundlessly. Hands outstretched, I place myself between the man and the boy. Again, I try to scream. I see the man's finger on the trigger. I see him pull it back. I jump at the loud bang. I feel my heart stop and I fall. And then, I do scream.

My cry rises, loud and anguished. My tears fall. I know the boy is dead. My body shakes just as his must have. But I no longer see him. Suddenly, I feel the cold floor beneath me. I feel hands struggling to pick me up.

"Doctor Thornhill, are you all right?" someone asks.

I think that maybe I say something. I remember being out of breath, trying hard to fill my lungs with air as I realize that I am back in the asylum. I sit, doubled over. Someone gives me water and I drink. And I look around.

All is as it was. The sun still shines through the window, and beside it, Margaret sits, calm and still.

I straighten in the chair. I drink more water. I finally start to breathe easier but then realize that each breath I take is tinged with the progressively fainter smell of gunpowder.

That dream is as real to me as the cup of tea I had earlier this morning or this pen I now hold in my hand. Yet I wonder how could it be real? And I wonder too, if this dream were real, then what of the terrible dreams that had been tormenting me over the past months? Were those real too?

If I had been an observer that day in room 106, I would have been convinced that Doctor Thornhill had just experienced a bout of temporary insanity probably brought on by some kind of emotional stress. In her report the next day, that was the exact conclusion of Nurse Ellen, so I couldn't blame her.

Yet, I know better.

Amelia closed the journal. "So, this first journal ends there. It covers her first two years at the Windward Asylum."

"Her dreams don't sound like any dream I've ever had," said Ben.

Howe gave him a skeptical glance then sighed as if reconsidering what he was going to say. "I'm certain that, for her, the experience *was* real." He cleared his throat. "Look, we have a lot of work ahead of us, Detective. There are four journals in all and from other historical accounts, we do know that your Grandma Lydia ends up having progressively more frequent...episodes of this kind which ultimately led to her being committed."

"She doesn't write like she's insane," said Ben feeling like he had to come to his grandmother's defense.

"No, she doesn't," agreed Amelia. "But this is just the first of her journals. The rest may become progressively erratic and nonsensical as the insanity takes hold."

Howe got to his feet. "I don't know about the two of you, but I'm bone tired. I suggest we get something to eat then get some sleep. I need to get back to the office tomorrow and want to get an early start in the morning."

Ben nodded. "Food sounds good to me. And I should get an early start too."

"Have you lined up a place to stay yet?" asked Amelia, grabbing her purse. "There may be an open spot in the dorm at the university. I can check for you."

"That'd be great, thanks."

At the diner next door, they grabbed a quick meal over which Howe and Amelia did most of the talking while Ben kept his rambling thoughts about Grandma Lydia to himself. He had a hard time erasing the memory of those empty eye-sockets of hers. It was as if he could still feel her stare and, as a result, he didn't eat much. On returning alone to his room he found Stump sleeping peacefully in the corner. Ben flipped off the light, undressed quickly and got into bed. Rolling onto his side, he pulled up the covers trying to ignore their musty smell. In the dim light cast through the curtains by the security light outside, he could see the journals laying in a neat stack on the coffee table waiting, maybe impatiently now, to be read.

"You look like shit," Amelia told him the next morning when he emerged from his room.

Ben shrugged, tossing his suitcase into his car. "Had trouble getting to sleep." He glanced at the cloudy sky. "Looks like more rain."

"Thinking about your grandmother?"

"Guess so. I've never dug up a grave before. It's a little hard to get it out of my head."

"That's understandable, especially with it being the grave of one of your ancestors." She slid her bag into the back of Howe's Saab. "How about you giving me the first journal? I'll read it in detail on the way back. You should keep the others for now but remember, I'll need access to all of them. That was our understanding, right? You give me access, I give you a professional assessment and maybe get something publishable out of it so I can reeducate people about the importance of your grandmother in the history of psychology."

Ben ignored the reluctance he felt. "I don't remember actually discussing an 'understanding' but yes, that sounds right to me." He pulled the first journal from his pack and handed it to her. His eyes caught hers.

"We're doing a good thing, Ben."

"Yeah, I suppose. Sure doesn't feel right though. Anyhow, right now I just want to get back. I've got to check out my burned-out place. I've also got a couple of funerals to go to."

"Right, sorry, I forgot about them." She paused. "I'll let you know about that dorm room."

"Not a big deal. I'll figure out something." He was about to ask where Howe was when he showed up walking back from the front office of the motel.

"We're all checked out," he said, getting into his car. "I covered your bill, detective."

"You didn't need to do that," said Ben. But Howe had already shut the door and was buckling up. Ben glanced at Amelia. "What? He thinks I'm a charity case or something?"

She gave a dismissive wave. "Don't worry about it, Ben. He can afford it. I'll check in with you later today or tomorrow." Not waiting for a reply, she got in the car.

Ben watched them pull out then, ten minutes later, with Stump in the back and the journals riding shotgun, he took the main road back to the freeway heading south.

On the way he called Ginny and arranged to crash at her place for a couple of nights. Relieved about that, he called Amelia and let her know she didn't have to check on a dorm room for him. He then dug a worn business card from his wallet and called Henry Gibbons, his landlord. Like Ginny, Gibbons expressed his relief that Ben hadn't died in the fire and, from him Ben learned there'd already been a small private service for Rob-Roy. Maddie's funeral would take place the next morning. Gibbons also told him that he'd already made a renters' insurance claim for him. Ben thanked him then ended the call and turned up the radio.

Predictably, the driving slowed at the outskirts of Boston. He worked his way back onto familiar streets then did a slow drive past his building. Yellow caution tape stretched across the steps. The front door was boarded up. Black soot framed the doorway and windows which were all boarded up. It looked just like any other abandoned building in the city and, around it, life carried on as it always had. People passed by, paying no attention to the place where two people had burned to death. Well, that was life in the big city for you. Everybody had worries of their own, didn't they? Take me, for instance—I'm going nuts, my career is gone, I'm descended from some sort of crazy lady whose grave I dug up, and my flat was just burned out. "Yeah," he said aloud, "everyone has worries."

From the car-rental Ben took an Uber to Ginny's. She buzzed him up.

In a pink dress and black sweater, she stood in the open doorway at the top of the stairs. She gave Ben a big hug. "You don't know how relieved I was to hear your voice over the phone the other day. I couldn't bear to think of you actually being, you know...dead."

Ben hugged her back. He could tell she cared about him and, at that moment, he cared about her. A few years back their hug would have melted into a passionate kiss, escalating from there. But that was then, not today.

Stump barked and walked past them into the apartment. Ben picked up his suitcase.

"That all your stuff?"

"I travel light."

Ben used her shower and got a load of laundry going, then joined Ginny in her front room. She sat curled in her recliner, nursing a glass of white wine. There was an open MGD on the coffee table. Ben took a long swig then sat. “Mmmm, that tastes good. Thanks, Ginny. It’s been a rough week.”

“I gave Stump some water and some Cheerios. Did you know he likes Cheerios?”

“He’ll eat anything.”

“So Maine, huh? Do you have friends up there?”

“No, I don’t know a soul. But I have a long lost relative who lived there. She’s dead now.”

“It’s a long way to go to visit a dead relative. It doesn’t sound like something you’d do.”

“Well, there’s a little more to it.” He pulled a photo up on his phone. “This is her right here—my great, great grandmother Lydia.” He handed her the phone.

Ginny held it steady, just staring. Then her mouth twisted. “Shit, Ben. She’s in her grave? You took a picture of her in her grave?”

“No, no. Not me. I didn’t take the picture. See how fuzzy it is? It’s black and white, taken a long time ago.”

“She’s why you went up there?”

“She died back in the 1920’s and she was kind of famous. She was a doctor and had a house there. It’s mine now, I guess, if I want it. But it’s kind of a dump.”

She handed the phone back. “Why was she famous?” she asked, sitting up now with arms folded as if from a sudden chill.

“She wrote a book about mental disorders and prison reform. And she’s also been written up in some psychology books.” He leaned closer, holding the phone so she could see the photo again. “Did you notice that she’s holding on to something? Those are her journals. I’ve got a couple of psychologist friends who’re pretty excited about them. Well, they’re not friends exactly.”

“What do they want with her journals?”

“They think they have some kind of historical value.”

“They want to sell them?”

“No, they’re not like that. They want to study them.”

Ginny looked back at the phone. “But you said that this is your grandmother and she’s holding them in her grave, for God’s sake. How exactly do they propose to get their hands on them?”

Ben cocked his head and Ginny's eyes widened.

"Christ, Ben, they aren't thinking of digging her up to get her journals, are they?"

Ben cleared his throat. "Well, actually, they already have. Well, all right, it was me really."

Ginny went pale. She sank back into her chair, her eyes no longer on Ben but roaming the room as if searching for a safe place to settle. Finding none, she closed them and took a deep breath. "Shit, Ben. You dug up your own grandmother?"

"It sounds pretty bad when you put it that way."

"Ben, I don't know how else to put it. It *is* pretty bad. Ugh, how could you do that?" She got up, walked to the window and pulled it open. Fresh air filtered in along with the sounds of the street. She turned back to him. "So what happens now? Are you planning to publish those journals, make a few bucks off your poor dead grandmother?"

"No, it isn't like that—I'm not like that."

"Yes you are. You're an ass-hole."

"I think my grandmother *wanted* someone to have the journals."

"That's horseshit. If she wanted someone to have them why would she have taken them to her grave?"

"Yeah, I'm kind of bothered by that too."

"Kind of bothered? Ben, you dug up a dead body. That's just...creepy."

Ben nodded, his eyes dropping to the floor for a moment then raising but failing to catch hers. "It *was* creepy," he said, his voice low.

Ginny sat back down and took a swallow of wine. "So, you have her journals with you?"

Ben smiled a little. "You're curious about them, aren't you?"

She didn't answer.

"There are four in all, I've got three of them. I've got a psychologist reading the other one—it's one I've already started to read."

"That's one of the psychologists who's not really a friend of yours?"

"Yeah, the one who saw me when I was in the hospital. Well, they both saw me, but she's the one who told me about my grandmother. She's pretty excited about the journals. Supposedly, there've been rumors about them for nearly a hundred years." He paused. "Want to see them?"

She put her wine down and seemed to sulk for a moment. "I don't know. Well, I guess maybe I do. You've already done the creepy part so..."

Ben retrieved the journals from his suitcase and put them on the coffee table between them.

Ginny stared, making a face. "Oh God, Ben. They even smell like...death."

"They're just dirty."

"Dirty from the grave" she whispered, her eyes glued to them. "What did she write about?"

"She wrote about her experiences at an asylum."

"An insane asylum?"

"She was a doctor there but then became a patient. It seems she had dreams, mostly about people dying, I think."

"People dying?"

"Yeah. Strange huh?"

"So at the asylum, that's how she became a patient?"

Ben shrugged. "Guess so. But I'm not so sure that she was crazy like they say in some of the psych books."

"But she did become a patient. That's what you said. So she must have been insane."

Ben shrugged, watching her hesitate, staring at the journals. "Go ahead. It's okay if you want to read one of them. You can read all of them if you want."

Almost as if she was holding her breath, she leaned closer to them. Using the tip of one finger against her thumb, she picked up the journal on top. With a grimace, she placed it on her lap, then opened it.

"That's the second journal you've got. Careful, the pages are a little brittle," Ben cautioned, but Ginny had already started reading and seemed not to hear.

As she read, Ben finished his beer and grabbed another after he'd switched his clothes from washer to drier. Ginny looked pretty intent with her reading and Ben could see that she'd already covered a few pages. He watched her unchanging expression as she read more.

Then, Ginny looked back at him. "Have you read any of this?"

"No, I've just read a little of the first journal. There're a couple of years between the time she wrote the one I read from and this one."

"It's frightening, Ben. The things she writes. Listen to this." She flipped back a few pages. "This passage is dated April 2 1907." She began reading aloud:

"I have endured more than thirty episodes in all and have documented each of them in two notebooks, this being the second. I have given the first to my daughter Abigail for safe keeping. I know that she has read from it and I know that she has been warned about me by Nurse Ellen. She is wary of me. She fears me. And I fear myself.

I struggle to understand what is happening. My flights of dreadful fantasy come over me now without need of Silent Margaret's presence and they come without warning sometimes two to a week, sometimes none for a month. I ask myself, have I gone insane? Dr. Woodhouse thinks so, and so does the rest of the staff here. But I sense that some of the patients here know better. Even though I rarely see her now, I sense that Margaret is one of those who knows better for I feel that I am becoming very much like her. No, not silent, but similar in other ways.

As a doctor I've been trained to observe, to document, to analyze, and to form logical conclusions. But now, as my only patient, everything about my condition that I've observed, documented and analyzed leads to the most illogical, the most impossible of conclusions:

First: My mind seems not to be limited to the confines of my immediate surroundings. At any given moment, my awareness can be swept away as if sucked from the body of Lydia Thornhill and injected into the world of someone else.

Second: Without exception, I witness the death of a young child."

At this, Ginny sighed, glanced at Ben, then continued.

"Third: Within each dream, or spell as I've come to call them, I feel connected to that child in such a way that I'm actually able at times to feel their terror, their pain and their agony as they endure the throes of death.

Fourth: At the instant of the child's death, I am violently returned to my own body, still feeling and still reacting to the child's death exactly as if it had been my own.

Fifth, and most speculative: I sense a purpose behind these death events, as if I am somehow supposed to do something that will save these children from their terrible deaths. I've come to think of them almost as my own children. With each one lost, I feel I've lost part of myself and, in not knowing how to save them, I can't begin to save myself.

Ginny closed the journal. "It's terrible what your grandmother went through."

"The Thornhill Disorder, that's what some of the textbooks call it."

"So other people have had this...condition?"

"I guess so, otherwise they wouldn't have given it a name, would they?"

She put the journal back on the coffee table and reclined her chair. She closed her eyes then opened them again. "I'm sorry I gave you a hard time. I think you're right, your grandmother wrote those journals for a reason. She must have wanted someone to read them—maybe make some sense of them even if she couldn't."

"Yes, well I'm sure that I won't be the one to make sense of them. I'll leave that to the shrinks."

Neither of them spoke for a while, then Ginny broke the silence. "What will you do, Ben? You don't have a place to stay and you don't have a job. I'm sorry but I can't put you up here for long. I wish things could be like they once were, but..."

"Yeah, I know. Look, I don't want you worrying about having

to put up with me. I'll figure something out. I just got back into town and I've got a funeral to go to tomorrow so it might take a few days. I'll make some calls. No big deal, I'll work it out." He spoke with as much confidence as he could muster, then finished his beer.

CHAPTER 17

July 3, 1907

Lydia walked the halls conscious of the stares from both the staff and from patients. She longed for the days when things had been normal. How many years ago was that now?—too many to count. Had she once been that girl on the hillside in Michigan when Danny had taken her for the first time? Yes, she had once been young and naïve. But maybe not so naïve—hadn't it been she who'd taken him? The wine they'd had after being left alone, her caresses, soft at first then more aggressive as the sun sank behind the trees, yes, it had been she who'd taken him that day and he'd been under her control every day since, up until the day he died.

Or had even his death been within her control? Yes, she supposed even that was true.

Had she always harbored a streak of the sinister? Had she always been a woman who knew what she wanted, intolerant of anything that stood in her way? Her mind went back to her days at the reformatory and the secret, then not so secret titillation she'd felt when treating the wounds and sometimes the carnal needs of the inmates she knew were going to die. No, that hadn't been normal. Yet, for her, it had all been ever so natural and right. With the passing of each year, she'd left the world of the normal farther behind as like a mole burrowing deeper and deeper under the earth, searching for God knows what. And now, in these visions of hers, perhaps she'd found what she'd been looking for.

Her journals were her only link to the more rational side of her existence and she kept them up with a passion, trying desperately to create some kind of pathway back to the respectable world of *Doctor* Lydia Thornhill.

So now, on this bright summer morning she was as normal and respectable as she could be. She had twenty patients to see and, after handling the sixth of these, she walked into the ward where number seven sat waiting. She saw the woman's head turn toward her. Their eyes collided in a jarring, physical way. A feeling of dread overtook Lydia and everything went black. By now she knew the routine. Another vision was on its way. Squeezing her eyes shut, she braced herself.

The next thing she felt was a hard, cold rain pelting her face. With a shrill whistle a fierce wind tore at her hair. She opened her eyes. Though dark as night, she sensed that it was day. All around her tall, white-capped waves rolled and thundered as the little boat she was in rose then plummeted, riding them like a rodeo bull from crest to trough and then back up again. With both hands she gripped a rope and was able to keep her footing. That was when she realized that this vision was different from the others. She saw the white knuckles of her fingers on the rope. She looked down and saw her legs and feet, struggling to keep herself upright. This time, within this vision, she was actually here. But no, this wasn't her body was it? These were the hands, and these were the feet, of a child of ten, maybe twelve. Yet, somehow at this moment, Lydia found her consciousness inhabiting this body.

"Give me your hand, Maggie," she heard someone shout from behind.

She turned and, through the rain saw a man only a few feet from her, reaching for her.

But Lydia, Maggie now, couldn't let go of the rope that ran taught from the bow up to the boat's wooden mast. "I can't," she yelled back. "I can't."

The man struggled closer, his face buffeted by the rain, terror filling his eyes. "Yes, you can, Maggie," he shouted again, still reaching out with one hand while holding onto the mast with the other. He extended his arms a little more and inched closer to her, his fingers nearly brushing her shoulder. "Come on now. You can do it, Maggie. Grab onto me."

Lydia looked into his eyes. This was a good man, she thought.

She hoped he would survive this storm because she knew that she would not. She held her breath and, with her right hand, let go of the rope, reaching back for him.

She felt his reassuring grasp and held on tight as he pulled her back toward the base of the mast where they crouched together against the wind and rain. "There, now. You're okay. We're going to be okay. You understand?"

Lydia, who was now Maggie, nodded as he snugged up the orange life vest she wore. She hadn't noticed the vest before and she saw that he wore one too. Great, she thought, maybe, just maybe, we're going to make it out of this mess.

The little boat wasn't much more than a rowboat. What was left of the sail clung to the mast, whipping in the wind above her head. They were taking on water. It filled the hull up to her hips with more coming over the sides with each wave.

The man embraced her with his free arm. "I love you, Maggie. You know that, don't you?"

Numb with cold, all she could do was look up at him and nod. A scream escaped her lips as, at that moment, a shadow loomed over them. Her vision cleared and Lydia saw a single wave, taller than the rest rise over them. The man, who must be Maggie's father saw it too. He held her close as it crashed down on them.

Lydia flailed as the power of the water ripped her from the man's arms and off the boat. Underwater, she held her breath in pitch darkness fighting for the surface with her last ounce of strength. But the waves pushed her down, holding her under. She fought against them until she thought her lungs would burst. Still tumbling, falling still deeper, Lydia's strength finally faded and involuntarily, her mouth opened, searching for air. But it drew in only water. 'I'm sorry I couldn't save us, dear child,' she thought with despair as the blackness around her became blacker still. Suddenly without feeling, without a sensation of any kind, Lydia knew she must be dead. Her life was over and she was almost relieved by the revelation.

But then, just as suddenly, her senses came roaring back and she knew she was alive. She could feel the coolness of the floor on which she lay curled up in the same posture as she'd been while succumbing to the waves. But there were no waves now. And no wind. Strong arms on either side of her were struggling to pull her up. She was back at the asylum yet, like a distant echo, the storm raged in her mind and the power of the waves still held her under. She gasped for breath.

"Dr. Thornhill, Dr. Thornhill. Can you hear me? Are you all right?" the orderlies shouted. She could feel them struggle as they positioned her on the edge of a bed.

She doubled over, coughing in a violent spasm, trying desperately to expel the water she'd sucked in. But there was none. She took in a deep, desperate breath. She tried to calm herself. She waited, not moving until her breathing steadied. Slowly, she opened her eyes. She cleared the hair from her face, the strands wet, not with seawater but with sweat. Feeling nausea build, she tried to stand. The room swayed around her and an orderly grabbed her shoulders as she bent over in a dry wretch that sent her into another fit of coughing.

"I'm all right. I'm all right. Just leave me be for a moment," she gasped, finally able to straighten. With the back of her hand, she dried her eyes and stared back at the ring of concerned faces around her. The orderlies looked familiar but she could not recall their names. Just coming up behind them was a shocked Nurse Ellen, her face pale.

"My God, what's happening here?" she shouted.

Lydia shook her head. "I...I don't know," she muttered, catching Ellen's wide eyes. "I was somewhere else for a time and...now I'm back." She felt her body begin to shake, but through a force of will, she brought herself back under control. She spread her feet farther apart. The room was still rocking as if still settling itself back into reality. "I'm all right now," she repeated, swallowing and taking another long breath. "I need to get back to my office."

With a hand at her elbow, Ellen guided her out of the room into the corridor where Dr. Woodhouse stood with an expression less of concern than one of hardened resolve. Lydia caught his eyes then turned and shook off Ellen's help. With increasingly more confident strides, she made her way back to her office where she closed the door, sat at her desk and cradled her face in her hands. Remembering the look Doctor Woodhouse had given her, she knew at that moment that she could no longer consider herself to be a doctor on staff here at the asylum. Today she had become a patient.

Maybe that hole she'd been digging for herself over the years had finally reached a fitting end. She swiveled to face the window. Outside, the sun shined and a gentle wind bent the apple tree, rippling its leaves and bending its branches. All seemed to be as it was but Lydia knew that, for her, everything had changed. She knew she had crossed a line today. Her visions were no longer just visions and she was no longer just an observer in them. Today she had now become a participant. And, more than that, my God, she had actually become that little girl named Maggie. And of one thing she had no doubt: Yes, that poor child really had died in that storm.

The next day, Dr. Woodhouse stepped into her office flanked by two orderlies. He held a few sheets of paper. Of course, Lydia knew what was coming and didn't bother listening to what he had to say. When he handed her the papers, she signed each of them, formally consenting to her admittance to Windward Asylum as a patient suffering from—what did he call it? Oh yes:

Spells of mental instability that sometimes endangered herself and those around her.

"I am very sorry, Doctor Thornhill," he'd said with a polite nod on his way out.

From that day, the months and years passed in a blur and, over that time, the death-spells came without warning. Through it all, Lydia continued making her meticulous notes, documenting each spell and occasionally speculating as to what was happening to her. Had Silent Margaret been merely a catalyst in bringing on these spells? In the same way as one might catch a cold from someone's sneeze, had she somehow sniffed up some kind of cerebral contagion from Margaret? And was it her immersion in death and evil at the reformatory that made her susceptible to that contagion? *A mental disorder that was contagious*—now there was a new concept for the eminent Dr. Thornhill to puzzle out. But then again, she wasn't a doctor anymore. No, just like Margaret, she was a patient in an asylum for the insane.

But, unlike Margaret, Lydia had become violent, leaving in the aftermath of her most recent spells, bloody bite marks, deep scratches, and even broken bones among those who were only trying to help.

Lydia had been appalled at first by this but knew she had no control over her body as, in the death throes that ended every spell, she was fighting desperately to save her own life. Yes, her condition seemed different from Margaret's but still she wondered if, behind those shining black eyes and that placid composure of hers, could Margaret be experiencing similar horrors?

So, yes, days, months and years passed in a blur. The spells came and went. She'd just finished the third journal documenting them, still wondering if they'd ever make sense. It was mid-August now, 1912 and she'd been at Windward for twelve long years—five of those years as a patient.

Lydia sank into her pillow, depressed at so much lost time. Through the window, the midday sun beat down, focusing its beams on Lydia as if she were a specimen under a microscope. They had placed leather restraints on her wrists following her last spasm. That's what they called them now: spasms. That last one had been particularly violent nearly resulting in a broken jaw for one orderly. No, she couldn't blame Woodhouse for ordering the restraints. Had she been the one in charge, she would have done the same.

Lunch came with two muscular orderlies. The restraints were removed so she could feed herself in their presence as, the whole time, they observed her while keeping their distance. Once finished with her food, the restraints were retied.

Abigail, now eighteen, visited faithfully every Wednesday. Mercifully, she had yet to see Lydia during one of her spasms but Lydia could tell that she knew of them. Dr. Woodhouse had no doubt kept her informed of every last embarrassing detail. Lydia knew that her daughter was afraid of her now and it probably took every ounce of courage she possessed to keep up with her visits.

"Hello, Mother." She said timidly from the doorway when she arrived a few hours later, today being Wednesday.

Lydia had been staring out the window. She flopped her head around to see her daughter standing in the doorway. Such a pretty girl she was. Too bad she's stuck with me for a mother, Lydia thought. "Hello, dear. Good of you to come."

Abigail walked in, bent close and brushed her mother's cheek with her own.

"They've got me tied down now."

"Yes. Nurse Ellen told me about that. I'm sorry Mother."

"I am too, dear. But, in a short time, it won't matter."

"What was that? Why won't it matter?"

Was that a suddenly hopeful expression on Abigail's face? Perhaps she thinks I'm about to die. Sorry, dear, that's not the case. "They'll be closing the place down in a few months. Didn't Nurse Ellen tell you?"

"What? No, she didn't say anything about that." Abigail sat, her hands fidgeting in her lap.

"Well, I suppose she may not even know. She'll be out of a job soon, poor woman. I think she has a young child at home. It's lucky for me that you're old enough to take care of yourself."

"Who told you they were closing Windward?"

Lydia shook her head. "No one told me. I see Dr. Woodhouse every now and again, people come in and they talk. I listen and I notice things. It's something I just know. Apparently they've got funding problems."

"Maybe you're wrong."

"I'm not wrong, child."

"But where will you go?"

"*Timbervale*, of course. You and I both. Oh, don't worry, I'm quite normal most of the time. And when I'm not, you can lock me in my room."

Abigail's laced fingers whitened in her lap. "It's been years since we've been there," she said quietly. "Father was still with us the last time."

"Yes, he was. It was the time that you caught that frog of yours."

Abigail's lips formed a smile that quickly vanished. She pulled out a handkerchief and dabbed her nose but said nothing.

"You will need to write Samuel to let him know we'll be coming," Lydia went on, referring to the son of a shopkeeper in Randell who'd helped keep both the house and pantry in good order over the years. "Ask him to get us some supplies and to make sure the house is in decent shape."

As if not hearing, Abigail kept her fingers tightly woven, the tension visibly running up her arms and into her shoulders as if, with her whole body, she was trying to keep from shaking.

"I know you've got your own life to live, Abigail, and I know we've talked about you going off to college back in Michigan. I want that for you. But I'm sorry, I need you now and those plans will just have to wait."

Abigail's face hardened. "You mean, wait until you get better? You're a doctor. Do you really think you'll ever get better?"

Lydia closed her eyes for a moment, holding back tears of regret. Had her hands not been tied to the bed-rail, she would have reached out to comfort her daughter. "No my dear, I don't expect that I'll ever escape this thing that has taken hold of me. But, I'm not going to live forever." She paused, taking in a deep breath. "We'll be just fine, Abigail. You'll see."

Abigail averted her eyes, nodding in a familiar, herky-jerky way that belied her words. "Yes, I know, Mother. You're right. You always are."

It was a cold November morning when Lydia, guided by an orderly named Jeffery, walked with a cardboard suitcase down the darkened main hall of Windward for what she knew would be the last time. The walls echoed their footsteps. Most of the patients and much of the staff had left weeks earlier and over that time, the rooms and halls and staircases of the asylum had grown progressively silent and stark, the floors littered with debris that no one cared enough to pick up. 'Disgusting,' thought Lydia. It wasn't right that this institution run by supposed professionals had come to this inglorious end. Twenty steps further took them past room 106, empty now like all the rooms. Lydia kept her eyes straight.

Silent Margaret had come to her own inglorious end a month ago with an apparent cerebral hemorrhage that left her bleeding from her eyes. A fitting end, thought Lydia without much emotion. Perhaps the same end awaited her.

Dr. Woodhouse had abandoned ship the previous week, leaving for a lucrative position in New York City, and Nurse Ellen had gone her way only yesterday. Funny, Lydia half-expected Ellen to stop in and say good-bye. But no, she was never really a friend, was she? None of them were. How could they be, when they were all afraid of her?

Jeffery took a few steps ahead, opening a pair of inner doors before finally opening the outer door itself. The comparative brightness of the overcast day flooded in, bringing with it a whoosh of cold air that ruffled the longer strands of Lydia's hair that poked out from under her woolen cap.

"You should wait inside," advised Jeffery.

"Nonsense," said Lydia, stepping out onto the crowded porch, putting her suitcase down. "My daughter will be here shortly. You may go now, thank you."

Both porch and steps were lined with patients, former patients now, all bundled up like Lydia, all with suitcases, all waiting for the long line of buggies and automobiles to snake its way forward, pick them up and take them to God knows where. Among the throng of people, Lydia recognized a few but kept her distance. After all, she was still a doctor.

Slowly, the line of vehicles shortened and the crowed dwindled. Lydia could see Abigail now, near the end of the line, driving a single-horse buggy with a black cloth canopy. Abigail had tried to talk Lydia into buying an automobile but Lydia wouldn't hear of it. "It's too rugged a trip up there for one of those things," she had said. "And when it breaks down, who will fix it?"

Lydia was among the last to leave the asylum that morning.

An orderly loaded her suitcase into the buggy then helped her up onto the seat beside Abigail who sat bundled up, a scarf tightly wrapped around her neck and chin. "Hello, Mother," she said, making eye contact only briefly but long enough for Lydia to notice that her daughter's eyes were moist and red. Lydia moved to take the reins from her but Abigail held onto them tightly and slapped the horse forward, her eyes fixed on the road ahead.

After twelve years at Windward, Lydia found herself neither happy nor sad to be leaving. She didn't look back. The wind whipped the little buggy and tore at the blankets gathered around Lydia's legs and feet. The horse labored.

The trip they'd planned should have gotten them to *Timbervale* well before dark and all had been going well until, on the two-track in the woods, a spasm caught hold of Lydia. From the cold buggy she was pulled in an instant into the body of a child who stood in warm, knee-deep water. A hand gripped her throat, forcing her off her feet, pushing her back until her face sank under the waves. My God! Someone was trying to kill this child. Lydia gathered her strength. She fought and kicked. She was able to break the surface of the water for a moment and saw the face of a man, no, a woman, her features obscured by the light of the sun that blazed just over the crown of her head.

Lydia screamed in terror. She tried to harden her emotions, but could not. She fought the woman's grip, trying to rip the woman's fingers from her throat. With irresistible force, the woman plunged Lydia underwater again. Lydia reached up. She tore at the woman's face with her fingers, the woman flinching, pulling back until suddenly, Lydia broke free. She stood and ran, stumbling and splashing toward a beach, empty except for a man standing in the distance in front of a white house with a red roof. She screamed but the man was too far away to hear. She kept running, thinking that she might be able to escape. She forced her legs to move faster, sloshing through the wet sand and up onto the beach itself where she picked up speed. Yes, maybe she really could escape.

"Not so fast you little brat," a man's voice shouted from behind. A hand fell on her shoulder, knocking her down, erasing any thought of escape. Lydia hit the sand hard. The soft grains felt strangely warm and comforting on the side of her head and, in that instant, she wanted to just lay there, close her eyes and be safe. But a cold, strong hand grabbed her by the foot. Lydia screamed, feeling the water engulf her now as she was dragged back out away from shore, under the waves. Two hands now pressed her face down into the sandy bottom. She tasted the sand and gagged, desperately coughing it out even as her lungs sucked in the water to the point of bursting. She kicked and struggled hopelessly.

Panicked, knowing there wasn't much time left, Lydia shouted within her mind to the girl whose life was about to be lost. "Give me your name, child."

And from somewhere deep within, came a feeble response: "I am Mary."

And knowing that, at that moment, the child was gone, Lydia cried from within, her tears mingling with the waves: "Oh, dear Mary I'm sorry I couldn't save you."

As with all of her recent visions, Lydia was, for a moment, caught up in two realities. She could still feel her last gasping attempt to draw air into her lungs, still feel the warm waves against her body even as the dark of night intruded, and the wind whipped cold. Then, when cold was all she felt, she opened her eyes.

She lay flat on her back. Between the leafless trees that towered around her, a silvered half-moon shown down and a few stars twinkled. Snow covered the ground beneath her. Her teeth chattered and her body shivered. She could feel the snow and the cold air sucking the heat from her body. She rolled to her side and doubled over in a fit of coughing that ended with a sobbing scream. She pounded her fists into the snow and screamed: "Why? Why? What have I done to deserve this curse?"

But her words were lost in the wind. Her tears turned icy on her cheeks and her breath rose from her lungs in thick vaporous clouds. She struggled to get to her feet and leaned against a tree to keep from falling. Finally, she breathed easier. She held her hands to her neck, where only moments earlier she'd felt the grip of a killer. But something was wrong with her own hands. She looked at them and, in the moonlight, saw blood dripping from her fingertips. Her fingernails, three of them on each hand, were gone, pulled out from the fighting and scratching of the poor drowned child. To stem the bleeding, Lydia folded her arms, squeezing her hands within the folds of her coat.

She breathed deeply again, the chill stinging her lungs. She looked around. Trees surrounded her and every direction looked the same, but she knew she couldn't be too far from the road. She called out: "Abigail. Abigail. I am here Abigail." But there was no response.

She began shivering violently. She had to get moving or the cold would kill her. *Timbervale* should be uphill from where she stood so she started off in that direction, shouting out her daughter's name every now and again.

But why should I even want to live? She thought as she trudged along. Wouldn't it be better if I just died here and now? Better for me, better for Abigail. Yes, poor Abigail. A curse had befallen her too, condemned to carry the terrible burden of a deranged mother.

But Lydia knew she wouldn't just lay down and die. After all, she was still the eminent Doctor Lydia Thornhill and she had still not given up trying to solve the riddle of just what had gone wrong with her mind.

As she walked, frozen snow-covered leaves crunched beneath her boots. Numbness spread from her toes to her feet and ankles causing her to stumble. The grade grew steeper and she rested more often, while calling out for Abigail less frequently. She trudged, shivering through the night. Trying to keep the moon on her right shoulder so she wouldn't be walking in circles.

The wind whistled. The forest seemed to go on forever.

Finally, morning came, dull and cold and with it, came a parting of the trees. Suddenly, Lydia realized that she knew this frozen field of tall grass that lay before her. *Timbervale* bordered a field like this. Hoping it to be that same field, she started out across it, feeling ice, not ground beneath her feet, hardly able to bend her knees, hardly able to see anything but the spotty green of the grass against the white of the snow. The wind tore at her coat that had long since lost its warmth.

Frozen and shivering and wondering if maybe she was in just another one of her death-spells, Lydia stopped and rested. She kept her body bent against the wind and tried to look across the field. There. Wait! Was there something on the other side? A dark speck? Was it moving? She cleared the hair from her eyes. Yes, it was moving. Yes, my God, someone was on the other side.

Lydia's knees nearly buckled as she broke down sobbing with relief. She raised an arm in a feeble wave then willed her unfeeling legs and feet to start moving again. Faster now, with her destination in sight, she kept her eyes focused. Hope rising as she went, she began to make out features in the distant figure: a red scarf, a black, knee-length coat. And finally, she saw it was her daughter standing there. "Oh, my God, Abigail," she cried out. She hurried closer, expecting Abigail to come out to meet her, to help her. Instead, she saw Abigail retreat a few steps, her arms bent forward, her mouth a little agape as if ready to let loose a shout.

Sensing something amiss, Lydia slowed and stopped. Only ten paces from Abigail now, she was able to see more clearly and she stumbled back, horrified by the deep red scratches that ran down her daughter's cheeks. Lydia tried to speak. "Oh, my darling Abigail, I am so sorry," she wanted to say, but could not force the words past her frozen lips.

Abigail stared for a moment then turned and began walking toward the house, visible now within the trees. And Lydia followed.

Samuel had a good fire going and, before he left, Lydia paid him for his time and for the supplies he'd brought. "Thank you too for watching out for Abigail while I was...wandering around out there." She glanced out through the window where the snow was starting to fall. She scooted her chair closer to the fire.

"No trouble, Dr. Thornhill. I'll stop by and check on you in a week or so. Looks like it's going to be a hard winter." He turned to Abigail as he said this.

Abigail remained silent.

"Don't worry, Samuel, we'll be fine," said Lydia, standing. With her hands warming, the fingers with their torn nails had begun to bleed again. She tried hiding them from Samuel within her folded arms but saw that he'd noticed.

Apparently deciding not to complicate his morning any further, he turned and started gathering his things. "All right then, I'm just up the road if you need me."

After he left, Lydia returned to her chair and waited for Abigail to say something, but she didn't. "It must have been terrible for you. I am sorry, my dear girl. I am so terribly sorry," said Lydia finally.

They both remained silent for a long while, with only the sound of the fire and an occasional whistle from the wind outside. Then, Abigail spoke: "You were like a wild animal."

Lydia nodded. "Did I say anything?"

"No. You just yelled. Not words, just terrible screams. After you...scratched me, I jumped from the buggy. I started to run, then stopped and looked back at you. You sat there, still in the buggy, screaming—just screaming. Then, almost like you'd been pushed, you slid off your seat and fell to the ground. Right away you got to your feet and ran off into the woods. I could hear your screams, I wanted to help, but I didn't know what to do. I know I should have stayed and looked for you, but I was afraid. I just got back into the buggy. I whipped the horse something terrible, racing for the house."

"Trying to get away from me."

"I'm sorry."

Lydia's eyes filled with tears. She went to Abigail and tried to hold her close, to comfort her, but she felt her daughter stiffen in her arms, pulling away. "You did the right thing, child. When I'm like that, I'm...dangerous."

"Samuel was here when I got here. I told him you'd taken a separate horse and would be along soon. I didn't tell him what really happened."

"He didn't ask about your face?"

"He did. I told him I fell. He helped me wash my face clean."

Lydia stared again at the terrible red streaks running down both of Abigail's cheeks. She lowered her head. How could she possibly continue on as her mother after causing her daughter so much pain?

"What are they like for you, these spasms?" asked Abigail quietly.

Lydia lifted her head and saw that Abigail was staring dry-eyed into the fire, its flickering light giving her daughter's eyes an intensity she hadn't seen before. Without a word, Lydia got up and went to her suitcase. From it she pulled one of her journals. She gave it to her. "This will give you somc idea."

Abigail took it and began to read.

CHAPTER 18

Ben woke up on the couch. It took him a moment to remember he'd just returned from Maine and had just spent the night in Ginny's apartment. He looked around, realizing she had already left for work. He brushed his teeth, got dressed, and took Stump out for a walk. On returning, he stood for a while by the window drinking the last of the coffee Ginny had made— a decaffeinated, pre-sweetened, aromatic French-almond blend. It wasn't the kind Ben needed to think straight right now.

He checked the time. The church service for Maddie started at 10. If he left now, he could just make it. Going to a funeral Mass was the last thing he wanted to do. But it was for Maddie and it was the least he could do. He glanced down at his slacks and tennis shoes, not the best church apparel but, since all his good clothes had been lost in the fire, these would have to do. He took one more sip of impotent coffee and gave Stump a pat on the head on his way out.

Saint Mike's was an older church, gothic, dark and a little cold inside. Red vigil lights glowed on either side of the altar. The incense-laden air was still. Ben intended to sit in back but, when he saw how few people were gathered up front, he decided to move closer. The coffin had already been wheeled up the center aisle and, on either side of it, about fifteen people dotted the pews. Ben genuflected then picked a spot as the priest came out and the service began.

Ben had been raised Catholic and had even been an altar boy for a couple of years but he'd long since lost the little faith he'd had. He stood, knelt, and sat at all the right times and surprised himself by remembering most of the congregational responses. What had it been—fifteen years at least since he'd been inside a church? But, for as long as Ben had known her, Maddie had been a faithful church-goer, making the long walk to Saint Mike's every Sunday morning, dressed properly, with her gray hair flowing down from beneath her flowered hat.

Her son's short, stuttering, but sincere attempt at a eulogy was followed up by the priest saying a few well-chosen words that ran on for about ten minutes. The priest then invited others to offer some comments of their own. The clergyman scanned the pews but no one moved. When his eyes fell upon Ben, almost as a reflex Ben stood and cleared his throat, having no idea what he was going to say.

"I didn't know Maddie well," he began. "I lived two floors above hers and, on coming home each night from work, there she'd be at her door, greeting me back," *with a loaded 45,* he wanted to add with a slight chuckle, but didn't. "The smells from her kitchen told me that she was a good cook who liked to eat. And..." He hesitated, not knowing where to go from there and felt embarrassed that, after sharing the building with the old woman for so many years, he knew so little about her. "Well," he went on, "I live alone. And I guess she made me feel like she was welcoming me back home each night." He paused then caught the kind eye of the priest. "In that sense, she was a little like a mom to me and I'll miss her."

A few others got up and said a few things that made Ben realize how alone Maddie had been. He tried to imagine her years earlier as a playful little girl then as a young woman with hopes and dreams. She had a good, long life, but it was too bad it ended like it did.

The service lasted another 30 minutes before Maddie was wheeled out, everyone trailing slowly behind. Ben waited for them to pass, then followed them out, down the long aisle. When he stepped outside into the bright sunshine he put his hands in his pockets, thinking about Maddie, saddened again at how few people knew her and how few would care that she was gone. Well, that's life isn't it? How many people would be missing Ben right now if he had died in that fire along with Maddie and Rob?

Yeah, he hated funerals.

He started walking down the steps of the church when an older man who looked vaguely familiar stopped him.

"Excuse me, Mr. Marshall, I'm Henry Gibbons. Do you have a moment?"

"Mr. Gibbons, yes, hello," said Ben, more familiar with his landlord's voice than his face, having only met him once before.

They shook hands.

"Tragic about what happened," Gibbons went on, "I was so glad to hear that you were out of town when the fire hit."

"Yeah, me too. Any word on the cause?"

Gibbons sighed and turned to where the hearse had pulled out with a short line of cars following. "Looks like the fire started in Maddie's kitchen—poor woman. It's good that you made it here to the funeral mass. It wasn't much of a turn out for her. Nice of you to say a few words."

Ben shook his head. "I didn't...well, I wish I'd known her better."

"Yes, I can't say I knew her well either and I didn't want to get up in there just to say that she was a good tenant." Gibbons ran a hand over his square chin on which a pinkish mole poked out. Ben wondered if he had trouble shaving around it. "Listen, Ben, sorry, can I call you Ben? I know you'll be needing another place to stay now. I own a few other properties in Boston and have an opening at one of them. It's a little upscale but you can have it at your current rate if you want. We'll need to make an adjustment when your current lease ends but we should be able to work something out." He paused. "You don't already have another place, do you?"

"What? No, no I don't," said Ben, unable to believe his good luck. "I'm staying with a friend right now but that's just temporary. So yes, sure, your other place would be great, Mr. Gibbons. I'd really appreciate that."

"Please, call me Henry. And I'm glad to help out. Besides, I know you're with the force so it's the least I can do for one of our boys in blue. You know I've always supported you guys, right? You can move in tomorrow if you like. I'll leave the key with building security. Just show them your I.D., they'll give it to you and let you up." He gave Ben the address, handed him his card then clamped a hand on his shoulder. "If you need anything, you know, to get you through the transition and all, give me a call. I'll be glad to do what I can."

Ben shook his hand, thanked him again and, with one less thing to worry about, walked back to Ginny's. He was anxious to check out his new place but decided he couldn't just leave Ginny without seeing her. He stopped on the way for a bag of real coffee, brewed a full pot and made himself a sandwich. As he ate, he found himself staring at the journals, still lying were he'd left them on the coffee table. He knew he should get on his computer and start looking for a job. But no, that could wait. He should read one of the journals—the last one. Yeah, he'd do that then give the whole stack to Amelia and let her and Howe do their research and make themselves famous. Who knows, maybe they'd even make Grandma Lydia famous. Besides, he'd be glad to be finally done with his distant grandmother and glad to set aside all the creepiness he felt at having dug up her grave.

Done with the sandwich, he poured himself another cup of coffee and sat down on the sofa. From the stack of journals he slid out the bottom one and began reading. He started by skimming over the first few pages but then felt lured in, almost as if he could hear his grandmother lending a chilling voice to each word as he read about death after horrifying death that she'd experienced—all of them, children.

Instead of just being an observer of these deaths, Grandma Lydia now imagined herself to be the children, inhabiting their bodies as they faced their terrors. Her handwriting, once stylish and precise was now ragged. Her thoughts rambled across the page as if tired and spent. But every so often that shrinking part of her that was still sane, that part of her that was still a doctor looking for answers, seemed to take over. And Ben read almost spellbound:

Logic tells me my death experiences cannot be real. They can only be fabrications pieced together by my own mind, from my own experiences and from my own dark imaginings. Yet, in my heart, I discard logic and ask myself: How can they not be real? To decide this and to learn the cause of these terrible visions, I am determined to observe better. As I live and die through these experiences I must see my surroundings more clearly and, most important, I must learn something about these people, these children I become. I must try to somehow talk to them before they die. Only then can I judge them as being fantasy or reality and by so-doing, judge the condition of my own sanity. And then the question might become: If I'm not insane, what am I? What have I become?

Funny, thought Ben, that was the same question he was trying to answer.

After that entry, the next death event was a drowning—another little girl, held under by strong hands at her throat. The date was November 18, 1912.

Tell me your name, child, Lydia had shouted with an inner voice even as she struggled to free herself from the murderer's grip. And at that terrible moment, from some distant corner of the little girl's mind came a tiny voice, crying, scared and alone. *I am Mary,* it said. And that was all. Death for Mary came too quickly to learn more.

So Grandma Lydia had had two names to go on, but just first names—one Maggie, the other Mary, both of them drowning victims. Ben knew, just as Lydia must have known, he'd need more than just that to go on.

On his computer, Ben checked the information he'd collected from the state archives in Augusta. Yes, it was in November of 1912 that the Windward Asylum closed and Lydia had gone up to *Timbervale* to live with Abigail. He picked up the journal again and, flipping ahead, noticed the larger time gaps from one spell to the next. She covered the whole period from 1912 to 1920, the year of her death, in just ten pages. Yes, the spells were much less frequent, and her descriptions of them less detailed. Maybe Lydia was just tiring of keeping up the journal. Or, could it be that now, away from Windward, she was able to recover some of her sanity?

Ben checked his watch. It was later than he thought but, without much farther to go, he pressed on and started to read the entry dated May 11, 1920:

On entering the body of this poor child, I feel my eyes—her eyes, squeezed shut. I force them open and tears spill out. I shrink in horror from what I see. There is a man's face, inches from mine drenched in sweat. His breath is hot but oddly fragrant as if perfumed. He holds a large knife to my throat. I can see the shine of it. I feel its edge cold against my skin. My chest heaves. I try to breathe but the man presses his body hard against mine. I realize now that I am standing naked, my hands tied behind me to a post in what looks to be a cellar or crude basement. A light from somewhere casts long shadows. My bare feet feel the sandy earth beneath them. I cringe with fear even as I try to think.

The man speaks softly. "I warned you not to scream. Now you will die. Are you ready to die, my dear girl?"

I want to shout back at the man but, at that moment, from the floor above I hear a light scraping sound and I lift my eyes to the wooden supports of the floor above.

"Maybe you think my dog's going to save you. Is that what you think?"

My heart sinks. But I keep my gaze upward on the thick wooden beams grayed with age and by chance I see something. There, between the joists directly above me, two letters are carved into the wood: T and J. I stiffen. I try to shrink back from the knife still held at my throat, heartened that now I at least know something specific about this place and maybe about this monster in front of me.

I lower my gaze, my body suddenly charged with rage. I look my assailant straight in the eye, defiant. How dare this man take this innocent life? With all the strength left in me, I shout: "Say my name."

I feel the knife flinch. The man pulls back a little.

"Before you kill me, SAY MY NAME. And tell me yours. Are you TJ?"

He repositions his knife. I feel the sting of it moving slightly.

Slicing. Oh, God in heaven, I feel a burst of pain. I feel warm blood trickling down. I feel my body tremble yet I try to think clearly, even as I face his evil smile.

"You think you're so smart, don't you? All right, little miss, Cindy Brand. There, I spoke your name. But you will never know mine. That's because you are about to die."

And at that, I spit out the last words ever spoken by poor Cindy. "May you burn in hell for this. You are a worthless piece of shit. You animal!" Suddenly, more than anything, I just want to get this over with. I pull my knee up into his groin as hard as I can.

I hear his breath suck in just as the knife sliced deeper. Its sting burns through me like a bolt of lightning. I try to scream but cannot. I tremble and struggle, pulling at the rope that binds me to the post. I feel my blood pouring out in a torrent. My knees give out and I fall to the earthen floor. I squeeze my eyes shut again. Please let it be over, I scream within me as my strength drains away.

Ben closed the journal, his mouth dry, his hand shaking. As a cop he had known creeps just like the sadistic murderer who had killed that little girl. Knowing that there were such monsters in the world had been one of the reasons he'd become a cop in the first place. But fortunately, this was just his grandmother's dream, right? It never really happened. He glanced at his laptop on the counter. He felt a chill run up his spine. He had a name now, didn't he?—a full name. And he had a date. He got up and slowly walked over, feeling almost as if he were approaching a door that, once opened, could never be closed. Christ, what was he afraid of? He powered up his computer and, at the blinking curser, entered: *Cindy Brand, killed in 1920.*

He came up with dozens of Cindy Brands who were alive now, none dating back to 1920. If a Cindy Brand had been kidnapped and murdered back a hundred years ago, it would have made the papers, right? He entered *Cindy Brand Murdered 1920* then *Cindy Brand Kidnapped 1920.* He tried other words in other combinations but could find nothing that would suggest that any of the Cindy Brand's that ever existed had fallen victim to foul play.

Ben freshened his coffee, paced the floor a few times, then placed a call.

"Captain Nolan's office."

"Harriet? Hi, it's Ben...Ben Marshall."

"Oh, Ben. Hi, how're you doing?"

They chit-chatted a bit then Ben got to the point. "I'm working on something historical and I could use your help."

"You said historical right? Not hysterical?" She paused as if thinking that should get a laugh out of him. When it didn't, her voice turned stern. "This isn't some joke that Phil put you up to, is it? Because I've got other things to..."

"No, no. This isn't a joke. It's about a murder that would have taken place roughly a hundred years ago. The murder of a child."

"Ben, why would you...?"

"Look, it's a long story. But trust me, it's important. I thought I'd check in with you and maybe, if you had time, you could drill into the National Crime Info Center files and see what you can find. The records there go back quite a ways, right?"

"Well, yeah, it's got everything from 1900 on up to yesterday afternoon. But I can't just jump into it without a good reason. I've got to log in, give my ID number and password, sometimes it asks for a case number that would explain what I'm up to. Somebody somewhere is going to see that and maybe ask questions."

"The victim was a little girl named Cindy Brand. She died in a basement, her hands tied and her throat cut." Ben could hear Harriet take a breath. He knew that would get her attention. "Just take a quick look, will you Harriet? You can do it while you're on the net for an actual active case, can't you?"

"What's with you, Ben? Haven't you ever heard of Google? Just Google the name and see what you get."

"I tried that. Nothing came up."

"Well then NCIC probably won't come up with anything either. Why's this so important to you?"

The last thing Ben wanted to do was to tell her about his weird

Grandma Lydia. Once Harriet knew, it would be all over the department. "It's kind of personal. Come on, Harriet, just look into it. If you find anything at all, I promise, I'll give you all the background you'd like. And, I'll owe you, big-time.

"And If I don't find anything?"

"Well, I'll still owe you."

"Yeah, a lot of good that's going to do me." Harriet sighed.

Ben could tell she was at least considering it. "So, will you help me?"

"I suppose, I could." She paused. "You said it's important so I'll trust you on that. But just this once and you best not be shittin' me. And don't think you can make this a regular practice, asking for favors." She sighed again. "That was Cindy Brand right?" She spelled it out.

"Yeah, I think so. But you might try other spellings. And yes, it'll be just this once that I ask you for anything like this, I swear."

"All right, all right, Ben. I'll see what I can do. I'll text you to let you know if I find anything."

"That's great, Harriet. Thanks."

Ben ended the call and sat back in his chair, satisfied that he'd put Grandma Lydia to the test. One way or another he'd find out if her death experiences had any connection to reality. But how could they be real? How could any of it be real? The only sane answer was: they couldn't—simple as that. Yet, something in him couldn't believe that Grandma Lydia had made all this up. He stared at the journals, re-living anguish and terror that filled each page, convincing himself that, for her at least, all of that anguish and terror were real.

A call interrupted his thoughts. It was Amelia.

"I know I said I would wait until next week to call you but I wanted you to know that I made it through the first journal. Have you read any of the others?"

"I read a little of the third then skimmed most of the forth. I've been a little too busy to spend much time with them."

"Have you found a place to stay yet? Sorry, but there're no openings at the dorm."

"That's all right. Thanks for checking. As a matter of fact, I *was* able to find a place."

"That's great, Ben. Good for you."

"Yeah, Stump and I'll be moving in tomorrow. I just have the stuff in my suitcase so it'll be a pretty easy move."

"Glad to hear it. Sorry to rush this call but I'm between classes. So, all right, getting back to the journals, if you don't mind can you get them to me? I'd like to have them all together. I'm thinking that, through the course of writing them, your grandmother went through a series of stages as her condition worsened. I think it's important to document those stages. To do that, I really need them all."

Ben thought fast. "How about you stopping by tomorrow night for them?"

"Or we could just meet somewhere."

"We *can* meet somewhere—my place. Tomorrow night around seven, bring some Chinese, I'll furnish the wine...and the journals."

"Ben..."

"Oh come on. You don't have to be all business do you?"

"I suppose not."

He gave her his new address, ended the call then looked down at Stump. "Well, I've done it now boy. This new place of mine better look good."

Then he had another thought and stepped out to the corner grocery.

"This is good, Ben," said Ginny a few hours later, sitting at her kitchen table across from him. She took another bite, savoring the flavors. "I didn't know you could cook."

"Well, I can read a recipe on a box. It's the least I can do for you being such a good friend. You know, caring about me like you did."

"I'm impressed that you found a place to stay already."

Ben shrugged. "Yeah, well, like I said, all I needed to do was to make some calls." He knew she wouldn't have been impressed, knowing that the new place just kind of fell into his lap so he didn't furnish any details on how it all came about. "Still need a job, though. I'll be spending some time brushing up my résumé."

"You should file a claim with your insurance company for what you lost in the fire."

"Already coordinated that with my landlord."

Ginny gave him a glance that said she didn't quite believe him, but he knew she was impressed. "What's with you? I'm not used to you being..."

"So on top of things?"

"Yeah, you usually put things off. What happened? You turn over a new leaf or something?"

"Guess so," he said, knowing he really hadn't. Nope, sorry Ginny. Hate to disappoint but I'm still the same old procrastinating Ben. It'd take a lot more than narrowly escaping a fiery death or digging up my grandmother's grave, to change me.

They topped dinner off with some wine in front of the TV. She gave him a light kiss on the lips before they turned in. "Thanks, Ben. I enjoyed tonight. It was a lot like old times."

"Yeah, for me too."

She held his eyes. "You know we can't go back to those days though, right? I mean, be like we were. We've both decided to move on and I still think that's what's best."

Her words caught Ben off-guard. She was dumping him—again. There'd be no turning back now. Part of him had hoped he and Ginny might still have a chance together. Another part of him knew it was over and would be glad for a clean break. He tried to give her a smile. "Yeah, you're right. It's best we move on. Still friends though?"

She smiled back. "Yup, still friends. Look, I probably won't be seeing you in the morning. Good luck at your new place and with your job hunt. Let me know how things work out for you."

"Sure, I'll let you know."

Getting dumped twice by the same woman was not good for the ego. As he tossed and turned, trying to get to sleep that night, he was hounded by things he should have done or said that might have saved their relationship. But it wasn't really worth saving, was it? Ginny had been *okay* for him and he had been *okay* for her. And they both deserved better than *okay*. Yes, he concluded finally, a clean break was best.

In the morning he left Ginny a note, straightened things up the way he knew she liked, packed his things, and got Stump ready to go. Closing the door as he left, he felt as if he were leaving yet another part of his old life behind. First, had been his job, then his apartment, and now Ginny. He looked down at Stump. "At least you're still with me, huh, buddy. Ready to check out our new digs?"

Stump gave him an affirmative woof.

Ben jumped on the subway and got off two stops later near the waterfront in the middle of a high-rise jungle. His was a newer building, not the tallest but not the shortest either. After showing his I.D. at the security desk, he picked up the key and rode the elevator up to the seventh floor where he found room 714. On opening the door, he just stood for a moment, wondering if he was really in the right place. It was a corner apartment, open floor plan, spotless beige carpeting, sparkling white ceiling and recessed lighting. He flipped on the lights and closed the door behind him, then walked to the wall length windows in the far corner where a sliding door led out onto a wrap-around balcony. He opened it and walked out, Stump staying back a little. A light breeze and the noise of the city wafted up. "Man! This is quite a place. What do you think, boy?"

Stump woofed again.

"I'll bet there're no roaches either," said Ben walking back inside where he checked out the rest of the place. Four stools were lined against an eating island that fronted a full kitchen equipped with the latest gimmicky appliances. All the countertops were granite. A short hallway led to two bedrooms each with a full bath. The rent on this place had to be through the roof. There was only one downside: except for the stools in the kitchen, the place was completely empty—no furniture, no bed, no TV, and no curtains on the windows. Well, there'd be time to take care of all that. There'd be money coming in from his insurance claim and, if he was lucky, he might be able to afford a few things. He wondered how the stuff from the local thrift store might look in a place like this. Then he realized, he also needed new clothes. Shit, he needed everything.

For a while, Ben just sat on the floor looking at his new place, then decided he was hungry. He found an over-priced grocery where he bought some necessities along with two bottles of reasonably good wine and a couple of wine glasses. Once back, he made himself a sandwich, fed and watered Stump, then spent the rest of the day tinkering with his résumé. At six, he showered and at seven, his fancy-dancey door chime went off. Ben held down a button and spoke into it with his best British butler accent: "This is the Marshall residence, whom may I say is calling?"

"A...Amelia Silvers. Ben? That's you isn't it?"

"Ha, yeah it's me. Come on up." At her knock, he let her in.

She wore jeans and a tee-shirt and carried a white paper sack. She gave him a tentative smile and stepped inside. He hoped she wasn't nervous being alone with him.

He took the sack and put it on the counter, then gave her the two-minute tour.

"Nice place, Ben. Really, very nice."

"Not bad for a cop, hey? I just got access to the place today so I don't even have a table and chairs yet." Or a bed, he discretely didn't add. "It's a nice day though, I figure we can eat outside. That okay with you?"

"Sure."

He went to the fridge and pulled out the wine. "I've got a white and a red."

They went with the red and ate with legs stretched out, backs against the glass wall watching the sun through the railing as it made its way down behind the high-rise next door. The breeze had turned warm and the street noise was tapering off.

"This is lovely, Ben. I'm glad things are starting to go well for you."

"Cement's a little hard though, right?" he said, shifting his weight. "Chairs will be my first investment. My cut-rate lease here runs out in a few months. After that, the rent will likely double so unless I find a really good job I'll need to move. But, I'll enjoy it while I can." He took a sip of wine working the Mu Shu Pork with his chop-sticks.

"You said you finished the last journal?" she asked.

"I just jumped ahead to the last twenty pages so I'm almost to the end. It's really depressing with all the children dying these terrible deaths and Grandma Lydia caught up in it all, feeling their death agonies. It must have been horrible for her."

Amelia stopped eating. "Feeling them? What do you mean?"

"Oh yeah, you've only read from the first journal so you wouldn't know about that. Well, somewhere along the line it seems that, in these visions of hers, she started to actually become the child who's about to die."

"So she dies with the child? And she describes the death experience?"

"Yes. She's starting to think there must be a way for her to save the child but all her visions end the same way—the kid dies." Ben was silent for a moment, remembering the horror of the Cindy Brand death. He decided not to go into that. "You'll need to read it for yourself."

"You all right?"

"Yeah. It's pretty tough reading." He went back to his food, chewing thoughtfully. "Cindy Brand—that was the name of the girl who was murdered in the last passage I read. Knowing her name just makes it a little more personal." He stood up. "You done?"

He divvied up the rest of the wine and took care of the left-overs, bringing the bottle of white out with him.

"So you have a name: Cindy Brand."

"Yes. And I've checked the net for any info on a Cindy Brand who might have been murdered back then. You know, just in case these visions of hers were somehow real. I didn't find a thing. I guess I didn't really expect to. Grandma Lydia was just off her rocker, simple as that." He took a sip of wine. "Anyway, yes, you should take the journals, all of them. I'll be glad to be rid of them."

"Is that really all right with you? They'll remain your property, of course, but I am anxious to study them all. Dr. Howe is interested too. They'll be a very big deal in the psychology community."

"Well, at least they'll do someone some good."

They sat quietly for a while as the sky dimmed and the myriad of lights from the other buildings blinked on. The wind picked up a little.

"What made you want to be a psychologist," Ben asked, turning to take in the profile of her face in the dimming light.

She smiled as she considered the question. It was a charming, disarming smile showing Ben that she was comfortable being here with him. Or maybe it was just the wine.

"I've known for a long time that we humans are the strangest beings on earth. I just wanted to understand our species better—still do. How about you, Mr. Detective? What made you want to be a cop?"

"Comic books. I used to read them all the time when I was a kid—especially the super-hero ones."

"You wanted to be a super-hero?"

"Of course, all kids do." Ben folded his arms. "When I realized there were no such things as super-heroes, I just wanted to be one of the good guys. You know, the guy everyone looks to when they're in trouble and need to be saved."

"You're sounding like Holden Caulfield."

"Ha, yeah, *The Catcher in the Rye* guy, maybe so. I had to read it in high school. But I think I was really going for Iron-Man."

She shook her head. "You're far too sensitive a guy to be Iron Man."

"That's me, Mr. Sensitivity."

She put down her glass. "I should really be going."

Ben nodded and closed his eyes, the wine catching up to him. "Stay, I've got two bedrooms and a nice comfortable floor."

She stood. "Thanks, Ben, but no. Maybe some other time."

"Rats. Maybe I should have sprung for a third bottle."

"Yeah, that would have done it all right. Too bad you're such a cheap bastard." She gave him another smile, curls bouncing. "No, sorry. Look, don't read anything into that. I really do have to go."

Ben got up and they went inside. There was enough ambient

light coming in so he didn't turn on the lights. She walked to the front door as he retrieved the journals. He handed them to her.

"Thanks, Ben. And thanks for the company. I enjoyed it. You've got a great place here."

"Yup. All I need now is a job to pay for it." And someone to share it with, he didn't add.

"You're a good guy, Ben. You'll find something."

She left, and Ben closed the door. He put away the last of the wine then took Stump out. As they walked the still-busy street, he thought about Dr. Amelia Silvers. She'd been interested in him as a patient when he'd been in the hospital and she was interested in him because of the journals. Sure, she'd been friendly with him over dinner tonight but most of the talk had been about his grandmother. How unromantic was that? Maybe she'd planned on just being friendly enough to get the journals from him. Maybe that's all tonight had been about for her. Well, she had them now. She'd gotten what she'd come for and there was no longer any reason for her to give him a second thought.

It was mid-morning the next day when a text came in from Harriet:

Nothing on the murder of a Cindy Brand by any spelling I can think of. Seriously, Ben, don't ask me to do this kind of crap again.

CHAPTER 19

Harriet's text was exactly what Ben expected so he couldn't say he was disappointed. He replied, thanking her for looking into it and promised not to bug her again. So that was it. That was the end of the story of Grandma Lydia and her house in the woods and her journals. It was just as well. Ben had something much more important to worry about—he needed to find a job.

Three weeks passed with Ben filling out applications and sending out résumés for dozens of job openings, some of which he was actually qualified for. He received some call-backs, did an online interview which he thought went reasonably well and did three in-person interviews that didn't go well at all. It was a frustrating process and he was starting to get discouraged when he stumbled across an open position that looked like it fit him to a tee. After filling out the application, he received a call-back the same day. They wanted to see him the next morning.

For the occasion, Ben wore a second-rate suit he'd purchased from a bargain-basement outlet. On entering the building he'd eyed some of the other men in the busy lobby and, as discretely as possible, he pulled off his tie and stuffed it into his pocket. Guess nobody wore ties these days. He rode the elevator up to the 14th and found the offices of Masters and Green. "Ben Marshall here to see Mr. Green," he said, to the startlingly pretty receptionist who looked to be just out of high school. She gave him a pearly-white cheerleader smile and he handed her one of his old business cards.

"You're a police detective?"

"Was. I'm here about the Senior Case Manager position."

She gave him back his card, told him to have a seat, then picked up the phone and announced: "Your 10's here."

As Ben waited, his phone buzzed. He checked it and saw the call was from Captain Nolan. Now what could he want?

"You need to take that?" asked a tall man with a deep tan and slick black hair who'd just strode over. Under a dark sport jacket, he wore a darker tee shirt with a tight collar that made Ben glad he'd ditched the tie.

He stood and slipped the phone into his pocket. "No, I'll call them back. I'm Ben Marshall. You are Mr. Green?"

"Yes, but please, call me Clay." Another big white smile—must have a good dental plan here.

"Pleased to meet you Clay," said Ben.

They shook hands and walked past a line of desks occupied mostly by twenty-something men who were either on the phone or working their computers. "I have to tell you that we were excited to get your application," Green said as they reached the far wall where he opened an office door and waved Ben into a chair. "We have a few veterans of the force on staff here, but not near enough and only a couple with your level of experience."

The M&G Agency was the biggest PI firm in Boston and the case manager position would be a plumb job for Ben. He still felt bad about his forced retirement but, with a job like this, he'd have landed on his feet. He made sure to remember the line he'd honed over his first few interviews about having retired early from the force due to his desire to take on other, more rewarding challenges in the private sector. It played well with Green.

There was the usual battery of other questions about his willingness to work long hours and about his ability to write up comprehensive reports efficiently and concisely. Ben answered these along with a few personal questions in a way that seemed to play equally well.

When Clayton Green finally saw him out, he did so with another sparkling smile and shook his hand. "Thanks for your time, Ben. I have to say that I'm excited by the prospect of having you aboard. You'll be hearing from us soon."

"Believe me, I'm excited too, Clay," said Ben, thanking him with a smile of his own. Well, that went well, thought Ben on the elevator ride back down. Mentally, he assessed the timing of when he might draw his first check from M&G and when his next rent payment would be due. He knew it was going to be tight but he was feeling pretty good about things as he pushed his way outside through the revolving door. At that moment, his phone buzzed. Shit, he'd forgotten about Nolan's call. "Yeah, this is Ben."

"Ben, this is Nolan."

"Oh, sorry Captain, I meant to return..."

"I need you to come down to the precinct, Ben. Can you do that?"

"What? Sure, I suppose I can come in. Tomorrow okay?"

"Sorry, I need you here now."

"Why? What's this about?"

"Just get here, will you? I'll tell you more when you get here."

Ben sighed. "All right then, Captain. I'm on my way."

There was no 'Thanks, Ben,' from the other end. Nolan just clicked off, ending the call.

Ben caught a cab to the station and, on the way, was preoccupied more with thoughts about the Case Manager position at M&G than wondering what was up with Nolan. Once there, he trotted up the steps and walked into the building. It was all so strange not to be a part of this place. The sounds, the smells, the sight of familiar faces told him that this is where he should be. This is where he belonged. This is where the action is. But no, he was now Ben Marshall, the soon to be Case Manager for Green and Masters. As good as that sounded to Ben, it still didn't feel quite right.

Sergeant Mullins looked up from his spot a few desks back from the front desk. "Hey, Ben. How's it going?" he said, coming forward. "Captain Nolan said you were coming in. Here's your visitor pass. You can go right up."

Ben slipped the lanyard over his head so the glossy tag with a big V on it hung down to his belt buckle. He rode the elevator up to the third floor where he gave a nod to other familiar faces. From his desk Phil caught his eye with an expression that, even for Phil, looked a little grim. What was that all about? Well, there was no reason for Ben to worry, was there? He wasn't with the department any more. What could they do to him—cancel his pension? Shit. Maybe that's what this was about.

"How's it going, Benjie? How'd that thing up in Maine work

out?" asked Phil when he'd walked closer. They shook hands.

"Things are good. Maine was kind of a bust but I'm onto other things now. We can talk about that later." He lowered his voice. "So, what's going on, Phil? What's Nolan want with me?"

"All I know is, a couple of hot-shots from Internal Affairs met with the Captain this morning. They're in the conference room, waiting for you." He cocked his head in that direction.

Ben felt his stomach knot up. There was no way this was going to be anything good. He walked to the conference room door, knocked, and walked in.

Captain Nolan sat at the head of the table, farthest from the door. He lifted his head from the papers in front of him, gave Ben a blink of recognition, then went back to the papers. To Nolan's right sat two suits, both about Ben's age, both clean shaven with buzz cuts, one with black hair, the other brown. They each gave Ben a non-committal stare as Harriet, seated opposite them, handled the introductions.

"Detective Marshall, this is Larry Gerard and Richard Kindle from Internal Affairs. Please sit." Her eyes blazed at Ben as she waved him into the seat opposite Nolan. Shit. What was she pissed about?

Ben sat, took a few seconds to survey the faces around the table. The IA guys were just staring at him, Harriet had her arms folded with her eyes downcast. Ben tapped a finger on the table a few times. "Look, will someone tell me what's going on?"

No one answered.

At a glance from Nolan, Harriet placed a voice recorder at the center of the table and clicked it on. "We'll be recording this meeting and need your permission to do so, Mr. Marshall. Please state clearly that you approve."

A red LED started blinking on the device.

"Shit! What the hell is this?"

"Please state clearly that you approve of this meeting being recorded," Harriet repeated.

"Okay, okay, I approve," said Ben. "Just tell me what's going on."

Nolan looked up from his papers. "You are here because of

Cindy Brand."

Suddenly relieved, Ben sat back in his chair. "What? You've got to be kidding me. That's was this is all about? Look, Harriet, I'm sorry if I got you into trouble but I was just looking for information. Something about an old case."

"What kind of case?" asked black-haired Larry—or was that Richard?

"Well, I was thinking that it'd probably be kidnapping and murder. It would have happened in the early nineteen-twenties."

"The kidnapping and murder of Cindy Brand you mean?"

"Yes. But Harriet checked on it and didn't find a thing on it so I figured, it probably never happened."

"Where did you first hear the name Cindy Brand?"

"The name came up in something I was working on."

Nolan folded his arms. "And what were you working on, Detective?"

Ben felt his blood rise. "First of all, I'm no longer a detective. You canned my ass, remember? Second, what I work on these days is my own business."

"Not when you bring me in on it," said Harriet.

"Bring you in on what? I didn't bring you in on anything. I asked you for a favor; you obliged and that was the end of it."

The brown haired guy reached over to the papers in front of Nolan. He grabbed an 8x10 photograph and slid it in front of Ben. It was the picture of a young girl with blonde, braided hair. Maybe ten years old, she was smiling over a bouquet of wild flowers that she was holding out to whoever was behind the camera. "You ever see this girl before?"

Ben spread his hands. "What's she got to do with any of this?"

"Answer the question, Ben," said Nolan. "Have you ever seen her before?"

"No."

"She lives in Texas with her mom, dad, and two older sisters," explained Nolan. "She was reported missing three days ago. Her name is Cindy Brand. That's the same name you had Harriet run through the system a few weeks ago."

Ben froze. “Jesus,” he said under his breath. “Now, there’s a strange coincidence. I hope she’s all right.”

“The authorities in Austin have no leads. Except for you.”

“Me? I’m not a lead. How could I...I mean, here I am in Boston and she’s in Austin. How would I even know her?”

“That’s what we’re here to find out,” said Nolan.

Ben almost laughed. “No, no, no. Like I said, it’s just a crazy coincidence. The Cindy Brand I was interested, if she existed at all, would have died almost a hundred years ago.”

“And how did she die?”

Ben’s mouth went dry. “Somebody cut her throat,” he said quietly.

The brown haired guy shifted his chair, turning so he faced Ben more directly. “You said Cindy Brand’s name came up on something you’d been working on. Care to tell us about that now?”

“It goes back a few months to when I found out about my great, great grandmother.”

Nolan slammed his fist onto the table. “Damn it, Ben. You’d better start taking this seriously. A life is at stake. We’re not here to hear about your great, great grandmother.”

Ben kept his calm. “It’s the truth. You asked how I came up with Cindy Brand’s name and I’m telling you.”

The room was silent for a moment. “All right then, Ben,” said Nolan, speaking slowly. “Tell us about your great, great grandmother and what the hell she has to do with any of this.”

Ben hesitated, knowing how crazy this was going to sound. “She wrote about dreams she had. They were all about the death of children. One of those dreams was about a girl named Cindy Brand.”

“What exactly were these writings of hers, Mr. Marshall,” asked brown-hair. “Did she write about her in a letter that was passed down to you over the years?”

“She wrote journals—four of them. She was a medical doctor, born in the 1880’s. She was interested in studying the human brain. She wrote a book on the prison system back then. After that, she worked in an insane asylum where she ended up going nuts herself. When I got...after I retired from the force, I had a little time on my hands so I thought I'd see what more I could find out about her. She'd lived up in Maine so it wasn't far. She had a place up there. Turned out that she kept a written record documenting her bouts of insanity. I managed to find them." Ben paused, everyone around the table staring back at him. Ben waited for a moment, then continued. "Her name was Lydia Thornhill."

"When did your Grandma Lydia die?" asked the black-haired guy.

"1920, I think."

"And how is it that you were able to find these writings of hers?"

"I found her grave..."

"I'm sorry, could you speak a little louder?" asked Harriet.

"I found her grave. Her journals had been buried with her."

Harriet's eyes went wide. "You dug her up?"

"Yes."

Nolan sighed, keeping his eyes on Ben. "I think we're getting a little off track here."

The black-haired guy shifted in his seat. "Have you ever been to Texas, Mr. Marshall?"

Ben thought for a moment. "I spent a few days there back maybe five years ago. You probably remember the case, Captain. We were extraditing some guy on drug charges."

"Yes, I remember. And that was in Austin, I think, right?"

"Yes, it was. But I was never there before or since."

"While you were there, did you interact with anyone besides the people related to the case?"

Ben thought for a moment. "No. I was only there for a few days, like I said."

"We'll check on that," said brown-hair. He scribbled a note, then continued. "You said that your grandmother wrote about the death of children. How do you mean that?"

"She was a little...weird about that. She wrote as if she herself was the child; as if she herself was dying. She had these death-visions, you know. That's what drove her nuts." Ben glanced down at the photo. "But her Cindy Brand couldn't possibly be this girl.

She couldn't be."

"We'll need to see your grandmother's writings," said brown-hair. "We can have them analyzed and authenticated."

"That'll take too much time," said Nolan. "The Austin PD is desperate for information. We can't derail their investigation with hundred year old evidence dug up from some grave. That little girl has been missing for three days now. We might already be too late." He turned to the IA guys. "I've known Ben Marshall a long time. I've never known him to lie. So I guess I agree with him. This has to be just some kind of crazy coincidence."

Brown-hair tapped his pad with his pencil. "I suppose the name Cindy Brand isn't all that unusual."

Nolan thought for a moment then glanced at Harriet. "Tell Austin we can't help them."

Harriet flicked off the recorder.

Everybody stood and filed out but Nolan took Ben aside. "Where are these journals of your grandmother's?"

"They're a series of journals—four of them. They're at BU. I know a psychologist there."

"Howe's associate, you mean. Yeah, I know her. Well, get them back. I want to see them."

Ben nodded and rose to leave.

"Just covering all the bases, Ben," Nolan told him on his way out.

CHAPTER 20

Once outside, Ben pulled out his phone. His call to Amelia went straight to voice-mail so he left a message. Then he sent her a follow up text: *Call me; it's important. I need the journals back.* He put the phone in his pocket, only then noticing that he'd been walking the wrong way. He stopped. Coming out of the station house he'd automatically taken a right to get back to his old place. He didn't miss the roaches but he missed just about everything else about the third-floor of the old brownstone. His new apartment was nice but seemed sterile in comparison.

He turned and headed for the subway.

Too many white walls, he concluded once back. And too empty. He had a bed now, he had a TV, he had a used recliner, and he had two folding chairs out on the balcony. No, it didn't feel like home yet and, with money getting tight, he wondered if he'd be staying here long enough for it ever to feel like home. Well, the job at M&G might change all that.

But this thought passed through his mind only for an instant. Just a distraction from the picture of little Cindy Brand and her flowers. What kind of animal would ever want to harm such a beautiful child? He reminded himself that it was all just a strange coincidence. This girl in Austin would probably turn up okay—just lost, or maybe just with a family member. Then Ben thought about the Cindy Brand his Grandma Lydia had written about.

She'd been tied to a pole in a basement—a dirt floor basement. She'd looked up to see the initials *TJ* carved into the rafters overhead. The guy had a knife at her throat. His blazing eyes were wild and tinged deep with blood. His muscular arms glistened with sweat. And there was something else, wasn't there? Something on one arm beneath the sweat, a dark purple something on his skin moving with the flex of his muscles. A tattoo? No, maybe a scar?

As if seeing the vision himself, Ben watched the knife move against Cindy's throat. Blood. My God, so much blood. A wave of nausea hit him. Almost doubling over, tears suddenly filled his eyes and his vision went blank. Almost like an echo, he heard himself speak: "I'm so sorry, Cindy, I couldn't...I just couldn't help you." He squeezed his eyes shut but that couldn't stop his tears. Then, through his funk, he felt his phone go off. He had a knee on the carpet and a hand on the seat of the recliner. He looked around, for a moment unsure of where he was. Almost breathless, he pulled out his phone. He swallowed, tasting bile. "Yeah?"

"It's me, Ben. I was in class when you called. What's up?"

Ben got to his feet. "Oh, hi. Yeah, I..."

"Are you all right, Ben?"

"Yeah, yeah, I'm fine." He struggled to rearrange his thoughts. "I sent you a text. I need the journals back."

"Really? All of them? I've managed to get through most of them but really, there's a lot more work to be done. They are remarkable, just as I thought. I need to go over them in more detail, take notes, write some observations. That's what I'm doing now. But it's going to take a while. Why do you need them?"

"Cindy Brand. She's one of the girls who dies in the last journal."

"Okay, so what about her?"

Ben shook his head as if clearing out cobwebs. "She's missing, in Austin. A girl with the same name. The police think I know something about it."

"What do you mean, missing? You mean missing now?"

"Yes."

"Well, that's just... wait, the police? How do the police know anything about the journals? Oh, I'll bet Howe told them. But how did they know about Cindy Brand?"

"Look just get the journals back to me. I suppose I only need the last one, the one that covers her death. You can keep the others. Are you at BU? I can meet you somewhere to pick it up."

"I don't have that one with me, Ben. It's at my apartment."

"I'll meet you there." He was already out the door, heading for the elevator.

"What? You mean now?"

A strange feeling of urgency came over Ben. He felt queasy again. The vivid image of the words on his grandmother's wall flashed through his mind. Two of those words screamed out:

SAVE THEM!

In that unnerving moment, Ben knew the terrible, unbelievable truth. There was no time for him to try and rationalize what was happening. All Ben knew was that he had to hurry. "Yes, I need it now," he almost shouted into the phone. "Give me your address."

Ten minutes later the cab pulled up to the steps of a campus brownstone not unlike Ben's old place. He stepped out. With his thumb hooked through a belt loop, his hand began a nervous pat, pat, pat on his jeans. He looked up and down the block then saw Amelia peddling toward him on a bike. Shit—a bike. He told the cab to wait, then waived for her to peddle faster until she finally made it to him.

"Get the journal. Hurry," he told her. She ran inside as Ben grabbed the bike carrying it up and leaving it on the porch.

Two minutes later she was back down, the journal in her hand. "Here, you go, Ben. But I don't see why..."

Ben opened the door to the cab. "Get in, you're coming with me."

"What? Why? Ben, you're not making any sense," she complained, getting in.

Ben gave the cabbie the address of the station. "Step on it!"

The cabbie gave him an 'Everyone's in a hurry these days,' sigh, then pulled out.

"You're acting crazy," Amelia told Ben.

"Yeah, I know." He was looking over the cabbie's shoulder as if willing him to go faster. "Look, I don't understand any of this, but I'm sure now that this is no coincidence. That girl out in Austin. She *is* the same Cindy Brand that my grandmother wrote about." With the journal in his lap, he tapped it with his thumb. "I know it's her; we have to save her."

"She's in Austin?—Texas you mean?"

"Yes."

Amelia stared at Ben then faced forward and didn't say anything the rest of the way.

"Ben Marshall, here to see Captain Nolan," shouted Ben, storming inside the station.

"Whoa, whoa there buddy," shouted the man at the front desk. "Oh, you're Detective Marshall...or were, I guess. Sorry but you've got to sign in. And you need one of these." He held up a visitors pass. "She does too. Who're you here to see?"

"Just stopping by to see Captain Nolan. You know, old times and all."

"Sorry, still need a pass."

They signed in and headed up to the third floor where Ben led the way, striding past a startled Harriet. He gave Nolan's door a single rap and walked in.

Nolan was on the phone, nodding politely and hmm-hmming to whoever was on the other end. He gave Ben a look then glanced over Ben's shoulder where Amelia stood beside a silently irate Harriet.

Ben gave Nolan a hurry-up gesture.

"Sorry, Mike," said Nolan. "Gotta run. Something just came up." He hung up and gave an okay indication to Harriet who left with a shrug, leaving the door open.

"It's about Cindy Brand, Captain. I remember now that in my grandmother's journal she said that there were initials carved in the wood ceiling of the basement. There was also a thing on the guy's arm, either a tattoo or a scar. I know it's nuts but I'd feel a lot better if you got that info down to Austin."

"You said the whole thing with your grandmother was just a coincidence."

"Maybe it is. Hell, it probably is. But I don't know now. I just have this feeling."

Nolan's brows went up. "Another one of your visions, Detective? Like when you shot that guy in the white overcoat?"

Ben had been leaning forward, both hands on the front of Nolan's desk. He straightened suddenly as a chill ran up his spine and he realized—my God, it *was* like that. Shit. What the hell's going on? His mind went blank for a moment and he sank into a chair.

Brows still up, Nolan turned to Amelia.

"All I know is that Detective Marshall thinks he's telling the truth," she explained. "He's somehow convinced himself that the girl his grandmother wrote about is the same girl whose gone missing in Texas. I have no idea why he thinks this, but...well, I'd hate to end up with the body of a dead child proving he was right."

Nolan placed his folded elbows on his desk eying the journal in her hand. "Is that his grandmother's notebook?"

"Yeah." Amelia flipped through it, then put it in front of Nolan, her finger at a spot halfway down the page. "The passage about Cindy Brand starts here."

Nolan read it then lifted his eyes and stared at Ben who'd managed by that time to compose himself, at least outwardly.

"All right," said Nolan, after a while. "I'll call Austin about the TJ thing but there's nothing here about the mark on the guys arm."

Ben blinked. "What? Of course there is." He turned the journal around and skimmed twice through the passage confirming Nolan's observation. "But...I swear, I read it."

Amelia put a hand on his shoulder. "You're just remembering it wrong, Ben."

Ben's mind was a muddle. He felt numb. All he could do was shake his head.

Nolan picked up the phone, dialed, and waited. "Hello Dick? I might have something for you on the Brand case." He gave him the details about the basement and the initials adding, as an afterthought, that the guy who had the girl might have a tattoo or scar on his arm. "Yeah, that's right. Now I can't exactly vouch for this info but it may give you something to go on. Yes, it came through on an anonymous tip. No, I don't know anything else. Sure, I'll get back to you if we learn something more." He hung up.

Ben took a breath. "Thanks, Captain," he said quietly.

Nolan closed the journal and handed it to Amelia. "I don't know why I just did what I did. I hope it doesn't lead them down a rabbit hole. You two better hope so too."

Ben got to his feet. "You'll let me know?"

"I'll let you know," said Nolan. There was pity in his voice, like he was talking to an old man with Alzheimer's. And Ben couldn't blame him because that was exactly how he felt. On his way out he gave a nod and a forced smile to Harriet and Phil.

Once outside, Ben just stood stock-still at the base of the steps.

"What now?" asked Amelia after a moment.

"Ha, you're asking *me* that? I'm crazy Ben. Just like my crazy grandmother."

She didn't answer.

Ben looked up the street. "I suppose I'll just head up to my place. Sorry I dragged you out here."

"Want some company?"

"Don't worry, I'm not going to jump off my balcony."

"Ben, stop it," said Amelia grabbing his arm. "Come on. Let's go to your place. How about you take me out to dinner tonight?"

He hesitated, turning to her. "I don't want your sympathy. Or do you just want another lunatic to study?"

"You're not going to get any sympathy from me. You should know me better than that."

Ben looked into her eyes. They were honest, sincere eyes. Without thinking, he pulled her closer in an embrace that she willingly stepped into. It was a relief to feel her body against his, her cheek on his. He felt as if he'd been cast adrift but now had something to hold on to. A wave of fatigue washed over him. "I don't know what's happening to me. I just don't know."

"It's all right, Ben. You had a premonition. It's something everyone has sometimes. There's the life of a little girl on the line and you did what you had to do. You did the right thing."

He nodded as they parted and they started walking again. "I don't think Nolan would have called Austin if you weren't there supporting me."

"I haven't known him as long as you, Ben, but he seems like a straight-shooter to me. Do you think he'll get back to you?"

Ben shook his head. "No. For one, I do think I'm nuts. And, for another, I don't think Captain Nolan wants anything more to do with me."

They had an early dinner at an Italian restaurant over which Ben learned that she'd only just started reading the fourth journal. "I'm taking notes as I go along. It slows me down and I'm a slow reader anyway," she explained munching on a slice of garlic bread. "I've noticed that she's getting into more details now. You know, the thing with Cindy Brand, learning her name and all. There's another one too, a drowning where she mentions seeing a white house with a red roof."

"She said the name of the kid that time though, didn't she?"

"Yes. She was Mary. Just the first name, no last."

Ben used his napkin. "Sure puts you in a foul mood though, reading about all those deaths. All children. That's why I gave you all the journals back. I didn't want anything to do with them." He shook his head. "I have no idea why I thought that Grandma Lydia's Cindy is the same girl that's missing in Austin."

A short time later, the waiter came by with the bill which Ben picked up.

"Look, Ben. I know you're still out of work right now. I can..."

"Not a chance. I've got this," he said. "I'm the one who dragged you out to the station. It's the least I can do."

On the walk to his apartment, he did let her spring for a bottle of wine.

"Love what you've done to the place," she exclaimed, walking in, surveying the bare walls as Stump barked and jumped and sniffed her feet.

"Yeah, yeah. I probably won't be staying here much longer so, you know, why bother?"

"You mentioned over dinner that you had a line on a good job."

"I do. I'm hoping for the best but I can't count on it." He

opened the wine and poured. "I've got better glasses this time."

"I'm impressed, Mr. Marshall."

Stump kept up with his sniffing. "He's got a nose for good quality foot powder," Ben explained.

They drank sitting on Ben's folding chairs out on the balcony. A golden glow was all that could be seen of the sun that had fallen behind the neighboring buildings. It had been a warm day but now a cooling breeze blew.

Amelia swirled her wine, took a sip, then put it down. "Ben, you don't really think anything will come of this Cindy Brand thing, do you? You seemed to be so sure of yourself in Nolan's office—at least at first."

He shook his head. "It really doesn't make any sense, does it? All I know is that when I first left the station house after finding out about her, I came back here and somehow became utterly convinced that it was in my power to save that kid. In my head, word for word, I played back Grandma Lydia's description of Cindy's death until I felt I was actually in that basement with her. And at that moment, I could see the killer. I could see the evil and the hate in his eyes."

"You could see his face?"

"No, just his eyes. It was as if everything else was out of focus."

"You saw something on his arm though."

"Yeah, I saw that too." Ben felt his heart pounding again. He closed his eyes and leaned back in his chair, resting the back of his head against the glass window of the building. His head was spinning. He thought about Grandma Lydia's first line in her book: *I remember the date, almost the exact hour that the feeling of normalcy left me.* Is that what this moment had been for him? Was he the one losing touch now? But aloud he said: "No, I don't think anything will come of any of this. Kids like Cindy go missing all the time and the stats are not in their favor. They usually end up dead or never found at all."

"*'Save them.'* That's what your grandmother wrote on the wall of that house up in Maine. Why would she say that?"

"Now you're the one talking crazy."

They sat in silence for a while as the lights from the buildings and from the street below took over for the sun.

"When you called me from Maine you said you were up there gathering information from the state records about your grandmother. What did you find?"

"Just a bunch of normal stuff: Birth certificate, death certificate, medical records, documents from when she was working for the reformatory then the asylum after that. Nothing really important but I took pics of it all."

"They're on your phone?"

"Yeah. I can send them to you if you want."

Amelia didn't answer right away.

"What are you thinking?"

"Oh, sorry. Nothing really. Yes, send them to me. Or put them on a thumb-drive. I'd like to have a look." She checked her watch. "Sorry, Ben. I have to be going. I teach an early class tomorrow."

Hmmm...always the same excuse, he mused.

She got up and so did Ben. She declined his offer to walk her to the subway then kissed him on the lips. It was just a peck and she pulled away too quickly for him to make anything more of it. "Thanks, Ben. I enjoyed tonight." She picked up the journal from the kitchen counter where she'd left it. "All right if I take this? I'd like to keep all of them together."

Ben hesitated. He'd wanted to go over the Cindy Brand part again but now thought, well what good would that do? Maybe it would be best to get Grandma Lydia out of his head for a while.

"I won't keep it long," Amelia added.

"No, no. There's no problem. You're right, they should all be kept together."

"They all belong to you anyway, Ben and, if you don't already know, they are extremely valuable. I want to get them all on computer. They offer a great insight to what exactly happened to your Grandma Lydia and what might be happening to a host of other patients suffering mental disorders."

He walked with her to the door. "How about I come over to your place sometime and we can go over them. I'm sure you have more furniture than me. Besides, it's your turn. I've had you here twice already."

Her face soured a little. "That wouldn't be a good idea."

"Why not? I could..." His voice trailed off. "You're living with someone."

"I've been with him a long time."

"Why did you come up here with me then?"

"I...I don't know, Ben. It wasn't like I was leading you on. I care about you, I really do. I just know it would be a little sticky having you over."

"I thought you shrinks are supposed to be good at handling sticky situations."

Amelia formed a slight smile. "Not all the time," she said in a whisper, her eyes glistening. She took a step toward him, gently placing her hand on the back of his neck. Pulling him closer, she kissed him hard, her lips moving, Ben moving his, lost in the unexpected ecstasy of the moment. Then, as abruptly as she'd began it, she broke off the kiss. "Good night, Ben," she said, turning for the door and leaving without another word.

Dumbfounded, Ben leaned his back against the closed door as Stump came over and gave him an affirmative look, head cocked and both ears peaked.

CHAPTER 21

Ben slept well that night with the feel and scent of Amelia's lips lingering on his. He could still feel her body close to his and, dreaming, had imagined it closer still. He was surprised to see it was already nine when he got up the next morning.

He had a breakfast routine: Cheerios on Mondays and Thursdays, Rice Krispies on Tuesdays and Fridays, and Shredded Wheat on Wednesdays. Eggs, which he loved, were reserved for weekends. Still bleary-eyed, he flicked on the TV and, this being a Thursday, poured out the Cheerios. He had just retrieved the milk from the fridge when, from the TV, he heard the name, *Cindy Brand*. He fumbled with the remote and turned up the volume, his now wide-awake eyes glued to the screen.

A woman, late forties maybe, was speaking through tears to a crowd of reporters. "Please, please, if anyone knows anything about where our little Cindy might be, call us. I think there's a hotline number you can call?" She turned nervously to a cop standing next to her who nodded and stepped closer to the cluster of microphones to give the number. As he did this, Cindy's picture, the one with the flowers, flashed on the screen with the hotline number below it. Then, the woman came back on screen.

"Cindy dear, if you can hear me, don't be afraid. We're looking for you and we're going to find you and bring you home." She tried to wipe her cheeks dry but let out a sob, shaking her head. She took a step back and was embraced by a man who looked equally distraught. Ben could almost feel the pain and heartbreak of Cindy's parents and these feelings became all the more real for him because somehow, some small part of him believed that there was something he could have done, maybe something he could still do, to save their little girl.

With the parents still clinging to each other, the Chief of Police stepped up and made a brief statement about having no solid leads. He took a few questions before the news anchors in New York broke in with sad faces, said a few words about hopes and prayers then went to commercial.

Ben flicked the TV off.

Shit. No solid leads. That's what the chief said. What about the initials, the dirt-floor basement, the arm thing? Were they following up on all that? Ben shook his head. Had he really thought they would?

Ben had had a missing-person case two years back. They'd set up a hotline too and he remembered all the idiot calls they got from people saying they'd had a dream and "saw" things. He knew back then that such information was worthless and he knew now that, had he received a call from someone claiming to have relevant info passed down to him from some long lost relative, he would have just hung up on the guy. At least Nolan, in his call to Austin yesterday, hadn't mentioned that the source of the info was somebody's long dead grandmother. As far as Austin was concerned, that anonymous tip had been passed on to them from a brother officer, a chief of police no less. That should give it some credibility. Yeah, Nolan had stuck his head out for him on that one.

Ben checked the buzz on the internet about the Brand case but found nothing new. Shit, he should just call that hotline number himself. But what was he going to say that Nolan hadn't already said?

He started pacing. Maybe he should catch a plane to Austin. Maybe there was something he could do there that he couldn't do here. He was about to check the flight schedules, then got another idea. He called Nolan.

Harriet picked up. "Sorry, Ben. The Captain's tied up right now. Something's...well, I can't put you through."

"I need to talk to him, Harriet. It's about Austin."

"What about Austin? Do you have something new?" There was an anxiousness in her voice.

"No, nothing new but..." Suddenly it hit him. "It's about Cindy

Brand isn't it? That's what Nolan's tied up with right now. Shit! Look, tell him I'm coming over there and he'd better see me." He ended the call, rode the elevator down and was nearly run down trying to flag a cab.

Twenty minutes later he ran into the station and, not bothering with the visitor pass bull-shit, headed straight for the stairs taking them two at a time up to the third floor.

Harriet was standing on the last step. Shit, the last thing he needed right now was a confrontation with her. But the anger he expected to see in her face wasn't there.

"The boys at the front desk told me you were on your way up," she said with the same anxiousness as on the phone. "The Captain's up on the fourth in conference room A. He's expecting you. Here, take this." She handed him a pass.

"Thanks, Harriet. You're a honey."

"Yeah, I am. And don't you forget it."

Ben ran up to the fourth floor and stepped out of the stairwell out of breath. He spotted a line of closed doors along the far wall and found Conference Room A. He knocked once and went in.

The room was dark except for a large flat screen TV on one wall. The screen was solid blue with a red dot and a time-date stamp blinking in the lower left corner. Central time, Ben noted.

"Close the damn door, Ben," growled Nolan who was standing only two feet away.

Ben closed the door, his eyes adjusting.

"It's a live feed from Austin. They've got a SWAT team on the way to an address somewhere outside the city. They should be there in about thirty minutes. Turns out they know of a guy with a scar on his arm from a knife-fight in prison. He also happens to have the initials TJ. His parole officer saw our tip and fingered him." Nolan lowered his voice. "However this turns out, Ben. Austin's going to be very curious as to where our info came from."

Ben saw Phil sitting on the other side of the table and gave him a nod. The two other guys sitting at the table where ones he knew but not well. He was pleased to see that Frick and Frack from Internal Affairs weren't in the room.

"Coffee's over there," said Phil from his seat.

Ben grabbed a cup along with a glazed doughnut. He sat and had the doughnut gone in three bites. A tense silence filled the room as they all waited.

After a while, a female voice spoke from the blue-screen: "Ten minutes out. Coms check."

Ben had been in on hits like this before but never from this end. The female voice had to be the team-lead and the screen in front of him had to be the same screen she was looking at in her control van. Ben pictured that van leading a line of cop cars, racing down a Texas highway, sirens blaring.

"Blue one, come in," said the lead, her voice ice-cold.

"One here."

The blue screen became a grid of nine smaller screens, each showing black at the moment.

"Blue two, come in."

They counted off until Blue nine had checked in.

"A-V coms good. Eight minutes out."

Ben's heart thumped madly. Hang in there, Cindy, hang in there. The good guys are coming.

"Five minutes out, sirens off."

The seconds dragged. "Two minutes. Everybody go?"

In order, the men shouted their status: "Blue 1, go. Blue 2, go..."

"Sixty seconds. Pulling up now. Remember, quiet approach routine. Safeties off, flash-bangs ready." There was no waver in that steady voice. Seconds later, the sound of tires braking over sand was followed by a shout: "Go. Go. Go. Come on boys let's get that ass-hole."

The nine screens went from pitch black to bright daylight as van doors flew open. At first all of the helmet-cams showed the same thing, the jerky image of a ramshackle single-story house coming closer. An old pick-up was parked in front. Boots rumbled over the hard-pack ground. There were no shouts but plenty of hard breathing as the men ran, then separated, some going to the front, some the back. The screens steadied out.

"Positions," said the lead.

"Ready," said two voices.

"All right! Go! Go! Go! Get in there. Get to the basement."

A crash sounded as two doors flew off their hinges. The men ran in shouting: Police! Police!"

Ben stood. His stomach churning. Both hands curled into fists. Come on, get that bastard. Get him!

"Back clear," someone yelled. "Front clear," shouted another.

Boots rumbled. Two screens showed a kitchen, two others, the front room. Ben's eyes were drawn to the screen that showed a narrow hallway. A door was flung open. Stairs led down. The cop leaped down them shouting, "Hands up mother fucker! Hands up! This is the police." The screen rocked then steadied and adjusted to the dim lighting.

Ben held his breath.

The camera panned with the tip of the cop's rifle visible as he searched for a target. But there was none.

A support post came into view.

"Oh, my God in heaven," said the cop, almost in a whisper.

The camera dropped lower.

Ben froze.

There was Cindy Brand. Her hands were still tied to the post behind her. Her neck glistened with blood that ran scarlet along her bent body and pooled in the dirt floor all around. Tangled hair, tinged red, covered her face like a shroud.

The team lead screamed: "Is there a pulse? Check for a pulse!"

A hand lifted Cindy's wrist. Her fingers hung limp. "No pulse."

Ben slumped down into his chair, head in his hands. Oh, God. They were too late. Cindy darling, I'm so sorry. I should have found a way but...I couldn't...I just...

At that same instant, the lead let out an anguished cry that seemed to speak for everyone in that house and everyone watching in Conference Room A. Her voice shook as she pressed on, doing what had to be done: "All points, all points, we...we have a fatality. Secure the crime scene. I want this entire area cordoned off—five mile radius. Got that? Nothing gets in or out. We're going to get this son-of-a-bitch."

As the stunned Austin PD moved back into action, Ben stared in a daze at the multiple screens, some blank now, some following the men as they searched the house and the basement. "They should check the ceiling," Ben said quietly as if he were talking to himself. He cleared his throat, then spoke louder. "Have them check the ceiling—the basement ceiling between the joists, just above the post."

Nolan hesitated, then made a call, relaying the request directly to the team lead who gave the order: "Hey, Blue 3, point your cam up to the ceiling right by the post. I want a clear shot of it all around."

One of the screens moved closer to the body then angled up. The optics adjusted to reveal bare wood and the support beams for the floor above. The cam circled around slowly, then stopped.

"Shit. There it is," muttered Ben, staring open mouthed at the initials *TJ* carved deep into the wood. He felt limp. He had been right. His grandmother had been right. And God damn it to hell, he should have found a way to save that poor little girl.

Nolan terminated the video feed a moment later. He threw open the door, his eyes blazing in the light that poured in. "Clear the room. Ben, you stay. Everybody else out, now." He turned up the lights.

Nolan closed the door behind Phil who'd been the last to leave. He slid his chair over and pulled another one next to him. "You're sitting here, Ben, next to me. Austin's going to be all fired up about how you knew what you knew. They'll want to find out what else you know. This'll be a live, two way A-V feed. Better dry your eyes," he added quietly.

Ben did so with a handkerchief then swallowed hard. "What am I going to say to them? I don't know what to say. I can't tell them it was my dead grandmother who..."

"You're going to tell the truth, and that's it. Got that?"

"Shit, Captain..."

"Yeah, shit is right." Nolan keyed the video conferencing device then, they waited. Ben took a gulp of coffee gone cold. He realized that his eyes were brimming again. He wiped them. All he could think about was poor little Cindy and how he'd let her down.

The screen blinked then showed a head shot of a uniformed woman—forty maybe, with angry, red-tinged eyes. LED's blinked from a rack of black instrumentation behind her. It was the team lead, still in her van.

"Lieutenant Waldon here. This your guy, Captain?"

Nolan nodded.

"Former Detective Ben Marshall," said Ben.

"We've got a lot of questions for you Detective, but right now we've got an ass-hole murderer to catch." She held up a photo. "This is our killer, right?"

It was a mug shot of a guy with long wavy blondish hair down to his shoulders. He had a square jaw and flat nose. But it was his eyes, passive in the photograph, that Ben focused on. He stared into them almost reliving the moment he'd seen them when they'd been filled with hate. Ben stiffened in revulsion. "Yes, that's him."

"Good. I just wanted to be sure." She put the photo down. "What else do you know?"

Ben shook his head. "I've told all I know."

"You're sure."

"I'm sure."

She paused, her forehead creasing. "I have other questions for you, Detective, but I'm a little backed up here right now trying to catch this kid-killer animal that you somehow know. In the meantime, Captain, send over Detective Marshall's records, we'll want to have a good close look at them."

Ben was stunned. Did she really think that he had anything to do with Cindy Brand's killer? In an instant, the sorrow he'd felt for Cindy was replaced by anger. "Look Lieutenant, I had nothing to..."

"You'll have them this afternoon," interrupted Nolan forcefully. "Good luck chasing your guy down."

At this, Waldon's entire face darkened. "Oh, we'll get that piece of shit. Fuckin-A, we'll get him."

The screen went blue. Nolan got up and opened the door. "I'll call you when we need you back here. Until then, stay in the area. Don't try to leave town. And don't say a word about any of this to anyone—got it? We're letting Austin handle the info stream."

"Right," said Ben through a daze, still sitting there, alone. He buried his head in his hands for just a moment and, after taking a long deep breath, stood up suddenly needing to get out of the room and out of this building. He took the stairs down, his disjointed thoughts boiling over.

On the sidewalk he started walking in the general direction of his apartment, passing the usual hurried foot-traffic. For all of them it was just an ordinary Thursday, maybe less ordinary for some, but still ordinary—a day just like his had started out. A day for Cheerios and not Rice Krispies. None of them had any idea what had just happened almost two thousand miles away.

The sun shined down—hot for September.

After a few blocks, Ben spotted a bar and went in. "Double scotch," he said grabbing a stool at the otherwise empty bar. When it came, he drained it quickly and ordered another.

"Rough day, huh?" said the bartender, bringing it over. "It's still morning you know, things could get better."

Ben just shrugged, making it clear he was in no mood for conversation. He tried to piece things together. The only thing he knew for certain is that the journal's vision of Cindy Brand's death was real. But how could that be? And how could it have actually happened, not back then when Grandma Lydia was alive, but now, today? The Austin police would ask the same questions. And Ben had no answers. He remembered the look Waldon had given him, like he was complicit in the whole thing; that maybe he knew the killer and should have been able to stop him. Well, she was right about that, wasn't she? He should have done *something*. He should have found a way to save that little girl.

Ben brought the drink to his lips, downed half in one swallow then put the glass down. Staring at the remaining liquid, he ran a hand over his face, thinking again about the journal, thinking again about the words written on the wall of that dilapidated house up in the woods. SAVE THEM, it had said. Not HER but THEM. And he realized suddenly, that there were other children slated to die. His chance to save Cindy was gone, but maybe he could find a way to save the others.

He shoved the glass aside. He knew what he should be doing right now and getting drunk wasn't going to help. He pulled his phone surprised to see he had a missed call from the person he was just about to call—Amelia. He keyed the call-back and, after she picked up, he just told her straight out: "Cindy Brand is dead."

"What? What are you talking about? She's all over the news. I was trying to call you about it. I just saw her mother on the TV with the chief of police. Cindy Brand isn't dead. They're still looking for her."

"The media people don't know about it yet. It just happened, about an hour ago. I saw it at the station—a live feed from Austin. They raided a house." He stopped for a moment, having a difficult time thinking about it much less talking about it. But he forced the words out. "Cindy's body was in the basement. The cops almost got there in time. It looked like...like her blood hadn't even dried. Another hour or two sooner and they might have saved her." He waited for Amelia to react and, when she didn't, he went on. "It was all there, Amelia, the basement, the dirt floor, the post she was tied to. The initials were there too, carved into the wood—TJ, plain as day."

"Ben. I'm sorry Ben. How could...I don't know what to say."

"Look, I messed up on Cindy. Maybe she could have been saved, maybe not. But, if we forget about trying to make sense out of this, if we just believe the journal and stop asking questions we can't answer, we might be able to save the others."

"Ben, where are you now. I hear music in the background."

"I don't know, some bar..." He looked around spotting a sign above a mirror. "Hogan's...right, it's Hogan's Rest."

"Are you drunk?"

"Maybe just drunk enough to be finally thinking straight about all of this. Look, I need to get the journals from you. All of them."

"I know Hogan's. I'll grab a cab."

She ended the call and Ben downed the last of his drink thinking it might do him some good after all. Shifting his regrets about Cindy Brand to the back of his mind, he left a twenty on the bar and stepped outside. Fifteen minutes later he slid into the backseat of a cab beside Amelia, the stack of journals between them.

"You mind coming with me?" asked Ben.

"I'm coming with you whether you want me to or not. You're going to need the help."

Ben gave her a grim smile then gave the driver the address of his building as he reached for the journals.

"The fourth one is on top," said Amelia. "I bookmarked the Cindy Brand page.

Ben opened it as the cab peeled out.

"How many drinks have you had? You smell like scotch."

Ben didn't answer.

"I'll make some coffee when we get there. I could use some myself."

But Ben hardly heard. He was flipping past the Cindy Brand pages. "Okay, she saw Cindy's death on May 11, 1920. She sees the next one on May 16th, 1920. So, the next death happens in five days."

"You don't know that, Ben."

Ben looked up from the journal. "Yes, I think I do. Five days from now a girl named Jennifer Watts who lives right here in Boston, is going to die in a fire. We're going to find her and we're going to save her."

CHAPTER 22

The cold February winds howled, piling snow in tall drifts against the cedar walls of the house, some level with the windows. By this time, Abigail's cheeks had healed and Lydia was relieved to see that the terrible scratches had left no scars. For weeks Abigail had kept her silence about the incident, speaking only of mundane day to day things, passing each day as if only going through the motions of life, letting the tension between her and her mother build to the breaking point.

On this particular day they sat in chairs set apart on either side of the fireplace, both angled close to its warmth. Lydia kept her hands busy with her knitting but Abigail just sat, staring into the flames.

The fire crackled and seemed to give Abigail a start as if waking her from a daydream. Without missing a stitch, Lydia spoke the same words in the same frustrated tone as she'd used many times over the past weeks: "For God's sake, say what you need to say, child."

This time, Abigail surprised her with a response. "I'm not a child, Mother," she said quietly.

Lydia grew hopeful that their long impasse might be at an end. "You must have questions."

"A long time ago, when Daddy was...with us, did you have these spells then?"

Yes, that's the question she would have asked, thought Lydia. Back then Abigail was a fun loving, happy girl. It was after Danny's death that things changed—for both of them. Lydia chose her words carefully.

"When we lived in Portsmouth, my spells were just dreams I'd have at night. But they were terrible dreams. Always about dying.

It got so I'd be afraid to go to sleep. I was still at the reformatory when they started coming on me during the day. I'd be wide awake, sometimes right in the middle of something, and then I'd be lost as if in a trance." Lydia flinched at the memory of the time it had happened when she'd been alone with Danny. It was about the time she'd published that cursed book of hers and long before she'd begun the journals. She couldn't remember much about the dream she'd had that day but she certainly remembered the nightmare she endured when she snapped back into reality.

Danny lay there on the floor, bleeding, his head bent at an odd angle. From beneath his cheek a sea of blood grew and in that sea lay a flat-iron, a small bit of reddened flesh clinging to its tip.

Seeing him, Lydia fell to her knees but she didn't cry. She watched the shoreline of blood creep closer to the hem of her dress until it seemed as if she'd become an island in the middle of it all. It made no sense to check for a pulse. She knew Danny was dead and some dark part of her reveled in that fact. It was the same part of her that had succumbed to temptation at the reformatory. And it was the same dark part that welcomed her now into an exclusive club whose members included Jerimiah Foley and all those other men she'd helped up the gallows steps. She felt united with them now.

She was a murderer too.

But she hadn't meant to do it, had she? Re-living that moment, kneeling on the bloody wooden floor, staring down at her dead husband, she remembered how her head had spun with dark and terrible thoughts. And she knew that it was more from the anguish of uncertainty and confusion than from remorse that she had screamed loud enough for Mrs. Murphy to come running up from downstairs, to knock frantically at the door and, on opening it, to let out a scream of her own.

The police had come. They'd asked questions. And Lydia concocted a story about a violent intruder that they somehow believed.

After Danny's body had been taken away, she'd tried to clean up the floor but the stain would not come out. She imagined how it must have been, blood seeping through between the floorboards, dripping down into the room below. And she wondered whether it had been the seeping blood and not her scream that had caused Mrs. Murphy to run up the stairs.

Abigail had been in school that day and, like the police, she had believed her mother about the intruder. Lydia wondered if now, years later, having seen the violence of her spells, Abigail might suspect the truth.

But, while Lydia kept no other secrets from her daughter, she couldn't bring herself to tell her the truth about that day. So, she'd lied then and she lied now, "My dreams were just dreams back when your father was with us. The violent spells didn't begin until long after he was gone."

Abigail stared back in response as if wanting to believe her mother's words but possibly knowing better. The fire crackled again and the logs in the fireplace shifted, sending up red sparks. "Are you insane?" she asked

"Some would call it that. But I'm a doctor. I've been trained to analyze symptoms and to develop prognoses and no, I wouldn't call it insanity. It's exactly as I've written in my journals. In these spells of mine, the way they are now, I occupy someone else's body at their moment of death. It's as if I'm bearing their fear and their pain for them."

"But why is it always children? And all girls except for that first boy."

Lydia thought back to that first vision of the boy who was shot and then to the one of Jeremiah Foley about to be hung. Yes, except for those two, all her visions had been about young girls. She'd wondered herself why this was but had no answer. "I don't know," she said quietly, putting down her knitting. "The important thing is that, when the spells are over, as you see, I revert to my normal self."

"No Mother, not your normal self," Abigail blurted out, her voice shaking. "I remember how you used to be. You used to laugh. You used to hug me tight and pick me up. You used to love me. You used to be fun. You haven't been that way for a long time. Not since Daddy..."

At this, Lydia rose from her chair and placed a hand on her daughter's cheek. Kneeling, her tear-filled eyes met Abigail's. "Oh, dear daughter. All of this has taken a terrible toll on me—on you too, I know. But I swear to you, I am still trying to learn more about what's happening to me and more about the children who are dying. They are so real to me. And by now they must number in the dozens."

"Fifty-three. I've read all your journals, even the one you're writing now. There've been fifty-three deaths in all."

"Not many more to come now, I think," said Lydia

"How do you know there'll be more? You haven't had a spell since that one when we first got here when you...came at me. Maybe that was the last one. Maybe getting you out of that asylum cured you and you'll never have another spell again."

"It wasn't the last, Abigail. There will be more. But maybe not many. It's as if I can feel them out there. I can almost hear them crying out, every bit as afraid as I am about what is to come."

Lydia got up from her knees and sat back in her chair. "Maybe I am insane after all. When I was younger, just out of medical school, this was exactly the condition I wanted to study. I had a theory at the time that the outlandish actions and emotions exhibited by those we call the insane were actually the same actions and emotions that a perfectly sane person would exhibit if faced with their strange realities. I thought that, from their point of view, they'd been transplanted into a different world, a world with an entirely different set of rules governing what it means to be rational. My plan was to learn as much as I could about those realities."

"Is that still your plan?"

Lydia felt a grim smile stretch and crack her dry lips. "Yes, I suppose it is."

"Then, let me help you."

Lydia shifted in her chair to look more directly at her daughter. "And how do you think you can help?"

"I don't know. You're the doctor. You tell me what you want me to do. For one thing, I can observe what you do when you're in one of your spells."

"You've already seen what that's like, me fighting and scratching you like I did. I'm dangerous."

Abigail was silent for a long while then took in a deep breath. "So, you will never get better? You'll never be cured?"

"There was a time when I thought that I might conquer this...this thing that's happening to me. Or that I at least might understand it better. But I am getting old now and I see there is no hope of that. There never was. Yet, strange as it is, I'm beginning to see some kind of purpose for..." She stopped there, unable to form words to express the new idea that was just starting to take root within her.

"A purpose for these spells of yours?" asked Abigail

"No, no child. It's just foolishness. I'm getting old and my thinking's starting to ramble. That's all." Lydia went back to her knitting and Abigail went back to staring at the fire.

Over time, Lydia taught Abigail how to tell when one of her spells were coming on. She had Samuel strengthen the door to Abigail's room and equip it with a heavy inside lock so that, at the first sign, Abigail would run there and lock herself in until Lydia became herself again. They had a safe-word that Lydia would use to announce through the closed door all was safe and normal.

"Wake up, bluebird," Lydia would call out each morning, and only then would Abigail unlock her door and come down to breakfast.

In this way, they learned to live with things as they were. Both developed their own day to day routines while, over the years, the trees closest to the house grew taller, drooping down until some touched the eaves. Samuel stopped by less and less to maintain the place. Lydia kept having her spells, though not as frequently as at the asylum. With Abigail's help she worked to keep up her journals, always believing her spells were not just dreams. Her descriptions of them grew more and more detailed.

Lydia tried several times to link her death-spells to reality. She wrote the police and newspapers, inquiring about actual deaths that might be similar to the ones she'd experienced. But the replies, when she got them, were always negative.

So, they must be just dreams then, concluded the rational side of Lydia Thornhill. Yet, in her irrational heart of hearts, she never stopped thinking otherwise and, while she despaired of ever rescuing any of the children herself, she came to believe that saving them might just be the work of someone else.

In May of 1920, another spell came. It was a fire. Those were the worst: Seeing the blaze; feeling the heat while trapped in a corner with no place to go as the flames marched closer and closer; the awful, stinging pain building, becoming unbearable; her hair and clothing igniting with a whoosh while tongues of bright orange licked up her legs blackening then consuming her flesh as if hungry for her life. Her last memory of it were the echoes of her own futile screams melting into the roar of the blaze.

That girl's name was Jenifer Watts. Lydia had learned that much from the things the girl had in her purse. She'd been older than many of the other girls, maybe thirteen or fourteen. These facts were apparent to Lydia when the spell ended and she'd found herself sitting on the floor in a corner, huddled there, entirely limp, wet from sweat, her breathing coming in desperate, rasping spasms that slowly evened out.

She noticed it was daytime and the wind outside was rattling the windows. The kitchen table just beyond her outstretched legs was overturned. Broken dishes littered the floor.

"How do you feel?" asked Abigail, her voice calm but her face drained white. She stood in the doorway that led out into the mudroom. She held a pencil and notepad.

Lydia struggled for a moment, trying to get up but found she had no strength. She rested her head against the wall, her eyes on Abigail.

"How do you feel, Mother?" her daughter asked again, taking a step back.

A burning pain shot through Lydia's shoulder and she grimaced. But it was nothing compared to what she'd just been through. "Don't worry, Abigail. It's over. I'm all right now. Help me up would you?" When Abigail still didn't move, Lydia realized why and she smiled slightly. "It's all right, bluebird. It's all right."

Abigail got her into a chair and pulled the table back up. She poured some water for both of them then sat. "It was another fire, wasn't it?"

Lydia finished the water in a few quick gulps not caring that much of it dribbled down her chin. She leaned back and would have closed her eyes were it not for her fear of again seeing the flames. "Yes. The fires are the worst. Were you watching the whole time?" She straightened. "Did I come at you?"

"I was up in bed when I heard you, near dawn but still dark. I was quiet coming down the stairs. I watched you from the front room. I could see you beating your hands against the walls. You tore open the cupboards, throwing everything out, trying to crawl inside."

Lydia nodded, remembering her desperate attempts to break through the walls that had trapped her. "There was so much smoke, dark smoke with a terrible, unnatural stench to it."

"But was it daytime or night?—where you were, I mean?"

Lydia thought for a moment. "Yes, I remember at first seeing daylight through the windows up beyond the flames. They were large windows. And up in the ceiling, it was a very high ceiling, there were lamps that glowed a brilliant white. One by one they seemed to explode as the fire burned closer."

"What kind of building was it? It doesn't sound like a house."

"No, a factory maybe. Yes, there were a lot of shelves. It could have been a warehouse. Wait..." Lydia brought her hands to her face, covering her eyes, sickened but forcing herself to re-live the terror. "Yes. There were shelves. Rows of them, each filled with brightly colored things that began to twist with the heat as if they were somehow alive. It was as if they were trying to get away from the fire just as I was. Then, with the heat, they blackened and melted like wax."

Abigail looked to her notepad. "You shouted a name. I didn't hear it clearly."

"Yes. She had a purse, the girl did. I tossed everything out looking for any clues as to who she might be. That's when I saw a card. A name was on it. She was Jennifer Watts. The word *Boston* was on the card."

"That was where she lived?"

"Yes, maybe."

"And she died?"

Lydia just nodded.

"What's it like to die?"

Lydia met Abigail's eyes. "There is a terrible, agonizing pain. But there is an instant of time, just as the pain is most intense, that it suddenly ceases and all is quiet and dark. At that briefest of moments, the child and I seem to be standing over a deep chasm our hands together, fingers intertwined. Then, abruptly, as if repelled by an unseen force, we let go of each other and I am brought back."

"And what of the child?"

Lydia shook her head, feeling her eyes brim. "I don't know."

CHAPTER 23

When they arrived at his apartment, Ben got some coffee going and called out for a pizza while Amelia sat in his recliner and set up her laptop, ready to do a search for teenaged girls named Jennifer Watts living in the Boston area. Then, with her hands poised over the keyboard, she stopped.

"What now?" asked Ben catching her eye as he poured the coffee and brought it over.

"How do we really know we've only got five days? You're only thinking that because you're assuming that there's a consistent timeline to your grandmother's visions. What if her visions came in an entirely random order? What if Jennifer Watts actually died in a fire ten years ago? Or what if she dies ten years from now?"

Ben saw what she was getting at. He sat in a folding chair beside her and took a sip from his coffee. He could still feel the scotch fogging his head. "Well yeah, I suppose if her visions were random then we're out of luck. To have any chance of saving Jennifer we have to assume they're not random."

Amelia brushed off a curl that had sprung down over her forehead. She took a sip of coffee. "There might be a way to confirm the timeline," she said, putting her cup down and turning back to her computer, her fingers working the keyboard. "There are some crazy sites on the internet that compute the number of days between any two dates. Yes, here we are. Get the journal. Tell me the date that your grandmother had her vision of Cindy."

Ben finally saw what she was getting at. He picked up the fourth journal and flipped some pages. "All right, her vision of Cindy came on May 11, 1920." He looked over her shoulder as she entered that date, then, in the next box over, entered today's date then hit the ENTER key.

"35,150 days," she read off. "Okay, so now we..."

"We check the date of the vision just before Cindy's," interrupted Ben, flipping back a page. "That would be Mary's death. It was a drowning. All we have is her first name but, yes, we have a date for that vision: November 21, 1912."

"Yes, I remember wondering about that. She went eight years without a vision. Why do you suppose that was?"

Ben shrugged, impatient. "Maybe she had the visions but got tired of documenting them. Look, just enter the date and add 35,150 days to it."

"Right." Amelia began plunking away again, talking as she worked. "This site is a little more awkward to use when you know the number of days but don't know one of the dates. It's kind of an iterative process."

Ben had finished off his coffee by the time Amelia finally looked up.

"Okay, got it. Mary would have died on August 31, 2009. So now we just start a new search for drowning deaths occurring on that day." She worked for a time then shook her head. "I'm coming up empty. Here, let me try some different search terms."

"Check the following day," said Ben. "There might be some discrepancy with the time of death."

"September first, then." She turned back to the screen and changed the date. Immediately, the screen referenced a newspaper article. She clicked on it and froze. "My God, Ben, here it is. Mary Foster, eight years old, died from drowning. Somewhere near Jacksonville Florida. It says they're looking for her aunt and uncle who were supposed to be watching her." Amelia straightened and backed away a little.

"So Mary's death was real and so was Cindy's. And the timeline for the visions isn't random."

"I guess you're right. Jennifer Watts dies in five days. That doesn't give us much time. At least Lydia pins her down to the Boston area. I'll do an area search and see what comes up."

The pizza came and they ate as they worked.

"Think she's old enough to be on Facebook?" asked Ben, wolfing down the first slice.

"Maybe. She should have a digital footprint somewhere." Amelia ate, using a napkin on her knee as a plate, chewing as she bent closer to the screen. "The first three are a middle-aged singer, a writer of poetry who sounds like an older lady, and an eye-blackened EMO with purple hair. Looks like there're a few more pages of Jennifer Watts's, maybe more if we look into first name variations like Jen or Jena."

Ben stared over her shoulder at her screen, his attention immediately drawn to the bright blue eyes of the EMO girl sitting in sockets of jet black like she'd just looked through a pair of those old joke binoculars that left black rings around your eyes. Hers stared out big and round with bloodshot whites above a ring-pierced nose and full lips painted brilliant red. She wore her bright green hair in a Lady-Di cut. "Never cared for that look," he said. "How many Jennifer Watts's are there?"

It took her a minute to go through them. "I count 28 in all."

"So, what do we do? Just text a warning to each of them?"

Amelia leaned back in the recliner. "The ID your grandmother saw might have been a drivers' license, so maybe we can assume that our Jennifer's a teenager. That'll help whittle down the 28. But wait, Ben. Let's think this through. These things your grandmother saw, they're happening now. Why now? Why not back in her own time? Why not twenty years ago or twenty years from now?" Her face clouded into a frown. "And why these particular children? Kids die all the time and your grandmother couldn't have experienced all their deaths. She only experienced certain ones."

"You're thinking there must be something special about Mary and Cindy and Jennifer and maybe all the other deaths that allowed Grandma Lydia to pick up on them?"

Amelia shrugged. "What if there's something that all these girls have in common—I mean besides having experienced violent deaths? If we knew what that thing was, maybe we could use it to find the right Jennifer Watts."

"It's worth a shot," said Ben. He retrieved his laptop from the bedroom. "I'll get all the details I can on Mary, you do the same for

Cindy and we'll see what we come up with."

They were quiet for a while, both working their keyboards until Ben leaned closer to her putting his laptop next to hers. A whiff of her perfume suddenly brought him back to last night. Remembering her warm lips moving against his.

But Amelia's head was in the game at hand and she ran through a comparison, her eyes flitting from his computer screen then back to hers. "All right, both female, they're within maybe 6 years of being the same age, and one of them comes from a broken home, the other not. They lived a couple of hundred miles apart so they didn't attend the same school. I suppose they could have both been born at the same hospital." When Ben didn't respond right away, she looked up at him.

"Uh, yeah. Same hospital? But if they were born 6 years apart, that probably wouldn't make a difference."

"Right. Either of them have any siblings?"

They both scrolled down their respective screens both seeing none.

"Maybe they're both only-children," suggested Ben. "Maybe that's important."

"Could be. Would the police have more info on them?"

"Maybe..." said Ben, knowing that police investigations into suspicious deaths always turned up mountains of mostly useless details. He sighed and reluctantly pulled his phone and keyed in Nolan's direct number. He put the call on speaker just before Harriet answered.

"What now Detective?" she asked in her tired voice.

Ben glanced at his watch—it was nearly quitting time for her. "Sorry to bug you so late, but I need another favor." There was silence on Harriet's end so he continued. "I need you to check the details on two young girls who were recently murdered."

"And why is that, Detective."

"I think there's a connection between them."

"The same killer you mean?"

"No. I just think there has to be some connection between the victims themselves because they were both..."

Harriet's sigh cut him off. "This is about your grandmother

again, isn't it? Shit, Ben I... Well, all right. Give me their names."

Ben did so and added Jennifer Watts to the list.

"I thought you said only two murdered girls. You've got three now?"

"Sorry. I meant three." He didn't say that Jennifer was still alive nor did he say that she wouldn't be murdered but would die in a fire. No, that would be a bit too much for Harriet to process. "I really appreciate this Harriet."

"Yeah, yeah. Look, I'm only going along with this because you've somehow bamboozled the captain into believing all this crazy shit."

"Well at least we agree on that. This *is* some really crazy shit."

"So what kind of info do you want?" asked Harriet after a long pause.

"Just get me everything you can on them, birthdates, birth locations, family history, I need everything. Email it to me and I'll sort through it all."

"Okay, I'll get you what I can and I'll try to get to it in the morning. I've got lots of other things going on around here, you know." Harriet ended the call.

"She didn't sound too motivated," said Amelia.

"She's more of a morning person. It's never a good idea to try to get her to tackle anything new after four. But it'll be okay. She'll come through." Ben put down his phone hoping he was right about that. He got up and walked to the kitchen counter. He took a bite of his fourth slice of pizza as he had a new thought. "I don't think it's a warehouse. No warehouse has big windows. I think it's a store. Maybe one of those big-box warehouse stores."

"Ben, we've been through this. We don't have enough to go on to even begin to track down where the fire will be. High ceiling, bright lights, lots of shelves with bright colored things on them—that's all we know. Our only hope is to find Jennifer. And if your gal Harriet doesn't come through, we're stuck. We'll just have the 28 Jennifer's on the internet." She paused and got up from the recliner, walking over to him. "Ben, how did you manage to come up with those things about Cindy's killer? You know, his eyes and the scar on his arm?"

Ben shivered at the memory of seeing her killer's eyes so clearly—almost as if he'd been there in that Texas basement himself. "You're thinking that I can just do that for Jennifer? Look, I have no idea how that happened. I thought I was just remembering it from the journal."

"But you said you could actually see him. When we talked on the phone that day. You sounded out of breath like you'd just run a marathon or something."

"I was just feeling a little queasy."

"Because you'd found out that Cindy Brand was real and that she'd just gone missing."

"Well, I didn't believe any of it at that point." Ben ran his hand through his hair, remembering the moment. "What are you getting at? Are you thinking that I had some kind of vision like my grandmother had?"

"Ben, like Nolan said, you had a vision about a guy in a white overcoat who wasn't there. And whether you admit it or not, I think you had a vision about Cindy."

"So I have this thing my grandmother had? This Thornhill Disorder? Is that what you think?"

"Well, now that we have her journals, all the textbooks on the Thornhill Disorder will have to be re-written. Plus, we've got kids dying in ways that match the journals. We're on strange new ground here where, what we once thought was a simple and rare disorder, may be something much more." She leaned her elbows on the kitchen counter across from him. "It's a fact that everyone inherits certain traits from their ancestors and it's a fact that some traits skip generations. You having her...condition, could be a good thing if we can use it to save Jennifer."

Ben put down the pizza, suddenly nauseated. He shook his head, glancing toward the balcony. The lights of the city were starting to come on. Time seemed to be passing these days at break-neck speed. What if he did have the same thing as his grandmother? What if this was just the start of it and at some point he would begin to live through terrible deaths-visions that would ultimately drive him insane? "I'm not like my grandmother," he said.

"I'm sorry, Ben, but in some ways, I think you are. And in some ways I think that..." Her voice trailed off. She blinked a few times. "Wait, Ben. I just had a thought. But, hold on, I need some time." She hurried back to the recliner and picked up her purse. "I think I've still got your grandmothers book in here."

"What does that have to do with anything?" He was thinking that he needed another scotch—a double.

"Yes, here it is." She pulled out the faded green book, flipped to the first page, then sat down. "It may be nothing, but give me a minute." She grabbed her laptop.

As she worked, Ben cleaned up, put the leftovers in the fridge, and poured each of them a glass of wine. He placed hers beside her then waited by the counter sipping his own, staring off absently, lost in a jumble of fragmented thoughts. His wine was gone by the time Amelia came back to the counter with her notepad.

"Do you remember in Lydia's book, she talks about the actual day that changed her—the day she said normalcy left her? She pins that date down as September 29, 1886."

Ben gave a sigh, seeing now what she'd been up to. "I'll bet you added 35,150 days to that date."

"Yes, I wanted to see if maybe something important happened on that date."

"What did you come up with?"

"Well, the date was July 9, 1983 but..."

"Oh Christ, come on now," interrupted Ben, standing. "You're just messing with me. You saw my file."

"What? No, I'm not...wait, what about your file? Yes, I've seen it but..."

Ben shook his head, "July 9th 1983—that's the day I was born. Come on, you must have known."

Amelia turned pale, mouth open. She said nothing.

Ben stood there, stunned. He studied her face expecting her to break out laughing, telling him the joke was on him—but she didn't. "You're serious. Shit. You're serious. What the hell is this supposed to mean? Are you thinking that my being born caused my grandmother's insanity?"

"I...I don't know, Ben. Yes, maybe. God, Ben, I don't know." She picked up her untouched wine and drained half the glass in one gulp. "All right, all right, let's think this through. What if your birth did have some kind of effect on her? What if somehow, from all those years ago, she was somehow aware of you, and it changed her."

"You're forgetting that something else happened that day in my grandmother's time," said Ben. "It was that execution she was involved with. That's what changed her. My being born couldn't have had anything to do with it. How about we just get back to trying to find Jennifer Watts."

Amelia was silent for a while. "Ben, what if *you* are the connection between those children. And what if, through you, they're connected back to your grandmother."

Ben felt his heart pounding, rushing a flood of blood to his head. This was all just too much. "No! Shit no! I had nothing to do with those kids. They all die terrible deaths. God, how could I possibly have anything to do with that?"

"Keep calm will you? I'm just speculating here but I don't think it's a coincidence that your grandmother's departure from normalcy occurred exactly 35,150 days before your birth. I think that's important and I think it might lead us to a way to save Jennifer."

Ben tried to think logically. He walked to the balcony doors, opened them and breathed in the cool air. The lights and the sounds of the city had an almost soothing effect. He closed his eyes and let his mind drift. He half expected to be overtaken by another vision like the one he'd had of Cindy, but none came. And he was thankful for that. He opened his eyes and put his hands in his pockets. He waited a long while. "Jennifer's out there somewhere," he said. "All we have to do is find her."

Amelia, close behind him now, placed a hand on his shoulder.

At her touch, thoughts of his grandmother and of Jennifer slowly drifted away. "You kissed me last night," he said. "It was a real kiss."

"Yes, Ben. It was a real kiss. And you kissed me back."

"But you said you're living with someone."

"I lied. I don't know why, I just did. I say and do a lot of things. That doesn't mean they all make sense."

"Nothing that's happened in the last few months makes a whole lot of sense." He turned to her and saw a slight smile tug at the corners of her lips. She closed her eyes and he pulled her close. They kissed. Almost desperately, he held her tight, feeling as if she might be his last link to reality. "All these things happening. I feel like an old man slipping into...I don't know, maybe it's Alzheimer's. People with Alzheimer's have visions, don't they?"

"Ben, this is not Alzheimer's. This is nothing like that. It's nothing like anything I've seen or heard of—but we'll figure it out. Somehow, we're going to figure this out and we're going to save that girl."

Ben slowly loosened his embrace. When they parted, he saw how late it had gotten. "You missed your class," he said.

"I texted my students a while ago. I canceled class and gave them an assignment. I'm sure they're all happy to get the night off. But I've got an early class tomorrow morning and I can't miss that. I've cancelled too many classes already this semester." She walked over to the recliner put on her jacket and grabbed her things. "I'll be over early afternoon tomorrow. All right?"

"Stay for dinner."

"You're still hungry after all that pizza?"

"Have lunch with me tomorrow then."

She smiled. "Okay. Yes, I'd like that."

They agreed on a spot and, after she left, Ben eyed Stump stretched out on the floor in the corner. "Bet you need to go out, huh boy?" He grabbed the leash and Stump came over, tail wagging.

Outside, Ben and Stump walked slowly. It was a weekday night and there weren't many people on the sidewalks. The air had grown crisp. They stayed out for more than an hour.

CHAPTER 24

In the dark of his bedroom that night, Ben lay, staring up at the ceiling. From the window, the lights of the city filtered in, painting it in blotches of yellows and reds. A few days earlier he had gotten a good deal on the bed that squeaked with every shift of his weight. It sounded off now as he rolled onto his side. Had his being born really had some kind of effect on his grandmother? And was she having some kind of effect on him? Was she there in his head right now, listening to him, maybe slightly amused as he pondered these questions?

He tried to think back. Back to his childhood. Back to a memory he never knew he had. And, as if through a haze, the smells of it came first.

Freshly cured varnish and the warm steam of simmering vegetables combined with his mother's peachy perfume. It defined for him what home smelled like. He, little Ben Marshall, sat on the floor. Towering above him, Mom tended to her cooking while Dad leaned against the kitchen sink alternately trading the cigar at his lips with the brown bottle he held loosely.

They were talking, then yelling. Then Mom fell.

The adult Ben almost jumped remembering the sound of it—a thud. Her shoulder hit the floor first but it was her head hitting the floor next that had made that sound. At no more than an arms-reach from him her head crashed against the shiny linoleum and she lay there for a moment as if she was going to play with him as she sometimes did. Her eyes were open, staring back at him, tears falling from them.

Ben fought to remember what happened next but could not. He only remembered his mother's tears and then his own.

The sound of a police siren wailing in the distance brought him back to the present. Shit. Had his childhood really been that awful? He couldn't ever remember his father hitting his mother. Then another thought hit him—he couldn't remember his father smoking. Not cigars, not cigarettes, not anything. Guess he must have quit. With that thought, Ben rolled onto his other side. Ignoring the squeaks, he gathering the covers up to his chin, closed his eyes, and slept.

Over Cheerios the next morning, Ben checked each of the Jennifer Watts girls Amelia had come up with. Again, he was drawn to the picture of the EMO girl. She lived in the Boston area, was twenty-three years of age, and listed her FB status as: *Involved but always interested.* Now there was an invitation for trouble. She was a lot older than the other girls in the journal so that probably ruled her out but still, there was something about her that Ben found intriguing. He supposed he was just horny and his mind quickly shifted to Amelia.

He could still smell her perfume, feel her lips soft on his. He could even...no, he shook his head, no, damn it, that was the last thing he should be thinking about right now. He took a breath followed by two quick spoons of cereal.

According to Grandma Lydia's vision, not only Jennifer would die but maybe a dozen more would die, trapped at a locked exit trying to escape the fire. He refocused and time dragged slowly as he completed a page and a half of what he knew were useless notes on all twenty-eight of the Jennifer Watts's in the Boston area. He hoped Harriet would call or text soon with something new to go on.

At one, he left to meet Amelia for lunch.

He spotted her right away. Seated in a back booth, she was staring at her phone as he walked over. He wanted to steal a casual kiss as if they were lovers but settled for placing a hand on hers as he sat.

She gave him a smile then right away turned serious. "Did you hear from Harriet?"

"No. I took a few notes on all the internet Jennifers you found but none look promising. Most are grown women." He handed her his notes which she quickly scanned and set aside.

"You should call her—Harriet, I mean. We haven't much time. Just four days now."

After a waitress came over and took their orders, Ben pulled his phone and called Harriet but was only able to leave a voicemail. He put the phone down but, almost immediately, a call came in—it was Nolan.

The captain's voice was laced with irritation. "Damn it Ben. I heard the message you just left Harriet. What the fuck is with you? Now you're off trying to save some other poor kid? Don't you realize the trouble you and I are in?"

"What are you talking about?"

"The Austin PD wants us down there. They want to know how you knew what you knew about Cindy Brand. They're figuring you for a possible accomplice."

"Accomplice? But how would I...?"

"Look, I don't know what they're thinking and I wasn't about to tell them you got the info from your dead grandmother's journals. I'll let you try and explain that. But whatever happens, I'm not letting myself get jammed up along with you. You got that?"

Ben sighed, his eyes on Amelia as he talked. "Yeah, I got it."

"We fly out tomorrow morning. I'll meet you at the airport. And make sure you bring the fucking journals—all of them."

"What? Wait, tomorrow morning?" All Ben could think about was Jennifer Watts. How could he leave? He had to find her.

"Yes, tomorrow morning. And don't tell me you can't make it. Nothing you have going on could possibly be more important than this. I'll send a damn squad car for you and put you on the plane in cuffs if I have to."

Amelia leaned closer. "What about Harriet? Did she find anything?"

Ben swallowed. He needed to think this through. "Can you put Harriet on, Captain?"

"Shit, you just don't give up do you? Christ! All right, here she is. She can give you the flight info. But you'd better be at the airport and you better be there on time. Got that?"

"Right. I got it."

Harriet came on, exhaled heavily into the phone then gave him the flight information.

"And what about the girls I asked you about? Did you find anything?"

There was another long, heavy breath. "All right. I got a boatload of stuff on Mary Foster and Cindy Brand but not much on the Jennifer Watts girl, which is odd. If she was murdered there would have been a lot of case info in the files. You did say she was murdered, right?"

There was no point in confusing things any more than they already were. "Yeah, murdered," said Ben.

"Well, I did see that there was a Jennifer Watts who attended one of our *Meet the Force* things. And so far as I know, she's still alive though so she can't be the girl you're looking for. I've got her picture here. Funny thing, I kind of remember her—bright, outgoing. She lives just a few blocks from the station."

"She lives close to the station? Do you have her address?" Ben tensed, his eyes caught Amelia's.

"Yeah, I guess I have her address. She's on one of our mailing lists. But, like I said, she's alive and well so far as we know, so she can't be the girl you're..."

"Just give me her address."

"All right, all right. I don't know why you have to have a bug up your butt all the time. I have to look it up. I'll text it to you."

"Great, but can you please do it right away? And tell the captain that I'll see him at the airport in the morning."

"I'll let him know."

"And you'll send me the address?"

"Shit. I told you I would. Why not? I'll do anything for my favorite former fucking detective." She ended the call.

Ben put down his phone.

Amelia stared back, her eyes wide having absorbed Ben's half of the conversation. "They found her?"

"I think, maybe so," said Ben. "She's about the right age but there's no way of knowing for certain. Harriet's sending me her address. She lives close to the station and was actually there about a year ago at one of our outreach events. We'll have plenty of time right now to go to her place and warn her about the fire."

"Wait, she was at your precinct? So you might have met her?"

"Yeah, I suppose I might have. I sometimes get involved in those outreach things—crazy huh?"

She shook her head as if burying a thought. "Yeah, crazy."

Half an hour later, the address for Jennifer Watts came in from Harriet. A cab took Ben and Amelia to a respectable two-story duplex. On the way they'd rehearsed what they were going to say to Jennifer or her parents or whoever answered the door. Warning them that Jennifer would be killed in a fire four days from now wouldn't be easy. There was nothing they could think to do to make their warning believable, but they had to try.

They stepped onto the porch and rang the bell. A middle aged woman in jeans and a sweatshirt answered the door. She was holding a mop.

"Is this the Watts residence?" asked Ben.

The woman looked them both up and down. "Yes."

"And you are Mrs. Watts?"

"No, Mrs. Watts isn't in right now. I'm the cleaning lady and I'm a little busy right now."

"It's very important that we talk to Mrs. Watts, or her husband."

In a casual move, the woman locked the screen door. "And who might you be? If you really knew Mrs. Watts, you'd know that her husband died two years ago."

"No, you're right, we don't know her. But we still need to talk to her," said Amelia. She fished around in her pockets then produced a card. "Is her daughter Jennifer in?"

The woman hesitated then unlocked the door, opened it a crack and took the card.

"You're psychologists?"

"She is. I'm from the police department." Ben gave her his old card. "But I'm...we're not here on official business."

"And you don't want to say what this is about?"

Ben could see she was really curious now. "It's about Jennifer."

"Is she in?" asked Amelia again.

With a distressed look, the woman shook her head. "She's in trouble again, isn't she? Look, they're both out of town right now, back tonight. If you want to write out a note, I'll make sure Mrs. Watts gets it."

"Just have Mrs. Watts contact me at that number," said Amelia. "It's very important. I'd like to stop in tomorrow to talk with her."

"All right then, I'll tell her." The woman gave them a last glance up and down then closed the inside door.

They stepped off the porch.

"I'll be in Austin tomorrow," said Ben. "Whatever happens here will be up to you. What if she doesn't call?"

"Don't worry, I'll handle things here," said Amelia. "Whatever it takes, I'll make sure that Jennifer is safe. I think it's important that you go to Austin and learn all you can about Cindy and her killer."

Ben nodded, not quite convinced. He didn't like leaving things entirely on Amelia's shoulders. But hell, maybe she, by herself, would have a better chance of convincing Jennifer's mom of the danger her daughter was in. Then, another thought hit him. "What if she's not the one?"

"Look, I've got your notes on all the other Jennifer's. I'll go through them to cover all the bases but, really Ben, I think this Jennifer is the one we're looking for."

"Because I might have met her once. Is that what you're thinking?"

She hesitated only for a moment. "Yes, that's what I'm thinking."

They walked back to the main road and flagged down separate cabs—Amelia heading to BU, Ben back to his apartment to pack.

The next morning, in suit and tie, Ben met Nolan at the gate as the plane was just boarding. The captain was similarly dressed and, like Ben, carried a black briefcase.

"You bring the journals?" asked Nolan.

"Yeah. Who're we meeting with?"

"Lieutenant Waldon will be there along with her precinct captain. There'll be a few others who've been tacked onto the Brand case."

"Have they found the guy?"

"No, he's still out there. But they say they're closing in on him. They've brought in a couple of FBI agents from the Austin office. They'll be the ones who'll be grilling you. From what I understand, we'll be going out to the crime scene first. It's out past the airport."

Ben's stomach turned at the thought of that dark basement, and the pillar with blood on the floor around it. Guilt at having not been able to save little Cindy rose up inside him again.

They spoke only a little on the plane which touched down on time in Austin at 11am local time.

Out in the terminal Ben recognized Lieutenant Waldon. She stood twenty paces away, flanked by a couple of crew-cut suits. She wore a black business outfit, her dirty blonde hair falling to her shoulders. He remembered her from the video feed back in Boston. She was taller than he'd imagined.

As if it were the start of a football game, they introduced themselves and shook hands. The only thing missing was the coin toss. Agent Mike Bradly and Agent Chuck Harris were the FBI guys, but it was Lieutenant Sarah Waldon who immediately took charge. "This way," she said striding off under the *Ground Transportation* arrow. Moments later they got into a waiting black Ford Flex fitted with blue and red flashers on the roof and a steel ram over the grill. Ben and Nolan took the third-row seat and they pulled out.

From the front seat, Waldon twisted around. "The suspect's name is Thomas Francis Jamison. His wrap sheet's a mile long. Robberies, drugs, and other petty stuff, no offenses like this though. We think he picked Cindy up on her way to school. She'd been missing for four days and we had no leads until we heard from you."

With almost a thud, her eyes fell on Ben.

"Your tip eventually led us to Jamison's place south of here, out in the boonies. You know how that turned out." She took a breath and Ben realized that she probably felt as guilty as he did about not being able to save the girl.

"Based on time of death," she continued, "we figure we were 30 to 90 minutes late. We got things cordoned off but either Jamison was already gone or else he somehow managed to slip through. Lots of open land out there. We believe that he worked his way out to the main road where he hijacked a vehicle—late model Chevy sedan, dark blue. We have the plates but he might have already dumped that car for another. We also assume he's armed."

Questions flew back and forth for the next few miles then everyone grew silent, watching the desert brush roll by—blue sky, bright sun, hot. There wasn't much AC drifting back to the back seat.

Finally they took a left onto a road that didn't even look like a road. The car bounced. With a glance over his shoulder, Ben watched the dust rise up in a yellow cloud that quickly caked the rear window. After cresting a small rise, he saw a wood frame house through the windshield. It looked ready to fall over if a decent wind came along. He recognized it as the dump from the video feed. Yellow crime-tape was draped all around. The car slowed. Ben saw a squad car parked around back.

Waldon turned to them again. "All right guys, this is still an active crime scene, evidence procedures are in place. You know the drill." She tossed back some white shoe covers. "Put them on before you enter and after you've kicked off the dust. We don't want you tracking anything inside. The car stopped and they got out. The heat hit Ben like a blast furnace.

Fifteen strides got them around to the back door. "If you want to touch or pick up anything," said Waldon, "let me know, I'll give you some gloves. If you discover anything that might be important, let me know immediately. I've got some evidence bags."

They all slipped on their shoe covers and trooped inside. Last one in, Ben let the rickety screen door slam behind him. Then, he stopped.

He stood in a kitchen. An ancient stove and fridge sat against the wall to his right. A still-dirty pot tilted in a rust-stained sink beneath a window where flies buzzed in and out through a hole in the screen. An open door to his left revealed a walk-in pantry, its shelves stocked with sacks and large cans. Survivalist, thought Ben. Then he saw a few bags of dog food. "What about the dog?" he shouted up to Waldon.

"Jamison shot it. We found the body outside. He was in a hurry. Guess he didn't want it slowing him down."

"How'd Jamison know you were coming for him?"

"We don't know. That's something we'll want to talk to you about."

Ben almost gagged. "Shit. You think I tipped him off?"

"We don't know. We're not ruling anything out."

"What did Jamison do for money?" asked Nolan quickly with a glance at Ben that told him he needed to tread lightly here.

"He was a cook," said Waldon as she walked. "Not a bad one either, from what we've been able to learn. There's a restaurant about twenty miles further south of here. That's where he worked for the past five years. His boss was shocked when we told him what he'd done."

Ben followed the others, continuing on through a hallway passing open doors to bedrooms on either side. In one, a dresser sat against the wall opposite a double bed with rumpled bedding. On the far wall a dented air conditioner, still running, was mounted in the window. Beside it hung a mirror in which his own reflection looked back at him, strange and out of place with his suit and tie in a dump like this.

Ben turned to the other bedroom and managed only a glance at a cot positioned in the center of the room with a bare, stripped mattress. He flinched, knowing without asking that this must have been where Cindy Brand had been assaulted more than once.

Next came a bathroom that looked surprisingly orderly and clean, then the living room where the group had gathered.

"Captain Gregory and my partner Lieutenant Fisher are already in the basement," said Waldon. "Any questions or comments before we go down?"

There were none.

Through a door opposite the bathroom, she led the way down the dark stairs. The wood creaked under the weight. The coppery-iron smell of blood tinged the stifling air that got only a little cooler as they descended. Ben imagined how much more intense this must have been for the cop who discovered the body. Or, worse yet, for Cindy herself who must have known that this basement would be her tomb. He stepped off the last step onto the soft, sandy earth, the basement lit by a single bulb that hung from a wire near the wall. There were no windows.

"I am Precinct Captain Gregory," said a tall, gray-haired man in full police uniform standing near the center of the basement. Cap in hand, he stood beside the metal post in the center of the room. Ben's stomach twisted at the sight of it.

Gregory wasted no time, he pointed to Ben. "You're Detective Marshall, is that right?"

"Yes, sir."

He motioned him closer.

Lieutenant Waldon who'd been standing in front of Ben, stepped aside to let him pass.

Despite the heat, Ben shivered as he moved forward. He stopped at the post and turned to Gregory who flicked on a flashlight and pointed it up toward the top of the post. Almost involuntarily, Ben's eyes followed the beam up to where it illuminated the initials that were carved into the floorboards. He spoke in a deep voice, strained and tired. "Captain Nolan filled me in on your great, great grandmother's journals and I know about these visions she supposedly had. I know that she'd written about those initials up there and I know about the markings on Jamison's arm that only you knew about."

Captain Gregory lowered the flashlight and turned to face Ben directly. "I know that this world is full of things that I can't explain or begin to understand. We have a dead child, Detective. This is where it happened, only a few days ago. Reach out now. Touch this post. And on the sacred life of that poor, innocent child, tell us what more you know."

A dull hollow feeling overtook Ben. He shook his head then opened his mouth but had no words. What could he say? He knew nothing more.

But the old cop's gaze was insistent. Demanding, yet patient. "Put your hand on the post, Detective."

Suppressing another shiver, Ben placed the palm of his left hand on the rough, round surface. It was cool to the touch and seemed to suck the breath from him. His mouth turned dry. What was Captain Gregory expecting? Did he think that maybe he'd have a sudden revelation about the killer? That maybe he'd somehow know where Jamison was? But Ben knew nothing more. He just shook his head. After only a moment, he pulled his hand away. "I'm sorry Captain. I don't know any more than I've already told you. I have no idea how I knew about the arm. I thought I'd read it in my grandmother's journal but you're right, there was no mention of it there. I can't explain any of this."

As if not accepting this answer, Gregory just stared back, waiting.

Ben felt his nausea build and, even as he was repulsed by it, he put his hand on the post again for support. He almost felt like wrapping his arms around it as he would have to embrace little Cindy if she'd been there, still alive. His voice came out as a hoarse whisper. "I swear, Captain, on the life of that poor girl, I don't know anything more. I wish I did."

Gregory held Ben's eyes for a moment longer then flicked off the flashlight. "All right, Detective. I believe you. It might take a bit longer to convince the FBI, but yes, I believe you. Waldon, do you have anything more?"

"No, sir."

"Harris, Bradly, you can ask your questions back at the station. Right now, I need some air. Let's get out of here."

Ben was the last to leave and, alone, still near the post, he shuddered. He remembered his own vision. The black, blazing eyes of Cindy's killer, the sweat on the arm of the hand that held the knife, the markings that rippled with the working of the muscles beneath the skin as he struck and sliced. But no. He remembered nothing else. He headed up the stairs and out the front door, wincing as his eyes adjusted to the bright sun. It was as if he were leaving a darkened theater after a matinee horror movie. But this horror was real.

The cars were starting up.

Waldon came up beside him. "You okay?" she asked in a tone without sympathy.

"Yeah. I'm fine."

She fixed her eyes on his for only a moment then headed for the Flex where she slid into the shotgun seat.

Ben retook his seat in the back of the car beside Nolan. He closed his eyes and didn't say a word until an hour later when his phone went off. He didn't recognize the number. "This is Marshall," he said, quietly.

"Hey, Ben. How're you doing buddy? This is Clay from M & G."

Ben's mind was slow to adjust. It felt like a year ago that he'd met with the guy. Oh that's right, he needed a job. But that didn't seem at all important now. He saw through the window that traffic was picking up. They were on the freeway just getting back into the city. He cleared his throat. "Hi Clay. What's up?" he asked, keeping his voice low.

"You in the middle of something?"

"Yeah. A little bit. But it's all right. What's up?"

"What's up is, we want to make you an offer, buddy. When can you come in? Monday work for you? We can do it over lunch."

Ben struggled to remember what day of the week it was. "Yeah, that's good. Thanks. Monday'll be fine."

"Great. See you then," said Clay, ending the call.

"Got yourself a new job?" asked Nolan.

"Yeah, looks that way."

"Good for you."

Ben sensed that Nolan still had some regrets over firing him and that now he might be feeling a little better knowing that he might be landing on his feet. Hell, he himself should be feeling better about things now too. At least he might not have to worry about his next rent payment.

But Ben didn't feel better at all.

Once at police HQ Ben hit the john along with Nolan.

"I thought you hadn't told them about the journals," said Ben from the next urinal over.

"They called me late yesterday and pressed me on it. I had to tell them. I probably should have given you a heads-up on that."

"Captain Gregory at least seems to be taking the journals seriously."

"Hard to say. I know the guy. He can be a stone-faced prick, then pretend to be your best friend, then turn on you like a snake all in the span of sixty seconds. He's got good interrogation skills, I've got to give him that. But it's not him you have to worry about. You need to worry about those two FBI guys."

"They don't talk much," said Ben washing up.

"No. But you can bet they were listening to every word you and I said today."

After getting some food in the cafeteria, Ben was ushered alone into an interrogation room where Harris and Bradly sat waiting at a wooden table. Ben took the lone empty chair and stared back at them. They had their sunglasses off but still had their ties tight against the collars of their white shirts. Square jaws and clean shaven their only distinguishing feature were their ties—one red, one black. Ben figured them to be just like all the other pompous, FBI dip-shits he'd ever met.

"Just to be clear," said red-tie, "I'm Agent Bradly, this is Agent Harris. Unless there are complications, we won't keep you long."

Right, step one—give the subject a little hope. Ben wondered just what complications they might be expecting but decided not to ask.

"Have you ever been to Austin, Detective?" asked Harris.

"Yes. A few years back. It was an extradition thing. It was only for a couple of days."

"Did you get out much, hit any night spots, take in any of the sights?"

Step two—a little small talk. Get your victim to think you really care about them. He hadn't been planning to be belligerent but, Jesus, did they really think they had to warm up to him before hitting him with a fastball? "Maybe a few bars, not much else," replied Ben.

"Have you ever met Cindy Brand?"

"No. I only know of her from my grandmother's journals."

Neither of them reacted. All right, here comes the fastball thought Ben.

Bradly flipped over a page in the yellow notepad in front of him. It was covered with writing in blue-ink. "You were in Austin on October 9, 2010. You stayed for three days in room 583 at the Holiday Inn downtown. For two of those three days, Colleen Brand and her daughter Cindy took part in a custody hearing. It was held in courtroom number 4 in the Municipal Courthouse downtown. The hearing on your extradition case was held in that same courtroom right after theirs." Bradly looked up from the page.

"That's quite a coincidence, wouldn't you say, Detective?" asked Harris.

Ben tried to relax but felt his body stiffen just like he would have expected of a perp who was guilty as sin. These guys couldn't think that he had anything to do with Cindy Brand's murder, could they? "Well, yeah, quite a coincidence. I didn't know anything about them though. Not back then."

"And you haven't had any contact with the Brands since?"

"Look, I didn't really have any contact with them then or since. It sounds like circumstances brought us to that same courthouse at the same date and time without our knowing it. Or at least without me knowing it."

Harris produced a photo and slid it in front of Ben. "This is how she looked back then. Does she look familiar?"

It was a black and white of a smiling little girl holding a balloon. She was missing a front baby tooth. Her smile looked forced in the same way that Ben remembered some of his early birthday smiles being. 'Smile for the camera, Ben,' his mother would say and he'd pretend he was happy. That looked like what

Cindy was doing in the photo—just pretending.

Ben shook his head. “No. I don’t think I’ve ever seen her.”

“Have you ever seen this man?” He held up the photo of a guy leaning against a big shiny Harley. He wore black leathers. A cigarette dangled from his grinning mouth.

Ben recognized him immediately. “It’s Jamison.”

“And how do you know him?”

“I don’t know him. I just saw him in...”

“Yeah, in a vision, just like your grandma did a hundred years ago.”

Ben felt his blood pressure spike but he knew he had to keep his shit together. “Yes, that’s right. I had a vision. Look, I’ve already told you that I can’t explain any of this. It’s all nuts. But I’m telling the truth and you can believe me or not, that’s up to you. But I...” Ben’s voice trailed off. He felt his skin go prickly. He glanced down at his briefcase. Inside it were the journals, all four of them. He sat back in his chair. “You don’t know about the others, do you? No, of course you don’t. I didn’t tell you and neither did Nolan.”

“Tell us what?”

Ben retrieved the journals. He placed them on the table, found the fourth one and opened it to the Cindy Brand page. He turned one more page then slid it across the table. “There are other kids besides Cindy who have died and two more who *will* die. A girl in Boston named Jennifer Watts is next, but I think we’ve already found a way to save her.”

Ben sat back in his chair and, as Harris and Bradly read, he thought about Amelia, hoping to God that she’d been able to warn Jennifer or her mother. He decided to give her a call as soon as frick and frack were done with him.

CHAPTER 25

Ten the next morning was the earliest flight they could get out of Austin. Ben sat next to Nolan, tapping a finger on the armrest between them. Four rows behind them sat Harris and Bradly, still black-tie, red-tie but Ben had stopped trying to remember which was which.

He'd called Amelia last night from his hotel. Everything looked set. She'd been able to meet with Mrs. Watts and with Jennifer herself. Neither of them had been convinced of the danger but she did get a promise from them that Jennifer, instead of stopping by a shopping mall as she normally did, would just come straight home after school. To be sure, Amelia planned to tail her home from school but didn't tell them that.

Amelia had given Ben the name of the mall and, just in case, Ben had twisted Nolan's arm into giving the mall management and the local cops a heads up that there might be trouble there: trouble as in *a fire*.

So, it looked like all bases were covered. Still, Ben's finger thumped on the armrest. Just like in the dozens of other police operations he'd been a part of, he asked himself now, 'What could possibly go wrong?" The answer was the same as always: *Plenty*.

They landed on time at 1pm Boston time and were picked up curbside by a squad car.

Nolan sat in front leaving Ben stuck in back mashed between Harris and Bradly.

"Not too roomy back there I'm afraid. Sorry about that," said the driver with a grin as he pulled out. He glanced at Nolan. "Station house right?"

"Yeah," said Nolan who was on the phone.

"Nothing going on at the mall yet," said Nolan when he'd

ended his call.

"And no other fires anywhere else close by?" asked Ben.

"Nothing so far."

Ben felt a sinking feeling take hold. What if they had the date wrong? What if they had the wrong Jennifer Watts? It didn't help him being buried left and right by the broad shouldered FBI pricks.

Then Ben's phone went off. He shoved himself forward and twisted to pull it from his jacket pocket. It was Amelia.

She was breathless. "Ben, is that you Ben? Thank God I got you. We've got a problem. You're back here in Boston right? Tell me you are."

"Yeah, we're just on our way to..."

"Shit Ben. There was a school field trip today. I had no idea. A bus left an hour ago with Jenny and most of her classmates. I just found out about it."

Over the phone Ben heard the screech of tires.

"Damn it all, I'm catching all the reds. Shit Ben, if she dies..." Her voice shook.

Ben tightened his grip on the phone. "Where's the field trip Amelia? Where are they going?"

"It's a factory, Ben. A plastics plant. They do injection molding. The field trip's part of a career day thing. Here, I've got an address."

Ben reached forward and banged on the screen that separated front from back. "We've got a new destination, driver and we've got to hurry. All right Amelia, give it to me."

She gave him the address of *Custom Engineering and Fabricators* that Ben repeated for Nolan who was entering it into GPS.

"Shit," said the driver, "that's way back the other way." He jerked the wheel. The car swerved as he took a quick left, then a right. "You said we're in a hurry, right?" Not waiting for an answer, the driver flipped on his sirens and flashers then floored it. The car accelerated. He glanced at Nolan. "Why are we going there again?"

"ETA, twenty-two minutes," shouted Nolan to the driver,

ignoring his question. "Get us there in ten. You got that?"

Ben turned his attention back to the phone. "All right, we're on it, Amelia. We're not too far out and Nolan's calling the fire department. Where are you?"

"Almost there, Ben. I should see it soon. Oh Christ, Ben. I see smoke up ahead. Shit! Shit! Shit! That poor girl. And others too. I don't know how many. Oh, Jesus. Jesus Christ, Ben I..."

"All right, all right. Just don't get into an accident. And, whatever you do, don't go into that building. Do you hear me? We're coming at it from the opposite direction. We'll be there right away."

"Yeah, right. Okay. Good, okay."

Ben could almost hear her tears falling. "We're going to get her, Amelia. And the others too. They're all going to be okay. I'm hanging up now. You just focus on your driving and get there in one piece. I'll see you in a few minutes."

"Yes. Yeah, good. Just hurry."

"We will." Ben ended the call.

The siren wailed. The car weaved through traffic, still picking up speed.

In the front seat Nolan held his phone, eyes fixed on the GPS screen. He screamed at the driver: "ETA fifteen minutes. That's not good enough. Move this fucking car, damn it!"

But Ben knew the driver was doing all he could.

"Who was that on the phone with you?" one of the FBI guys asked Ben as casually as he would have if they'd been out on a Sunday drive.

"A psychologist from BU. She's been helping me make sense of the journals."

"We'll want to talk with her."

Shit. Not if I can help it, Ben thought but didn't say.

Ten long minutes passed.

Nolan pointed through the windshield. "There's the smoke."

It floated dark on the horizon, darkening further as they got closer. The next five miles seem to take an eternity. They took an exit and, drawing closer, Ben could see how huge the black cloud was as it curled and billowed into the blue sky. Beneath it was a modern brick structure fronted by large reflective windows that spanned its length. Tongues of orange flame flicked up from the roof. Parked in front of the building was a school bus. A few people were milling around, some with blackened faces, some bent over with their hands on their knees. Two lay flat on the grass just off the parking lot.

Their squad car took a sharp left and raced into the parking lot. It pulled up with a screech.

"Shit, we're the first ones here," shouted Ben. "Where the fuck's the Goddamn fire department?"

The FBI guys were already out of the car racing for the building. Ben got out and ran over to a car parked askew beside the bus. Its driver side door was open, its key alarm going off. Ben spotted a thick book sitting on the front passenger seat. He didn't need to look closer to guess that this was Amelia's rental car. "Shit." He turned to the building where thickening smoke streamed from an open side door. Harris and Bradly were already there. One of them had a handkerchief over his mouth. He went in. Jesus, good for him, thought Ben.

Ben stripped off his jacket and balled it up, running for the door.

The other FBI guy held up his hand. "Don't do it. You'll never make it without a respirator. Bradly's already inside checking things out."

"I'm going in," shouted Ben just as Bradly staggered out through the door, bent over, wrenching out the foul air.

Ben heard sirens in the distance. It had to be fire trucks on their way. About time.

"There's still some clear air in there," said Bradly managing to cough out the words. "An aisle way off to the right. Don't go left—that's what nearly got me."

"How far to the right did you get?" asked Ben.

"Maybe twenty feet."

"Anybody there?"

Bradly shook his head, overcome by more coughing. "I heard screams. But didn't see anybody. Just heard them, but shit, I'd taken in too much smoke. Barely made it back. Shit, the screaming..."

Ben didn't wait for him to say more. He took a deep breath, held his jacket to his face and ran inside.

Everything was black. Ben kept running until, just as Bradly said, the air cleared a little. His eyes burned but he could see maybe ten feet down an aisle way marked by black and yellow striped floor-tape. Big machines towered on either side. Then he heard the screams.

They pierced shrill through the deep roar of the fire creating a fearsome and terrible chorus.

Ben drew in a half breath then took off down the aisle. The screams grew louder and the smoke thinned a little but not enough to see clearly. Then, just ahead, a shadow appeared on the floor—the body of a man on all fours. With his free hand, Ben grabbed his arm. "Get up. Get the fuck up."

The man struggled to stand just as Harris got there. "Take him out," Ben shouted running further up the aisle. He took another smoke-filled breath through his jacket. Shit, what the fuck do I think I'm doing? By the time I get to Amelia and those kids, I won't have the strength to help them. I'll be trapped, just like them. He slowed, then saw rows of shelves. The hairs on the back of his neck stood on end. His mind registered that here, on these shelves, were the brightly colored objects, plastic parts warping and twisting with the heat. Christ, it was just as Lydia had seen them.

He staggered on until finally he saw the back wall of the building. The screams overwhelmed even the roar of the blaze. Smoke burned his eyes. Then he saw the kids, huddled just beyond the shelves almost in a pile against the back wall. Ben tried to yell to them but choked instead. He raised his hand. There, someone saw him. There was movement, a face. He took another step closer but couldn't quite get one foot in front of the other. He fell hard onto the cement floor, stunned for a moment. But there was less smoke here, just off the floor.

He took another breath of gritty air and got up on all fours about to crawl forward. But his legs wouldn't move. Shit, I can't do this. I can't...I can't reach them. They're too far. He tried to yell: "Get up. Get up. There's a way out. This way. This way..." But his words faded, lost in the roar of the fire. He had no breath left.

A loud popping sound came from overhead. Sparks and shards of glass flew down from the bright halogens as one by one they exploded. Except for the raging orange of the flames, the place went dark.

Ben's arms gave out. His face hit the floor. He might have been out for a few seconds but he regained consciousness and tried to move again. His entire body felt as if it were glued solid to the floor. His lungs wouldn't work. Shit. Jennifer Watts would die today just as Grandma Lydia said. And he was going to die with her.

And Amelia would die too. Oh God, where was she? He tried to scream but couldn't. He had no breath left. The flames were louder now, roaring, coming for him. He couldn't move. He couldn't think. Then everything went blank.

Ben felt a coarse canvas glove at the back of his head, lowering it down onto the...grass? Yes, grass. He was laying on grass. He could feel it through his fingers. And there were sounds. Lots of sounds that he couldn't make sense of. He was alive. He was pretty sure about that, but not much else. He tried to open his eyes but couldn't.

His throat burned raw and gritty with every breath but the air gave sweet refreshment to his lungs.

He winced as a calloused hand slapped his cheek, once and then again.

"Ben, you there Ben? You're all right. Can you hear me?"

He recognized the gruff tenor voice. "Captain?"

"Yeah. Can you open your eyes? Guess not. Your lids are glued down with soot."

"Where's Amelia? Did she get out?" He raised his head as much as he could.

"Yeah, she's out. I saw her being loaded into an ambulance. She's on her way to Boston General but I hear it's just minor stuff.

She should be all right. I'm not sure about the Jennifer girl but we got a lot of the kids out."

Ben sank back with blessed relief about Amelia. "Oh, thank God." Then the rest of what Nolan had said registered. "Only some kids? Some didn't make it?"

"We're still working on a head-count. Just rest easy. It's over. You swallowed a lot of smoke. Shit, you're nearly as black as me."

Ben swallowed hard, grit caking the walls of his mouth and throat. He tried to sit up.

"Here's some water. Don't drink, just swish and spit for now." Nolan held a paper cup to his lips then eased him back down.

Ben coughed, his throat feeling a little better.

"Here, they gave me a wet towel for you. Not used to playing nursemaid to one of my detectives," he grumbled as he wiped Ben's face and eyes.

Ben's hearing was no longer muffled: motors running, men shouting, screaming, high pressure hoses hissing, and behind it all the cracking and whooshing of the fire still going. He forced his eyes open. The first thing he saw was Nolan's big face blocking out the sun. The water had helped. He swallowed more easily now, his strength slowly returning. With Nolan's help, he sat up.

Ben stared at the building only fifty feet away. The front of it had collapsed, smoldering under the spray of a fire hose. Orange flames still licked up through the roof of the rest of the building where two more hoses were in play. Above it all, black smoke billowed, towering like a vengeful dragon.

"You, Bradly, and Harris saved a lot of kids today."

Ben brought his knees up and rested his arms on them. He shook his head. "We fucked up, Captain. We knew there was going to be a fire, we just didn't know where."

Nolan stood. Ben could see the soot on the captain's face, his uniform was torn. He realized that he must have run into the fire too.

"Don't beat yourself up over this," said Nolan. "For one thing, you've got a few more believers on your side. Me for one. Bradly and Harris for two more."

Ben squinted up at him. “Believers in what?”

“Believers in those journals of yours. Between me and the FBI we’re going to get our best people on them. I don’t care if anyone thinks we’re crazy. We’re going to figure things out, we’re going to get out there, and we’re going to save some kids.”

“Shit, Captain, there’s only one more to save. The next death in the journals is the last one.” Ben shook his head. “All those other kids who’ve died and we’re just now figuring things out.”

“Then we’ll just do our damnedest to save that last one.”

A fireman came by with a water jug and offered it to them both. Nolan was able to swallow his, but Ben just did the swish ‘n spit routine twice again.

“And another thing,” said Nolan. “I’ve decided to reinstate you. Higher pay grade. And you’ll have your carry permit back. You’ll be the lead guy on that last kid in the journals and, after that, who knows. You’ve got your career back, buddy. You up for it?”

Ben allowed himself a tight smile. This is what he wanted, right? Hell yes, it’s what he wanted. He felt relief, but more than that, he felt vindication. Breathing almost normally now he got to his feet without help.

“You need to be nicer to Harriet, though,” said Nolan. Think you can manage that?”

“I’ll give it a shot.”

His head still clearing, Ben again looked out on the scene in front of him. Fire engines, with their lights blinking, were angled close to the ruins of the building. Firemen directed their hoses, the spray deepening the puddles in the parking lot. On the hill behind, a long line of slow-moving cars jammed the ramp off the freeway. Most were driven by frantic parents trying to get to their kids, Ben figured. Off to the right, on a grassy rise bordering the parking lot, a group of teenagers were gathered, some drinking, some crying, some bent over puking their guts out, some just lying there. He was too far away to see their faces well.

Ben took a step in that direction. “Come on. I need to find Jennifer Watts.”

CHAPTER 26

As soon as Ben spotted the girl, he knew it was Jennifer. Yes, he remembered her now from the outreach event at the stationhouse. She'd been full of energy that day, sharp-eyed and full of questions. He remembered her smile and he remembered a little mole just below her left ear. Strange that he was able to picture her so vividly. As he drew closer, he saw that she wasn't moving. Then, yes, he saw her chest rising and falling slightly and ever so slowly. She was alive. And her eyes were open wide, looking up.

Black soot streaked her skin and clothing. With one shoe off, she wore tight jeans and a peach colored top torn at both shoulders. Ben moved to her other side. Yes, there was the mole. Ben knelt beside her and might have reached for her were it not for an EMT who cautioned him not to disturb her medicated burns. "Jennifer? Jennifer? Can you hear me?" Ben asked.

She blinked once but Ben couldn't tell if it was a reaction to his voice or if it was just a random thing.

"She's been like that since we got her out. You know her?" asked the EMT.

"She's Jennifer Watts. No, I don't know her but I met her once and recognize her."

"She's got a bad burn on her right leg but that should heal up okay. She may have other burns too. That's why we need to be careful with her.

Ben glanced at her leg, the one without the shoe, and saw that the rescue team had cut her jeans up to her thigh. Over her calf some white salve had been applied to her red-blistered skin.

"She'll get the next bus out."

"Bus?"

"Ambulance. We need to get some fluids into her. We can't do that too well here."

Ben slowly waved his hand a few inches over Jennifer's face. Her eyes remained wide, staring up. There was no reaction.

The EMT shook his head. "Like I said, she's been like that for a while. Probably nothing to worry about though. It was pretty traumatic. These kids were pretty lucky though. Things could have been a lot worse."

"Any fatalities that you know of?" asked Nolan.

"Five, I think, two of them were kids. Wrong place wrong time, you know. There were a couple of criticals. They were the first to be bussed out. No word on them."

A sudden feeling of dread overtook Ben. "Criticals? Was one of them a woman?"

"Yeah, burns to her back. Poor lady. Might have been one of the teachers. They say she was trying to shield these kids from the fire."

Ben was stunned. He got to his feet, glaring at Nolan. "Shit. That has to be Amelia. I thought you said she was okay."

"That's what they told me, Ben. Now don't go off..."

If Nolan said anything else, Ben didn't hear it. His eyes darted. He spotted their squad car. He ran to it and saw that the keys were still in the ignition. With a screech of rubber he pulled out of the lot heading for the interstate, siren blaring.

Four hours later Ben put down the magazine he'd been reading.

He'd been told three hours earlier that Amelia Silvers had been admitted to the burn unit with second and third degree burns on her back. "That's all we know right now," the receptionist had said. "Are you family?"

"No. A friend. A good friend. I'm a detective with the Boston PD."

The woman had nodded sympathetically. "You look like you were at the fire too."

"How soon will you know anything? How soon can I see her?"

"She's receiving treatment now, Detective, that's all I know. Just have a seat. I'll call up there every 30 minutes and will give you a shout as soon as I hear anything. As for visiting, the family will have priority. But if she asks for you, and if it's all right with the family, I'm sure we can get you in"

"Her family is here?"

"Not yet, but they've been notified. I think they're driving in from out of state. Hard to say how long that might take."

Ben had simply nodded then took a seat facing the desk, closing his eyes that still burned from the fire. Again and again his mind replayed the scene inside the burning building, the screams, the huddle of people hopelessly jammed against the back wall. One of them had to have been Amelia and one had to have been Jennifer but, to Ben, it had all been a blur, seen through the dense smoke that had driven him to his knees nearly suffocating him. He leaned forward, hands cupped over his knees, eyes open, staring down at the waiting room floor.

Ambulances discharged their loads through another entrance so Ben had no idea if or when other burn victims were coming in. The ER waiting room was crowded. Among the gaggle of people waiting to be admitted and others waiting for word about loved ones, he spotted a few who, he imagined, might be the parents of kids hurt in the fire. He wondered if Jennifer's mom was among them but then remembered that Jennifer's burns were minor, yeah, she was one of the lucky ones. Her mom was probably with her now, thanking God that her daughter was alive and probably wondering how it was that, only a day ago, someone had contacted her warning her that there was going to be a fire.

Now, after putting down the last in the stack of magazines beside him, Ben saw an older man and woman come in and stop at the front desk. They were talking to the same woman Ben had and he saw her gesture in his direction. The couple turned to him for a moment. Ben met their eyes. They looked tired. The woman's eyes were red. Ben stood as they came over.

The man spoke. "We're Jason and Colleen Silvers, Dr. Silvers...Amelia's mom and dad. I guess you know our daughter?"

"Yes, I do," said Ben knowing it wasn't out of rudeness that they didn't shake hands. ER's were not places for formalities. He guided them to a spot with three empty chairs then explained who he was and how he knew Amelia. The two of them listened attentively but every now and then the mom threw nervous glances back to the ER desk. The dad was more focused.

"How is it," he asked, "that Amelia happened to be there at the fire? Do you know anything about that, Detective?"

Ben improvised. "She did a lot of volunteer work in the community. I think she was there helping out with the students who were touring the place."

The dad had just nodded, turning to his wife. "She's always been like that, hasn't she, dear?"

Ben didn't tell them about the journals.

Finally, the ER receptionist came over. They all stood. She spoke to the parents. "Your daughter is doing as well as can be expected. They've been taking her through the burn protocol and that's why this has taken so long."

"Is she in pain?" asked her mother, eyes brimming.

"Can we see her now?" asked Dad.

"Yes, we can allow the family to see her now. Just the two of you for now. She's conscious and is able to talk. We've got someone here who'll take you up." She extended a hand in the direction of an orderly who then guided them through a set of double doors.

"They'll need some time with her alone," the receptionist explained to Ben. "I told them that you'd like to visit too but that'll be up to them."

"She *is* in pain, isn't she?"

"I'm not a doctor, but yes, burns are the worst."

Ben just nodded and sat back down.

Nolan arrived a little later but didn't sit. "You stole one of my squad cars, Detective. Care to give me back the keys?"

Ben pulled them from his pocket and tossed them over. "It's parked over by..."

"We'll find it." He put his hands on his hips. "You look like shit. Go home, Detective. Come back tomorrow."

Ben shrugged. He was beat. Every breath and every swallow was tainted with soot. He needed to brush his teeth, he needed some food and he needed a shower. He glanced at his watch, then realized he must have lost it. "Her folks are with her."

"That's good, Ben. Look, you've done all you can here. You can come by in the morning."

Reluctantly, Ben stood.

"I've got a squad car outside waiting to take you back to your place. You can take your luggage from the other car but the journals stay with me. Harris and Bradly have already checked in with their people. They're going to be sticking around here for a while and they want to start going over the journals ASAP. They'll be working the next case with you."

"Yeah, I suppose that makes sense," said Ben, nodding. Sharing a case with the FBI would normally have incensed him but, Harris and Bradly had both shown their metal today. They were okay in his book.

On the way out, Ben told the ER receptionist that he'd be back in the morning.

"Give me your number. I'll call you when I know something."

"That all right with her folks?"

She gave him a little smile. "I'd heard that you were one of the men who saved their daughter's life and I think they might have gotten wind of that too. So yeah, I'd say it's okay with them."

As soon as Ben inserted his key in the door to his apartment, he heard Stump wining and scratching from the other side. He opened it and dropped to a knee as Stump jumped into his arms. "Hey, boy. How ya been? Yeah, I was bad leaving you like that, wasn't I? But I'm back now."

Ben had paid extra for the doorman to walk him and feed him while he was gone but he could tell that Stump was pissed at him leaving. "Yeah, I'm back now, boy. I'm back." He gave him a couple of treats, then hit the bathroom, doubling up on tooth paste and mouthwash before taking a long hot shower. He made himself a sandwich and ate it while taking Stump out for a short walk.

Getting back, Ben was bone tired and should have slept well that night, but didn't. His head was clouded first by the strange stare he'd seen from Jennifer Watts as she lay there on the grass and then by thoughts of Amelia and the pain she must be going through.

It was mid-morning the next day, when he saw her. The vaporous smells of medicines filled the small private room nearly knocking Ben back as he entered.

His heart sank when he saw her. She lay on her stomach with a white sheet tented over her, her face turned away from the door. Her lovely curls were gone from the back of her head, her exposed scalp in that area coated with a white salve. He thought about the fire and the huddle of kids he'd seen against the wall just before he'd collapsed. Amelia must have been among them, her back blistered and her hair singed as she tried to shield the kids from the heat. He drew in a shaky breath. He should have been there for her. He should have never left. He came closer, up to the foot of her bed, then walked around to the window side of the room. Tubes ran out from under the sheets, one up to a bag of clear liquid atop an IV pole, another down to a bag attached to the side of the bed. Instruments beeped and a screen displayed an array of numbers. Then he saw her face.

Eyes closed, what was left of her red curls were gathered around her cheeks. Her lips were slightly parted, she seemed to be sleeping peacefully, as if nothing at all was wrong. Ben just stood there for a moment, guilt rising within him for the pain she must be experiencing. He tried to keep his breathing and his movements quiet but, after a moment, her eyes fluttered opened, startling Ben.

She blinked a couple of times then looked up at him. "Hey, Ben," she said in a sleepy voice.

"Sorry, didn't mean to wake you."

"It's okay. The docs say it's not so bad. They're second degree burns, mostly." She shifted her hips under the sheet and winced. "Hurts like hell though."

"I shouldn't have gone to Texas. I shouldn't have left you alone."

"No, no. It all worked out. I hear that Jennifer's alive. We saved her Ben. We actually saved her."

"Yeah, and you almost died. You shouldn't have gone inside that building."

"I had to, Ben. I wasn't going to just stand there and wait for you and the fire department to show up." She paused, but kept her eyes on him. "There's something else, Ben." She shifted again, wincing again. "Pull that chair over so I don't have to look up at you. My neck is killing me. Besides, you probably want to be sitting down for this."

Ben complied, searching her eyes for any hint about what she was about to say. In them he could see worry, maybe even a little fright.

"I talked with her, Ben. In the fire...I talked to her."

"What do you mean? Who did you talk to? You mean you talked with Jennifer?"

"No. Not Jennifer. It was your grandmother. *She* was your grandmother. Your great, great grandmother." Her lips spread in a wavering smile. "I talked with Lydia."

For a split second, Ben couldn't move. A goose-bumpy chill ran up his spine.

"It was her, Ben. No, I wasn't imagining things. It was real. I talked to her just as I'm talking to you right now. Well, all right, things were a little frantic at the time with the fire and all, but it was no hallucination. It was real! I'm sure of it."

Ben swallowed. He wondered if maybe the hospital might have her on some funny drugs. But no, Amelia seemed to be wide awake and rational. Then he remembered the strange look on the face of Jennifer Watts as she lay there on the grass.

Amelia blinked. "You don't believe me."

"I don't know, I...Here, let's back up. Tell me exactly what happened after I talked with you on the phone. You were driving. You saw the smoke. Then what?"

She spoke slowly, "I got there as quickly as I could, Ben. I couldn't bear to think that we'd just let Jennifer die like that. I pulled into the parking lot and got out and just stood there for a second. The flames were high and getting higher. I could feel the heat but it seemed like the fire was just in the front of the building. I could see a few men staggering out the front door. They stumbled and crawled, some just collapsed right there in the lot. I saw that going in the front door wasn't an option. I found the side door and went in.

"The lights were still on and smoke was everywhere but not so dense that I couldn't see where I was going. I took off my blouse and breathed through it. I shouted but couldn't hear myself over the roar of the fire. I remembered that the journal mentioned a back wall. I found the center aisle and ran down it until I saw them—a bunch of kids and a few adults gathered around a door that was marked *exit*. It must have been locked Ben. Shit. That company should be sued. They..."

"What happened then?"

Amelia's smile re-formed. "I recognized Jennifer. While all the others were trying to beat down the door, she faced the front. With a look of complete terror, she saw me. Our eyes locked. I shouted her name—Jennifer. 'Yes, yes, I am Jennifer. Do you know me?' she asked.

"I ran to her. 'Yes, we're going to get you out of here,' I told her. 'The others too. There's a way out. That way.' I pointed in the direction of the fire, but at that instant, the flames reared up almost like a thick curtain. The heat was terrible.

We both backed away from the flames, closer to the others now. I could hear them banging on the door. Screaming for help. 'It's too late. This poor child will be dead soon,' said Jennifer. 'No. You don't know that,' I screamed. But then I realized what she'd said. You know, she referred to herself as *this child*. Right away, it hit me. I grabbed her by both shoulders. I could feel her body shaking in my hands like a leaf in the wind. 'You're not Jennifer, are you? Is that you Lydia? Lydia Thornhill?'

"She stared at me then lost her balance and almost collapsed, but I was able to hold her up. I pulled her close. All she could do was mumble: 'How...how do you know...Is this all a dream?' There was a pop-pop-pop sound, loud as if gunshots. Glass showered down on us. The lights went out. 'Help is coming,' I shouted, even though I didn't believe it myself. 'We're going to be saved.' I backed away from her and tried to get everyone away from the locked door, telling them that we needed to go to the front.' But even as I said this, all we could see in that direction was a sheet of flame. There seemed to be no way to run through them. All we could do was wait for help. It was then that I realized that Jennifer was still staring at me, her eyes wide. 'Do you know me? Do you know who I am?' She said it clearly this time.

"I told her that we knew about her from her journals and that we've been trying to save these kids. I told her that we were not going to let her die again. Then I watched Jennifer's face change from a look of terror to a look of…I guess I'd call it wonder. 'My journals?' she said. 'Almighty God in heaven, you've read my journals?' It was amazing, Ben. And for a moment, I forgot my own terror.

"I told her about you and she became excited. 'Ben? Is that his name?' she asked. But, at that moment, there was a muffled explosion. The flames died a little but then black smoke started curling up. I could see the racks of colorful plastic parts twisting in the heat, then igniting—just as she'd described in her journals. Dark smoke billowed and rushed toward us.

"Everyone screamed. I screamed too. At that moment I really felt I was going to die. We all pressed against each other then, through it all, I could hear your grandmother's screams. 'Why? Why is this happening?' she cried. 'I can carry this curse no longer.' I tried to console her and I can't remember exactly what I said. I had no time to think because, in that instant, the fire was on us. I felt my back, my neck…my skin burning, blistering. Like sausage on a skillet, I thought to myself, as I braced my body against the pain. I couldn't breathe. I must have passed out. I don't even remember being carried out of the building. When I woke up, I was in an ambulance on my way here."

Ben had been staring at the floor as she spoke. Shaken, he lifted his eyes to hers and with his hand, brushed aside a curl of hair that had fallen across her forehead. "I'm sorry you had to go through all that. I tried to get to you but the smoke was too much. I was gagging and crawling, down on all fours but I caught a glimpse of all of you pressed against the wall. I heard the awful screams. I tried to get up. I tried to get to you, but couldn't. I was so close."

"You did all you could, Ben. Just like me."

"The fire department guys had respirators. They must have followed me in, maybe a minute or two behind. They found me, and they found all of you."

A tear slid down her cheek. "Not all. I hear five didn't make it, two of them kids."

Ben nodded. At that moment he wanted to hold her in his arms. But knew he couldn't. He leaned close and placed a lingering kiss on her forehead. "I'm just glad you're going to be all right." He straightened in his chair and took a shaky breath realizing that, at this moment, this woman was the most important person in his life.

Ben ran a hand over his face as if to clear his thinking. "I saw Jennifer. It was right after she'd been rescued."

"I heard she was okay."

"She was laying on the grass with the others who made it out. Just some burns to her leg, not too bad I think."

"Did you talk to her?"

"I tried to. I called her name but she didn't respond. She was just staring up at the sky. Like she was in shock or something. Probably was."

Amelia's eyes darkened. "It could be more than that, Ben. When I was with her in the fire, she was really and truly, Lydia Thornhill."

Ben hesitated. "Wait a minute. You aren't saying that she might still be Lydia are you? That she's somehow still inside her? Like the girl's possessed or something?" He was stunned at the thought.

"I don't know, Ben. With all the others, their deaths seemed to set her free. Since Jennifer didn't die...yes, I suppose she may still be there. You need to talk to her."

Ben gave a reluctant nod. "I'll get in touch with her mom. She may not even let me see her."

"Ben, her life was saved because of you. She'll let you see her."

"But what should I say to her?"

"I don't know, Ben. You'll think of something." She struggled to move her legs, wincing.

"Damn it, I wish I could trade places with you."

"I wish you could too. But you've got work to do now. Besides seeing Jennifer you have to get working on the next death from the journals. We've got one more life to try to save. It's the last one, right?"

Ben almost shivered remembering his grandmother's account of that last killing. "Yes, it's the last. It's supposed to happen in fifteen days."

"Not much time."

"It's more time than we had for Jennifer."

"We got lucky with her."

"The FBI'll be helping out with this last one so maybe we'll catch a break." They were both quiet for a while.

"I heard Nolan reinstated you. Good for you, Ben."

"How do you know about that?"

"Nolan sent me a text—you know, 'get well soon' and all that. He also wanted more background on the journals. He mentioned you as an oh-by-the-way. My parents read it to me off my phone." She paused. "They said they met you. They said you looked like hell."

"Yeah, I didn't make a good first impression."

"It was *the best* first impression, Ben. They know you helped save me."

"Yeah, but what they don't know is that, if it weren't for me, you wouldn't have been in that building in the first place."

She smiled slightly again. "You, me, and your grandmother, we saved lives, Ben. That's all that matters."

Ben held her gaze. And, in a wordless moment, gave her back a thin smile of his own.

CHAPTER 27

The next morning, Ben paced his apartment floor working to get his words straight in his mind before placing the call. When he couldn't delay it any longer, he picked up his phone and dialed. It rang twice before someone picked up at the other end, but didn't speak.

"Hello. Is this Mrs. Watts?" Ben asked.

"Yes. Who is this?"

"It's Detective Ben Marshall, Mrs. Watts. I'm with the Boston Police Department. I think you spoke to a colleague of mine, Dr. Amelia Silvers a few days ago."

Mrs. Watts hesitated then spoke tentatively. "Oh...yes. How is she doing? I heard she was hurt."

"She's still in the hospital. She's in a lot of pain, but she'll be all right."

"Poor woman. She saved my Jenny's life, you know. Were you there too? At the fire?"

"Yes, I was. How is your daughter doing?"

She paused again. "First tell me how Dr. Silvers knew about the fire. I didn't believe her, you know." Tears filled her voice. "I should have listened to her and just kept Jenny home from school that day like she wanted me to."

"Mrs. Watts, I'd like to come over to talk with you, and with Jennifer too, if that's all right." Ben paused, waiting for a response but none came. "Your daughter's not behaving normally, is she?"

"No, no she's not," said Mrs. Watts quietly. "She...the pain from her burns seem to be lessening but...it's as if..." her words faded.

"Mrs. Watts. I know this is a hard time for you, but I think I might be able to help."

She let out a long sigh that shook with emotion. "I don't know what you can do. You're not a doctor. The doctors tell me that Jenny's okay, but she's not. She's..." Mrs. Watts started to sob but quickly recovered. "All right. Come then. But you can't upset her. Don't you dare upset my child. She's a good girl. This shouldn't be happening to her. None of this should be happening."

Well, he had to agree with her there—none of this should be happening. "I can be there at two this afternoon. Will that work for you?"

"Yes," she said, ending the call.

Ben had the use of an unmarked police car and he took the long way to the Watts's house. He arrived five minutes early. Wearing jeans and a faded top Mrs. Watts was already waiting at the door. Her eyes were red, her hair unkempt. Ben held out his ID which she glanced at briefly. Without a word she let him inside then took him to Jennifer's room where, together, they stood for a moment by her half-open door.

Dressed in a gray woolen bathrobe, Jennifer sat arms folded beside a window, staring blankly.

"She hasn't said anything since the fire," Mrs. Watts explained. "She just sits. When I talk to her I don't even think she hears me. She takes food if I spoon it to her and at night she seems to sleep—she closes her eyes anyway. The doctor says this is common after a trauma like she's been through. They say she's fine and it'll pass."

Ben just nodded, still wondering to himself what he could possibly do to help the girl.

Mrs. Watts was a short woman. Her nervous eyes looked up at Ben. "I've never seen her like this, Detective Marshall. I know she's been through a lot, but I'm scared. If you think you can help her, I'm not going to stand in your way."

"Thank you for your understanding. I'd like to ask her some questions. Is that all right? Please, you can stay while I try to talk to her."

Mrs. Watts nodded. She pushed the door fully open and walked in, Ben following. From in front of a dressing table she pulled a chair in front of Jennifer and waived Ben into it. She then sat on the edge of the unmade bed.

Ben sat and looked into Jennifer's eyes that, with her pupils dilated, looked more like dark pools of glistening black surrounded by thin rings of lighter brown. They gave no hint that she even knew he was there. "Jennifer, I'm Detective Ben Marshall. Can you hear me?"

No reaction.

"There was a fire, Jennifer. It was a bad fire. You have burns on your leg but you're going to be all right. You know that, don't you? You're going to be all right. You mother's here. Nothing's going to hurt you."

Still no reaction.

Ben plodded on. "Jennifer. I'm going to ask you if you know someone. It's very important that you hear me now. You need to think hard about this." Ben swallowed, his eyes still fixed on hers. "Does the name Lydia Thornhill mean anything to you?"

Jennifer's face remained blank.

"Think hard now—Lydia Thornhill. Do you know that name? Did she come to you in the fire?" Ben could sense Mrs. Watts shifting uneasily, still sitting on the bed. Probably wondering what this Thornhill person had to do with anything. But from Jennifer, there was still no reaction. Nor did he get a reaction from his next few questions.

Ben sat back in his chair, unsure about what to do next. He took a breath. Then he saw Jennifer's hand twitch slightly then move toward him ever so slowly.

Ben leaned closer. He smelled the salve that covered her burns. His mouth was dry. He held out his own hand, palm up, just an inch from hers and, with his eyes still fixed on hers, he waited, his heart pounding. He sensed that something important was about to happen. His mind flashed back briefly to Grandma Lydia's description of her first meeting with Silent Margaret.

Jennifer's hand twitched again. Her fingertips brushed against his and with a lightning speed that made Ben jump, she grabbed his hand. Her head turned. Her eyes fastened on his almost with a force of their own. Her skin grew warmer, her grip even tighter so that he couldn't pull away even if he wanted to. And with all this happening, Jennifer suddenly smiled. It was a sweet, almost angelic smile.

"You are...Ben."

Ben's heart raced. He felt his body shake. He fought to get the words out: "Yes, I am Ben," was all he could manage.

The room seemed to grow dim and distant. Jennifer's smile vanished even as her eyes continued to drill into his. Then, with what could only be described as a flash of terror, her eyes roll back in their sockets. Her mouth opened wide but made no sound.

The room around Ben seemed to tremble and shake but, through it all, Ben was remotely conscious. In his periphery he saw Mrs. Watts stand. He could hear her screams, muffled as if coming from far away. "What's happening? What are you doing? Oh, God. Get away from my daughter." He could feel her grab at him, trying to pull him away. But Ben couldn't pull away. His hand, his entire arm stiffened involuntarily as if it wasn't his own, as if an electric current was passing through it from Jennifer's vice-like grip. Ben's heart thundered, beating like a machine gun. He felt his own mouth spring open. His muscles, every part of his body suddenly went rigid as stone. He couldn't move. He couldn't breathe.

Then, just as suddenly, it was over.

Ben's body went limp. His hand lifted from Jennifer's almost as if it were repelled. He fell forward, down onto his knees, just in front of Jennifer. He took in one enormous breath as if he'd just come up from being underwater too long. His body shuddered, craving more and more air and slowly, reality came back into focus.

Mrs. Watts was still screaming. "Oh, God. What did you do? What did you do to my Jenny?"

On his knees, slowly gathering strength, Ben couldn't respond. He tried to get up and, on his second try, made it onto his feet. Still bent over, he managed a look at Jennifer. Somehow she had slumped out of her chair and lay on the floor passed out in her mother's arms.

Mrs. Watts was crying, tears flowing. "Oh, baby, my poor

baby."

"Is she breathing?" asked Ben.

Mrs. Watts jerked her head up, her face twisted in rage. "Get out. Get out. I should have never let you in. You almost killed her."

But just then, the corner of Jennifer's mouth quivered and, as if waking up from a long night's sleep, her head lifted and she opened her eyes.

Seeing this, Mrs. Watts looked down at her daughter. "Oh my God, Jenny, my Jenny, are you all right?"

Jennifer yawned and looked around. "Mom, what's wrong? Of course I'm all right." She moved to sit up. "What are we doing on the floor?" Then she saw Ben. "Who are you?"

Relieved to see that Jennifer was looking tired but otherwise normal, Ben gave her a shaky smile. "I'm just a friend. How are you feeling, Jennifer?"

"Tired, but okay. Just really tired," she said, getting to her feet. She winced in pain then looked down to see the burn on her leg. Her face darkened. "Oh, there was a fire, wasn't there. I thought I dreamed it but there was really a fire. Is that right?"

"That's all over now, Jenny," said her mother. "You don't have to worry about that. You have a burn on your leg but you'll be just fine in a few days." She looked at Ben and shook her head. "I'm sorry, Detective. I was upset. I didn't know..."

"I understand, Mrs. Watts. Don't worry about it. You just take care of your daughter," said Ben, getting to his feet.

"And then I left," said Ben after recounting his visit to the Watt's house for Amelia at the hospital later that day.

"Sounds like a scene from *The Exorcist*. How about you? Are you all right?"

"Yeah, I guess. Still weirded out by the whole thing. She just touched my hand, that's all it took. But man, I felt like I'd been hit square in the jaw. I think I was nearly out cold at one point."

"But Jennifer seems all right now?"

"Yeah, she does. I guess I should have stayed to make sure, but I had to get out of there. You know, get some air. Man, it was like the life was being sucked right out of me through that girl's grip."

Amelia didn't say anything for a moment. "Interesting you put it that way. It's like you gave her a jump-start. Like her battery was drained and you had to recharge it. But the other thing is that many people had touched Jennifer after the fire—the EMT's, the doctors, her mother. None of them got the reaction you did. Ben, you were the only one who could have helped her, and you did."

"You're back to thinking I've got some kind of a connection to these kids."

"You said you'd met her a year or so ago at the station. Did you talk with her then? Did you touch her?"

"What do you mean, did I touch her? Of course I didn't..." Then he remembered. "No, that's wrong. I think maybe I shook hands with her. Or maybe it was just a high-five thing. I sometimes do that when we have stuff going on for the neighborhood kids."

Amelia shifted her head on her pillow. "Ten years on the force, that's a lot of kids you've come in contact with."

"What are you saying?" asked Ben slowly.

"You deal with people every day of your life. As a cop for ten years you deal with more than most, sometimes dozens in a day, many of them from deprived, crime-prone family situations. Many of them kids. You have to admit that it's one hell of a coincidence that you once met the same Jennifer Watts that your grandmother had written about in her journal."

Ben leaned forward in his chair, elbows on knees, his right foot tapping. "I think I met Cindy Brand too," he said in a low voice.

Amelia blinked.

"Turns out I was in Austin a while back. She and her mother had a custody hearing on the same day, in the same courtroom as the hearing I was involved with."

"You remember that?"

"No, I don't remember it at all. But the Austin PD was trying to link me to Cindy and that's what they came up with."

"And you might have inadvertently brushed her hand or..."

"Yeah, who knows? I guess I could have."

"This keeps getting stranger and stranger, doesn't it?" she said with a grim smile from beneath her tented sheets.

Ben rubbed his eyes. He'd had enough talk about his grandmother and dying kids that he should have been able to save. He straightened. "You any better today? What do the doctors say?"

"I'm better. They say I'll be like this for a few more days. They're giving me all kinds of meds. Sometimes I feel like I'm floating." She was quiet for a moment. "Your grandmother saved Jennifer from the fire, Ben. And with your touch you somehow saved your grandmother."

Mentally exhausted, Ben had no reply but his mind flashed back to the words on the wall. *SAVE ME* it had said. Had he really just saved his great, great grandmother?

"I'm thirsty, Ben," said Amelia. "There's a glass of ice-chips over there." He helped her with it until she nodded that she had enough. She waited another moment then asked: "Have you ever been in a hospital for the mentally ill?"

Now why would she ask that? Ben wondered. "Well, you know that I was a patient in one after that coma I was in, right? Is that what you mean?"

"No. I mean have you ever visited an asylum. You know, a long term care facility where people might be institutionalized for years." She took a breath, her throat a little raspy. "Most times the patients there act like they're totally rational then, other times, it's like they're in another world. And, for some, that other world often seems full of pain and violence. I imagine that's how it was for your grandmother and she, in her rational moments, was just trying to understand it all. That's why she wrote her journals. So, even though she couldn't figure things out, she hoped that someday, someone else could."

"But she kept her journals a secret. Hell, she had them buried with her."

Amelia took another long breath, as if she were tiring. "She left them where she knew that only you would find them."

"But how could she possibly know that I would be the one to stumble across them?"

"You didn't just stumble across those journals, Ben. She left you clues, and you followed them." With an effort, Amelia smiled. "She also knew for certain that one day you would be the one to find them."

"And how could she actually *know* that?"

Amelia sighed as if he was slow to catch on. "She knew because, in the fire, I told her."

"But, in the journal, Jennifer Watts dies and my grandmother makes no reference to having met you."

"I don't know, Ben. I don't know," she said wearily. "Look, this is all really confusing to me and the drugs I'm on aren't helping. I just need to..." She closed her eyes and, a moment later, was sound asleep.

Ben watched her for a moment. Yes, sleep is what she needed most right now. He left the hospital a short time later and it was only on the drive back to the station that it occurred to him to wonder what his experience with Jennifer earlier that day must have been like for his grandmother.

But it had been like nothing he could have imagined.

She'd floated, neither body nor spirit, neither seeing nor feeling, yet somehow managing to hold onto the fragile thread of her existence. All was blackness and time stood balanced and dangerously still. Was it hours or days or months or years? Or was it just a second or two? Somehow Lydia knew that time had no meaning here.

And she also knew that this death, the death of Jennifer Watts, had been different from all the others. Maybe the woman had been a dream, coming to her as she did in the midst of the blaze. But that woman knew her. She knew *her*—not Jennifer, but Lydia Thornhill. She knew that this terrified girl who had been Jennifer Watts an instant earlier was, at that terrible moment, Lydia Thornhill. But how could she know? Maybe that mysterious woman had been just another part of the dream—the dream conjured up by the mind of the insane part of Lydia Thornhill in the hope that there was actually some sense to be made of this hell to which she'd been condemned.

But they had talked. In that brief, desperate time, they *had* talked. Maybe not as much in words as in thoughts that seemed muffled and unclear now. But one thought, one word, had come through most clearly. It was a name—Ben. Yes, Ben. But who was Ben? She wondered as she floated.

Suddenly these thoughts fractured and Lydia became conscious again of her body. Her skin tingled and the space around her seemed to sparkle with energy. A warm flickering glow fell on her. And she could see. There was her hand. Yes, and she could move it. She could feel it. But still she floated.

Around her the glow intensified and with it came a deep rumble. Like an approaching tidal wave the rumble grew. The light grew. A feeling of irrepressible dread consumed her. Her heart pounded with the power of a fist trying to break out from her body through her chest. She screamed. She tried to curl up in a ball, like a child in bed afraid of a storm but found she couldn't move. She cried out in a failing, defeated whimper: "Take me now. Put an end to this. Kill me! Kill me! Please!"

And with these words, the light became suddenly blinding, the sound deafening. Her body shook. She squeezed her eyes shut and felt herself swept up. Higher and higher she rose and, as she ascended, the sound dissipated; the bright light bled away.

Then, with a jolt, she was back. Breathless and spent, she shook in her chair, crying a wailing, tearless cry even as her chest heaved desperately craving more air. Finally she slumped, exhausted.

"Mother?"

Lydia opened her eyes and, through the watery film covering them, pulled the form of her daughter into focus. "Abigail. Oh, dear Abigail," she cried in blessed relief. She tried to raise her arms, then felt her restraints. And she was thankful for them. No harm had come to Abigail as it had that one time. She took a deep, deep breath. Her trembling subsided. It was over. At least for now it was over. "It is all right now, child. I am all right now, little bluebird," she said, almost in a whisper.

Abigail stood and untied the rope from her wrists. She leaned over and brought both arms together in a warm embrace. "I was so scared for you, Mother. You were never like this."

Lydia felt her daughter's tears mingle with her own as their cheeks met. They held each other for a long while, both sobbing.

When they parted, Lydia just sat, breathing in the fresh breeze flowing through the kitchen window. She sensed that it was morning. And she sensed something else, "I am hungry, dear. I need something to eat."

Abigail prepared a breakfast of bread, eggs, and sliced apples. "This spell was different, wasn't it?" asked Abigail quietly as she watched her eat. "You were violent for a time, like always, but then you fell quiet, as if you were in some kind of a trance. It lasted more than two days. I was scared. I thought you might never come back."

Lydia nodded. "I think someone knows about me, Abigail. Someone in that place where I go to die knows about me."

"But that place you go isn't real. How can it be? Whenever you have one of your spells, you stay right here. You don't go anywhere."

Lydia gave her a grim smile. "That place is real. I know that now."

Abigail just stared back.

"I'm not insane. At least no more insane than you already know me to be."

Abigail got up and filled her water glass from the pump at the sink. "You said that someone there knows about you. How do you know that?"

Lydia nodded. "There was a woman. She came to me in the midst of a terrible fire. She came to me as if she'd been looking for me. My memory of her words is jumbled, but she knew me. She *knew* me, Abigail. She spoke my name: Doctor Lydia Thornhill."

"She knew you were a doctor?"

"Yes. And I asked her how she knew me. She said that she'd read my journals. She knew about me and she knew about Jennifer Watts—that's the girl who died. At least I think she died but maybe..."

Abigail sat back down. “Anything can happen in dreams.”

Lydia shook her head. “Maybe you’ll never believe me but these are not dreams. That place was real and that woman was real.”

It was late that night, after Abigail had gone to bed, that Lydia put her pen down and closed her journal. It was the fourth and she wondered if it would be her last. She blew out the lamp and sat in the darkness listening to the wind outside. Tree branches brushed against the window. She knew she should cut those back, but knew she wouldn’t. Then she thought again about the woman who had come to her in the fire. How could she have seen her journals? And how could she have known about the girl, Jennifer Watts, when she, Lydia, had only just now written about her? She shook her head knowing it was futile to ponder questions she couldn’t answer.

She stood. Then, after taking a few steps toward her bedroom, she stopped as a new recollection and a new revelation washed over her.

CHAPTER 28

Parked at the hospital entrance, Ben tapped his thumbs against the steering wheel of his unmarked police vehicle. He'd been surprised to get Amelia's call earlier that morning telling him she was about to be released and needed a lift home.

"They'd keep me longer," she'd explained, her voice still sounding weak over the phone, "but my recovery's going pretty well so they're shoving me out the door."

"You're really feeling good enough to go home?"

"I think they need the room for someone else and, besides, my insurance isn't all that great. My folks already left for home so I thought I'd ask you—for a lift."

Ben had left the station right away.

Five days had passed since his trip to the Watts home. Each night he'd visited Amelia and each day he'd spent working long hours at the station with Harris and Bradly. Ben had asked them if they'd been miffed, in getting assigned to a spooky case involving someone's great, great grandmother.

"Are you kidding?" Bradly had responded. "We wanted to be assigned to the Thornhill case and had to call in some favors to make it happen."

"The Thornhill Case? That's what they're calling it?" Ben had asked.

Bradly had smiled. "Well, that's what we're calling it. It'd be a little tough opening a formal case on someone who died a hundred years ago. As far as Austin knows we're staying here to do some follow up work on the Brand murder. Like I said, we called in a few favors. We've got a guy running interference for us."

"We also had some personal time coming," Bradly offered.

Ben appreciated them sticking around but worried that, even

with their help, they'd made no progress on the next journal killing. Too bad there was so little to go on, he thought as he stared through the passenger-side window at the glass doors to the hospital.

Her name was Sandra—no last name, just Sandra. Ben swallowed hard. As if he himself had written Grandma Lydia's terrifying account, he remembered it almost verbatim:

I open my eyes. It is dark. I'm lying on a thin smelly mattress that sits on a small bed. My hands and feet are spread, tied to the bedframe. From the pain in my wrists and ankles I know that I've been lying like this for a long time. There is a chill in the room yet I feel beads of sweat on my forehead. I need to pee. A light goes on but not in the room I am in. It illuminates a hallway and slightly brightens the ceiling and walls around me. There are pictures on the walls but I can make none of them out. Something hangs over my head, a chandelier I think. Its crystals weakly scatter the light like fairy dust in dots that float around the room. I see my feet. They are bare but the rest of me is clothed—in a dress, I think. I sense that my body is small. I pull at the ropes that bind me and wince as they chaff the sores on my wrists.

I hear something from the other room.

I shout: 'Hello. Who are you? Untie me now and I won't tell anyone about you.'

There is no reply and, for a moment I hear nothing. Then, there is music. It's classical music, Beethoven, one of his symphonies. It seems to be coming from everywhere, softly at first, then gradually louder. Then the light from the hallway is blocked and I realize that someone is standing there. I hear breathing.

I shout again: 'Please. Please, let me go. I won't tell anyone about you.' I wait, but hear no reply. Fear overtakes me. Though somehow I know this to be the last of my deaths I shrink from the thought of the pain and suffering I know is coming. I cry out: 'I can't do this again. I can't do this.' I cry. Tears flow down my cheeks. My body—her body—starts to shake inside. Then I hear a voice, a woman's voice.

'There, there child. There's no need to be afraid. You should

know by now that we mean you no harm.' Footsteps come soft against the carpeted floor. She is closer. Her shadow leans over me. Touching my face, wiping my cheeks with the rough skin of her hand.

'I am not who you think I am,' I say, trying to calm myself. 'I am not a child and I know that somewhere the police are coming for you.'

The woman bares her teeth through a smile that quickly transforms into an ugly smirk. Her touch becomes a harsh grip, her fingers pressing hard into my cheeks. 'There's no one coming, my dear. You know that, don't you? Well, Jack is coming. He'll be here soon. You'll need to look pretty for him. Can you do that for him? I've brought a brush for your hair.' She begins using the brush, pulling hard against the snarls.

I feel like Jesus in Gethsemane awaiting His fate, but I do not pray. No, I am too angry for that.

'Tell me my name,' I demand of the woman.

The brushing stops for a moment. It was a question she hadn't expected. 'Have you forgotten, dear? Your name is Sandra. Such a pretty name for such a pretty girl.'

A door opens. It's a door to the outside and cool air rushes in. I hear the wind and I hear nighttime sounds like maybe from a nearby woods. I smell cologne. The door closes.

I hear breathing. A man's breathing. I see his profile in the dimness staring down at me. 'Yes, she will do just fine,' he says to the woman. He hands her something, an envelope maybe. The woman says nothing. I hear her moving around, then she comes back to me. She brushes my cheek with the back of her hand. Then, she is gone and I am alone with the man.

A lamp comes on. I can see better now. The man is tall, fat, and unshaven with a horseshoe of black hair around his balding head. He's wearing a black suit and tie. His cologne fills the air. I breathe it in and start to gag. 'Who the fuck are you?' I say in the harshest voice I can manage.

He winces, then seems to collect himself, smiling. 'Well, it sounds like little miss pure and innocent isn't as pure as she looks.'

'Untie me and I'll show you just how impure I am. Would you like that?'

He lets out a breath, like he's been punched in the gut. No, he didn't like that.

I think that maybe I've got a chance with this animal. I think maybe, if I can get him to untie my hands, I can hit him with something when he's least expecting it then run for help. But even as these thoughts run through my head, I know there's little hope of that. I know I wouldn't be here unless this poor girl was going to die. But then I have an idea.

Treat him like a patient. I am a doctor after all. Yes, now there's a new thought!

'Your mother didn't love you, did she?' I say. 'Is that why you do these things? You're angry with her, I think.'

He just stares down at me but I hear his breathing quicken. 'Shut the fuck up you little bitch. You don't know anything about me.'

'You're wrong. I know all about you. I know that you've killed before. Were they all little girls? Yeah, I'll bet they were. You're too much of a coward to take on a grown woman.'

At that, his big beefy head puffs out, turning a bright red. He lets out an animal-like snarl and mutters something in a foreign language. It sounds Slavic maybe. He reaches for his collar and whips off his tie. He puts a knee on my chest, forcing the air out. I can't breathe. I try to resist. I pull at the ropes that bind me. He loops his tie around my head, gagging me with it, drawing it tight, stretching the corners of my mouth. I taste a trickle of blood. His knee still hard against me, I gasp for air, struggling against his weight. But even through this, I keep my eyes on him, trying to show anger instead of the fear he expects and needs. Finally, he pulls back, panting for breath nearly as much as I am. 'You are quite the little bitch, aren't you?' he says, standing now, hands on hips.

He takes off his clothes, carefully laying them over the back of a chair, like he's afraid they might get wrinkled.

My body, Sandra's body, begins to shake again as he stands over me. He straddles me then positions himself and suddenly drops his entire weight onto me. I try to cry out but am breathless as he forces himself into me. Heavy, flabby, sweaty, he pounds himself into me again and again and again. I squeeze my eyes shut. I cry. I pray for it to be over. My lungs strain against his body, exploding, desperate again for air. I scream through the gag, I scream and sweet God in heaven, I scream again and again. When he's finally finished, he rolls off me, tumbling down onto the floor.

Again, I struggle against the ropes. I force my eyes open and see him get to his feet.

He smiles, almost in a fatherly way. Then he raises his open hand and slaps me hard across the face. A tooth snaps. My jaw flares with pain. Blood fills my mouth. It dribbles down my chin. I cry. My body shakes again and I cannot stop it.

Without a word, he walks to a table then comes back. In one hand he's holding something black and shiny. I feel my eyes go wide and, though I shrink back, I am glad that it's a gun and not a knife. It will be quicker this way. A calm feeling comes over me as he takes his aim. I sense his frustration in staring at my face and not seeing the fear he expects. The look of terror, that's what he needs to see. But I will not give it to him. He lowers the gun and rips off my gag. He takes aim again, pointing the gun at my face. His thumb pulls back and I hear the mechanical click as he cocks the weapon. 'It is okay, my dear. You can scream. Go ahead.' Again I hear what I think is a Slavic accent in his voice.

I shout: 'Your name isn't Jack, is it? Tell me your name, you ass-hole. I want to know the name of my killer.'

'You speak bravely for a girl about to die.'

I surprise myself for, though I am still shaking, I manage a slight smile. 'You have no idea who I am. I am the woman that will haunt you until you die.'

'No! You're just a dirty little bitch, that's all you are, and this bullet is the only thing you'll get from me."

Then, I utter what I know will be Sandra's angry last words: 'You're a chicken-shit ass-hole. Your mother was right not to love you. She hated your guts.'

I see his finger pull the trigger. I see the gun kick and I hear, not a bang, but a popping sound. My head kicks back into the mattress but I feel nothing except for blessed release. It is over. This last death, except for my own, is over.

Ben took a tense breath, his stomach knotted up in the same anger Grandma Lydia must have felt at the moment that ass-hole pulled the trigger. The monster who would kill Sandra was out there now, probably planning his kill. And Sandra was out there too, probably just playing and doing all the things a carefree little girl should be doing having no inkling of the horrors to come.

He realized that both of his hands had a white-knuckle grip on the wheel. He relaxed a little, drying his palms against his pants. He and Bradly and Harris had wasted nearly a week searching for any leads at all. Time was running out and each second's passing was one less they'd have to find Sandra. It was as if a clock the size of Big Ben was ticking off those seconds inside his head and, according to the journal, that clock would stop in five days, not with a deep, majestic gong of a giant bell, but with a gunshot that would take a little girl's life.

At a rap on the passenger-side window, Ben jumped and saw a hospital orderly there. Behind him Amelia sat in a wheelchair looking a little miffed that Ben hadn't opened the door for her. Her face was a pasty white. Ben unlocked the door and, after wheeling her closer, the orderly guided her in. With each movement she bit her lip, letting loose a grunt when she finally eased herself into the seat. The guy helped her with the seat belt, put a hospital blanket over her lap then said, "Thanks for choosing Boston General."

"Like I had a fricking choice," Amelia muttered as the door slammed shut. She drew the blanket up around her arms. "Is it cold, Ben? I feel cold."

Ben turned on the heat and, though it was a warm day in October he said, "Yeah, guess it is a little chilly." Ben saw that she was shivering. "Do you need another blanket? I..."

"Just drive, Ben. Stop staring at me. I'm all right. Really, I'm all right."

They were silent for the first few miles, she wincing at every bump in the road while staring straight ahead. Then she spoke. "We need to talk with Jennifer. And I need to look at your grandmother's journals again."

"I have number four here." He tapped it where it lay on the console between them. "But you need to rest. You look like shit."

She shook her head. "Ben, I've been cooped up in the hospital, living in a med-fog and I'm just now beginning to realize what happened in that fire and it's a lot more important than how I look or how I feel."

"What happened in that fire was: We saved Jennifer and we saved most of the kids with her. You got hurt and you need to take care of yourself. Now, thanks to my grandmother, we have a chance at saving one more life."

"Yes, I remember reading about that last one. Sandra somebody, right? Anything new?"

Ben shook his head. "Not so far. There isn't much to go on."

"We didn't have much info on Jennifer but we managed to save her. We can't give up."

The tires screeched as Ben steered the car a little too fast around a curve. "Nobody's giving up."

"Slow down, will you? I know it's frustrating. But we'll find her and we'll save her. Maybe we just need to back off a little to see what's really happening."

"How do you mean, back off?"

She yawned. "Man, I'm tired all of a sudden."

"You need to rest."

"Okay, okay, I'll rest. But hear me out. Somehow, your grandmother experienced all these death's she's written about. Early on, she was just an observer but, eventually, she became the victim and she actually experienced death over and over again. That's what the journal says. It says Cindy died in a dirt basement and Jennifer died in that fire along with most, if not all of her classmates. But Jennifer didn't die and neither did most of those kids."

Ben stopped for a light. "So the journal's wrong."

“Not wrong exactly.” With an effort, she shifted a little in her seat to face Ben.

Ben put a hand on her knee. “Stay still will you?”

“These burns are a bitch,” she said, leaning her head back, catching her breath. Her lips were twisted with tension as if bracing for another wave of pain. A tear escaped from one of her closed eyes and Ben moved his hand from her knee to dry it then placed his palm lightly against her cheek. He saw the tension drain a little from her face. He cleared a few strands of hair from her forehead. “You need to take care of yourself.”

“I will, I will. There’ll be time enough for that later.”

The car behind honked and Ben started driving again.

Amelia took a breath. “No, the journal isn’t wrong. It just tells of a different reality. Maybe only a *possible* reality. Your grandmother simply wrote what she experienced.”

“Which is what would have happened if she hadn’t warned us about it in her journals.”

“Yes.”

“But you said that you talked to my grandmother. You know, in the fire. Now, if you were her, wouldn’t you write a little note in the journal about that conversation? Wouldn’t you also write about Jennifer Watts being saved? Yet there’s no mention of you and no mention of anyone being saved, is there? Look, it’s like you said, my grandmother left clues for me to find her journals. She wrote on the wall of that house, *Save Me, Save Them*. That tells me that she thought there might be a way to prevent these deaths.”

“She also wrote, *Save Yourself*. What do you think she meant by that?”

“That was about the fire in my apartment. I should have died in that fire but I was up in Maine as she must have known I would be.”

“But what led you to go to Maine? What led you to that house of hers where you saw her message on the wall, where you found that camera, where we dug up her journals? Don’t you see, Ben? It all goes back to you getting kicked off the force. It goes back to you shooting at something you thought you saw in the street. That’s what started the dominoes falling.”

Ben hadn't made that connection before but he could see it now. "You're saying that my grandmother somehow caused that?"

"I don't know. When I spoke to her in the fire she seemed as baffled at these death experiences of hers as we are. It's hard to believe that she would have been able to manipulate the future like that."

They were both quiet until Ben turned onto her street and double parked. He got out, grabbed her bag and helped her up into her apartment. It was a cozy little place with a Formica counter separating the kitchenette from the living space. She had a small flat-screen. The walls were lined with books. It seemed to Ben to be almost too neat and tidy for someone who had left as unexpectedly as Amelia had when she'd found out about Jennifer's field trip. He glanced passed an open door into the bedroom where her bed was neatly made. "Your roommate must be a neat-freak," he said.

She smiled at that. "No. I'm the neat freak. I don't have a roommate."

"I thought you said..."

"I had one a while ago. He and I were good together for a time, but it didn't last." She turned to him. "I lied to you, Ben. I just don't need a man in my life right now to...complicate things. Lying seemed to be the easiest thing to do."

"Do you still feel that way?—about not wanting to complicate your life, I mean."

She raised her eyes to his. "I'm sorry I lied. I know that much. I wasn't being fair to you or to myself. I like you, Ben," she added. "But I need some time. My back hurts like hell. Give me a few days and ask me that again."

"Are you going to be all right here by yourself?"

She smiled. "Yes, Ben, I'll be just fine." She poured herself some water and took a few long swallows. "They say to drink plenty of water," she explained, putting the glass down. "But there is one thing you can do. When you were up in Maine, before Howe and I met you there, you said you collected a lot of info on your grandmother—you know, employment records, her case history from when she was institutionalized. Do you have copies of all that?"

"I wouldn't be much of a detective if I didn't, now would I? But all that seemed to be a waste of time. I didn't really find anything significant."

"You found her house. You found her grave. You found her journals."

"I mean I didn't find anything *else* significant."

"Just get me what you found, will you? Email them to me. I'm going to be cooped up here for a while. I want to look them over."

Ben shrugged. "Sure thing. But call me if you need anything. Help, I mean...with anything. You need me to pick up some food or something? Your fridge must be full of spoiled stuff."

She yawned.

"Okay, okay. I get the message. Just call if you need anything, will you?" At a honk from a car backed up behind Ben's double-parked car, he left. That night he sent Amelia an email with a long list of attachments.

The next morning turned cold and Ben's trek from his subway stop to the station had been a brisk one. Brisk or otherwise, he usually enjoyed these walks and found them to be a good way to clear his mind. But, on entering the precinct at 7:35, his head was anything but clear. He grabbed some coffee and made it into the third floor conference room they'd been using for the Sandra case. Harris and Bradly were already there, seated next to each other at the paper-strewn table. With them this morning was Nolan who sat on the opposite side.

"Hey, Captain," said Ben a little wary. Nolan had been a part-time participant in their meetings but hadn't been involved for the last two sessions.

"Thought I'd join you this morning," said Nolan to Ben. He pointed over Ben's shoulder to a whiteboard covered with writing and post-it notes. "From what I can see, you've hit a wall. You're no farther ahead than when I was here last."

Ben sat as, brows raised, Bradly looked up from behind his laptop.

"Besides that," Nolan went on, "Austin's been asking about

when they can have their agents back. I'm sorry gentlemen, but until we get something concrete to go on, I'm going to have to put things on hold."

Ben was shocked. "But you can't..."

"Yes I can and you know it, Detective," said Nolan calmly. "But no. I'm only putting the brakes on the FBI part of things. You can continue on your own, Detective. According to the journal that's only what, five more days?"

"Four as of today," said Ben.

"Stopping a crime from happening isn't easy, Captain," muttered Bradly.

Nolan lifted his hand to keep Ben from interrupting. "I'm sorry gentlemen. We can't investigate all rich fat guys with Slavic accents and we can't protect all the little girls in the country named Sandra. All we can do is hope that she's somewhere in the Boston area and be poised to act and..."

"We don't have to protect *all* the girls named Sandra," said Ben. "I had contact with Cindy and with Jennifer long before the incidents that put them in danger. At some point I must have met Sandra too. Chances are good that she lives around here."

Nolan shook his head. "So we search all the Sandra's you may have bumped into in the last five years? Exactly how would you suggest we do that?"

Ben had no answer.

Nolan stood. "All right then. Harris and Bradly, thanks for your help. You're welcome to catch the next flight out. Ben, you stay on the case, but I can't give you any help until you get something resembling a concrete lead." He looked around the table. "We clear?"

Looking nearly as upset as Ben felt, Harris glanced at Bradly then said, "I think we might stick around here a little longer, Captain. When something turns up, we want to be part of it."

"If you clear it with Austin, I'm okay with that. But I'm done running interference for you." Nolan put a hand on Ben's shoulder hesitating like he wanted to say more, but he left the room without another word.

“Hate to leave work undone,” said Bradly after the door closed. “Besides, I’ve got a new angle I want to try with the NSA database. Who knows we might get lucky.”

“I thought you needed a warrant for things like that.”

“Not for a statistical search, you know, just stats, no names. Our authorization for that came through this morning.” He pointed to the whiteboard. “If we want to match the stats to the names of actual people, that’s when we’ll need authorization at a higher level. That might be a little dicey, but first things first. Like I said, we might get lucky.”

“Why didn’t you tell the Captain about your stats idea?”

Harris gave him a dead-pan look. “All part of the FBI’s secret sauce. Besides, some people go bananas when they see what we can do with HUM-INT these days. “You aren’t going to go bananas on us are you, detective?”

“Are you kidding? We ordinary cops know all about *human intelligence*. We’re the ones who feed it to you every day. Don’t you know that? Besides, I’m way past going bananas, and I’m way past trying to make any sense of it.”

“There’s no reason for you to stick around here, Detective. We’ll let you know when we’ve got something. In the meantime, maybe you can try to track down all the Sandra’s you’ve ever known.”

Ben’s blood rose at the intimation that this would be a futile effort, yet he didn’t disagree with that assessment. Hell, this was all a long-shot effort. “All right, I’ll stay in touch,” he said, leaving the room. He headed for his desk across from which Phil appeared to be working diligently.

“Hey, Benjie. How’re things?” he asked as Ben sat.

“Not good.”

“The word is that you’ve got a line on a kidnapping and murder that haven’t happened yet. What kind of shit is that?”

Ben smiled grimly. The work on the Thornhill Case had been considered confidential but the grapevine at the station was a strong one and word about it had somehow gotten out. “Strange shit. That’s what it is, Phil, very strange shit.” He gave him the details and was just finishing up when his phone went off. Ben saw that it was Clayton Green. Wonderful. "Hello, Clay. This is Ben."

"Shit, what happened, Ben? I cleared my whole afternoon for your sorry ass. You could have at least called."

"Sorry, I've been tied up with something. Look, I appreciate you offering me the position, really I do, but I'm back on the force now so I'll just have to turn you down. I'm really very sorry about..." But Green had already ended the call.

"You got a line on another job?" asked Phil.

"Had. I'm back on the force now, remember?"

"Turned down the big bucks just so you could get back to being a cop?"

"Go ahead, call me an idiot."

Phil's face took on the stern expression of an irate father. "You're a God damned idiot, Benjie. Just like me."

CHAPTER 29

Ben spent the afternoon again going over the departmental database for anyone named Sandra. Of the names that came up, most were female criminals already incarcerated, a few were past employees of the department and a few were listed as witnesses in the case-files. All were well into adulthood. Even the neighborhood outreach mailing list where Jennifer's name had been found, had come up empty.

Ben slouched in his chair, thumb and forefinger massaging his tired eyes, pinching the bridge of his nose. The Big Ben clock in his head was still ticking away, getting louder. "If I did have contact with a Sandra, it must have been outside the department."

Phil sighed then glanced at his watch. It was almost quitting time. "Wish I could help you, but one guy banging his head against this brick wall of yours is better than two." He gathered his things and headed for the door. "It seems to me that you'll just have to wait for this Sandra girl to go missing before you can do anything at all."

Ben just shook his head. He left an hour later and spent the better part of the night and most of the next morning at home, scouring old photos and old newspaper clippings coming up with nothing.

Then a call came in from Harriet. Ben picked it up quickly. "Any news?" he asked.

"Not about Sandra, if that's what you mean. But you need to get in here."

"What's up?"

"You know that girl you saved in the fire? She's here with her mom. They want to talk to you about something. Dr. Silvers is here with them, she said she tried calling you but her phone died."

Ben wondered what Mrs. Watts might want with him. He also wondered if Amelia was in good enough shape to be up and around. "Okay, tell them I'm on my way."

Harriet was waiting for him when the elevator doors opened.

"This way, Detective," she said, hurrying to one of the interrogation rooms. She opened the door.

Amelia stood against the far wall, her face unnaturally pale; her eyes a little glassy. She wore a tight fitting cap that covered her sparse hair. She gave him a tired smile then creased her brow, telling Ben in an unspoken way to be careful in the way he spoke to Jennifer and her mother who sat next to each other on one side of a table in the center of the room. With difficulty, she sat in a chair opposite them, Ben wincing as she did so then taking the chair next to her.

"Still hurts?" asked Mrs. Watts with sympathy.

"Yeah," managed Amelia with a slight smile. "Getting better every day though."

"Captain Nolan asked me to stay," said Harriet, opening a folding chair and setting it up beside the door. "Hope you don't mind."

Ben kept his gaze first on the mother, then shifted to the daughter. "It's good to see you both again. How are you feeling, Jennifer?" He tried but failed to make eye contact with Jennifer who seemed content to just stare down at the table. "You're looking well," he added.

Mrs. Watts nodded then, as if reading from a rehearsed script she spoke to Amelia in a low dispassionate voice. "You met with us two days before the fire to warn us about it. Now I know that my Jenny's life was saved because of you—because of both of you, but we have questions." With her hands on the table she gripped a white handkerchief. She glanced down at it then looked intently at Ben. "How could you have known about the fire? And why didn't you stop it? How could you let such a terrible thing happen?"

Three good questions, thought Ben. He wished he had three good answers. "Dr. Silvers and I only knew that there was going to be a fire somewhere on that day and we knew that a young girl named Jennifer Watts was going to...to be in danger. We had no idea where the fire would be and in the days leading up to it, we had no idea how to find the right Jennifer Watts. It's not an uncommon name and, for all we knew, the Jennifer we needed to find could have been living anywhere in the country. We just got lucky in finding the right one."

"I didn't believe you," said Jennifer, her voice shaking. "Neither of us believed you."

"How did you know?" Mrs. Watts asked, keeping her eyes on Ben while putting an arm around her daughter.

Before Ben could reply, Amelia pulled a folded sheet of paper from her jacket pocket, unfolded it and placed it in front of Jennifer and her mother. "This is the information we had."

Ben realized that it was a copy of a page from the journal. Mother and daughter both read silently.

Mrs. Watts blinked back a few tears as she looked up from the page. "I don't understand. How could this...? But it didn't happen this way. Jennifer only has burns on her ankle. How...?" She picked up the sheet of paper. "Who wrote this? How did you get this?"

"That's just a photocopy," said Amelia. "The original was written a long time ago by a woman named Lydia Thornhill."

Ben kept his eyes on Jennifer. Her mouth opened but she didn't speak. He leaned closer. "You know that name, don't you Jennifer?"

Jennifer folded her arms and held them close to her body. She seemed to be shivering as if from a cold wind. "It...It didn't happen like this. It didn't happen like she wrote."

Her mother pulled her close. "No, it didn't Jenny. You didn't burn. You didn't die. You're all right. You were saved, thank God."

But Jennifer shook her head. "No, you don't understand. None of this happened. I wasn't even in the fire."

"Where were you Jennifer," asked Amelia.

"I...I don't know where I was. At the start, we were in that building, you know, for the field trip. We were walking. The sounds of the factory were loud. The man taking us through the place was talking but I couldn't hear much of what he was saying. Then, from far behind us, I heard a hissing sound. I was about to turn to see what it was when something at the front of the building exploded. I felt a jolt of fear. It nearly knocked me off my feet."

"It was fear that almost knocked you over? Not the

explosion?" asked Amelia.

Jennifer shook her head. "No, it wasn't the explosion. I had a sudden rush of terrible fear...or maybe dread. I knew something bad was about to happen. I remember trying to scream but couldn't, because at that moment, I was gone. I was no longer in that building." She hesitated and her voice fell to a whisper. "And I was no longer afraid. It was dark and there was no sound that I can remember, but I do remember feeling warm and safe. I was...nowhere. I was nowhere for what seemed like just a short time. Of course I found out later that I was out of it for two whole days." She turned to Ben. "Then, suddenly, the darkness was gone and I could see through my own eyes again. And I saw you. And I was home."

"But you knew there'd been a fire, didn't you?" asked Amelia.

She looked mystified for a moment. "I...yes, I guess I did. But it seemed like it was happening far away—like I wasn't there at all." She leaned closer to her mother.

Mrs. Watts kissed the top of her daughter's head. "Will someone please explain? Who is this woman, Lydia Thornhill?"

"Lydia Thornhill was my great, great, grandmother," said Ben. "She was born on June 18, 1858, and died on July 9, 1920." He saw the eyes of Mrs. Watts go wide, while Jennifer showed no reaction. He continued on. "While my grandmother lived she wrote a series of journals about dozens of deaths that she believed she'd actually experienced. We only found out recently that these deaths were real and that they've been occurring now, in our time, long after my grandmother's death. We've been trying to prevent them."

Mrs. Watts's let out a sigh, then sat back in her chair. "I'm sorry, Detective, you can't really expect us to believe that. Please, just tell us the truth. I think you owe us that."

Jennifer shook her head. "No, Mother. What he says feels right to me. I was protected by something, or by someone. The warmth I felt. Yes...maybe it was her warmth. I can still feel it."

The room was silent for a moment. Then Amelia spoke: "What Detective Marshall told you, *is* the truth, Mrs. Watts. We can hardly believe it ourselves."

"Right now we're trying to save another young girl," said Ben, "just like we saved Jennifer. Her name is Sandra. We have no last name. She's the last of the deaths my grandmother wrote about."

"How could she write about things that haven't happened yet?" asked Mrs. Watts. "You're playing her up to be some kind of a Nostradamus?—like a prophet or something."

"I suppose you could call her that," said Ben. "It was only because of her journals, we were able to save your daughter."

Jennifer, straightened. "You said there were other deaths. How many others have you saved?"

"You're the only one," said Ben quietly.

The room was quiet again. Then Jennifer got up and walked to Amelia. "I know about your burns. And, it's hard for me to believe it, but I know you saved me. You and Detective Marshall both." She touched Amelia's arm. "Thank you," she whispered

Ben stood as did Mrs. Watts.

"I'll see you out," said Harriet, standing while quickly brushing a tear from her cheek.

After they left, Ben was alone with Amelia. All he could do was put both hands on the back of his chair and stare down at the floor. He felt empty. Useless. "All those girls we could have saved but didn't. We only saved Jennifer."

"And maybe Sandra," said Amelia.

"Yeah, and maybe Sandra. But right now, we're nowhere on that. And time's running out."

Amelia reached for his hand, taking it in hers. "We can't give up on her, Ben. We can't let Sandra die. We're all she's got."

Ben took a breath then lightly kissed her cheek. "Yeah," he said softly, "we're all she's got. And that's what scares me."

The rest of the day passed slowly and through it all Ben had the nagging feeling that there was something he should be doing but wasn't. He slept poorly that night and left for the station-house early the next morning. He was just trotting up the steps outside when his cell went off.

It was Nolan. "Where are you, Ben?"

Ben could hear the urgency in the captain's voice. He felt a surge of hope. Something must be happening—finally. He broke into long strides pushing through the outer door. "In the building. On my way up. What's going on?"

"It's happening. Sandra Menendez, age twelve was just reported missing."

Ben's heart jumped into his throat. "Be right there." He killed the call and broke into a run, taking the stairs two at a time, making it to Nolan's office seconds later. Bradly and Harris were just coming over as was Phil.

Seeing Ben, Nolan broke off a conversation he was having with Harriet. "All right. It's Sandra Menendez, age twelve. She lives down in Brockton. Her mom reported her missing. She left for school but never made it there."

"Where's Brockton?" asked Harris.

"About an hour south of here. The local PD's interviewing the mom now."

"Anything on the dad?" asked Ben.

"Don't know. This is just coming over now. They're still interviewing Sandra's mother. They're doing other interviews at the school too—you know, friends and teachers who know her." He locked eyes with Ben. "I Notified Dr. Silvers right after I called you. She'd asked me to call her as soon as we got a break. She's on her way here."

"And just what the hell good is a shrink going to be?" asked Phil.

"She needs to be here, Phil, that's all you need to know," said Ben tersely before turning back to the captain. "Do we have a picture of the girl?"

"Give it a minute," shouted Harriet from behind Nolan where an outdated fax machine chugged away. "It's coming through now." Seconds later, she handed the page to Nolan who passed it over to Ben. "Says here, it was taken on her last birthday," she added, reading from the second page just off the fax as she gave that to Nolan.

Ben stared at the image. The girl's black hair hung in long braids, her mouth forming a half-hearted smile. She wore a bright red dress. Her black eyes peered back at Ben as if imploring him to do something—*anything* to save her. But Ben was trying to remember where he might have seen the girl. He shook his head. She didn't look the least bit familiar.

"All right, here's more," said Nolan, reading off the second page. "She's been raised by a single mom, who's been divorced for a few years now. No siblings. The girl gets average grades and is something of a loner at school."

"Do you have a picture of the mother?" asked Ben.

"Not yet."

"I want to talk to her. Maybe she remembers me from somewhere." Ben felt his conviction rising. Yes, that's what he needed to do.

"So what, if she remembers you? How does that help us find the girl?" asked Phil.

Ben ignored him, his eyes on Nolan. "You have an address?"

"I'll get it. And Phil, since it seems like you've already wrangled your way into this case, you stay here and work with the Feds, see what other info you can get on the girl or her mother. Harriet can help you too."

"Aye, Captain," said Phil.

Harriet gathered up all the info, created two folders and handed one to Ben just as Amelia arrived, her face a little brighter than the last time Ben had seen her. "Feeling better?" he asked.

"Yeah, a lot better. I hear the girl's from Brockton."

"You and I are heading there right now." Ben handed her the folder, noticing that her movements seemed tentative. "You sure you're up for this?"

"Try and stop me."

They took an unmarked police vehicle. As Amelia studied the few pages in the folder, Ben weaved through traffic, siren blaring, then merged onto the freeway.

"Not much here," said Amelia. "I take it the girl didn't look familiar to you?"

"Right, not at all familiar. I'm hoping the mother'll be able to help me place where I might have met her. One thing might lead to another."

Ben's phone went off. It was Phil. "The mom's left her house. She's driving toward her daughter's school."

"Probably tracing her daughter's route again," said Ben. "It's got to be tough on her. Is she violent? Do they expect trouble?"

"No, not violent. They say she's just really upset and shouldn't be driving. Where you at?"

Ben read off the mile-marker. "Should be in the general area in ten. We'll head for the school."

Phil gave him the address then ended the call.

When they pulled into the parking lot of Brandeis Elementary, they found the lot mostly empty. Two black and whites were angle-parked at the entrance.

"Looks like they called off classes for the day," said Amelia as they got out.

Ben flashed his badge to the cop standing beside the door.

"Been expecting you, Detective," said the cop who, with a nod, added "Ma'am," as Amelia passed. The cop guided them in through a set of double-doors, the cuffs at his belt jingling in time with his strides as he led the way down a brightly lit corridor bordered on both sides by rows of lockers, classroom doors and an occasional poster. A trophy case to the left proclaimed the glorious achievements of the Brandeis Bulldogs.

The setting took Ben back to his own elementary school with the smell of paper and white glue in the air mingling with the slight whiff of a plugged up urinal. From up ahead he heard the sound of a woman crying, then talking—too faint to pick out any words.

"That's the mom," the cop explained as he walked.

"Yeah, I figured," said Ben.

They stopped at a door to the right, the sounds of the mother clear now even through the closed door. "My baby. My poor baby," she muttered through sobs.

"She just got here a few minutes ago," the cop explained, his voice low. "There's a social worker and a few teachers with her right now trying to calm her down."

Ben caught Amelia with a glance then gave the cop a nod.

At the sound of the opening door, the sobs stopped. The woman, who had been sitting on a low stool with her back toward Ben stood and turned.

Her long black hair hung tangled down to her shoulders, strands of it clinging to her cheeks. From deep in their sockets her reddened eyes stared back at Ben, imploring, hopeful. “Have you found her? Have you found my Sandy?” But her words faded as she read the truth on Ben’s face. Her arms dropped to her side and she sat back down, her back straight. She put a hand over her eyes, her lower lip quivering as she tried not to cry.

Ben kept his eyes on her. Had he seen her before? No, he didn’t think so. And he’d seen no hint of recognition on her face either. They walked closer.

“This is Detective Marshall, Mrs. Menendez,” the cop explained. “He just drove down from Boston.”

The woman took her hand from her eyes “Boston?” she asked. “What would...?” Her eyes widened and suddenly flashed to Ben’s. “Did David send you? Was it David?” She stood abruptly. “Oh God, does he have my Sandy?” She reached out, grabbing Ben’s wrist.

“Who’s David, Mrs. Menendez?” asked the cop.

Ben allowed her to pull him closer “I’m sorry Mrs. Menendez, I don’t know the David you’re talking about. Is he Sandra’s father?”

Her grip slackened. “He didn’t send you?”

A woman who Ben took to be the social worker, moved closer from behind, placing a gentle hand on both her shoulders. She handed her a glass of water which, as she drank, seemed to calm her somewhat. She sat back down.

“Who is this David, Mrs. Menendez?” asked the cop more softly after a moment.

“Rico’s brother.”

“All right. So, he’s Sandra’s uncle.” The cop turned to Ben. “Rico’s the dad. Died a few years back. This is the first I’ve heard of this Dave fellow.”

“Does David live in Boston?” asked Ben. “Is there any reason that he might have Sandra? Were the two of them close?”

She shook her head. “No, no. I don’t know. No, there’s no

reason he'd have her. I just thought...yes, he lives in Boston. I haven't seen him in a long time. He sends a Christmas card every year though, and a birthday card for Sandy."

"Do you have a phone number for him? An address?"

Mrs. Menendez didn't move. She closed her eyes.

"It's important that you help them, Mrs. Menendez," said the social worker, a hand still on her shoulder.

Watching, Ben realized that Mrs. Menendez was praying. When she opened her eyes a moment later, they seemed clearer than before, her face more resolute. She reached for her purse and pulled out her phone. She tapped the screen with her index finger then handed it to the cop who handed it to Ben.

The screen showed the contact page for a David Burchini. Ben felt a chill run up his spine. The guy's Boston address showed that he lived on Elmhurst—Ben's old street, the address close, maybe only a block up from Ben's place. He swallowed, certain now that Sandra Menendez, God help her, was the Sandra from the journal. He handed the phone to Amelia. "When's the last time you saw David, Mrs. Menendez?"

"A year ago. No, maybe two years ago. We stayed with him for a few days while he showed us around the city."

"You haven't seen him since?"

"No."

"Are you on good terms with your brother-in-law?" This was from the cop.

Mrs. Menendez shook her head slowly. "After my husband died, he and I became close for a while. He wanted us to get together. When I decided I wasn't interested, he got angry."

"Angry enough to want to hurt Sandra?" asked Ben.

She shook her head. "No, oh no. He would never do anything like that. He..." She motioned for more water and took a swallow. She spoke slowly. "David was always playing the big-shot. He gambled and he drank and he always seemed to be needing money. He was everything his brother Rico wasn't, but he seemed all right back when Sandy and I visited him."

"Was he involved with the mob in Boston? Maybe the Russian

mob?" asked Ben.

She shook her head. "The Russian mob? No. Why would you ask that? David had his faults but he knew how to stay out of trouble. He was always talking about a guy named Vito and how he owed his life to the guy. He spoke of him like he was a saint or something."

A thought struck Ben. "Vito Ronaldi?"

"Yes, maybe. It was something like that. He only mentioned his last name once. I don't think he meant to say his full name, it just slipped out the one time. I didn't pay much attention but yes, it was something like Ronaldi or maybe Rondozi. I can't be sure. But David was always good to us, especially to Sandy. Even though he didn't have much of anything himself, he always managed to send her a little something on her birthday and at Christmas. He would never..."

But Ben had already taken a few steps away. He placed a call to Phil, talked quietly then walked back. "We're bringing your brother-in-law in for questioning, Mrs. Menendez. Is there anything else you can tell us about him?"

"So maybe he has Sandy? Maybe she's safe with him? I don't know why that would be but..." She looked up hopefully at Ben. "Is that what you're thinking?"

"It's possible," said Ben, doubtful. The journal made no mention of the killer knowing the girl or of she knowing him. And a Latino accent could never be mistaken for Slavic.

After a few more questions the social worker talked Mrs. Menendez into going home, offering to stay with her for a few hours so she could rest. At that point, Ben and Amelia were already on their way out.

"This David guy lives on your street," said Amelia as they walked down the hall. "So, the last time Sandy and her mom visited with him, you might well have had some incidental contact with the girl."

"Yeah, I picked up on that."

"So who's Vito Ronaldi?" asked Amelia when she and Ben stepped outside, heading for their car.

"He's a dead guy. Used to head up the east-side mob along

with his brother. They're both dead."

"Killed?"

"Yeah, knocked off by the Russian mob, we figured. Phil was working it. I think the case is still open."

"Russian, huh?" said Amelia, easing herself into the car. "That's a Slavic language."

"Yeah, guess it is." He pulled out of the lot.

"Where to now?"

"Back to the station," said Ben, his foot hitting the accelerator. "We're going to see what the brother-in-law has to say." Sirens and flashers on, they were nearly there when Phil called confirming that the guy had been picked up. "Does he know anything about Sandra?" shouted Ben over the road noise.

"Shit, Benjie, he's higher than a kite on something. He hasn't responded to any of our questions. I don't think he knows his own name right now. We had to check his ID to make sure we had the right guy."

"I'm betting he knows something, Phil. Get some coffee into him. We're almost there." He ended the call then gave Amelia a nervous glance. "He damn well better know something."

Thirty minutes later, they stood beside Phil in a darkened room staring through a two-way mirror at the sparse hulk of a man named David Burchini who, in jeans and sweatshirt sat slumped in a chair with both arms hanging limp. On thin shoulders his head drooped so that Ben could only see enough of his face to know that he needed a shave. The table in front of him seemed to be the only thing keeping him from falling forward onto the floor. "Is he asleep?" he asked Phil.

"Seems to me that he's coming in for a crash landing from a crack high." Phil took out some notes and gave them the rundown: "Forty-seven years old, last known place of employment was an auto-parts store in south Boston. We were able to get a few things out of him since I called you. He hasn't been in touch with Mrs. Menendez or the girl in more than a year. When we mentioned them he told us he used to send cards to Sandy—that's what he called her. He seemed a little surprised to hear the girl was missing. He's got no priors and lives on Elmhurst, two blocks up from where you used to live. Odd coincidence, huh?"

"You picked him up at his place?" asked Ben. "Did he let you in?"

"Yeah, he was cooperative but, you know, not really there. Didn't make a fuss when we asked him to come down here. He's got no priors."

"Did you see any pictures in his place?" asked Amelia. "You know, of the girl or her mother?"

Phil thought about that one then shook his head. "Didn't see any. The place smelled heavy of scotch though. I saw an empty bottle on the kitchen table. Saw a few needles in the bathroom so he's definitely a user, but his arms—he had his sleeves rolled up when we got there, they didn't have the look of a long-time junkie.

Amelia stared at the guy. "In that shape it's going to be tough getting anything useful out of him." She paused and looked closer. "But wait, see there?"

"See what?" asked Ben.

"His right index finger—he's tapping it on the table. He's doing it very slowly, thinking hard about something. I'll bet he's faking the high."

Ben had missed that but saw it now—the finger moving ever so slightly up and down every twenty seconds or so. "I'm going in," he said, reaching for the door.

"Hold on Ben," said Amelia. "If he does know something we need to get that information out of him fast. You want me in there with you?"

Ben considered this only for a moment. No, he had to do this by himself. He didn't want Burchini to feel like they were ganging up on him. He shook his head. "I'll let you know if I need help."

When Ben entered the holding room, the guy slowly looked up and, through half-opened eyes, followed the fresh cup of coffee Ben put in front of him.

As if cold, Burchini wrapped both hands around the cup but didn't drink.

Ben sat. "I'm Detective Marshall, Mr. Burchini. I've talked to my partner and..."

"Who are you?"

"Ben. Just call me Ben."

"Hello Ben." Shakily, he raised the cup to his lips only managing to wet his lower lip before setting it back down. "I don't know why I'm here."

"Your niece Sandy is missing and we think she's in danger. We thought you could help us find her."

Burchini stared blankly then lifted the coffee to his mouth again, this time taking an actual sip. "This is about her, isn't it?"

"Yes. It is. Do you know where Sandy is?"

Burchini shook his head.

"She lives in Brockton. But she's gone missing and we need to find her. Her mother is very worried. Can you help us?"

Burchini's hands began to shake. Coffee from the cup he still held began to splash out and puddle the table.

"Take a deep breath, Mr. Burchini," said Ben, calmly. "No one's going to hurt you here."

After a while, Burchini's hands steadied. After putting the cup down, he wrung them together, staring at the coffee puddles.

Ben's heart pounded. He fought to keep his patience. He knew he had to be careful with this guy. "Can you help us find Sandy, Mr. Burchini?"

No answer.

With few options, Ben decided to go with the only hardball question he had. "Do you know a man named Vito Ronaldi?"

There! It was much more than a flinch: a blink, a twitch at the corner of one eye and a mouth opening half way then quickly closing. This guy *does* know something.

Burchini began tapping a finger in the largest of the puddles. "What does he have to do with anything?"

"So you know him. You know he's dead, right? I'll bet you know his dead brother too."

Burchini folded his arms, not in a belligerent way but more as if he was trying to hold himself together. He spoke in a quiet voice. "He was my best friend. They both were. They were like family to me."

"Look, Mr. Burchini. We're not after you but we know you had dealings with the Ronaldi's. Do those dealings have anything to do with Sandy's disappearance?"

"No, no. Of course not."

"Are you in some kind of trouble, Mr. Burchini? If you are, you have to put that out of your head right now. Think of Sandy. We know she's in danger. Is there anything you can tell us about where she is right now?"

"She's with good people. You don't have to worry about her. She's with good people."

Good people. Ben felt his heart skip a beat. He spoke slowly now. "We know she's with good people, Mr. Burchini—David. Can I call you David?"

David shrugged his shoulders.

"We have to talk to her, David. Her mother needs her. Do you know how we can reach Sandy?"

Suddenly, David smiled. "She's with Anna. Don't worry, she's with Anna."

"Who is Anna?"

"A good person. She's beautiful. She gets me whatever I need. She does whatever I..."

"Do you have a way to get in touch with Anna—an address or phone number?"

David was silent again.

"Do you know Anna's last name? Think, David. This is important."

David shook his head and smiled again, his eyes almost closing as if on the brink of sleep. "It's a funny name. She's Russian. I can never remember it, Moldova maybe? I just call her Anna. But, she's a good person. There's no need to worry. She brings me whatever I need to make me happy. She's good to me."

At that moment there was a rap on the mirror behind Ben. He turned and Phil, it had to be Phil, rapped again—more insistent this time. "Excuse me for a moment, David. I'll be right back."

Phil met Ben just outside the door.

"I know the woman, Benjie—Anna Monderovna. That's just an

alias she sometimes uses. She's with the Russian mob. She's got a job at an import-export outfit at a swanky address downtown. We've had a tail on her for months looking for her to lead us to a bigger fish."

"What could she have to do with Sandy?"

"The mob has a big thing going with child porn and under-age prostitutes. It would make sense for them to put a woman in charge of that part of the business—you know, who'd suspect a woman of being involved in that kind of shit?"

"So she used Burchini to get to Sandy?" asked Amelia. "Does that make sense?"

"Procuring the girls is the riskiest part of operations like that. If they have some kind of an in with the girl that reduces the risk, so yeah, it makes sense. Burchini being her uncle, he might have even been the one who picked her up and delivered her to Anna. In his condition, he probably thought she was just planning to take her to an amusement park."

"Any idea where Anna is right now?" asked Ben, his mind churning and, behind it all, Big Ben ticking.

"We dropped the tail on her a few weeks back but I'm pretty sure she's up where she works. She seemed to keep to a strict routine. With the info we've got from Burchini we should be able to get a warrant to at least bring her in for questioning."

"Sandy dies tonight. There's no time for that," said Amelia.

Ben nodded, checking his watch. It was just past noon. "We know Anna will be at the scene of the murder tonight. All we have to do is find her and follow her there."

"She could be there already," said Amelia.

"If she is, Sandy's as good as dead," said Ben. "Our only hope is to assume she's at work, find her and follow her." He turned to Phil. "Do you have a picture of Anna?"

Phil gave him a thin smile. "We have tons of pictures of her and this guy Burchini's right about one thing—she *is* beautiful."

CHAPTER 30

In the heart of Boston, Karenina Enterprises took up the entire 18th floor of the stately Millburn building. In his best suit, with collar buttoned and tie straight, Ben stepped out of the elevator and strode through a pair of glass doors as if he was about to become their biggest client. At the reception desk a woman, not Anna, was staring at her computer screen and working her keyboard. Ben didn't wait for her to look up.

"I'm here on important business and I don't have much time. I need to speak to someone about a bill of lading for a shipment of American machine parts being exported into Russia."

"Do you have an appointment, sir?" asked the woman, still fixated on her screen.

"No."

Behind the woman was an open office area with a dozen desks where white-shirted men and a few women, worked. Ben scanned the women then settled on a gaggle of three women gathered around a copy machine. Two of them were clearly not Anna while the face of the third was hidden by the others.

The receptionist kept up with her work a little longer then looked up with feigned sympathy. "I'm sorry, sir. You'll need an appointment. I can get you in to see Mr. Vronsky on Thursday, will that...?"

Wondering why that name seemed familiar, Ben interrupted, raising his voice a notch. "No. I told you that time is short. I need to speak to someone now."

"I'm sorry sir, there's nothing I can do," said the receptionist, shaking her head just as the face of the third woman at the copier became visible—not Anna. "Who are you with? Do you have a card? Mr....?"

Ben slapped his hand down on the granite counter and raised

his voice to an irate shout. "I am Benjamin David Marshall. I'm with the BDM Consortium and I guarantee that, whoever this Mr. Vronsky of yours is with right now, my business will be ten times more lucrative for him and for your firm."

At this outburst, heads in the office area turned in Ben's direction. The eyes of the receptionist went wide and her face reddened. She backed her chair up and picked up her phone. Ben hoped she was calling her supervisor and not building security.

Ben waited for a moment then, in the office area out beyond the desks, an office door swung open. A gray haired man in suit and tie took a few steps out and, hands on hips, stared out at Ben. But Ben took little note of him because, standing in the shadow of the doorway just behind him stood Anna. And there was no mistaking her. She wore a tight red skirt and seemed to be straightening the matching vest that draped the sensual curves of her white blouse. There was no hint that she'd seen Ben and he looked away quickly. He didn't wait for the receptionist to complete her call. "All right, then," he shouted as if offended. "Thank you for your time. I'll take my business elsewhere."

He strode out, rode the elevator back down and stepped outside. To avoid scrutiny, he took a meandering route across the street, back to where Amelia waited in Ben's unmarked squad car. "She's there," he said, getting in behind the wheel. "Now we wait." It was 3pm.

At 6:30pm the woman known as Anna Monderovna left the Millburn building walking east up Central Avenue. Ben started the car. From Phil, he knew that she always parked at a parking structure two blocks away and that was where Phil waited in his car. Harris and Bradly waited in a third car at a random spot nearby in case Anna did something unexpected.

She walked at a brisk pace causing her calf-length green coat to shift back and forth. Her shiny black hair flowed back over her shoulders. She glanced at her watch. "She's definitely in a hurry to get somewhere," said Ben. He waited for her to reach the corner then pulled out, following slowly. "Turning on to Belmont," he said to Phil through the radio, losing sight of her momentarily.

"Don't see her yet," said Phil. "Oh yeah, there she is." And a moment later, "She's walking into the parking structure now."

"Harris? You guys set?" asked Ben.

"Ready here."

Ben pulled slowly around onto Belmont and did one pass of the parking structure giving Phil a glance as he passed by. On the next block up he double-parked and waited. He adjusted his side mirror so he could see the exit from the parking garage. The next move should be Anna pulling out in her late model, black Buick.

Over the next five minutes maybe ten cars pulled out, none of them a black Buick.

Ben was starting to worry. He flicked on the radio again. "You keeping an eyeball on the drivers coming out? Maybe she's in a different car."

"A little hard to see from this spot with the sun's glare off the windshields. But yeah, I've been watching," said Phil.

Another few minutes went by and another ten or so cars pulled out of the garage.

"Damn, I hate this," Ben muttered to Amelia, his thumbs tapping the wheel. "Maybe we missed her."

"Don't even think that, Ben. We can't let that happen."

At that moment, Phil's voice came over the radio. "Wait, what's this?"

In the mirror Ben saw a white pick-up emerge from the garage. Its left turn-signal came on. He gripped the wheel staring into the mirror trying to see the driver, but he was too far away. "What? You think that's her, Phil?" He had a hand on the gear-shift, ready to throw it into drive.

"Shit, I can't be sure. I know I saw long black hair and she might have taken off her coat. But her driving an old pickup, that doesn't seem right. No, that can't be her." The pickup took the turn. "Damn, I just don't know, Benjie."

"Shit. This is taking too long. I'm on it." Ben hit his siren and flashers. With only a glance back at traffic, he screeched into a U-turn, heading back toward the garage. "You guys stay in position in case I'm wrong."

He cut his siren and flashers then took another turn that took him past the garage. He leaned forward as he drove, his eyes frantic, scanning the cars ahead. "Don't see the pickup yet."

"Wait, there it is," said Amelia craning her neck, pointing. "She's a light ahead of us."

"Yeah, got her." Ben shouted into the radio: "Still no ID on her. You guys just stay put. I'll try to get closer."

"Stay to the right, Ben," Amelia shouted. "I think she turned up there on Fisher—probably heading for the freeway."

Ben hit the gas, dodging his way through a red light then jerked the wheel into the turn. With relief, he spotted the pickup, then slowed, maneuvering only two cars behind. He dropped back and eased into the left lane. Accelerating slowly, he began inching closer until they were even with the tailgate. Ben could see a feminine hand on the wheel, he could see a full head of long black hair but not much else. "I think it's her. But hold on. Don't look in her direction. We don't want to spook her."

The car in front of Ben slowed and the pickup pulled farther ahead. "Hold on," he shouted. He pulled into the left turn lane and hit the gas to get around the guy in front. Falling back into the left lane, he was now nearly even alongside the pick-up. He spotted a well-rouged cheek and a cigarette hanging from the woman's mouth. "This gal smoke, Phil?"

"Yeah, like a Dutch oven."

Ben slowed and took a breath. "All right. That's enough for me. It's her." He dropped back again then shouted the plate number into the radio.

"Great. I'll have 'em run it," said Phil.

"I think she might have seen us," said Amelia.

"She didn't." But Ben couldn't be sure. He spoke into the radio again. "Phil and Harris, both of you form on me but stay well behind and no cowboy maneuvering. She could be onto us." He slowed.

"How do your guys know where we are?" asked Amelia.

"I activated our GPS beacon. They'll just home-in on us."

They drove for another ten minutes in the left lane. The road began to veer left when, four cars ahead, the pickup suddenly shifted into the right lane causing Ben to momentarily lose sight it. When the road straightened, his heart stopped. It was gone.

Oh God, we lost her," said Amelia, peering around the car in front of them.

Ben shifted lanes trying to get a better line of sight. "She must have taken the turn-off back there. She was in the left lane, then went right. I didn't think she'd...shit! There's a new ramp onto the freeway back there. That's where she's heading."

Ben flipped his siren and flashers on again and jerked the wheel fishtailing into a frantic U-turn. "I lost her guys," he shouted into the radio. "I think she's going for the southbound I-93. We're heading there now. Phil, you take 93 north, just in case I'm wrong. Harris, you're on me. Anything on that plate yet, Phil?"

"Not yet."

Ben raced through traffic, following the signs to I-93. He accelerated down the newly constructed entrance ramp, bouncing along the shoulder for an extra hundred feet before weaving into the slow-moving traffic.

"Don't see her," said Amelia.

Ben peered ahead. He didn't see her either. His heart sank. He hit the radio call button and checked in with the station. "Need back up here. An old Ford Ranger pickup. Off Fisher, heading south we think on 93. I'm betting they'll be taking I-24 South. We got anybody over that way?" He gave the plate number.

"Checking..." said a female voice over the static. "No, you're the closest."

"Patch me into the Brockton PD." Two minutes later he gave them a description of the truck and the driver. "Do not apprehend. Repeat. Do not apprehend. Follow at distance. The driver is a person of interest in the Menendez case."

Ben signed off, continuing to weave through traffic. "Shit, how could I have lost her?" He smacked the wheel.

Amelia put a hand on his knee. "We'll find her, Ben. Keep your cool."

"Sorry, but I lost my cool a few miles back."

Siren still blaring, grill lights still flashing, traffic began to clear just a little and Ben coaxed the unmarked squad car up to ninety, then ninety-five. Cars veered sharply to get out of his way. He took the exit to I-24 south nearly skidding off the shoulder as he took the ramp too fast.

Beside him, Amelia sat stiffly, her left hand gripping the console. She shouted over the noise. "Shit, Ben it won't help anyone if we do a flip and fly into a ditch out here."

He backed off the gas, but only slightly. He was surprised to see that it was already getting dark. He knew he'd have to slow down for a road construction site a few miles up. He had to make good time now, while he could.

Moments later he saw a long chain of brake lights ahead. He jerked the car onto the shoulder, kicking up gravel. His headlights picked up a bright orange line of traffic cones. They were coming up fast and with a thwump-thwump-thwump, his right front bumper knocked them aside. Ben knew he should slow down and was about to do just that when the car hit a rut and flew upward.

They were airborne for a full second. Amelia screamed when they slammed back down, Ben fighting the wheel as the car careened first right toward a ditch, then left toward the line of stopped cars. He kept his grip and backed off to fifty, gaining control again. Shit! His mind flashed back to every chase movie he'd ever seen and wondered now how many cars they went through during filming. Here he was in a real chase and he only had the one car—he'd better make it last. The car rumbled and shook, still speeding along the shoulder.

Phil came on the radio. "The pickup's owned by an outfit that rents out junkers. They show it being signed out to a woman named Phyllis Reed who has an address in New Bedford."

"Roger that," said Ben. He did a position check then signed off. Up ahead he saw a work crew blocking off the shoulder and the entire right lane. He slowed and, as his heart rate climbed, he pried his way back into the lineup of cars, barely moving now.

"There's an exit half a mile ahead. It goes east to Whitman," said Amelia.

Ben was limp with frustration, inching the car forward only a few feet at a time. He knew there was no way they were going to find that pickup. Sandy Menendez was going to die just like his grandmother said. He put his hand on Amelia's and took a deep breath.

Ten long minutes later he took the exit.

At the top of the ramp he took a left onto route 27. He blinked into the distance, clearing his eyes a little, feeling better now that they were moving again. But no, there was something more, wasn't there? "This feels right, Amelia," he said under his breath without understanding why.

"What do you mean, Ben? What feels right?"

He shook his head staring at the road ahead. "Damned if I know." A mist was building. Ben put on his wipers. He cut the siren but kept the flashers going. Gas stations, a Walmart and strip malls dotted both sides of the road. He bent closer to the windshield as the mist grew thicker then backed off on the accelerator, his mind suddenly cluttered with a maze of thoughts which seemed to gather his senses gently up, away from his body, detached and floating free, twisting and turning along darkened corridors of what-if's. He could feel his foot hit the brake and, as if from a great distance, he heard Amelia shouting. But her words were lost in the wind that seemed to envelope him. As if he were flying, he looked down and far below saw a little girl lying on a bed, a dark, menacing form bending over her. She was crying then screaming.

Sickened, Ben forced himself to turn and look at the room: table, chairs, bed, lamp and there was something else—a sound. A sound as if from a swarm of bees. It came from somewhere outside. He felt his body jerk upright. He heard the girl scream. Louder now. It was happening. It was happening right now!

And suddenly, he was back.

"Ben! Ben, you can't stop here. What's happening, Ben? Are you all right?" It was Amelia. He could hear her clearly now.

His hands, cold and clammy squeezed the wheel. He looked around. The mist had cleared. Their car was at a dead stop in the left lane, cars whizzing by, horns blaring. Amelia was leaning close. He smelled the salve that coated her burns. He felt her hand brush his cheek, then feel his forehead. He could feel the beads of sweat that had formed there and suddenly he was very cold.

"Take a breath, Ben. Breathe easy."

Ben cleared his eyes and his mind. "It's happening now. I know it." He straightened and stared into the windshield. "I know it." He checked the rear view mirror, took his foot off the brake and hit the accelerator. He flipped the siren back on and gripped the wheel, flying down the road.

"Ben. What just happened? You had a vision, didn't you?"

"They're miles ahead somewhere. In a house I think. A big one. I saw her, Amelia. Somehow I actually *saw* Sandy. But I don't know where. But I think we're headed in the right direction. Check the map, tell me what's ahead."

"A map. You mean a paper map?"

He reached over and popped the glovebox, pointing. "It's sometimes the best way. Should be a penlight in there too."

She found both, then said: "We'll be getting into farmland pretty soon then Whitman's seven or eight miles up. But Ben, I don't understand. You saw the girl?"

"Yes. I saw her. I felt like I was actually there, just like with Cindy. I was looking down at her as she tried to fight...as she fought for her life. But there was nothing I could do. Shit! We can't let her die, Amelia. We are *not* going to let her die."

In another mile, trees and open fields began to border the road. There was little traffic and Ben, cut the siren and flashers. "Wait, what's that?"

"What's what?"

"Did you hear it?" Ben slowed and lowered his window. He slowed further until, just above the wind noise, he heard it again. "There, that buzzing. That's the sound. That's what I heard."

Amelia was silent for a moment as a few cars passed by and Ben steered off onto the shoulder and pulled to a stop. "That's a plane."

"Yeah, a small one, prop-driven. Is there an airport around here?"

Amelia checked the map. "Not according to this map. Let me

check the map on my phone. There might be a new one somewhere around here." And after a moment: "Yes, there's an airport ahead. A small, private one. Green Sky airport."

"Set your GPS to take us there," said Ben.

"You think they have the girl at an airport?"

"Maybe not *at* the airport, but near it." Ben shook his head in frustration. "Look, I don't know exactly, but I know what I heard. I..."

"All right. All right. I believe you, Ben. Let's go."

Ben took a breath, hopeful but knowing at the same time that the info he was acting on was pretty flimsy. He wasn't even sure now if what he'd had seen and heard a few miles back, hadn't been a fabrication of his own confused mind. But there was nothing else to go on, was there?

Ben let an oncoming pair of headlights go by then pulled out, off the shoulder and onto the road.

Amelia jumped, then turned in her seat as best she could to look through the rear window. "There! There, Ben! That's a white pickup that just went by, wasn't it?"

Ben hadn't seen it. "What? You think it's her? You think it was Anna and she just left Sandy with...? Shit." Frantic, Ben floored the gas pedal and peeled out in a spray of gravel. He shouted into the radio. "Suspect heading west on route 27 in a white pickup. Apprehend! Repeat, apprehend!"

"We're five miles out," said Harris through the static. "We'll get her. What about the girl?"

"On it," shouted Ben, breaking the connection. "Anna whatever-her-name-is has got her blood money," he said to Amelia. "The guy's alone with her now. And, God, we're out of time. How far is Whitman?"

"About four miles."

"All right, we're looking for a large house, someplace secluded so it wouldn't be in the town itself, and it's within earshot of the airport. It can't be far."

He drove hard for the next two miles, through a wooded area then out to where the road went into a curve and banked into a straight-away. He saw lights ahead. "No, this is wrong." He pulled over and lowered his window. "I can't hear the planes."

"Probably not the busiest of airports," said Amelia.

He did a quick U-turn and drove slowly back. As they approached the wooded area, he slowed further and flipped on his brights. He turned on the spotter light mounted just above his side mirror directing its beam into the trees, first on one side of the road, then the other.

"I still don't hear the planes," said Amelia.

"I know," said Ben in a near whisper, listening through his still-open window, peering through the crowded trees. He directed the beam more forward and caught his breath "There, what's that?"

"Yeah, I see it. Looks like it might be a driveway."

He pulled closer, lowering the light so it only penetrated the first ten feet or so of a gravel road that ran off to the left. He cut the spotter and turned in, then cut his head lamps. It was pitch dark. He lowered both front windows. The car crept along, the gravel crunching under the tires, the air thick with moisture and swampy smells.

The sounds of the woods were all around—crickets mostly, but Ben thought he could hear a few bull frogs in the mix. And, behind those sounds—yes, behind them, he heard the buzz of a light aircraft. "We're close."

He watched the odometer slowly count off the tenths of a mile.

"A bit long for somebody's driveway," whispered Amelia. She swatted a bug. "Do we really need these windows open?" She raised hers.

"Can't be too much farther," said Ben, thankful that the half-moon overhead was helping to keep him on the road which, after a few slight bends, began a gentle uphill grade. Then something caught his eye. "There, what's that?—a sign I think. He flipped the spotter light back on and read the black on yellow words:

YOU ARE ON PRIVATE PROPERTY
TRESPASSERS WILL BE PROCECUTED

IF YOU PROCEED FURTHER AN ALARM WILL SOUND

Ben shifted the light to the center of the road. 50 yards ahead a chain link fence topped with coils of razor wire blocked off the road. "Shit, with all this other stuff, they could have security cameras up there. The guy might already know we're here." He kept the spotter centered, hardly moving now. "Well, I've always preferred the direct approach anyway. Hold on."

Ben turned his brights back on, hit the siren and flashers, then stomped the accelerator.

He felt the rear wheels grind into the road-bed. There was a slight fish-tail but, as they gained traction, the car shot forward. Ben's head snapped back, pinned to the head rest. Ahead, the fence grew larger, its frame looking beefier than Ben had thought. Both hands on the wheel, he grit his teeth.

From the fence, a blinding light came on. A deafening alarm sounded. Ben braced himself keeping his foot hard on the gas.

The car hit with an enormous bang. The windshield shattered. A high pitched screech cut the air. The airbags blew, blocking Ben's vision for an instant. He kept his grip on the wheel. The car was still roaring ahead so he figured that they had to be through the fence by now. The airbag fell away and Ben could see again. The windshield was gone. The sheared off remnants of the fence clung to the grill, shaking and scraping with the rumbling of the car. Ben fought the headwind and kept his eyes forward. All he could see ahead was a blur of tall weeds. They pelted and scraped the under-carriage as the car tore through them.

Amelia was shouting. "Turn, Ben. To the left. Up the hill. There's a building up there."

Ben didn't see the building and didn't take the time to look. He veered left, heading up a grade where he found firmer ground. Just low grass here. When he saw the lights of the building, he turned more directly for it, only 100 yards ahead now.

It was a sprawling two-story structure, log construction with a single-level portion at one end. A few upstairs lights were on and, just as Ben caught sight of it, a first-floor light went on.

He drew back on the accelerator and glanced in Amelia's

direction but couldn't really see her. "You all right?"

"Yeah. I just hope this is the right place. It's big. Looks like this might be a golf course and that's the clubhouse up there."

"Shit, what kind of a golf club tops its fences with razor wire?" Ben pulled up to the front of the place and hit the brakes, skidding to a stop. He killed the siren but kept the engine and the flashers going. Getting out, he could hear from far below, the fence alarm still going off. "Come on," he shouted to Amelia. "Front door's there."

With his hand on his shoulder holster, he ran toward a set of large wooden double-doors going into a crouch as he came up beside them. He stopped and pulled his gun just as Amelia caught up, out of breath. He turned to her seeing a shiny rivulet of blood trailing down the side of her face. But there was no time to be concerned about that. "Stay close," he whispered. "And keep your head down."

He waited for a second, listening, then leaned forward. With the heel of his gun, he banged hard on the door. "Police! Open up! Open up now!"

Then he heard it—on the other side of the door a rifle was being cocked. Ben jumped quickly to the side, barreling into Amelia just as the shot went off.

With a huge bang, the doors flew open in a hail of splintering wood.

The blast echoed Ben's head. He repositioned himself. From both knees, he extended his gun forward, firing three shots blindly through the shattered doors into the building. He waited, listening, knowing how unlikely it was that he'd actually hit the guy inside. Then he thought, shit, he might have hit the girl. "I've got to get in there," he whispered more to himself than to Amelia. He turned to her.

She was on her knees leaning against the wall of the building, breathing hard, her back toward him. He put a hand on her shoulder feeling her flinch at his touch. "You okay?"

"Yeah, I'm good." She angled herself to face him, fresh blood glistening on her forehead.

"You're hurt."

"Damn it Ben, I'm good. Just got the shakes. You go on, get in there. Get the bastard. But be careful. Don't shoot the girl."

Keeping low, Ben turned back to the door. The blast from inside had ruptured the lock and had nearly blown the doors off their hinges. Using the barrel of his gun, he swung the far door out farther and crept forward. He could hear breathing inside now. No, it was crying, a whimpering strained with fear. It was Sandy. It could only be her, he thought with relief. She was still alive. Ben had to make his move now.

In one motion he jumped to his feet and shouldered his way inside. In the darkness, he took a quick left then fell back into a crouch, his back braced against the inside wall. With both arms outstretched, he held his gun at the ready. He could see that there was a chair beside him but his eyes were still adjusting. He still heard the girl's breathing. "Sandy. We're here for you honey. I'm a policeman. No one's going to hurt you." He waited for a moment. "Do you understand? You're safe now."

Slowly, Ben stood. He could see her now. She lay naked, spread-eagled on what looked to be an inflatable mattress positioned on a frame in the center of the room. "Oh, Christ," he shuddered, thinking about what the guy might have been doing to her only minutes ago.

At a sound from behind him Ben's heart leaped into his throat. He swung around. It was Amelia. He saw her eyes go wide when she saw the girl. Without hesitation, she ran to her, dropping to her knees. "Oh, baby. You poor baby." She placed a hand on the side of Sandy's face and kissed her forehead. "You're all right now. You're all right. We're going to get you home to your mother."

But the girl didn't make a sound.

"Is she okay?" asked Ben.

Amelia was working to remove the ropes that held her wrists and ankles. "Yes. I think she passed out. She's got a strong pulse. Oh God, Ben. You've got to get that monster."

At that moment, a low hum came from within the building.

"Shit," said Ben, recognizing the sound of a garage door opening. He rushed back outside, past the ruins of the front door.

He raced for the far end of the building where he'd seen a paved driveway. As he ran he heard a car start up. He made it to the driveway just as a pair of tail lights flashed on from inside the garage. The guy was backing out.

Ben held his position, arms out and steady, sighting down the gun barrel as if he were at the firing range. He shouted, "Police! Police! Stop you fucking creep. I'm going to blow your fucking head off."

Tires squealed. Ben saw the rear end of a huge off-road SUV charging straight at him. He aimed through the rear window up to where the driver's head should be. He fired five shots in quick succession. But the SUV didn't stop. Still in reverse, it picked up speed, closing on Ben. He took a last shot then jumped to the side—too late. The rear corner of the SUV hit him hard. The engine roared.

Ben fell back, his head hitting the hard driveway just as a spinning tire rolled over his right hand. A blaze of pain shot up his arm. Instinctively, he pulled his feet in and curled his body between the wheels as the entire vehicle backed over him and continued into a backwards turn. He couldn't move. Pain thundered through his arm. He wondered if his hand was still attached. Shit. He was going to bleed out. Yeah, he could feel the blood pumping out at his wrist. A sick numbness hit him. Then, from behind he heard a rumbling and a loud thump.

Ben shifted his body and saw that the SUV had flipped onto its side, wheels still spinning. He smiled grimly. The ass-hole wasn't going to get away after all. Then he heard another sound. He saw the upside door of the truck open. The guy was climbing out and, shit, he had a rifle. The guy jumped down off the side of the SUV, heading for Ben.

He could see him more clearly as the headlights from the overturned SUV caught him in their glare. He seemed to be limping. His silhouette sent a shiver through Ben. The guy wore an overcoat and held the rifle in one hand. Like the phantom of death he walked, the hem of his overcoat flaring out on both sides like wings, his arms lifting the rifle into position.

Ben struggled to move. He no longer had his gun. Maybe it was close by but hell, there was no use in looking for it. He couldn't even feel his left arm and there probably wasn't enough left of his right hand to even lift the gun much less pull the trigger. He strained as if against binding chains. But he couldn't move. There was nothing he could do. With each throb of his heart, the blood continued to pump out of him. He felt a terrible chill in the air. He hoped Sandy was all right. Thoughts of Amelia flashed by. He hoped she was all right too. Shit, he would have liked to know her better. And maybe that was his biggest regret. A strange sense of calmness overtook him as time seemed to flow in slow-motion. He remembered Maddie's funeral and the question he'd asked himself there—who would really miss him if he died? Phil probably, Stump maybe. But no, he was going to be one more dead cop added to the list that hung on the wall of honor back at the station, and that was all.

It took only an instant for these thoughts to course through Ben's mind. He turned again to the gunmen and realized that no, his biggest regret would be that he never had the chance to kill that bastard.

In the light of the moon Ben saw him lift the butt of the rifle to his shoulder and aim the barrel down at him. In one pull of the trigger—in one loud bang—in one horrific burst of pain—Ben's life would be over and he would know what death was like. Well, that was worth something, wasn't it? He closed his eyes.

Then, from somewhere overhead, Ben heard the tinkle of falling glass. He opened his eyes and turned his head. As if through a fog, he saw some kind of commotion at a window high over the garage. Then he heard an echoing shout from somewhere. "Kill him, Ben! Kill him!"

Two shots rang out. Ben's body jerked at the sound but he felt no pain. Instead, it was the gunman who cried out in agony. Ben twisted back around, amazed to see him fall to his knees. Like a statue, his face frozen in shock, he knelt there for a moment, his wide eyes staring at Ben. Then, he fell forward, hitting the ground with a hard thump, his face settling only two feet from Ben's. His eyes still stared at Ben. Blood leaked from his mouth. He gasped for air in short rapid breaths. His body shuddered then finally became still.

Ben stared back at his lifeless black eyes. His gray, balding hair and his ruddy skin put him in his mid-fifties. Ben wondered how such evil could have been hidden within such an ordinary looking man. "Rot in Hell, you piece of..."

But Ben cut his words short. He gasped. He jerked back, and a sickening shiver hitting him like a knife. He squeezed his eyes shut then opened them. Lifting his head, he could not believe what he saw. "God in heaven. It's you!" Ben felt his face contort. He felt his stomach twist. "No! No! Shit, no!" he struggled to sit up. He had to get away from here. How could...? No, it's not possible. He tried to get up.

"Ben, Ben. Are you all right?"

On some level, Ben knew it was Amelia's voice, but he was still staring, fixated on the gunman.

"Oh Ben, your arm."

He felt her raise his arm up and wrap something tightly around his wrist. "You'll be okay, Ben. Do you hear me? You're going to be okay."

But Ben could only stare at the man, lost in the evil that seemed to radiate from his still open eyes. The blood that had streamed from his mouth had slowed to a steady drip, drip, drip pooling on the ground around his cheek.

"Can you move? Try to move, Ben."

He tore his gaze away and found he was able to move his legs, first one, then the other. With Amelia's help, he got into a sitting position. He then turned back to the dead man, staring down at the overcoat splayed out over his body—the *white* overcoat. "It's him," he mumbled almost in a cry. "It's him, Amelia. That's the guy I shot back at the stakeout." He tore his eyes off the dead man and turned to her. "Shit, this is..."

Ben started trembling and couldn't stop. His arm blazed but he no longer felt the blood pumping out. Suddenly without strength, he lowered himself back down.

"Stay down, Ben, just rest. Your partners know where we are.

They'll be here soon."

Ben swallowed, his throat dry. "You should radio Phil," he rasped, still shaking, his entire arm ablaze. But he felt the warmth of Amelia's touch.

She ran a hand along the side of his face down to his shoulder. "You killed him, Ben. You killed him. And we saved the girl."

Ben forced in a deep breath. He let it out slowly then took in another. With an effort, he was able to sit up again. "Where is the girl? Is she okay?"

Amelia leaned closer, resting her cheek against his. He felt the warmth of her kiss. "You're still shaking. Just rest now. There's no danger." She drew back a little. "Yes. Sandra's going to be all right. I untied her. She's a little dazed right now. We saw everything from the door. The guy was going to kill you, Ben. I saw him standing over you, raising his rifle. But you weren't moving. I was frantic. I thought you were dead. Then you shot him twice and he fell."

"I heard you shout."

"That wasn't me, Ben. It was the girl."

Ben shook his head, confused now. "I thought it was you. There was nothing I could do. I didn't have my gun." He thought for a moment. "I must have hit him with one of my shots when he was backing out, trying to run me down. Yeah, that makes sense." He started to relax but was distracted by a shadow just over Amelia's shoulder. Amelia turned to look too. It was Sandra, her bruised face calm, almost serene as she moved into the light. She wore Amelia's jacket over a robe.

"You are Ben," said the girl. "I've seen you once, I think."

Ben attempted a smile, feeling his eyes brim. "Yes. And you are Sandra."

The girl nodded. "Tonight I am Sandra. She didn't die. You saved her."

Amelia hesitated, "You are Lydia, aren't you?"

The girl turned to her. "I remember you from...from the fire. That girl, she still lives?"

"Yes, she still lives. And now Sandra lives too."

Ben felt his lips shake as he tried to form a smile. "We know your journals, Grandma Lydia. I am Ben, your great, great grandson."

She nodded and backed away a step. "I've felt your presence for a long time. You're the one who started all of this."

Ben shook his head. "What do you mean? I don't understand."

"It makes no difference. Not now. It's almost finished, I think."

"What's finished?" asked Ben.

"The nightmares. The terrible nightmares." She looked around, her gaze drifting over the dead body on the ground. "All of this. All of this death. It is finished. I am finished. The thread will be cut soon—I can feel it." She turned to Amelia. "I will be dying soon. I can feel it. Did my journals tell you when? Did it tell you when I will die?"

"Are you sure you want to know?" asked Amelia.

The girl, old beyond her years, smiled. "Just tell me, dear."

"Your last journal ends with a note that must have been written by your daughter Abigail. I remember exactly what it said:

"My mother, Lydia Thornhill, died on July 9th 1920 at three in the afternoon. In her life she carried a heavy burden but through it all, she was a good mother. I will love her always. May she rest in peace at last."

"Abigail was a good daughter but she always was shit for a liar. I was the most terrible of mothers. Do you know what became of her?"

"All we know is, from Maine, she left for Boston. She had one daughter who became my grandmother."

Lydia nodded. "I hope she found some happiness, poor girl." She let out a long sigh then held her hand out close to Ben's. "You are a good man, Ben. I would like to stay longer. I would like to know you better...but can't. I sense that Sandra is ready to return." She turned to Amelia and gave her a tight-lipped smile that she held as she turned back to him. "Good-bye, Ben."

At her touch, a jolt of electricity hit Ben. He fell back. Rigid.

He felt his eyelids flutter then squeeze shut. He felt his body strain, his body arched backward until he thought his heart would launch like a rocket from his chest. Then, as suddenly as it had overtaken him, the seizure, if that's what it was, ended. His body went slack. He drew in a deep breath, then two more as he opened his eyes and saw the face of a child above his and, though he could not focus his tears he knew it was Sandra. This time it was really Sandra.

Seeing Ben for the first time, she drew back. "Who are...?"

"You're all right Sandra. You're all right now," said Amelia, her reassuring hands gently on the girl's shoulders. "You're safe. I'm a...I'm a doctor and this is Ben. He's a policeman. He's the one who rescued you."

Sandra was silent for a moment, her face still blank. Then, slowly she spoke. "A woman took me. She was bad."

"Yes, Sandra. She was bad. But she can't hurt you now. You'll see your mother soon. She's been very worried about you."

"I was with Uncle David."

"Yes, you were. He's worried too."

Sandra seemed to think this over for a moment before looking down at Ben with sudden concern. "You're hurt." She turned to Amelia. "The policeman's hurt. Is he going to be all right?"

Despite the pain that still throbbed like a pile-driver, Ben smiled up at her. "Yes, don't worry about me. I'm going to be just fine."

In the distance Ben heard sirens getting louder, coming closer. It had to be Harris and Bradly and it sounded like they'd brought the cavalry with them.

It was about time.

CHAPTER 31

In the hospital five days later, using his left hand, Ben signed off on his official statement, detailing what happened that night. His right hand remained bound up in bandages encased in a large rubberized mitten that pneumatically applied pressure, keeping blood flowing to each of his damaged fingers. Ben had gotten used to the hum of its pump that went on and off at intervals of exactly fifty seconds. Besides the injury to his hand, he had a few broken ribs but that was all. He knew he'd been a lot more than just lucky. He should have been dead.

The report he'd just signed with his barely legible left-hand scrawl, was a transcription of the audio statement he'd given the day before in the presence of Captain Nolan. Today's signature made it official.

The report told of him being fired upon from within a one-time hunting lodge where he had reason to believe Sandra Menendez was being held. It told of him returning fire then entering the building where he found the girl tied to a bed. It told of him trying to prevent the escape of the assailant by firing his weapon five times through the rear window of a black SUV that had been barreling backwards toward him at a high rate of speed. And it told of him being hit by the SUV, being knocked unconscious and, on regaining consciousness, finding the assailant lying dead beside him.

It was the truth—mostly.

A short time after the currier left, signed report in hand, Amelia walked in. "We have to stop meeting like this," she quipped, taking the chair beside him.

Ben smiled, happy to see her looking healthy and energetic again. Even her curls were starting to regain their bounciness.

"What?" she asked, conscious of his stare.

"You look good, Amelia."

"Yeah. I feel good. How is it though that one of us always seems to be in the hospital?"

"Just two more days they tell me. Then, after three months with this oven mitt, I'll be as good as new."

"How about up here?" she asked, tapping the side of her head. "Are you okay with everything that happened?"

Two days ago, Ben had told her everything. She knew how Ben had struggled to get up after being hit by the SUV. She knew about the gunman, rifle in hand, striding closer, the hem of his white overcoat flaring in a familiar way as he walked. She knew he'd taken dead aim at Ben as he lay helpless. She knew about Ben hearing a window break from somewhere overhead. She knew that Ben had seen the flash and heard two shots ring out, fired down from the window. And she knew, as did Ben, that it was those two shots, that he himself had fired almost eight months ago, that had actually killed the guy and saved his own life.

"Yeah, I am okay with it," he said. "In a strange way, everything seems to make sense now. I really wasn't imagining things back at that stakeout. I feel almost vindicated." He shook his head. "I had to leave a lot out of my report."

"Good thing too. If the truth ever came out, you'd be branded as a certifiable fruitcake and kicked off the force for good."

"It's too bad only you and I will ever know the whole truth," he said finally.

"I think Byron knows but, like us, he cares too much for his professional standing to actually say so." She paused then gave him a look of concern. "Are you ready for some more truth?"

"Truth about what?"

"I went over some of the documents you found when you were up in Maine. You know, when you were searching through the records for info on Lydia." She pulled some papers from the bag at her feet, maneuvered his hospital tray in front of him and placed four sheets of paper on it. "These are the birth records of your mother, your grandmother, her mother, and her mother who was Lydia Thornhill."

"Okay..." said Ben, wondering where she was going with this.

She then dealt out four more sheets of paper pairing them up with the first four.

Ben stared at them, still clueless. "These are death certificates."

"Yes, and look at the dates. And the names."

The name on the first one he checked was 'Baby Boy Thornhill'. It was lined up with Lydia's birth certificate. Then Ben saw the date. "The date of death is the same as on the birth certificate. But how...?"

"Your grandma Lydia had a twin—a still-born twin."

Ben looked at the others, the hairs on the back of his neck rising as he saw what she was getting at.

"That's right," said Amelia. "They all had still-born twins." She pulled out another two sheets of paper and placed them in front of him. "As did you."

Ben shook his head, staring. "I never knew."

"But," said Amelia raising a finger and smiling as if she were about to perform a trick of magic, "you were different. Your still-born twin was female, all the others were male."

"Is that supposed to mean something?"

"It might. I'm thinking that your being male could be the only reason that Lydia had a connection with you and not her other descendants." She gave a dismissive wave of her hand. "That's just a theory I have. Anyway, the odds against all these still-born twins occurring in a single unbroken maternal lineage are astronomical. This had to be what caused her to have an awareness of you and you to have an awareness of her."

"But I never had an awareness of her."

"So, how do you explain those visions of yours? In the case of Cindy, you actually saw the killer's eyes and that thing on his arm just as Lydia must have. In Sandra's case, you heard the buzz of a plane, just as she must have. None of those details were in the journals but you knew about them. Whether you care to admit it or not, there was a link between you and Lydia."

"Okay, I guess I can see that but..."

"And one thing more, there's an unusual medical phenomena called parasitic twins where an embryo actually absorbs portions of its unviable, embryonic twin. Some are born with an extra arm or even an extra head. The results are heartbreaking for the child as well as for the parents." She took a breath. "I think—and this is only what I think—I think that some part of your consciousness had been born with Lydia and that it became a viable part of your maternal lineage."

Ben felt his jaw drop. "Shit. You're saying that some part of me was actually born more than a hundred years ago?"

"Well, I hadn't actually thought of it that way, but yes. I guess that's right," she admitted, speaking slower now. "Look, I can't explain everything but I do know that your grandmother lived a good portion of her life in the alternate reality we call insanity. Maybe one day we'll learn that, in that alternate world, all of this makes perfect sense."

"Even me firing two bullets in March that ended up saving my life in September?"

"Yes Ben, even that."

Ben reclined his bed. He closed his eyes trying to absorb all that she'd said. Then his eyes blinked open. "Grandma Lydia talked about a connection, a thread between her and I. She said it would soon be broken."

Amelia nodded. "She knew she'd be dying soon—in her timeline I mean." She placed her hand on Lydia Thornhill's death certificate. "According to this, your grandma Lydia died exactly 35,154 days ago today. So that thread, that connection she'd had with you, would have been cut four days ago."

"So, no more visions, right? I'm back to being normal."

"Yes, I think so," she said with a hint of skepticism.

Ben hesitated. "You're thinking that maybe now I'll start up a connection with some future jerk born 35,150 days from now. Maybe I should start keeping a journal." He'd intended this as a joke but didn't get the laugh he'd expected.

"You can't worry about everything, Ben. We're all linked to our ancestors by the DNA that streams naturally from one generation to the next. That's a connection we all have with the past and it's apparently a connection that some small number of us, like your Grandma Lydia, possess with the future."

Shifting his weight in the bed, Ben shoved the tray back, out of the way. "I think I've had enough truth today." He closed his eyes again. No, he couldn't worry about everything. Besides, if there ever was some future jerk years from now he would have to be a descendant of his and he'd never given much thought to the prospect of ever having a kid. But, why was that? Why shouldn't he one day have a kid? He found himself wondering what kind of father he might be. He'd be a damn sight better than his own dad, he was sure of that much. He imagined himself having a daughter, maybe two daughters; maybe they'd be like Jennifer and little Sandy. Images of their faces flashed through his mind. With Grandma Lydia's help they'd been able to save each of those girls and the thought of them brought with it an emotion that he imagined must be something akin to a father's love.

"Are you all right, Ben?" asked Amelia, watching him. "What is it?"

Surprised and embarrassed that he'd let his feelings show, Ben shook his head. "I was just thinking...your father, he seems like a good man."

"Yes, he is, Ben."

"My father beat my mother. I know that now. I remember it. And he abandoned us when I was just a child. How could a man do that to his family?"

"Some men aren't meant to be fathers."

"Do you have any brothers or sisters?"

"Yes, two sisters."

Ben smiled. "Sounds like the perfect family."

"No family's perfect. But why are you...?"

"I don't know why I'm thinking about these things right now. I just am." Ben glanced at the clock on the wall. "You have a class coming up right?"

"Yes. The first of the new semester. I can't miss it."

"It's okay. You should go then."

She stood, leaned closer and kissed his forehead.

Ben gently placed his good hand on her cheek. "You know, when I was lying there on the ground waiting for that guy to come over and finish me off, I was sure I was going to die. At that moment my biggest regret, well, other than not getting to kill that creep, was not getting to know you better—not getting to love you—not knowing if you could ever...love me."

Amelia lifted her head. Her eyes met his and she spoke in a whisper through a gentle smile. "Funny thing, Ben, at that same moment, when I was running to you, I was thinking the same thing. I was afraid of losing you." She kissed him softly on the lips, then stood.

He raised the bed up watching her gather up her things. "A detective and a psychologist—what are the odds of that working out?" He said this in a casual way but his heart was thumping, wondering what she would say.

Amelia stopped what she was doing and reached for his good hand. She held it tightly then brought it up to her cheek. "I'd say our odds are pretty good, Detective Marshall."

EPILOGUE

In the months that followed, Ben often thought how strange it was that he and Amelia had been brought together by a woman who'd lived such a cursed life so many years ago. As his own years melted by, he came to believe that his happiness with Amelia and their three daughters had been Lydia Thornhill's priceless gift to him. In the giving of that gift, Ben hoped his great, great grandmother had somehow found her own salvation.

With Dr. Amelia Silvers' research and persistence, the name Lydia Thornhill became famous once again in the world of psychology as did what came to be known as, The Thornhill Deaths. For the first time, the possibility of an empathetical link between the world of the living and the transient world of the dying would get serious attention. Eventually, Dr. Thornhill's first three journals became required reading at most universities.

Fearing it could jeopardize the privacy of those it specifically named, Ben and Amelia mutually decided not to publish the fourth journal. For years Ben kept it in a nightstand on his side of the bed, a constant reminder of the woman who, though she'd lived so long ago, had been such an important part of his life.

In solitude, the ruins of the Thornhill house up in Maine forever marked the grave of the imperfect Lydia Thornhill, the words on its walls serving as her epitaph. Except for the creatures of the woods she would receive no visitors, yet she did not rest alone. For with her lay the memory of all those children she'd protected from fear and pain and tried to save. For them she'd wept a mother's tears and, perhaps in gratitude, their peace they ultimately gave back to her.

AUTHOR'S NOTE

Thank you for reading *Dr. Thornhill's Last Patient*. I hope you were able to guess that her last patient was her great-great grandson, Ben. If you can, please leave a review on my Amazon book page or on my website to let me, and others, know what you thought of it.

There is, of course, no scientific evidence of an active telepathic connection between the living and the dead or between the living and the dying. But empathy is unquestionably a strong emotion and who can place limits on the powers of the human mind to somehow hear the desperate but silent cries for help from those facing certain death? Perhaps those cries are the stuff of nightmares that occasionally haunt us. The whole idea is, at the very least, a point for all of us to ponder and, for some, to write stories about.

ABOUT THE AUTHOR

Tom is a lifelong resident of Michigan and presently lives in the Detroit area. He's proud to have three beautiful daughters and four grandchildren. A retired engineer and business executive, he holds several degrees from Wayne State University and enjoys travel, woodworking, guitar and, of course, writing. *Dr. Thornhill's Last Patient* is his 4th novel.

Tom's travels have taken him to Europe, China, Japan, South Korea and Russia. He has also enjoyed camping in the American West although he admits the ground now seems a little harder for sleeping than it used to.

Whenever practical, Tom tries to find time for author events and signings. For more on Tom, his books, and what he's up to now, visit him at tomulicny.com. Drop him a line on his contact page - he'd love to hear from you.

PRAISE FOR THE NOVELS OF TOM ULICNY

THE LOST REVOLUTION: Set in the era of Queen Victoria, a failed American journalist finds danger, adventure and love in the frontiers of the British Empire.
"Brilliant descriptions, a complex mystery, an exciting story well worth reading." Melinda Hills for Readers' Favorites.

THE CARUSO COLLECTION: Two artists. Two women. A dark secret. And a murder.
"Plenty of twists and turns, well developed characters. A good read with more to the story than meets the eye." Anne-Marie Reynolds for Readers' Favorites.

"A twisty, artsy thriller that demands to be read—Wow!" Aimee Ann, for The Redheaded Book Lover.

Also by Tom Ulicny with reviews still coming in:

THE SCIENTIST'S ACCOMPLICE: A hard luck drifter finds an unlikely woman and an astonishing cause worth risking his life for.

Check them all out on Amazon or at tomulicny.com

Made in United States
Orlando, FL
22 June 2023

34403970R00209